ACCLAIM FOR DOROTHY LOVE

"Dorothy Love effortlessly brings to life the setting and characters of *Every Perfect Gift* so that you'll feel right at home in Hickory Ridge. The love story is sweet and woven amidst secrets of the past that explore the various facets of prejudice. At the last page, you'll breathe a contented sigh and wish you didn't have to leave behind characters who feel like friends."

—JODY HEDLUND, BEST-SELLING
AUTHOR OF *THE PREACHER'S BRIDE*

"*Beauty for Ashes* is a touching story about finding joy and healing in the midst of heartache. Set in the small town of Hickory Ridge, Dorothy Love takes readers on a beautifully written journey into the heart of the South during the years that followed the Civil War. As her characters search for healing, they must choose to either cling to the past or trade the bitterness in their hearts for love."

—MELANIE DOBSON, AWARD-WINNING
AUTHOR OF *THE SILENT ORDER* AND
LOVE FINDS YOU IN LIBERTY, INDIANA

"Dorothy Love paints a vivid picture of the post–Civil War south [and] the need to rebuild hope. And she does it beautifully . . ."

—CATHY GOHLKE, AWARD-WINNING AUTHOR OF
PROMISE ME THIS, REGARDING *BEAUTY FOR ASHES*

"You'll adore this book from beginning to end. The story will capture your heart from the first line."

—*ROMANTIC TIMES*, 4½ STAR
REVIEW OF *BEYOND ALL MEASURE*

"With well-drawn characters and just enough suspense to keep the pages turning, this winning debut will be a hit with fans of Gilbert Morris and Lauraine Snelling."

—*LIBRARY JOURNAL* STARRED
REVIEW OF *BEYOND ALL MEASURE*

"Beautifully written and with descriptions so rich I'm still certain I caught a whiff of magnolia blossoms as I read. *Beyond All Measure* is pure Southern delight! Dorothy Love weaves a stirring romance that's both gloriously detailed with Tennessee history and that uplifts and inspires the heart."

—TAMERA ALEXANDER, BEST-SELLING AUTHOR
OF *THE INHERITANCE* AND *WITHIN MY HEART*

"Soft as a breeze from the Old South and as gentle as the haze hovering over the Great Smokies, the gifted flow of Dorothy Love's pen casts a spell of love, hate and hope in post–Civil War Tennessee. With rich, fluid prose, characters who breathe onto the page and a wealth of historical imagery, *Beyond All Measure* will steal both your heart and your sleep well beyond the last page."

—JULIE LESSMAN, BEST-SELLING
AUTHOR OF *A HOPE UNDAUNTED*

"Find a porch swing, pour yourself a tall glass of lemonade: [*Beyond All Measure*] is the perfect summer read!"

—SIRI MITCHELL, AUTHOR
OF *A HEART MOST WORTHY*

"Dorothy Love captures all the romance, charm and uncertainties of the postbellum South, delighting readers with her endearing characters, historical details and vivid writing style."

—MARGARET BROWNLEY, AUTHOR
OF *A LADY LIKE SARAH*, REGARDING
BEYOND ALL MEASURE

EVERY PERFECT GIFT

ALSO BY DOROTHY LOVE

EVERY PERFECT GIFT

A HICKORY RIDGE ROMANCE

DOROTHY LOVE

THOMAS NELSON

Since 1798

NASHVILLE   DALLAS   MEXICO CITY   RIO DE JANEIRO

Published in Nashville, Tennessee, by Thomas Nelson. Thomas Nelson is a registered trademark of Thomas Nelson, Inc.

Thomas Nelson, Inc., titles may be purchased in bulk for educational, business, fund-raising, or sales promotional use. For information, please e-mail SpecialMarkets@ThomasNelson.com.

All Scripture quotations are taken from the King James Version of the Bible.

Versification of Psalm 23 in chapter 5 is by the author. Hymn verse quoted in chapter 12 is from "Heavenly Father, Bless Me Now," words by Alexander Clark (1834–1879). Hymn verses quoted in chapter 33 are from "In the Bleak Midwinter," words by Christina Rossetti (1872), and "We Plow the Fields," words by Matthias Claudius (1782), translated by Jane M. Campbell (1861).

Publisher's Note: This novel is a work of fiction. Names, characters, places, and incidents are either products of the author's imagination or used fictitiously. All characters are fictional, and any similarity to people living or dead is purely coincidental.

Library of Congress Cataloging-in-Publication Data

Love, Dorothy, 1949-
  Every perfect gift / Dorothy Love.
      p. cm. -- (A Hickory Ridge romance ; 3)
  Summary: "Ethan and Sophie long to share a future together. But the secrets they're not sharing could tear them apart. Sophie Caldwell has returned to Hickory Ridge, Tennessee after years away. Despite the heartaches of her childhood, Sophie is determined to make a home, and a name, for herself in the growing town. A gifted writer, she plans to resurrect the local newspaper that so enchanted her as a girl. Ethan Heyward's idyllic childhood was shattered by a tragedy he has spent years trying to forget. An accomplished businessman and architect, he has built a majestic resort in the mountains above Hickory Ridge, drawing wealthy tourists from all over the country. When Sophie interviews Ethan for the paper, he is impressed with her intelligence and astounded by her beauty. She's equally intrigued with him but fears he will reject her if he learns about her shadowed past. Just as she summons the courage to tell him, Ethan's own past unexpectedly and violently catches up with him, threatening not only his life but their budding romance"-- Provided by publisher.
  ISBN 978-1-59554-902-0 (pbk.)
 1. Women journalists--Fiction. 2. Architects--Fiction. 3. Tennessee--Fiction. I. Title.
  PS3562.O8387E94 2012
  813'.54--dc23

                                     2012032476

Printed in the United States of America
12 13 14 15 16 17 QG 6 5 4 3 2 1

In memory of my brother, Lowell Dean Catlett
July 16, 1951–April 10, 2012
His life was a gift to all who knew him.

Every good gift and every perfect gift is from above,
and cometh down from the Father of lights,
with whom is no variableness, neither shadow of turning.
JAMES 1:17

ONE

The orphanage seemed so much smaller than she remembered.

Sophie Robillard Caldwell peered through the bars of the rusty gate, taking in the boarded-up windows, the weed-choked yard, the frayed remnants of a rope swing shivering in the sharp wind that seemed to whisper long-past taunts. *Mutt. Muddlebones. Mongrel.*

And worse.

Holding her hat in place with one hand, she looked up at the second-floor window of the room where she'd spent a lonely girl-hood daydreaming and spinning stories. She'd expected to feel a sense of familiarity upon returning here, a kind of homecoming. But the moment she stepped off the train, she realized that everything had changed.

True, Jasper Pruitt still ran the mercantile, and his wife still owned the dress shop that had once belonged to Norah Dudley. The bakery and Mr. Gilman's bank were thriving. The Hickory Ridge Inn, where she was currently staying, was full to overflowing every night. Miss Hattie's restaurant had reopened, and even now the smells of frying chicken drifted on the wind. She would write to her guardians, Ada and Wyatt Caldwell, about that. Despite their many years in Texas, Wyatt still rhapsodized about Miss Hattie's fried chicken.

But the pretty gazebo in the park was gone, and in its place was a statue honoring war veterans. And the riverbank where she had once played on her infrequent outings was covered with rows of new houses sporting gabled roofs and elaborate spindle-work porches. It wasn't only the physical details that made Hickory Ridge feel unfamiliar. It was the new busyness that permeated everything, erasing some of the small-town coziness that had so captured Ada's heart all those years ago.

With a final look at the deserted orphanage, Sophie climbed into her rented rig and clicked her tongue to the horse. According to Wyatt, Blue Smoke was responsible for much of the bustling activity. The massive luxury resort going up atop Hickory Ridge employed dozens of men who had come to town to build roads, mill timber, and construct the three-mile railway spur that took materials up the mountain. Soon a small army of farm girls would find work as housekeepers, laundresses, and serving girls for the moneyed guests arriving by train for weeks or months of tramping, fishing, and horseback riding.

The town was growing again, making this the perfect time to revive the long-defunct *Hickory Ridge Gazette*.

Wyatt and Ada were less than enthusiastic about Sophie's plan. But her work at the newspaper in Dallas had shown her how important a fair and independent newspaper could be to a town.

She guided her rig along the busy road past Mr. Pruitt's mercantile, her thoughts swirling. Of course the Caldwells were right. She could have stayed on at the paper in Dallas or even found a small Texas town in need of a paper of its own. But the notion that unfinished business awaited her in Hickory Ridge had captured her head and her heart, and here she was.

"Careful, miss!" A farmer, his arms laden with boxes of supplies, jumped back as she approached Mr. Tanner's livery. She slowed the rig and nodded an apology.

Truth to tell, she'd always felt she had something to prove. All those years at the orphanage, where she was treated as inferior, had left a mark on her soul. If she made a success of the *Gazette*, perhaps then she could vanquish those taunting voices in her head and prove she was as good as anybody, despite the whispers, rumors, and unanswered questions about who she was and where she came from.

Was that such a crazy thing to want?

She left the horse and rig at Tanner's livery and, drawing her shawl about her shoulders, walked the short distance to the newspaper office. The key slid into the rusty lock. The door groaned as she pushed it open. A dull gray light barely penetrated the dirt-streaked windows. In the corners, cobwebs undulated like ghosts. Wooden crates, an empty filing cabinet, and a broken-down bookcase littered the small space. The musty smell of old paper and lead mingled with the dust that rose in clouds when she plopped down in the chair behind the scarred walnut desk, bringing back a memory so sweet and sharp that her eyes filled.

What's that smell? She was ten years old and away from the orphanage for a glorious afternoon with the woman who soon would become her guardian. *Smells like an adventure!*

She still felt the same way. What could be more exciting than newspapering? Every day brought new stories that needed to be reported, examined, and remarked upon. As soon as her typewriting machine and her supplies arrived, the *Gazette* would be back in business. Assuming she ever got rid of all this infernal dirt and grime. She ran one hand along the dusty windowsill and checked the small gold watch she wore on a chain around her neck. It wasn't yet noon. There was time to do a bit of cleaning before leaving to conduct her first interview.

Ethan Heyward had been a hard man to pin down. It had taken three wires and two weeks' worth of handwritten notes before he finally agreed to talk to her about his role as codeveloper and manager of the new resort. Finally he'd promised to give her a brief tour of the grounds this afternoon.

Last night she'd tossed and turned, trying out interview questions in her head. The last thing she wanted was to have Mr. Heyward think she was frivolous and simpleminded. It might be 1886, but plenty of men—and women too—thought females were unsuited for business and their only place was in the home. Not that she didn't dream of falling in love with the most wonderful man on earth, making a life with him, having children. What woman didn't? But she didn't want to give up the newspaper business either.

She opened a desk drawer, thumbed through a dusty stack of old invoices, and slid the drawer shut. Why so many people of both sexes thought she had to choose one or the other was the mystery of the ages. Writing for newspapers and magazines was the perfect occupation for a woman who didn't mind persevering in a man's world, and there were plenty of women who agreed. Just look at Nellie Bly. And Mrs. Lydia McPherson, who not only wrote for but also owned one of the biggest newspapers in all of Texas. And Sophie's old boss at the Dallas paper was a woman too. The country was hurtling toward a brand-new century. It was high time for a new attitude about what women could accomplish.

She removed her shawl, rolled up her sleeves, and pumped water into the pail she'd left there yesterday. She dipped a rag into the water and tackled the grimy window overlooking the street, noticing with a sigh that several of the gold letters had worn away. She would have to fix that situation right away. Potential subscribers and advertising customers would be less than impressed by a shabby-looking façade.

She wiped the window clean inside and out and dried it, rubbing the glass until the streaks disappeared, then started on the woodwork. Potential interview questions for Mr. Heyward still swirled in her head. What was he like? She knew little about him, apart from what she'd gleaned from other newspaper accounts—that he was the scion of an old Georgia family, that he was an architect, and that he'd teamed up with a Maryland businessman named Horace Blakely to build the resort many compared to those in Saratoga, New York.

Coming up from Texas on the train, she'd bought a copy of the *Chattanooga Times* that carried a photograph of the balding and rotund Mr. Blakely. No doubt Mr. Heyward looked about the same. Birds of a feather flocked together, didn't they? Especially wealthy birds. And Mr. Heyward surely must be rich as Croesus to build such a palatial hotel. The *Times* article said Blue Smoke was meant to rival the Greenbrier, the plush West Virginia resort that attracted wealthy guests from all over the country.

After scrubbing the baseboards and windowsills and dusting the desk and the chair, Sophie straightened the picture on the wall behind the desk, a fanciful painting of ladies at tea on a calm lake. For a moment she stood still, drinking in its quiet beauty.

"Hello? Anyone here?" A slender young woman, her white-blond hair woven into a thick plait down her back, peered through the open doorway, looking for all the world like a water sprite in Sophie's favorite childhood storybook.

Sophie looked up. "May I help you?"

The water sprite stepped inside, holding a thin brown envelope sealed with a blob of blue wax. "Miss Caldwell?"

"Yes, but please call me Sophie." She pulled her sleeves down, buttoned her cuffs, and set aside her cleaning rag. "What can I do for you?"

"You probably don't remember me. I'm a few years older than

you." The woman leaned one hip on the corner of the desk. "But I remember you. It caused quite a stir in Hickory Ridge when Wyatt Caldwell and his Boston bride lit out for Texas and took you with them. Jasper Pruitt still marvels at it."

A mental picture of the hard-eyed mercantile owner rose in Sophie's mind. Had the intervening years softened his opinion of those who were different? Perhaps that was too much to hope for. "I'm sorry. I don't . . . I didn't have a chance to make many friends when I lived at Mrs. Lowell's orphanage."

"I'm Sabrina Gilman. But I much prefer to be called Gillie. My father owns the bank." She handed Sophie the envelope. "Your deposit receipt. Father said you left it in his office yesterday."

"So I did." Sophie smiled and dropped the envelope into the top drawer of her desk. "I was so eager to get settled and get over here to take a look at things that I forgot all about it." She studied her visitor. "I do remember you, though. You and Jacob Hargrove played Mary and Joseph at the Christmas pageant the year Mrs. Lowell brought us to church to sing carols. You aren't that much older than I am."

"Twenty-eight as of last week." Gillie sighed. "Well past my prime for marriage, according to Mother and her friends."

"I thought you and Jacob—"

"He left Hickory Ridge a couple of years after you and the Caldwells." Gillie shrugged. "I can't blame him. There was no work here for years. He finally got a job at a factory up north and married someone else."

"I'm sorry."

Gillie laughed. "Well, I'm not! It was only a childhood flirtation. Though I will admit, for a while I was in such a state that Father sought Dr. Spencer's help in sorting me out." She traced a scar on the wood desk with her fingers. "At first I couldn't imagine any other life than the one I'd dreamed of with Jacob. Watching our children grow up on our farm. Watching the seasons change. Growing old and wrinkled together." She sent Sophie a rueful smile. "Sentimental beyond all words, I know, but that's what I thought I was meant to do. God had other plans, though."

Sophie nodded. She had been visiting Ada Wentworth the day Robbie Whiting's father rode in to report that Wyatt Caldwell was taking the next train to Texas. That was the day Ada put her trust in God's plans and changed all their lives.

"I'm devoting my life to helping the sick," Gillie said. "It's my true calling. And I owe it all to a . . . woman of loose morals."

"A . . ." Sophie wasn't a prude, but she couldn't bring herself to speak a word polite ladies only hinted at.

"Exactly." Gillie bobbed her head. "Annie Cook. She owned a house of ill repute in Memphis. A very nice one, so they say. When the yellow fever epidemic broke out several years back, people left town like rats leaving a sinking ship, but she stayed and turned her place into a hospital. She took care of the sick folks till she herself died of the fever. It was in all the papers." Gillie looked up, her face full of light. "If that doesn't prove that God can use anybody for the good, I do not know what does. Annie Cook gave her life for other people."

Sophie made a mental note to look into Miss Cook's story. It might make an inspiring piece for the paper one day. "I hope you won't be called upon to go that far."

"So far my career has consisted mostly of tending colicky babies and patching up farming injuries. But Doc Spencer is teaching me to deliver babies. At nursing school we weren't allowed to attend a mother on our own."

Outside, the train whistle shrieked. Gillie shot to her feet. "My goodness—noon already. I didn't intend to take so much of your time."

"That's all right. Truthfully, I'm glad for your company. I'm afraid I don't have friends here. Except for Robbie Whiting, I never did."

"Their loss." Gillie's voice was warm with welcome. "But you've got one now."

Sophie returned Gillie's smile. How wonderful it would be to have someone near her own age to laugh with and confide in. "I hope so. Thanks for bringing my bank receipt."

"No trouble." Gillie waved one dainty hand and headed for the door. "I'll see you later."

Sophie emptied the dirty water from her cleaning bucket and draped the rag over the windowsill to dry, then headed for the hotel to freshen up before her trip up the mountain to Blue Smoke. Despite her education and practical experience contributing stories to the *Galveston News* and the *Oklahoma Star*, the mere thought of interviewing someone as powerful as Mr. Heyward made her stomach tight with nerves.

If she made a mess of this first real interview, folks would talk, as they always did in small Southern towns. If that happened, nobody would take her or her newspaper seriously. More than anything, she wanted her newspaper to succeed—to prove to the Caldwells that their faith in her was justified and to secure her future. She couldn't depend upon Wyatt Caldwell forever. He and Ada had their own children, Wade and Lilly, to consider.

The hotel parlor was quiet. A mother cradling a sleeping infant sat in the wing chair beside the window and gazed onto the busy street. Two salesmen in wool suits and bowler hats occupied the settee. Sophie retrieved her key from the room clerk and climbed the creaking stairs to her room. She changed into her best dress, a dark green frock with lace collar and cuffs, and picked up the new spring hat Ada had made for her. The jaunty little toque, adorned with netting and a single white silk flower, complemented her creamy skin and gray-green eyes.

She studied her reflection in the mottled mirror above the wash-stand and fought the fresh wave of apprehension moving through her. Despite her fair skin and straight hair, rumors that at least one of her parents carried African blood had marked her childhood and set her apart. Suppose she encountered the same thing now?

Back home in Texas, among Mexican *vaqueros* who worked Wyatt's ranch, hundreds of German and Czech immigrants, and African sugar plantation workers who sailed to Galveston to begin a new life, it had been easy to avoid questions about her family. Living with the Caldwells, moving through the world under their protection, had given her entrée into the finest homes and schools in Texas. Even so, without a blood family and a history to anchor her, she hadn't fit in with most of the other girls at Miss Halliday's School for Young Ladies. As much as she'd loved learning, graduating and starting her work in Dallas had come as an enormous relief.

She secured her hat with a pearl hatpin and brushed at a smudge of dirt on her nose. Maybe Wyatt was right and it was a mistake to come back to a place where some people—Mr. Pruitt at the mercantile, for instance—would remember the old gossip, and the hurt and rejection might well catch up with her again.

Fighting a wave of homesickness for Texas and the Caldwells, she gathered her bag, her notebook, and her pens and hurried from the inn to Mr. Tanner's livery. No sense in borrowing trouble. She'd made her choice. And the venerable Mr. Heyward must not be kept waiting.

TWO

"Mr. Heyward?" Tim O'Brien, the lanky, red-haired young Irishman Ethan had lured away from Gilman's bank with the promise of higher wages and shorter hours, stuck his head into the room. "That newspaper reporter is here."

Ethan set aside the payroll ledger he'd been perusing and glanced at the leather-bound appointment calendar lying open on his desk. He'd nearly forgotten his promise to give the reporter a tour of the facilities. Normally he enjoyed showing visitors around the marvel that was Blue Smoke, but today he was preoccupied with half a dozen headaches—delayed deliveries, absentee workers he'd been counting on to finish the flooring in the ballroom, and rumors of growing unrest among Negro workers and the Irish boys he'd imported from back east. Besides, the way he understood it, the *Gazette* was not actually in operation yet. It was only someone's dream—the way Blue Smoke was his.

Still, once the resort opened, he'd need the newspaper, not only to keep people apprised of goings-on atop the mountain, but to act as a jobber for printing stationery, menus, guest cards, and daily activity sheets. If an afternoon with the reporter would put the resort into the good graces of the paper's owner, perhaps he could negotiate more favorable terms when the time came.

"And, Mr. Heyward? Just a word of warning, sir. Mr. Blakely arrives tomorrow afternoon." The secretary waved a telegram in the air. "It says here he'll be wanting another powwow with you about the delay on the passenger car."

Ethan heaved a sigh, unrolled his sleeves, and slipped into his gray wool jacket. "One problem at a time, Tim. Show Mr. Caldwell in."

"'Tisn't a *Mr.* Caldwell, sir. She's a girl." The secretary grinned. "Pretty one too."

Ethan frowned. "Show her in."

He was prepared to be annoyed at having been misled, but one look at the young woman who stood framed in his doorway dispelled that thought. The only word that came to mind was *breathtaking.* He took her in—creamy skin, high cheekbones, eyes the most unusual shade of green. Glossy black hair tucked neatly into a stylish hat. A willowy figure. In the golden light coming through the Palladian windows, she reminded him of the portrait of his mother that had once graced his boyhood home.

"Mr. Heyward?" She crossed the carpet and inclined her head, a smile playing on her lips. "I'm—"

He bowed slightly. "S. R. Caldwell."

A faint blush crept into her cheeks. "Yes. Thank you for seeing me. I'm looking forward to touring the resort. The entrance is quite grand."

"Isn't it? The doors came from an abandoned castle in Scotland. My partner—"

"Excuse me." S. R. Caldwell opened her bag and took out a notebook and pen. "Your partner—that would be Mr. Blakely? Mr. Horace Blakely?"

"That's right." He waited while she scribbled, fascinated at the way her slender fingers gripped the steel pen.

She smiled up at him, her green eyes sparkling. His heart lurched. He lost his train of thought.

She flipped to a clean sheet in her small notebook. "Please continue, Mr. Heyward."

He cleared his throat. "Where was I? Oh yes, the doors. Horace—Mr. Blakely—happened upon the ruin during a tramping excursion and tracked down the owner, who was only too glad to sell the entire edifice for a song. We managed to salvage many of the old stones, some of the timbers, and that magnificent set of doors. As best we can tell, they date from the fifteenth century."

He watched her scribble some more. "Miss Caldwell, would you care for tea before we begin our tour? And perhaps your driver would like some too. The wind is sharp today, and it's quite a trip up here."

The reporter laughed, an infectious, bell-like sound. "I drove myself, Mr. Heyward, and yes, thank you. Tea would be delightful. If you don't mind my asking more questions while we pour."

Ethan nodded to his secretary, who scurried away, and motioned his guest to a chair.

"I'm happy to answer any question you may have. If you'll answer one for me."

She looked up, suddenly wary. "What kind of question?"

"I'm wondering why you took such care to disguise your identity. And why the newspaper owner would send someone so young up this mountain all by herself. Seems to me he should have come in your stead or, at the very least, provided you a suitable escort."

"That's two questions—and an opinion."

He smiled. "So it is."

She studied him, her expression calm, and folded her hands in her lap. "I signed my queries to you using my initials so as not to prejudice you against me from the outset. Here we are closing in on a brand-new century, and yet you'd be surprised at how many people don't want to give women a chance, no matter our qualifications."

He toyed with a small paperweight. "I can imagine."

She bobbed her head, and the white flower on her hat fluttered. "I'm not one for beating around the bush, Mr. Heyward. I may as well tell you I'm the owner of the *Gazette* too. There is no one else."

He considered himself a pretty good judge of women, and this one couldn't be many years past twenty-one. Even if she turned out to be a crack reporter, which he doubted—fine reporters, like fine wood, needed seasoning—what in the Sam Hill made her think she could run a newspaper, even a small one, all by herself?

But she was already on the defensive. Now was not the time to bring up *that* subject. "Do you mind yet another question? What does the S. R. stand for? After all, you know my name. Doesn't seem fair that I don't know yours."

Another lightning-quick smile. "Sophie Robillard."

He nodded. "Thank you. Ah, here comes tea."

He waited while O'Brien set down the tea tray and then quietly withdrew, shutting the door softly. "Shall I pour for you?"

"Yes, please."

He filled their cups, passed lemon and sugar, and took a long sip. "Now I'm all yours. Ask away."

Twenty minutes later, he recanted his assessment of her reportorial skills. This girl . . . woman . . . extracted facts and figures about the resort from him that he hadn't even realized he knew. By the time the teapot was empty, his mind swam with all he had told her. And with the intriguing realization that S. R. Caldwell was, in every significant way, more than his match.

A train whistle sounded as another load of furnishings arrived via the railway that had been built to ferry men and materials up to the ridge from the station in town. He rose. "Shall we take that tour now? I don't want you driving back down the mountain after dark."

"Oh, no need to worry about me. I'm sure I'll be perfectly safe." Clasping her notebook to her chest, she rose and followed him from his office into the grand lobby.

Something in her manner irked him. "Tell me, Miss Caldwell, are you always so sure of yourself?"

"I don't know what you mean." Wide green eyes, fringed with thick black lashes, held his.

"How can you be sure you'll come to no harm? Bad things happen to people when they are least expecting it."

"I know that. But don't you think it's better to assume the best will happen?" She indicated the room with a sweep of her arm. "Perhaps we'd better get back to the tour."

"As you wish." They continued along the broad hallway. "The ceiling was finished only last week. It was painted by Joshua Olmstead of New York. The flowers depicted in each panel are native plants that grow here on the mountain, and each is outlined in twenty-four-carat gold leaf."

Sophie Robillard flipped to a new page and made a quick sketch. If she was impressed with the paintings of blue gentians, yellow sunflowers, daisies, violets, and purple asters or with the carved moldings and the Oriental silk runners lying atop gleaming oak floors, she hid it well. She merely observed and scribbled.

Ethan frowned. Granted, reporters were supposed to be objective and impartial. But would it kill her to express a little enthusiasm for his masterpiece?

He led her from the lobby to the main ballroom and then to the east wing to see a suite of guest rooms. He took his time describing the antique furnishings, the expensive European linens adorning the canopied bed, the rosewood inlays in the fireplace mantel. She took in the brocade sofas, the Italian silk draperies framing the Palladian windows, her expression one of benign interest. Though his irritation persisted, he couldn't stop staring at her. Perhaps if he talked long enough, darkness would overtake them and he'd have to see the beautiful young reporter home himself.

Leaving her horse and rig at the livery, Sophie hurried to the inn as darkness fell. She was chilled from her long drive back from Blue Smoke, but at the same time she felt alive, energized. Ethan Heyward had been a very pleasant surprise. She'd detected some initial irritation at discovering her gender, but to his credit, he had taken her seriously and provided her with enough material for several stories. And there was no point in denying it: he was quite handsome—tall and well muscled, with thick brown hair and an engaging smile. Behind his thin, gold-rimmed spectacles were deep blue eyes that reminded her of the sky reflected in a clear mountain creek. He had about him an air of complete confidence. He moved easily between the hushed, rarefied atmosphere of the gilded resort and the rough-and-tumble army of men working to complete the buildings that were scattered across the lawns like pearls across a tapestry.

At the end of the afternoon, he had invited her to pay a return visit. Already she looked forward to it.

"Evening, Miss Caldwell." The hotel clerk handed her a stack of letters. "Mail came today."

"Thank you." She flipped though the stack, looking for an envelope bearing Ada's neat handwriting. A letter from home would be the perfect ending to this auspicious day, even though Ada's descriptions of everything going on at the ranch—Wade and Lilly's antics, Wyatt's latest cattle-buying trips—made her long for the familiar.

"Miss Lucy Partridge from over at the ladies' hotel came by to tell you your room is ready. You can move in anytime." He pulled a face. "Sure will miss you, but I reckon it's more proper for you to live at the Verandah."

"So I'm told." Personally she saw no purpose in having to move. Wasn't one hotel like another? But Wyatt and Ada had insisted she live at the Verandah. At one time she could have lived in the house Wyatt inherited from his Aunt Lillian and deeded to Ada before their marriage. But Ada had sold the house the year before and donated the money to the Ladies Suffrage Society. Even if it were available, it sat seven miles from town, too far to make living there practical. So the Verandah it was. She tucked away her mail and headed for the stairs.

"Oh, miss," the clerk said. "I nearly forgot. Railway agent says your shipment arrived this afternoon. You need to arrange for a delivery."

"I will. Thank you, Mr. Foster."

"You don't want any dinner, miss? Before the dining room closes?"

"I had tea at Blue Smoke. I'm not really very hungry."

He whistled. "Well, well. Tea at Blue Smoke. Is it as fancy as people say?"

"Yes. It's very grand."

The clerk grinned. "Too fancy for my blood. But I don't reckon I ought to worry about it. Ain't likely that ordinary folks like me can afford to stay there anyway. I can't—"

The door crashed open, and a disheveled man ran inside brandishing a shotgun. The clerk spun around. "Lord have mercy, Trotter. What in the world's going on?"

"Sheriff McCracken says to round up every man you can find and git on up to Blue Smoke. They's a riot going on."

The clerk darted from behind the desk. "You'll have to excuse me, miss. I got to go."

A riot? Sophie's reporter's instincts kicked in. Everything this afternoon had seemed so calm. What could have triggered such a disturbance?

She stuffed her mail into her reticule and drew her shawl tightly about her shoulders.

"I'm coming with you."

THREE

Sophie followed the clerk and Mr. Trotter into the street where half a dozen men were gathered by torchlight, rounding up horses and guns. In the middle of the chaos stood Sheriff Eli McCracken, barking orders.

"Hurry up with those—" He broke off when he spied Sophie standing next to Mr. Foster, her notebook propped on the hitching rail outside the inn. "What in the name of all that is holy are you doing here?"

Her pen stilled. "Reporting on the riot, of course. There isn't time to retrieve my rig. I'll have to ride up to Blue Smoke with one of you."

McCracken shook his head. "Absolutely not. Wyatt Caldwell would have my head on a platter if you got hurt."

"Sheriff?" Mr. Trotter jammed his brown felt hat onto his head and swung into his saddle. "We ought to get going."

"I couldn't agree more." Sophie snapped her notebook shut and looked up at Wyatt's old friend. "I'm sure I'll be perfectly safe with you."

"Out of the question." McCracken mounted up, saddle leather creaking, a torch in one hand. "Let's head out," he called. "Trotter, Foster, you two take the lead. The rest of you, follow me. We'll take the old logging trail and come in from behind."

Sophie grabbed the reins. "Then I suppose I'll have to take whatever mount is available from the livery and ride up there all alone. Unarmed. In the dark."

McCracken sighed. "This is dangerous business. And besides, it isn't proper." He looked down pointedly at her skirt.

"It's dark, Mr. McCracken. No one will be scandalized. And this is my first big story. Don't make me miss out just because we're short a horse."

"Sheriff, we're losing time," Trotter said.

The sheriff grunted in exasperation but held out his hand. "Are you going to be this much trouble every day?"

"Oh, no, sir." She grabbed his hand and vaulted onto the horse, settling herself behind him, arranging her skirt as best she could. "Some days I expect I'll be even more trouble."

The riders headed for the logging trail behind the train station and began the climb to Blue Smoke, Mr. Foster and Mr. Trotter in the lead. Sophie tucked her notebook inside her reticule and draped her shawl over her head to ward off the chilly mist shrouding the mountain. Light flickered through the thick stands of trees, the torch fires hissing in the damp.

As they neared the resort, shouts shattered the darkness. Gunfire erupted.

"Hold on." The sheriff dug his heels into the horse's flank and they flew through the darkness, passing the others and arriving just as another round of gunfire split the night.

Sheriff McCracken dismounted and helped her down. "Stay here," he ordered. "Do not move."

Sophie frowned. How in the world did he expect her to write a full account of this event without getting close to the action? It would be like getting one's nourishment by watching someone else eat. She waited until the sheriff had drawn his gun and moved toward the front entrance. Then she circled behind the waiting horses. Keeping to the shadows, she crossed the wide expanse of lawn to where a small knot of men huddled beside an empty freight wagon.

"What happened?" She addressed her question to a brown-haired young man dressed in denim pants and a blue-plaid shirt.

He spun around. "Holy cats. What's a girl doing in the middle of a fistfight?"

"Is that what it is, a fistfight? Who started it? What's it about?"

A string of shouted curses blued the air. A window shattered. A Chinese man, his pigtail flying, scurried from the shadows and disappeared around back.

A burly, red-bearded man frowned at Sophie. "Who wants to know?"

Brown Hair glared at him. "It started out as a fistfight, miss, but then O'Connor over there pulled his gun, and then Mr. Heyward ran out and—"

"Mr. Heyward. That would be Mr. Ethan Heyward?"

"One and the same. He doesn't allow gunplay up here. He took Jubal's rifle, and Jubal took a swing at Mr. Heyward. I reckon Jubal will be gone for good come daylight."

"Is anyone hurt?"

"Oh, no, ma'am. I don't think anybody was hit. The gunfire's just a way the men have of blowin' off steam. They don't mean anything by it."

"But someone told the sheriff a riot was in progress."

"Yes'm. This argument got out of hand, all right. The next thing we knew there was more'n thirty men slugging it out." He shook his head. "One of the younger boys on the logging crew got scared and sounded the alarm. Truth is, the Irish and the ni—uh, black folks don't like each other at all."

Sophie's stomach dropped at the man's use of the hated epithet, but she nodded.

"Both groups hate the Chinese." The young man jerked his

thumb toward the door to the kitchen. "Li Chung keeps to hisself mostly, but the others have been at each other's throats since this whole project began. And I for one'll be glad when it's over."

"What do the men fight about?"

Brown Hair's burly companion shrugged. "You name it. Women, whiskey, cards, somebody looks at somebody else the wrong way. You get nigh on a hundred men living in these conditions, fights are bound to break out. Two men got themselves killed last year. But Mr. Heyward don't like to admit there's problems up here."

Torchlight flared as Sheriff McCracken's men fanned out through the crowd, shouting orders and dispersing the men. Over her interviewee's shoulder, Sophie saw Ethan Heyward talking with one of his workers, one hand resting on the man's shoulder. "You mentioned problems. What kind of problems, exactly?"

The man took a step back. "I'm not saying. And I would appreciate it if you wouldn't tell nobody what I just said. I need this job." He frowned. "You never did say what you're doing up here with the sheriff."

The crowd melted into the darkness. McCracken spoke to Mr. Heyward before heading toward his mount. Sophie watched Mr. Heyward head back inside. He moved with the confidence of a man who understood his place in the world and reveled in it. She was attracted to his power and slightly afraid of it. Apparently his men felt the same way.

"I must go." Sophie hurried over and met the sheriff beneath the trees. Mr. Foster and Mr. Trotter, their torches burning low, joined them.

"Well, Miss Caldwell." McCracken swung into the saddle and held out his hand to her. "Looks like you came all this way for nothing. Just a few drunks letting off steam. Don't seem like there's much of an interesting newspaper story after all."

"I wouldn't say that, Sheriff." Sophie mounted up behind him, her brief conversation with the men playing in her mind. What sort of problems existed at Blue Smoke? And why was Mr. Heyward loath to speak of them?

The answers to those questions might prove interesting indeed.

⌒

Sheriff Eli McCracken, in the company of six townsmen, quelled a disagreement last week at the Blue Smoke resort. According to eyewitnesses, violence has marred the project from the beginning due to conditions the witnesses were unwilling to discuss. What does seem clear is that tensions among the various groups of men working on the resort erupt into gunfire on a regular basis, gunfire that has resulted in death for two workers. Steps should be taken to resolve whatever conditions are responsible for this atmosphere at Blue Smoke before some other unfortunate man loses his life.

Sophie rolled the paper from her typewriting machine and scanned it, then placed it in the wire basket with the other stories she was accumulating for her first issue of the *Gazette*. The piece still needed work. But today was Sunday, and she had promised to visit Ada's friend Carrie Daly Rutledge at her horse farm outside town.

She removed her reading spectacles and rose from her desk, glancing over at the steam press in the composing room. The new type trays and composing sticks she had ordered from Chicago had arrived. Too bad there was no time to begin setting the type for the first issue. Placing the lead letters one by one into the trays was a time-consuming and filthy task, the only part of newspapering she found tedious. It was always a relief when the trays were neatly filled and ready for ink.

The front door opened and a young man, his thick blond hair wind-tousled, peered in. He grinned. "Sophie Robillard Caldwell."

"Robbie? Oh my goodness." Her heart lifted at the sight of her only childhood friend. All grown up now, of course, but she'd know Robbie Whiting anywhere. He'd often accompanied his mother to the orphanage and kept Sophie company while the other children played or studied. Together they had roamed the hills in search of arrowheads, picked wild blackberries along the riverbank, shared penny candy from Mr. Pruitt's mercantile, and reveled in the dime novels Robbie bought from Mr. Chastain's bookshop. Her mixed-up parentage, whatever it was, had never mattered one whit to Robbie. For that alone, she was prepared to love him forever.

Robbie swept her into a bear hug, twirling her around until she felt dizzy. "Mother said Miss Ada wrote her that you were coming back here. I'd planned to surprise you at the train station, but I had to make a trip up to Muddy Hollow, and then a couple of days ago one of my flock fell ill and I—"

"Wait." She drew back and looked up at him. "One of your flock? The last I heard, you were reading law in Nashville."

He set her on her feet. "I was close to joining up with a couple of other lawyers once my studies were finished, but it turns out God had a completely different agenda. I'm the pastor here in town."

His laugh brought to mind the Robbie who had reveled in their childhood escapades. He'd idolized Wyatt Caldwell too, and more than once declared that his aim in life was to own a ranch in Texas, just like Wyatt's. For the first year after Ada and Wyatt took her to live with them there, she had hoped Robbie would visit, but he never had. And like most childhood friendships interrupted by distance, theirs had faded away. Now, looking into his bright blue eyes, she felt her old affection for him returning.

She took his arm and drew him into the office. "I'm on my way to visit Carrie Rutledge, but I've time for tea if you do."

"I'd love to stay and catch up, but Ethelinda and I promised to visit Deborah Patterson this afternoon. Her husband, Daniel, was the minister at the church up until the week before he took sick and passed on. I promised him I'd look after her."

Sophie's head swam. "I can't believe you're a preacher."

"Well, I am. As of last September."

"Good gravy. And Ethelinda is—"

"My wife. Also as of last September." Another burst of laughter. "I've had a pretty busy year."

"Apparently so. Why didn't I know any of this, Robbie Whiting?"

"Why didn't I know you were off in Dallas learning the newspaper game? Mother mentioned it only a few weeks ago when she learned you were coming back here." He smiled down at her. "Life hardly ever turns out the way we plan, does it?"

"Don't I know it? Mrs. Mills—she was head of my department at the paper in Dallas—offered me a job there last December. I said yes, but the longer I thought about it, the more I felt compelled to come back here."

"After the way you were treated at the orphanage?" He leaned against her desk and crossed his arms. "I don't understand."

"It didn't make any sense to Wyatt and Ada either. But I couldn't get the notion out of my head, so here I am."

He nodded. "I hope things will be different for you now. Lots of changes have taken place in Hickory Ridge since we were children."

"Yes, Blue Smoke is causing quite a stir, and not just locally. Even our paper ran a piece about it when construction first began."

"I was thinking of the orphanage. You know it's closed now."

"I went by there the other day. I couldn't help myself." She shrugged. "Even with all the broken windows and the locked gate, I still felt like Mrs. Lowell might stick her head out at any moment and yell at me to stop dawdling and get on inside."

"She could be fierce." He paused. "You remember the Wilcox children? A boy and girl who came here after their parents drowned?"

"I remember them. Jesse and . . ."

"Audrey. I ran into Jesse over in Knoxville last year. He works for a druggist now. His sister is married. I don't know where she's living. But Jesse told me Mrs. Lowell died of the yellow fever back in seventy-nine."

He picked up a book from her desk and flipped it open. "I remember when Ada bought this for you at Mr. Chastain's shop. I guess you heard he got married a few years back. Some fancy lady from New Orleans. But it didn't last long. I was away at school, but Mother told me his wife jumped on the train one day and never came back."

"That's terrible. Mr. Chastain is a good man."

"He is." Robbie set the book aside. "The strange thing is that after church last week, Lucy Partridge told Mother that Mrs. Chastain has written to the Verandah, asking for her old room back. Apparently she stayed there before she got married."

"Maybe she's had second thoughts and wants Mr. Chastain back."

"After all this time?" Robbie shook his head. "I doubt it."

"Remember how he read stories to us on Founders Day? And showed us his sleight-of-hand tricks? I should go by and see him."

"Oh, but that's another big change. Mr. Chastain left town shortly after his wife took off—sold the bookshop to one of Jasper Pruitt's cousins and never looked back. My folks bought it from Jasper's kin after Pa's accident."

Sophie nodded. "Ada told me about that. I was sorry to hear it. Mr. Whiting was always kind to me."

"It was pretty bad," Robbie said. "A load of timber slipped off a skip loader and pinned him underneath it. For a while it looked like he might lose his leg, but eventually it healed. He never could work the lumberyard again, though. He sits at a desk now. Hates it. Mother runs the bookshop."

"Mrs. Whiting is a bookseller now? Ada didn't tell me that."

"Mother took it over only recently. She seems to like it."

Setting the book aside, he peered over her shoulder into the back room, where the printing press stood amid a jumble of crates she'd recently unpacked. "You know how to work that thing?"

"Of course. I started hanging around the newspaper office back home when I was twelve or thirteen. Mr. Hadley—he's the owner of the *Inquirer*—showed me how to load type into the tray, but he wouldn't let me actually run the press till I was older." She grinned. "It's a dirty, tedious job, and slower than Christmas. Soon as I start making a profit, I'm going to look into replacing this old press with a more modern one." She tamped down a stab of uncertainty. "Assuming I actually make a profit. Sometimes I wake up and ask myself why on earth I came back here. Maybe I'm foolish for even trying."

"Not at all. I'm certain the Lord has a purpose for it."

She gazed past his shoulder to the street, quiet now in the cool spring afternoon. "Do you really believe that, Robbie? That there is a purpose to everything?"

"Yes, ma'am, I do." He smiled down at her. "I really have to go, but one of these days I want you to meet my wife."

"I'd love that."

"Come to services next Sunday. I'll save you a seat in the first pew."

He left the office whistling and jogged across the street to his waiting rig. Sophie watched as he turned the rig for home, her mind whirling. Heavenly days, but Hickory Ridge was all ajumble. People of every stripe milling around town like ants in a hill. Houses going up every which way. Mrs. Lowell dead and gone. Sweet Mr. Chastain all brokenhearted, no doubt, and off to who knew where, while his wife was on her way back to town.

Sophie frowned. Why would the former Mrs. Chastain come back here after so long a time? There was no accounting for human behavior and no telling what might happen next. But one thing was for sure: Lucy Partridge wouldn't have room for her at the Verandah. With Blue Smoke set to open in a matter of weeks, every room was taken or already reserved.

She grabbed her hat and shawl, locked the office, and headed for Mr. Tanner's livery. His rates were outrageous, but the Rutledge farm was too far to walk. Farther along the street, Eli McCracken emerged from his office and headed for Miss Hattie's. Sophie's stomach groaned. What she wouldn't give for one of Miss Hattie's legendary Sunday dinners. But Carrie Rutledge was expecting her.

She entered the livery, breathing in the familiar, dusty scent of hay, horses, and manure. "Mr. Tanner?"

He shuffled to the front of the building, wiping his hands on a faded towel. "Miss Caldwell. What can I do for you?"

"A horse and rig, please. That little chestnut mare I had last week will be perfect."

"She's a beauty all right, but I sold her yesterday to Blue Smoke. Mr. Rutledge usually takes care of anything related to the Blue Smoke horses, but Mr. Heyward himself come down from his mountaintop for a change and made me a right good offer for her. He said she'll make a good addition to that fancy riding stable they're building up there."

She fumbled in her reticule for her cash. "Mr. Heyward doesn't come to town that often?"

"Not hardly at all. Usually that young redheaded fellow shows up at the bank or the mercantile, but occasionally the boss man makes an appearance."

Sophie nodded and secured her hat against a sudden gust of late-March wind. "I'd love to stay and chat, but—"

"Oh, sure. You need a horse and buggy. Well, I've got Miss Pearl over there." He jerked his thumb toward a silver-gray horse munching hay, her tail swishing flies. "She ain't the fastest thing on four legs, but she's reliable."

"I'm sure she'll be fine."

While the liveryman harnessed Miss Pearl, Sophie retrieved Carrie's letter from her pocket and reread the directions to the Rutledge farm. The train whistle sounded just as Mr. Tanner led the horse and rig into the thin spring sunlight and helped Sophie inside. "Where you headed?"

"The Rutledge place. Mrs. Rutledge says it's adjacent to Mr. Gilman's. I hope it won't be too hard to find."

"You'll see the turnoff five miles or so past the train depot. The road's in bad shape, though. We had a lot of rain last month, and the ruts are pretty deep." He patted the side of the old rig, which had seen better days. "Just watch out that you don't damage my equipment. I'd hate to charge you extra for repairs."

Sophie flicked the reins and headed out of town. The liveryman's mention of Ethan Heyward had set her reporter's mind to working again. Why did Mr. Heyward keep to himself? Was something untoward going on at Blue Smoke, or was he merely one of those men, like Wyatt, who liked to keep a close eye on his interests?

She passed a Negro family on their way home from church, the women and girls dressed in bright calicos, the men and boys in denim pants and bleached white shirts. All were barefoot. A couple of the young girls offered a shy wave as their wagon and her rig negotiated the rutted road. By the time she finally arrived at the Rutledges' place, her dress was coated in a thin layer of dust and her mouth was parched.

The door opened and Carrie Daly Rutledge rushed out, her copper curls bound in a pale blue ribbon. "Sophie." Carrie wrapped both arms around Sophie and held her tight. "Our darling girl, here at last. Come in. I want you to meet Griff and Charlotte."

Sophie followed Carrie into the spacious, light-filled cottage. A bank of windows faced a lush meadow where five or six horses stood placidly cropping grass.

"Griff? Darling?"

"So this is the Caldwells' famous ward?" An extraordinarily handsome dark-haired man crossed in front of the fireplace and clasped both Sophie's hands. "Welcome to our home. Carrie has talked of little else but your arrival ever since we found out you were coming back here."

Sophie dropped her gaze. She loved the Caldwells with everything that was in her, and they loved her too. But Mr. Rutledge's use of the word *ward* reminded her that she didn't belong to anyone. Not really. Despite all the advantages Wyatt and Ada had provided her, the one thing they couldn't give her was a heritage. She was still a muddlebones, a mongrel, an orphan with two borrowed names and no real knowledge of who she was or where she came from. Sometimes a fragment of a song or story, a half-remembered dream, would feel oddly familiar, but her attempts to connect it to anything real brought only a vague sadness.

"We're delighted to see you." Mr. Rutledge, his dark eyes radiating warmth, kissed her hand just as a tiny replica of Carrie danced into the room, one shoe missing, her hair a tumble of dark curls.

"Papa, look what I found." She held out a fistful of violets.

Griff laughed and scooped her into his arms. "Where have you been, my sweet? And where on earth is your shoe?"

The girl's mother watched the exchange, obviously smitten with them both. "Sophie, this is our daughter, Charlotte."

"Hello." Sophie smiled at the little girl, who reminded her so much of the Caldwells' young daughter, Lilly, that a pang of homesickness shot through her. She nodded toward the meadow. "I was just admiring your papa's horses. Back home in Texas I have a young mare who is often too spirited for her own good. I have a horse named Cherokee too. She's almost too old to ride now, but she's very gentle, and I love her more than anything."

Griff set his daughter on her feet. Arms akimbo, Charlotte cocked one hip. "I'd want to ride the spirited one."

"Would you? Do you know how to ride yet?"

"Yes'm. I have a pony, but Mama won't let me ride her unless Papa is with me. 'Cause I fell off Majestic one time and bumped my head, and I couldn't even breathe."

"I heard about Majestic," Sophie said. "I heard he won the very first race ever held in Hickory Ridge."

Charlotte nodded. "Mama gots a picture of it. I'll show you."

She raced from the room. Mr. Rutledge smiled and caught his wife's eye. "Darling, I hate to rush things, but we should eat soon. I need to go back up to Blue Smoke."

"Oh, Griff, must you? On Sunday?"

"I'm afraid so. One of the riding trails still needs clearing, and I want to check on that new bay gelding. He's favoring a hind foot, and I don't want to continue training him until he's completely well."

Carrie turned to Sophie. "My husband is in charge of the entire equestrian program at Blue Smoke. As much as he loves the work, I do sometimes wish he weren't quite so indispensable."

"In another year or so I won't have to spend so much time there," Griff told Sophie. "I do enjoy it, but I'm looking forward to having more time to devote to my own stables."

"Here it is!" Charlotte ran to Sophie and handed her a framed photograph. "That's my papa and Majestic. I think he's the handsomest ever."

Griff laughed and ruffled his daughter's curls. "Are you talking about me or the horse?"

Carrie smiled and led Sophie to a chair at the table. "You just sit right here and relax. Everything is ready and warming on the stove. I'll be right back."

FOUR

Ethan Heyward tapped on the glass and opened the door to the *Gazette* office. "Anybody home?"

"Mr. Heyward." Sophie grabbed a rag, wiped the ink from her fingers, and removed the long apron she wore in the dusty composing room. Seating herself behind her desk, she motioned him into the chair across from her. "May I help you?"

He lowered his lanky frame into the chair and crossed his ankles. "I was in town and thought I should pay a call."

Aware of his intent gaze, she glanced away. Why hadn't she taken more care getting dressed this morning? She'd worn her old faded calico and pinned her hair up every which way, without even looking into the mirror. Ada was forever reminding her about her appearance, but she was usually too intent upon her work to bother. She should have paid more attention this morning, because Mr. Heyward was still watching her, his blue eyes behind his gold-rimmed spectacles full of undisguised interest. Despite her unanswered questions about the goings-on up at Blue Smoke, she couldn't help noticing that the expression in his eyes and the slight dimple in his chin made him seem at once studious and playful—a most attractive combination.

He swept one hand around the sunlit office. "I assume you're open for business."

"Yes. I'm behind schedule because I took half a day getting settled in at the ladies' hotel and catching up on my correspondence, but the first issue is almost ready for printing."

"Glad to hear it. We can't have a real town without a newspaper." He paused. "I don't suppose you'd give me an advance look?"

"Then you'd have no need to buy a copy, would you?"

"I suppose not," he said, smiling. "But if we're to do business together in the future—"

Understanding dawned. "I see. You expect to control what I write. A quid pro quo."

"I wouldn't call it that. Let's just say I like to be sure that whatever is printed about Blue Smoke is accurate."

She felt her blood heating. "That's an insult to any newspaper writer worth her salt. I trained at a big city newspaper, Mr. Heyward, a very respected one. Of course my reporting is accurate."

He shifted in his chair. "I don't mean to offend you. But one of the men told me that you came up to the resort with the sheriff the other night when that little skirmish broke out. To someone who doesn't understand how a large operation like Blue Smoke works, such a scuffle might give the wrong impression."

"I didn't get the wrong impression, but maybe you will clear something up for me."

"Certainly."

"When I toured there last week, you took pains to show me the grand ballroom and the twenty-four bedrooms and the thirty bathrooms and the grounds, but I learned very little about where the men live and work, what their lives are like."

"I didn't suppose it would interest you. Hardly anyone cares about how a project gets done, as long as it comes in on time and under budget." He leaned forward. "Besides, the workers' quarters are no place for a lady. I didn't wish to offend you. I'm the first to admit the shacks are not all that fancy. But the men who are here without their families have no reason to come and go from the mountain every day. It's more efficient for them to sleep at the site."

"And less expensive for you and Mr. Blakely too."

"We're paying more than fair wages. And we've no shortage of men wanting to work here. In fact, I've a few more men due in on this afternoon's train."

"So that's why you're on one of your rare visits to town?"

"Who says they're rare?"

She arched her brow and rose. "Confidential sources. Thank you for stopping by, but I must get back to work. Please don't worry, Mr. Heyward. I've reported the events accurately."

He rose and a small leather notebook fell from his pocket. Before he could retrieve it, she scooped it up and handed it back to him. "I intend to build the *Gazette* into the best paper in the region. I'm not planning on any sensationalism. But I will offer my opinion on things."

"That's your prerogative, I suppose." He tucked the notebook away and consulted his pocket watch. "The train isn't due in for another half hour, and I was heading over to Miss Hattie's for a bite to eat. Is there any chance you might join me?"

She considered. Work awaited, but Ethan Heyward, despite his take-charge attitude, charmed her. And she was hungry. This morning she'd overslept and had headed straight for work, bypassing the pot of sticky oatmeal bubbling on the stove in Lucy's kitchen.

"Let me get my hat."

He waited for her and offered his arm as they crossed the busy street, dodging a couple of empty freight wagons rumbling toward the station.

Inside Miss Hattie's, Ethan ordered a pot of tea and a plate of biscuits with butter and jam. Miss Hattie, her iron-gray hair pulled into a tight bun, shuffled to the table, the tea things rattling and tipping precariously on the tray. Ethan got to his feet to steady her. "Allow me, ma'am."

"Sit down, young man. I'm not completely incompetent yet." Miss Hattie set down the tray and squinted at Sophie. "Do I know you?"

"I lived here when I was a child. But I've been away for quite a long time."

"That's right. I remember now. You're the one Wyatt Caldwell took to Texas when he married that Yankee girl."

The door opened, and Miss Hattie spun away to greet her next customers.

Ethan added sugar to his tea and stirred. "Wyatt Caldwell is the first person I heard about when I got here. It seems he's a near legend in these parts."

"He owned the lumber mill back then. He sold it when his aunt, Miss Lillian Willis, passed on. His wife, Ada, worked for Miss Lillian and made hats too." She patted the blue silk toque atop her head. "Still does."

He smiled and buttered a biscuit. "Very fetching. How did you find life in Texas?"

"I loved it. Wyatt established a ranch west of Fort Worth. I grew up riding horses and branding longhorns. And helping Ada with her hatmaking business." She sipped the fragrant tea. "When I went away to school in Dallas, I fell in love with newspapering, so Wyatt arranged for me to work with Mrs. Mills at the *Telegraph*. She's a correspondent for papers all across Texas." She set down her cup. "I'm lucky to have had such good training."

He chewed and swallowed. "See, that's what puzzles me. Why would someone who could have gone to an established newspaper choose to come here and start from scratch?"

"Maybe for the same reason you came here to carve a resort out of a mountain." She smiled. "It's an adventure to build something from the ground up, isn't it?"

His eyes lit up. "Yes, that's exactly it. When Horace asked me to design Blue Smoke and oversee the construction, it was a dream come true."

Sophie buttered a biscuit and topped it off with a dollop of strawberry jam. "Do you still feel that way?"

"For the most part. Every endeavor has its challenges, and Blue Smoke is no different." He dropped a sugar cube into his cup and refilled it. "But everything is under control."

"No more riots?"

"There never was one. The entire episode was blown all out of proportion. Anytime you get a large group of men together, a few bad apples are bound to cause trouble."

His face closed down. Clearly he wanted to change the subject. Sophie finished her tea and watched the customers come and go from Miss Hattie's. The train whistle shrieked. Mr. Heyward stood and held her chair. "I'm sorry to rush off, but—"

"It's all right. I should get back to work myself." She rose. "Thank you for the tea and biscuits."

"My pleasure. I enjoyed our conversation." He smiled down at her, and she felt herself warming once more to his charm and intelligence. If he could resist the urge to control the content of her newspaper, perhaps they could forge a pleasant working relationship after all.

They left the restaurant as the train emptied and passengers scattered to await their baggage. At the end of the platform stood a knot of men, each carrying a small white bundle. Ethan frowned and his generous mouth formed a hard, straight line.

"Is something wrong?"

"When I wired my colleague out west for more laborers, I never dreamed he'd send a bunch of Chinese."

Sophie watched as the men chattered to each other, gesturing first toward the looming mountains and then to the train. Her heart ached for them. A few years back, the papers had been full of stories about the Chinese Exclusion Act the Congress had passed in an effort to end Chinese immigration. According to the editorials she read, people objected to the foreigners because they took American jobs laying railroad track and harvesting crops. Some writers called the Chinese "the yellow plague" and "slant-eyed Chinamen." It was disgusting.

"Well, they're here. And I can't afford to send them back." Ethan Heyward frowned, and Sophie's hope for a friendship with him dimmed. Apparently Ethan Heyward had little use for anyone who was different.

~

Ethan handed the five Chinese over to the cook and headed back inside. The newcomers seemed eager to work. With Li Chung to show them the ropes, they should adapt quickly to the routine. In the meantime, he had a million details to work out before the grand opening on the first Saturday in June. Only seven weeks remained to finish the landscaping, place the last of the furniture, hire the housekeepers, waiters, and valets, and plan the ball, to which he had invited everyone from Governor Bate on down.

"O'Brien?"

His secretary entered, pen and notebook in hand. "Sir?"

"How are the arrangements for the ball coming along?"

"So far, a hundred and twenty yeses, seven nos, and forty odd who haven't replied." O'Brien paused. "You got a lady in mind for yourself?"

"As a matter of fact, I do. Haven't asked her yet, though."

"Well, don't wait too long, sir. Ladies take a long time to pick out a fancy dress and such."

Ethan nodded and opened the leather ledger on his desk. "Be sure to pick up cash at the bank before payday."

"What about the Chinamen?"

Ethan thought for a minute. "Go ahead and pay them for the week. They're probably broke after their trip." He ran his finger down a column of the ledger. "I was worried that hiring more Chinese might cause a disturbance, but so far everything's quiet."

O'Brien scribbled in his notebook. "Speakin' of disturbances, Sean Murphy's been spreading it around that whoever talked to that lady reporter the night the sheriff came up here told her fights go on all the time. Murphy said the lady asked a lot of questions."

"So I heard. But I suppose that's what reporters do." Ethan signed a cash-withdrawal note and slid it across the desk. "Did Murphy say who it was that talked to her?"

"That boy who lives out near the mill. Works on the finish crew. I can't ever remember his name. I'll find out if you want."

"Don't bother. I'll handle it." Ethan sorted through a stack of mail and signed the purchase orders O'Brien had left on his desk earlier.

"All right." O'Brien scribbled on his notepad. "By the way, Mr. Blakely's looking for you."

Ethan took off his spectacles and rubbed his eyes. Last week his boss had moved from Baltimore to a palatial suite of rooms at Blue Smoke, bringing his wife and daughters with him. On the one hand, the move made it easier for Ethan to get a quick answer to any question that arose. On the other, having Horace constantly underfoot, second-guessing every decision Ethan made, was a trial. "If it's about the passenger car, nothing has changed. But I'll go see—"

"Ethan?" Horace loomed in the doorway. "I've been looking for you for hours."

O'Brien sent Ethan a sympathetic look and hurried out.

Ethan stood and reached across the desk to shake his boss's hand. "I had to go to town. What can I do for you, Horace?"

Horace collapsed heavily into the chair opposite Ethan's desk. "What you can do for me, boy, is get the American Railway Passenger Car Company to deliver the blasted car they promised me, preferably before our guests start arriving. I thought you had the situation under control."

"I had another wire last Friday. They're still waiting on that special leather you ordered from Italy. They can't finish install-ing the seats till it gets here." Ethan slipped his spectacles back on and reached for a thick folder. "After the first delay, I made some inquiries. I can get the same quality leather from a supplier down in Texas. I wired them last week, and they're ready to ship it to American Railway in Chicago as soon as you say the word."

He slid the folder across the desk to show his boss the com-pany's advertisement and a leather sample, but Horace refused to even look at it.

"I want Italian leather."

Ethan shoved the folder into his desk drawer and slammed it shut. People in Hades wanted ice water too, but that didn't mean they got it. He rose and walked to the window, his hands fisted in his pockets. Down by the stables, Griff Rutledge and his stableboy were working with a couple of the new horses. Ethan fought the desire to grab a horse and disappear into the woods.

"Well?" Horace yelled. "What are you going to do about this, Ethan?"

"I've already told you what I would do, but you won't listen."

"What are we going to do come June when our guests start arriving at the depot in Hickory Ridge and there is no train car to bring them up the mountain?"

"The four carriages we ordered last year have arrived, and I've already put Silas to work training more drivers. We'll have them meet the train and drive the guests up here."

"Along that bone-rattling road?"

"I give up." Ethan crossed the room and plucked his jacket from the back of his chair. "If you'll excuse me, I have business with the construction crew."

"Don't you walk away from me, Ethan. I haven't—"

"Mr. Heyward?" O'Brien hurried in. "Pardon the interruption, but the chef says the menus are all set and we ought to go ahead and have them printed. I can take care of it tomorrow if you like."

Ethan took a deep breath and let it out. "Never mind. I'll handle it. I need to talk to Sheriff McCracken anyway."

O'Brien nodded. "Mr. Blakely? Sir, I just saw your missus coming in. She's looking for you."

"What for?"

"She didn't say, sir."

Blakely muttered a curse word, got to his feet, and lumbered away, slamming the door on his way out.

O'Brien lifted one brow and grinned at Ethan. "Mr. Blakely is afraid of nothing. Except Mrs. Blakely."

"Thanks for rescuing me. I was close to punching him in the nose."

"He deserves it." O'Brien pulled his notebook from his pocket. "I could hear him shouting from the hallway. I'm guessing that was about his railway car."

"Yes. He's determined to be difficult. Some days I regret ever signing on with him."

"He's impossible, that's for certain. But you couldn't pass up a chance to work on something as beautiful as Blue Smoke. Quite a feather in your cap."

"I suppose."

O'Brien glanced at his notebook. "The replacement for the broken mirror in the library arrived. I told Joel Tipton to go ahead and install it. I hope that was all right."

"Fine." Ethan opened another folder and swallowed his lingering anger at Horace. Had Horace always been so difficult? Or were the pressures of the imminent opening wearing on his nerves, making him more demanding than usual? Now that Horace had left, Ethan realized just how close he had come to losing control.

"Forgot to tell you," O'Brien went on. "Lutrell Crocker showed up half-drunk again this morning and fell off the ladder. But he seems all right. And the cabinetmaker said to tell you he needs more varnish. I'll add it to the list."

"I can pick it up. I need to make a trip to the mercantile anyway."

O'Brien shrugged. "Whatever you say. Keep this up, and I'll be out of a job."

Ethan scribbled a few more orders. "No danger of that. Be sure these bills get paid, will you? And tell Crocker I'm looking for him."

O'Brien left. Too keyed up to concentrate after his argument with Horace, Ethan shoved the folders into the drawer and donned his jacket. He stepped onto the terrace and nearly tripped over an empty bucket the painters had left. With one swift kick he sent the bucket tumbling across the newly sprouted lawn.

The devil with Horace. The devil with all of it.

FIVE

Heavenly days, what an odious chore. Sophie massaged the knotted muscles in her back and frowned at the noisy steam press as if it were a living thing. She'd been here in the office since daylight, printing up the first edition of the *Gazette*. Now it was nearly noon, and she was less than halfway finished. An unexpectedly large number of subscriptions had poured in through the week, compelling her to increase her anticipated print run. Not that she didn't appreciate the subscriptions. Each one brought her a bit closer to repaying the money Wyatt had lent her and showing the profit she had promised him.

She eyed the small treadle-powered jobber press sitting in the corner, grateful that Patsy Greer had left it behind when she closed up shop more than a decade before. Smaller and lighter than the rotary press, it could be set up in a matter of minutes and spit out a thousand impressions an hour. If only the rotary press were so efficient. Perhaps in a year or two she could afford a feeder press like the one the *New York Times* had installed years ago. That press kept ten men busy feeding the paper into rollers that pressed it against the cylinder of inked type. For now, such efficiency at her newspaper was only a dream.

She laid her completed sheets of newsprint on the counter to dry and loaded the next tray of type into the press. Her stomach rumbled and she glanced at the clock in the outer office, realizing she'd completely missed the noon meal.

Oh well. The food at the Verandah Ladies' Hotel, though plentiful, tended to be quite plain. The original owner, Mrs. Whitcomb, had passed on a few years before, and now her widowed niece, Lucy Partridge, ran the place. And though Lucy was sweet as could be, cooking was not her strong suit. Flora Burke, who lived on the third floor, was doing her best to help Lucy bring her cooking skills up a notch. In the meantime, beans and fried fatback and occasionally a dried-apple pie were about the best one could hope for.

Sophie's stomach groaned again. Oh, for one of Wyatt's steaks, a baked potato oozing with butter, and a pan of Ada's buttermilk cornbread.

"Hello?"

Sophie peered into the outer office. "Mr. Heyward. Hello." She removed her apron and smoothed her hair before going out to greet him.

"Sorry to call without an appointment. I had a few errands to run and a bit of business with Sheriff McCracken—" He broke off and grinned at her. "And no, I won't answer any questions about it. It's a private matter."

"That's too bad." She smiled, enjoying their easy banter. "I've a spot to fill on the front page of next week's issue. Are you certain you can't give me a hint?"

"Maybe something newsworthy will happen before then." He perched on the corner of her desk. "I've business to discuss, if you have time."

"Certainly." She slid into her chair and rolled a fresh sheet of paper into her typewriting machine.

He placed a stack of papers on her desk. "I need six hundred copies of these menus. Can you handle it?"

"Of course. When do you need them?" She drew her calendar across her desk and flipped the page. April was already half over. Where had the time gone?

"No big hurry," he said. "We're opening the first weekend in June, but of course I want to handle as many details as possible ahead of time."

She nodded. "How about stationery? Business cards? Envelopes? If you place a larger order, I can give you a better price."

He laughed. "Did your boss at the Dallas newspaper teach you that?"

"Nope. Wyatt Caldwell did. I watched him sell off cattle all the time. Everything I know about business, I learned from him."

"Well then, I'll take a thousand sheets of stationery, a thousand envelopes, and . . . three hundred business cards. How's that?"

Her fingers flew across the typewriter keys. In a moment, she removed the completed order sheet and handed it to him. "There you are. My best price."

He whistled. "Pretty steep."

"I can do it for less if you want flimsy paper, but I wouldn't recommend it. Not for a fancy place like Blue Smoke."

"I want the best, of course." He reached into his inside pocket. "How much do you want on deposit?"

"Fifty percent will be fine. I'll have to order the better grade of paper, so the actual printing will take a little time, but I can have the proofs ready for you tomorrow. Shall I bring them to your office?" She handed him the order form and he signed it.

"That won't be necessary. Mr. O'Brien will call for them. He'll be coming into town anyway." He handed her a couple of crisp bills and waited.

She fidgeted at his intent gaze, her cheeks warming beneath his scrutiny. Ethan Heyward truly had the most beautiful eyes. "Is there anything else?"

"Actually, there is. Blue Smoke will be finished at the end of May. I'm conducting a reception and tour for the newspaper and magazine reporters. *Harper's* has agreed to send someone. So has the *Boston Globe* and several papers from around the state. I'm inviting you too. It'll be a chance to meet your colleagues and to see how everything turned out."

Feeling both pleased and surprised, Sophie could only nod. How wonderful it would be to meet others who shared her love of newspapering. But what on earth would she wear? The one fancy dress Ada had insisted she bring from Texas, just in case, wasn't quite right for such an occasion, but the plain dresses and jackets she wore to the newspaper office each day were unlikely to make a favorable first impression. Her bank account wouldn't allow for much extravagance. The sensible thing to do was to decline. And yet . . .

"Thank you." She smiled into his eyes. "I'd like that."

He nodded. "And something else. The Blakelys and I are hosting a ball the following night. Dinner, dancing, no expense spared. I'd be pleased to escort you." His eyes met hers. "Unless you've some objection to mixing business with pleasure."

She smoothed the folds of her skirt. Of course she wanted to spend a glittering evening at Blue Smoke. Who wouldn't? It was a once-in-a-lifetime opportunity. Most folks in Hickory Ridge, including her, would never have a chance to set foot inside the resort once the opening-week excitement died down. And she liked Mr. Heyward very much, or she would if she allowed herself to dwell on it. But she couldn't forget his apparent displeasure with the Chinese workers. If the taunts of her childhood were true, would he look at her in the same way? Maybe it was better to keep her distance despite her feelings. Keep their connection strictly business.

"I'm honored, Mr. Heyward, but—"

"O'Brien said I should ask you now, so you'd have time to buy a fancy dress."

He looked boyish, so hopeful and shy, that she forgave his earlier attempts to manage the news and tamped down the unsettling feeling that he might be just as prejudiced as some others in Hickory Ridge. Perhaps it was only her own insecurities talking and she had misread him altogether. Perhaps he deserved the benefit of the doubt.

"Thank you. I'd love to come. It sounds wonderful."

"I'll look forward to it." He headed for the door.

She leaned against the desk and watched him go. It was hard not to like Ethan Heyward, and she was flattered that he wanted her company for the ball. The question was, would he still want to dance with her once he read this week's *Gazette*?

~

"You're late," Gillie whispered, sliding down the pew to make room for Sophie.

"Sorry," Sophie whispered back.

The church was nearly full. Sophie spotted the Rutledges and Robbie's parents sitting a few rows ahead of her. Sheriff McCracken sat on the aisle next to Jasper and Jeanne Pruitt. But where was Mr. Heyward? She felt a stab of disappointment at his absence. Perhaps he was too busy to come all the way to town so early on Sunday morning. Or perhaps he attended services at Blue Smoke with his men.

Sophie plopped down beside her new friend. "I went by the office to check on one small thing. Next thing I knew, half an hour had evaporated, just like that." She snapped her fingers, causing the woman in front of her to turn around and frown.

Gillie elbowed Sophie and grinned. "There's a reason we're

not supposed to work on Sunday. It's too easy to forget about the Lord."

Robbie Whiting, dressed in a black suit, his wild blond hair slicked down, entered through a side door and crossed to the lectern, his Bible tucked under his arm. Sophie's mind filled with memories of their shared childhood, and she thanked God for the one boy who had accepted her when no one else would.

Until the Caldwells came along, of course. Sophie closed her eyes, picturing them at Sunday worship in the big white church near their ranch: Ada still slim and stylish in a new spring hat, Wyatt handsome and grave, holding Wade and Lilly by the hand. A perfect family who knew where they came from and where they belonged—and who had accepted Sophie as their own.

But though she was loved, accepted, and treated like a daughter, she wasn't a Caldwell and could never be. Who knew what she was?

Robbie welcomed everyone to the service, and the organist began playing an old hymn, one of Sophie's favorites. The notes floated softly on the spring air that drifted through the windows:

In pastures green he bids me lie
In peace beneath his loving eye.

As the words soared heavenward, Sophie remembered Miss Lillian and how she'd sung those words, her voice high and reedy, as she puttered in her garden. Wyatt's elderly aunt said contentment was a choice. But how was it possible to be truly at peace inside when there was so much she didn't know, might never know, about who she was and where she came from?

For years she'd dreamed that one day her mother might still find her. In her loneliest moments, she'd prayed for it, and for a brief moment years ago it seemed possible her prayers might be answered. When Wyatt and Ada learned that a woman had appeared in Hickory Ridge asking about a lost child, Wyatt hired the famous Pinkerton Detective Agency to investigate. But the woman disappeared, Pinkerton's gave up in defeat, and eventually Sophie ceased praying for the impossible. Clearly, God did not intend to intervene.

Robbie concluded his sermon and pronounced the benediction. Gillie looped her arm through Sophie's as the congregation filed out. "Now that we have paid our respects to the Almighty, how about some fun?"

Sophie studied her new friend. Since arriving in Hickory Ridge, she'd been so busy getting the paper up and running that fun had become a foreign idea. But the first issue was finally printed and out the door, and she felt like celebrating. "What did you have in mind?"

"Since the weather has been so warm lately, my parents invited a few people out to the house for a barbecue this afternoon. Daddy promised to let us ride the horses. You're from Texas, so I figured you might be homesick for the wild open range." She swept one hand toward the towering mountains. "Not exactly the same, but—"

"I'd love the chance to ride. I miss my horses something awful." They made their way out of the church and into the bright spring sunshine. "Of course I don't ride Cherokee anymore. She was Wyatt's when he lived here, but he shipped her down home and gave her to me when I lost my little mare, Hickory. Cherokee's getting pretty old, but I love her to bits."

"I'm sure we can find you a suitable mount. Too bad Mr. Rutledge bought Majestic from Daddy. Majestic would have given you quite a time of it."

"Sophie." Robbie waved to them and hurried over. "You came. Hello, Miss Gilman."

Gillie bobbed her head. "Reverend."

"I looked for you," Robbie said to Sophie, "but the church was so full I couldn't see you."

"A big congregation is a nice problem to have." Sophie smiled at her old friend. "Everyone seemed to enjoy your sermon."

"I try to keep it short and lively so Mr. Purdy and Mrs. Higginbottom won't fall asleep before the doxology." He grinned. "How are you? All settled in at the Verandah?"

"I'm fine. Missing Ada's good cooking, though."

The organist, a sweet-faced woman in a dark-blue bombazine dress and matching shawl, crossed the yard. "Good morning, Miss Gilman. I'm surprised to see you. Doc Spencer tells me you were up late last night helping him tend the Osborn girl."

"I was, but I'm glad to report she's much better. I'm exhausted, but I wouldn't miss church on account of it. Sunday isn't Sunday without Reverend Whiting's sermon."

Robbie smiled at Sophie and slid an arm around the woman's waist. "Sophie Caldwell, I'd like you to meet my wife, Ethelinda."

"I assumed as much." Sophie nodded to the woman. "Happy to meet you. Robbie and I are old friends."

"So I heard." Ethelinda smiled up at her husband. "He says you were quite a storyteller back then. I'm sure your newspaper enterprise will benefit from your skills. And the town will certainly benefit from having a local paper."

"I hope so."

Ethelinda laid a hand on her husband's arm. "Robert, dear, the Huffsteads are leaving, and the mister wants a word with you. I asked him to call at the parsonage this afternoon, but he insists it's urgent."

"I'd best see to him, then." Robbie clasped Sophie's hand. "We should go. I'm awfully glad you came today."

He and his wife hurried to greet the departing worshippers.

"You are coming out to the house, aren't you?" Gillie said. "I can promise you that Mother's barbecue will taste much better than anything you'll get at the Verandah."

"If we're going to ride, I'll need to change my dress."

"We can stop at the Verandah for your clothes." Gillie led the way to her rig. "You can change after dinner."

The two friends made the five-mile drive to the Gilmans' place in companionable silence, enjoying the beauty and the unusual warmth of the day. The lane leading to the house was crowded with wagons and rigs and carriages. People spilled from the porches onto the grass. Women gathered in groups near the house, enjoying the sun and chatting. The men lined up against the fence, studying the Gilmans' horses and those of the Rutledges next door.

Spying Sophie, Carrie Rutledge broke away and crossed the lawn to greet her. "I didn't know you were coming today, but I'm so glad you did. Charlotte will be delighted to see you. She was quite taken with you when you visited us."

"She's darling. I'm glad to see you too. You put me in mind of Ada. I miss her terribly."

Carrie patted Sophie's hand. "I'm sure she misses you too. Have you heard from her since you arrived here?"

"Two letters last week. Lilly twisted an ankle chasing after Wade, but otherwise they're all fine."

"Mrs. Rutledge, will you excuse us?" Gillie said. "We're starved. I hope Mother saved me a piece of pie."

"You might have to wrestle my husband for it. I have never met a man more in love with chess pie."

Gillie laughed. "Come on, Sophie. I'll introduce you to Mother, and then we can eat."

She led the way to the dining room where a large buffet was set with bone china and glittering crystal. A woman Sophie assumed was Mrs. Gilman moved among her guests, regal as a queen. Gillie caught her eye. "Mother, may I introduce Miss Sophie Caldwell? She's the new owner of the *Gazette*."

"So I hear." Mrs. Gilman crossed her ample arms and eyed Sophie from head to toe, taking in her ruffled shirtwaist and simple skirt.

Sophie felt her face go warm at such cold scrutiny, but she met the older woman's steady gaze.

"Of course my daughter's friends are always welcome here," Mrs. Gilman said. "But I do hope you won't monopolize Sabrina's time. There are several young men here who—"

"Come on, Sophie," Gillie said in a rush. "Let's get some barbecue before it's all gone."

They filled their plates and settled down on the porch steps to eat. While Sophie devoured slices of barbecued pork, mounds of mashed potatoes, and fruit compote served in a tiny hand-painted cup, Gillie regaled her with stories of her rounds with Dr. Spencer and her dream of opening an infirmary in town.

"Hickory Ridge is growing so much, Doc Spencer can't always get to everyone who needs him in a timely fashion." Gillie polished off her slice of pie and drained her glass. "And often mothers put off sending for the doctor for themselves. By the time Dr. Spencer sees them, they've gotten worse. We need a place where they can come and stay for treatment if necessary. I can handle the routine things, and Doc will have time for the more serious cases." She stood. "Come on. Ready to ride?"

They left their dishes in the kitchen, changed clothes in Gillie's room, and headed to the barn. Gillie lifted the bar on the door and they went inside. A sleek brown mare, her soft eyes fringed with thick lashes, bobbed her head and snuffled as they passed. Sophie breathed in the familiar smells of horses, hay, and liniment and paused to rest her cheek against the horse's muzzle, missing home and everything in it. Why had she insisted on coming back here, so far from everyone who loved her?

Well, it was too late now. She wasn't one to give up easily. She wouldn't go home until she'd accomplished what she set out to do.

"Look around if you wish," Gillie said. "I'll have Old Peter tack up a couple of mounts, and that will take awhile. He's ancient, but he loves it here, and Papa hasn't the heart to retire him." She disappeared into the dimness of the long barn.

Sophie stayed put and spoke quietly to the mare, running her hands over the animal's sleek, warm sides. The discomfort of Mrs. Gilman's cool reception vanished, replaced with the sense of peace that being around horses always brought her.

"Well, look who's here. Our newspaperwoman."

Sophie spun around, one hand over her heart. "Mr. Heyward. You startled me."

In a few long strides he covered the distance between them. "And you startled me, Miss Caldwell, with your editorial in the *Gazette*."

"Oh, that." She patted the horse. "Well, I'm sorry if I offended you, but it's my job to report the facts. And to remark upon them when I feel it's warranted."

"Thus giving readers the benefit of your vast experience." His voice was deadly serious, but a glint of amusement flashed in his eyes.

Was he making fun of her? She plucked a currycomb from the stall shelf and began grooming the horse. She hadn't meant to sound so didactic, but heavenly days, what did Mr. Heyward think she was supposed to do? Ignore the circumstances at the resort just to keep his good opinion?

He held out his hand, allowing the horse to sniff. "Of course, I can't tell you what to write, but your comments left the wrong impression. I'm not hiding anything up at Blue Smoke, and I didn't much care for the insinuation."

"I understand a couple of men died in fights up there. I'm only trying to prevent more bloodshed."

"Who told you that?"

"I don't know."

"You don't know? What happened to your high-and-mighty journalistic standards? Or are you now in the dirt with those sensationalist hacks who make up their so-called facts?"

She returned the currycomb to the shelf. "I did not make it up. One of your men told me about it the night I rode up there with Sheriff McCracken. The man did not tell me his name." She glared at him. "Apparently he's too afraid to speak out. He did tell me that fights are common among the workers. It seems to me like a dangerous situation."

He fixed her with a steady gaze. "I don't like it either, but human nature is what it is. So long as the coloreds and the Irish hate each other and they both hate the Chinese, there will be disagreements. I'm trying to keep the lid on things until Blue Smoke is finished. Editorials like yours don't help matters."

She waited, one hand resting on the mare's side.

Mr. Heyward propped one booted foot on the bottom rail of the stall door. "Besides, the situation is temporary. Another couple of months and most of them can go home. Problem solved."

"A lot can happen in the meantime."

The mare blew out and danced sideways in her stall, and he soothed her with a quiet word, his eyes on Sophie. "What would you have me do, Miss Caldwell?"

"I don't know. Maybe the men need something to do in the evenings. Something other than drinking whiskey and insulting each other."

"Maybe you'd like to have them join hands and sing hymns."

"It's better than firing weapons and beating up on each other with fists and broken bottles, don't you think?"

Just then Gillie and a gray-haired Negro man came out leading two horses. "Ready, Sophie?"

"How about if we make a pact?" Mr. Heyward kept his eyes fixed on Sophie. "Don't tell me how to run my resort, and I won't tell you how to run your newspaper."

"Mr. Heyward, I assure you, I—"

He jammed his fists into his pockets. "I'll leave you to your riding."

He turned and stalked off, leaving her staring after him.

SIX

Sophie pressed her palms to her tired eyes and sighed. After weeks of waiting, the fancy paper she'd ordered had finally arrived. This morning she'd begun printing Mr. Heyward's stationery, only to have the jobber press break smack-dab in the middle of the run. Repairing it had stolen an hour of work time. Now it was afternoon and the entire edition of this week's *Gazette* still awaited printing.

She rose and placed the finished sheets and envelopes in a large box for delivery to Blue Smoke, then headed to the back room to start the steam press. At least Mr. Heyward would have no reason to fault her for this week's editorial, a call for the establishment of a women's and children's infirmary in Hickory Ridge. Gillie was busy marshaling support for her idea. Robbie Whiting would do what he could, of course, and the Gilmans would support their daughter because the project meant everything to her. Perhaps Sheriff McCracken would back the idea too. According to Wyatt and Ada, he'd lost his wife to illness much too soon.

Outside, the train whistle shrieked. A buggy and a freight wagon rattled toward the depot. Sophie checked the ink supply and loaded the first sheet of newsprint onto the platen. She started the steam press, and the first proof slid onto the tray. She read through it, checking for errors.

The ad for Jasper Pruitt's mercantile occupied the bottom quarter of the page, advertising a new shipment of sewing notions and canning jars. The merchant's appearance to place an ad that first week had surprised Sophie. Years ago he'd voiced constant disapproval of her and had done everything possible to discourage Ada from having anything to do with the likes of her. Yet he continued to advertise with her, week after week. Perhaps Robbie was right and attitudes in town had changed.

She finished proofing the first page and paused to wipe her face and get a drink of water. A light breeze drifted through the open window, stirring the bouquet of violets Carrie Rutledge had dropped off on her trip to town yesterday. Sophie added water to the vase, admiring the delicate lavender petals and translucent green leaves, a welcome contrast to the inky, dust-laden composing room.

A face appeared at the open window. "Miss?"

Sophie set down her glass and motioned him to the door. He came in, and she recognized the man who had spoken to her the night of the fight at Blue Smoke. "May I help you?"

He sagged against her desk and shook his head. "I reckon I'm beyond help now. Mr. Heyward just fired me." He looked up at her, his eyes suspiciously bright, and she realized he was near her own age. In the darkness and confusion at Blue Smoke that night, she had thought he was older.

She picked up a rag and wiped her fingers. "Why would he fire you?"

"He found out I was the one who talked to you that night. He said he doesn't have room for me now up at Blue Smoke and I shouldn't have talked to you."

"That's ridiculous. Working for Mr. Heyward does not preclude your right to talk to anybody you want to. Good gravy, you aren't his slave." She plopped onto her chair. What was wrong with

Ethan Heyward that made him feel he had to control everything and everybody?

"That's what I told him, but he wouldn't listen. He paid me and told me to clear out."

"I'm truly sorry. I never meant to cause you any trouble. But I doubt there is anything I can do for you, Mr.—"

"Stanhope. Caleb Stanhope. And yes, ma'am, there is something you can do."

She waited, one brow raised in question.

"You can give me a job."

⁓

Ethan paused on the dirt trail leading upward from the resort and waited for his breathing to slow. The sounds of dozens of hammers echoed through the thick stand of trees, drowning out the calm burbling of the stream running parallel to the path.

He took off his jacket and sat down on a fallen log. Already he regretted firing Caleb Stanhope. Caleb was a good worker and one of the best finish carpenters on the crew, but he was quick tempered and loose-tongued. Since Miss Caldwell's editorial last month, the men had grown ever more restless and outspoken.

Last night Stanhope and a group of others had confronted the two new Chinese cooks with complaints about the food. Ethan happened upon the situation just in time to avert another melee. True, Stanhope didn't start it. One of the Chinamen threw the first punch. But Ethan depended on the cooks to keep the crews fed. Stanhope, despite his skill, was not so irreplaceable. He had to go.

Ethan studied a delicate trillium growing beside the log and sighed. It was all Sophie Caldwell's fault. How could such a willowy little thing stir up so much trouble? Still, he found himself devouring each edition of the *Gazette* and waiting impatiently for the next one. Miss S. R. Caldwell was a gifted writer who could tackle any subject from wildflowers to national politics and make readers care about it. If only she would stick to those topics and forget about the problems at Blue Smoke.

He took out his leather notebook and flipped to the sketch he'd started last night when sleep eluded him. Horace had mentioned that one of his colleagues back in Baltimore planned to build a new house on the shore. Ethan wasn't sure yet just how he could approach the man about designing his new home, but memories of growing up along the Chesapeake had fueled his ideas for a long, low building with plenty of windows opened to the water. A house on the shore had been his Aunt Eulalie's dearest wish, but he'd been too young and too poor to fulfill it.

He balanced his notebook on his knee and watched a couple of blue jays darting through the trees. If it hadn't been for Horace, maybe Ethan would still be knocking around Baltimore, aimless and angry at the tragedy that had befallen his family, picking up work on the crab boats or digging in the potato fields just up the road. He was grateful for the chance to escape his dead-end life, and he'd worked hard to justify Horace's faith in him. If only the man wasn't so stubborn when it came to getting his way about everything.

Just this morning they'd had another set-to about the long-delayed railway passenger car. Italian leather, Texas leather—what difference did it make? Their guests wouldn't notice. But Horace had gotten his dander up about it all over again. And once again, Ethan had nearly lost his temper.

Shaking off the memory of Horace's red-faced tantrum and his own less-than-temperate response, Ethan bent to his work, flipping the pages of his notebook as new ideas emerged. The quiet stream, the pure sunlight filtering through the stands of oak and hickory, calmed him and soon he found himself thinking of Sophie Caldwell again.

No doubt she'd get her dander up too when she found out he'd fired her informant, but that was how it had to be. Maybe she'd be over it by the time the reception for the press rolled around. He was eager to show her the resort once the last of the furnishings and the artwork was in place. Somehow it mattered to him that she respect and admire his accomplishments. Which made no sense at all. But the feeling lodged inside him, as immutable as the green mountains rising up behind him.

Leaving her rented horse and rig tethered near the riding stables, Sophie walked up the path toward the main entrance to Blue Smoke. Surely once she explained the situation to Mr. Heyward, he'd give Caleb Stanhope his job back. It was the only fair thing to do.

She passed through a shady stand of old oaks and stopped to watch a squirrel, tail flicking, jump from branch to branch. Something moved on the path and she peered through the thick undergrowth, her heart thudding. Wyatt had warned her about bears and the dangerous feral pigs that sometimes showed themselves in the area. The last thing she wanted was to surprise one of the ferocious critters.

Through the tangle of bushes and vines she saw another path leading upward and the gleam of metal. The roof of an old shack? Curious, she followed the narrow path farther into the forest. The path widened, and then she stepped into a clearing where a dozen windowless tin-roofed shacks stood cheek by jowl. The acrid smell of a recently doused campfire mixed with the stench of an open sewer, the smell so overpowering her eyes watered. A plaid shirt draped over a bush undulated in the spring breeze. Beneath the trees stood a stack of empty metal pails and a wooden water bucket.

She stood still, listening to the far-off sounds of hammers and saws and the occasional shout. So this was where Mr. Heyward's work crew lived.

She crossed the clearing, her shoes sinking into the spongy ground, and peered through an open doorway into a shack. Piles of blankets and clothes littered the dirt floor. Tools were stacked willy-nilly against the rough boarded walls. In one corner sat a banjo and a wooden chest; in another, a pile of dime novels and tattered magazines. A couple of candles in empty tin cans seemed to be the only source of light.

Sophie's stomach clenched. No wonder the men were in a constant state of anger. Who wouldn't be, living in such primitive conditions while spending their days building a palace that only the wealthiest people would ever see. The contrast was astonishing. And troubling. Why hadn't Mr. Heyward's partner provided better quarters for the men without whom his dream never could have materialized?

The sound of the supply-train whistle reverberated through the trees. She retraced her steps and hurried along the overgrown path. Something rustled in the bushes and she halted, the hairs on the back of her neck rising. A small child wearing only a filthy, sagging diaper darted into the path.

"Oh goodness." Sophie knelt and opened her arms. "Where in the world did you come from, darling?"

The little girl sucked her thumb and stared unblinking at Sophie.

"Are you lost? What's your name?" Sophie rose and pawed through her reticule, but she couldn't come up with anything that would tempt or delight a small child.

"She ain't lost."

Sophie spun around to find a young woman in a ragged calico dress staring back at her. "You scared me."

"Good. Maybe you'll stop sniffing around up here and leave us be."

Sophie took in the young woman's haggard face and febrile eyes. The unmistakable smell of vomit came off her in waves.

"You're sick."

"Ain't nothing wrong with me." She picked up the toddler and settled the child on her hip.

"You need a doctor." Sophie fumbled for her pen and notebook. She scribbled Gillie's name, tore out the page, and pressed it into the woman's hand. "This is my friend. She assists our town doctor, and she very much wants to help mothers and children. Will you go and see her?"

"Mind your own business." The woman wadded the paper and tossed it into the bushes. The baby wailed.

"My name is Sophie. I own the newspaper in town. Please tell me your name and where you live, and I'll send Miss Gilman to you. You must get well, or else who will look after your baby?"

The woman laughed, a harsh, bitter sound. "Do I look like I got money for a doctor?"

Sophie's heart ached as she looked at the weeping child. Had her own mother, whoever she was, been this desperate too? Desperate enough eventually to give up her child forever?

"I'll take care of the bill, I promise. Just go and see Miss Gilman. Or Doc Spencer."

The woman shifted the child to her other hip. "I reckon you mean well, but you don't know how things are up here. We don't have much, it's true. But my husband couldn't hold his head up high if I was to take charity."

"He'd rather you'd stay sick than admit he needs help?" Sophie clenched her fists. "How chivalrous of him."

"I got to go. And you ought to git on off this mountain and mind your own business."

Sophie frowned. How on earth did Gillie suppose people like this woman would come to an infirmary even if it was free?

Distance and lack of money seemed to be less an issue than pride. How could Gillie hope to overcome such thinking?

She watched the woman disappear along the trail, then turned and headed for the resort. She thought about Robbie's belief that God had a purpose in bringing her back to Hickory Ridge. Maybe that was true, because from where she stood, a lot of things in this town needed fixing.

She reached the entrance to Blue Smoke and stopped to check her hat and brush the dirt from the hem of her dress. Ada would say it was poor manners to arrive unannounced, but it couldn't be helped.

"Miss Caldwell?"

She looked up to see Mr. Heyward striding toward her. His hat was askew, his spectacles smudged, and his jacket sprigged with bits of foliage. Somehow his less than impeccable looks made him seem more approachable. Even though she was perturbed at him for firing Caleb and incensed at the deplorable conditions in the work camp, she couldn't help returning his smile. "Mr. Heyward. I was hoping to find you in. May I have a word with you?"

"Certainly, if you don't mind waiting while I make myself presentable to a lady." He blushed. "I was walking in the woods, and I'm afraid I'm in no state to receive guests."

She followed him through the antique door from Scotland, hiding a smile at the sight of his leather notebook protruding from the back pocket of his grass-stained trousers.

He showed her into his office and asked his red-haired secretary to bring tea. "I won't be long." Then he disappeared.

In a moment, Mr. O'Brien returned with a tea tray and filled her cup. "Anything else you need?"

"Maybe some information?" She lifted her cup.

O'Brien's eyes widened. "Now, that's the one thing I can't supply, miss, seein' as how anything I say is likely to wind up in that paper of yours."

She picked up the tongs, plopped a sugar cube into her cup, and stirred the tea with a silver spoon. "I understand. I was just curious about the work camp. It's so primitive, considering how long the men have worked here."

He frowned. "How would you know about that?"

"Oh, I . . . never mind." She sipped. "This is very good tea. No doubt it's the finest available."

The secretary relaxed and leaned against the door frame. "Of course it is. Mr. Blakely insists on the best of everything, but he wants it at a rock-bottom price. It's surely a burden to Mr. Heyward, trying to satisfy Mr. Blakely and keep the men happy and bring the project in on budget."

"I imagine so. What do you suppose Mr. Heyward will do once the resort is finished?"

"I really couldn't say. He keeps to himself, doesn't confide in me all that much. More tea?"

"The papers say he's from a long line of Georgia planters, so perhaps he'll return home when he's through."

She held out her cup for a refill. "Mr. Heyward seems to delight in building lovely things. Perhaps he'll go back and build something as beautiful as Blue Smoke."

"I don't think so, miss. They say something terrible happened there when he was a boy, and he hasn't been back there since. If the story is true, I wouldn't blame him for never wanting to set foot in Georgia again."

"What happened? Did someone—"

The door opened, and Mr. Heyward came in wearing fresh clothes, his shoes shined, his hair neatly combed. He nodded to his secretary. "I hope there's still some tea."

"Of course." O'Brien poured a cup for his boss. "Will you be needing anything else, sir?"

"Not at the moment. Supply train brought the mail up." Ethan took up the sugar tongs and dropped a couple of cubes into his cup. "You might get it sorted for me. And update the guest list for the ball. Li Chung will want to order his supplies soon, and I want to be sure Mr. Pruitt has enough of everything."

The secretary left, closing the door behind him. Mr. Heyward stirred his tea and took a long sip. "Now, Miss Caldwell, what brings you to Blue Smoke?"

"Caleb Stanhope needs his job back." Sophie set down her cup and folded her hands in her lap. "He told me he's supporting his mother and two younger brothers."

Mr. Heyward nodded. "Mary Bell. I understand she ran the telegraph office before she married. The boy told me her husband died shortly thereafter." He took a sip of tea. "Killed in a railway accident in Chicago. Tragic for all of them."

"Then how can you deprive him of his livelihood when the welfare of others is at stake?"

He sat forward in his chair. "Believe me, Miss Caldwell, I hated to let him go. But he shouldn't have discussed Blue Smoke with you."

"That isn't his fault. He didn't know I'd write about it, and now I'm sorry I did. Not because the situation here isn't utterly abominable, but because—"

"Pardon me. What do you know, really, about the 'situation,' as you put it?"

"I stumbled across the workers' camp just now. It's unfit for human habitation, in my opinion, and that open sewer is an invitation for serious illness. No wonder your men are prone to fighting. I'd be angry myself, having to live day after day in such deplorable conditions."

He opened his desk drawer, took out a couple of photographs, and slid them across the desk. "This is what the place looked like when I got here."

She studied the blurred images of haggard-looking men posing before a row of sagging canvas tents, their boots mired in a sea of mud. The pictures reminded her of Mr. Mathew Brady's heart-rending photographs of the war. Misery seemed etched onto every soldier's face.

"When Horace asked me to come on board to supervise this project, I said I wouldn't do it until he hired a decent cook and got those men out of tents and into permanent quarters." Mr. Heyward studied her, his deep-blue eyes serious behind his spectacles. "I realize the cabins aren't much to look at, but they're much more substantial than those tents. At least the men are kept warm and dry. And they have plenty to eat." He smiled. "Not that they don't complain daily about Li Chung's menu choices."

Sophie's heart softened as he spoke. Had she misjudged him? Perhaps Ethan Heyward was not as hard a man as he seemed. Still . . . "What about Caleb? Will you reconsider?"

"I'm afraid I cannot. Mr. Blakely is quite adamant that the men honor the promises they made when they were hired. One of those promises was not to say anything that could damage the reputation of Blue Smoke."

"I see." She rose. "Your stationery order is ready. Perhaps Mr. O'Brien can pick it up tomorrow."

"I'll ask him to call at your office." He walked her to the door. "Despite what you might think, I am truly sorry about Caleb. I understand what it's like to be young and without a father for guidance."

"But not sorry enough to take him back."

"Horace Blakely has the final say around here. About everything." He paused, his hand on the crystal doorknob. "I don't agree with his every opinion, but he's the boss. Caleb's smart enough. He's strong and willing to work. He'll land on his feet one way or the other."

She clutched her reticule to her chest. "If that is your final word on the matter and you won't help rectify a situation that was really my fault, I suppose I'll have to do something about it myself."

"I'd advise you to be careful what you print in that newspaper of yours from now on."

"Is that a threat, Mr. Heyward?"

He held up both hands, palms out. "Not at all. Just some friendly counsel."

They walked out into the brilliant May sunshine. Sophie climbed into her rig and turned it around in time to see Mr. Heyward raise one hand in farewell, the hint of a smile playing on his full lips.

He was infuriating. And yet impossible to ignore.

SEVEN

"Miss Caldwell?" Caleb Stanhope poked his head into the office and frowned. "Something's wrong with the jobbing press again."

Sophie rolled a sheet of paper from her typewriting machine and set it in the wire basket on the corner of her desk. "I'll be right there."

In the wake of Mr. Heyward's refusal to give Caleb his job back, Sophie had hired him to work at the *Gazette*. True, she could afford him only two days a week, but it was better than nothing, and Caleb was a fast learner. In the three weeks since she'd hired him, he'd learned to mix ink and had mastered the operation of the rotary press. Today he was printing up a notice for the upcoming meeting of the Ladies Benevolent Society to discuss the establishment of Gillie's infirmary. If the boy ever learned to spell, which seemed doubtful, she'd put him to work setting type.

She joined Caleb in the back room and bent over the small jobbing press.

"It's not my fault." Caleb jerked an ink-blackened thumb toward the press. "I didn't break it or anything."

"I know you didn't." She lifted the handle and shoved a worn coupling pin back into place. "This machine is so old, it breaks down most every time. Usually it's because this pin has slipped loose." She sat down and worked the treadle, and a clean copy of Gillie's flier slid into the tray. "There we are. Good as new."

Caleb grinned. "Thanks, Miss Caldwell."

"Caleb?" She smiled at the boy. "I'm not that much older than you. Could you please call me Sophie? 'Miss Caldwell' seems much too stuffy, and makes me feel older than dirt."

"Sure, Miss . . . Sophie. I've been meaning to thank you again for this job. I really like it, and my wages sure help out at home."

"I'm the one who got you fired. It was the least I could do."

He ducked his head. "Reckon I better finish this job before Miss Gilman gets here. She sure is all het up over that hospital idea of hers."

"The infirmary is a wonderful idea. I'm planning to run a series of articles about it as soon as we get the opening at Blue Smoke out of the way."

Caleb sat down at the press. "I heard you're going to the big party Mr. Heyward is throwing tonight."

"That's right. He's expecting a writer from *Harper's* magazine. A lot of other newspaper people will be there as well. I'm looking forward to meeting everyone."

Caleb cranked out a few more copies. "You going to the ball tomorrow too?"

"I am. Just like Cinderella."

"Don't lose your glass shoes."

She glanced at the clock on the wall. "It's after five already, so I suppose I should get going. Mr. Heyward is calling for me at six."

Caleb nodded. "You go on and get yourself all prettified. I can lock up for you when I'm finished here."

She took her key from her desk drawer and handed it to him. "Leave it at the front desk at the Verandah if you don't mind."

"No trouble. Have fun tonight."

She smiled. "I'm going there to work. I'll be so busy taking notes and talking to people I won't have time for much else. It is exciting, though. When I lived in Hickory Ridge as a child, I never dreamed I'd be back here one day running this paper, or that there would be anything as fancy as Blue Smoke in this little town."

"Ma's real excited about Blue Smoke. She says a fancy place like that adds to the quality of our town. But I reckon it's the people of a place that make it quality. Don't you?"

"I sure do." She headed for the door. "See you next week."

"Yep." Caleb rolled his eyes. "Give my regards to Prince Charming."

She crossed the street and headed for the hotel. Lucy Partridge had promised to have a warm bath waiting for her. The new dress she'd purchased from Jeanne Pruitt's shop, a cream-colored silk with a matching jacket trimmed in white braid, waited in a nest of tissue paper. It was too bad she couldn't afford a new gown for tomorrow night's ball. The dress she'd brought from Texas wasn't her fanciest, but it was nearly new, the silk fabric was of the best quality, and it fit her like a dream. And it had seemed more important to have a new dress for meeting her colleagues.

She hurried to the Verandah, eager for the evening to begin. After the difficulties of her childhood, she did feel a bit like a fairy-tale princess.

Not that Ethan Heyward would ever turn out to be her Prince Charming.

⁓

Ethan picked up his hat and gloves and sent O'Brien in search of his driver and carriage. The conveyance was nearly too wide to negotiate the narrow, bumpy mountain road, but tonight called for the best he had to offer. Waiting outside in the portico as the carriage arrived, imagining the glittering night ahead, he felt a jolt of anticipation and a sense of pride.

Every member of the press he'd invited to this evening's reception had accepted, eager to sample the food and admire the sumptuous rooms and the resort's breathtaking mountain setting. Already, to Horace's delight, some had begun calling Hickory Ridge the Saratoga of the South. Perhaps the comparison to New York's famous resort town was a bit too ambitious just now. But with time and the right management, the resort's reputation would grow until Blue Smoke became as impressive a destination as anything the country had to offer.

This afternoon, after a week in Baltimore attending to his interests there, Horace had returned for the summer with his wife and three lively daughters. Now, thank goodness, they were napping in their rooms, a small army of chambermaids at the ready to answer to their every whim. Despite disagreements over developing Blue Smoke, Horace was thrilled with the results. He'd pronounced Ethan's efforts nothing short of miraculous and proffered a generous bonus check. A check that had somehow failed to cheer him as much as he'd imagined.

Money was useful, of course. No Southerner who had lived through the years of privation during and after the war would ever dispute that. But now the job was done, and Ethan had no idea what would come next. He could stay on here and run Blue Smoke. But the prospect of continuing to work for Blakely, despite their long association, seemed vaguely depressing.

And Sophie Caldwell had more than a little to do with his feelings. He couldn't forget the sharp look of disapproval in her eyes when he refused her request to rehire the Stanhope boy. He didn't really blame her. He didn't like himself very much for giving in to Horace's iron will and rigid policies. On the other hand, he owed his boss some loyalty. Had he not met the man all those years ago, who knew how his life might have turned out?

"Your carriage, Mr. Heyward." The gray-haired driver halted beneath the portico, jumped down, and opened the door with a flourish. "Big night for you tonight."

Ethan nodded. "And for everyone at Blue Smoke. It's been a long time coming."

"Yes, sir, but I don't imagine there's anybody in Hickory Ridge that regrets that. Before you and Mr. Blakely got here, we were fadin' fast." He shook his grizzled head. "The depression just about did us all in. If it hadn't been for Mr. Gilman startin' that horse race and Mr. Blakely takin' a shine to our little town, well, I hate to think of what might have become of us."

He motioned Ethan into the carriage and closed the door. "You just sit back and relax, and I'll have you to the Verandah in no time."

Ethan settled onto the rich red leather seat and braced himself as the carriage rolled down the brick drive and onto the mountain road. The sun rode low in the trees. The air was heavy with the sweet smell of honeysuckle and the promise of the evening ahead.

An image of Sophie rose in his mind. He couldn't remember the last time he'd felt as excited about a woman as he did about Sophie Caldwell. Here lately she'd occupied more of his thoughts than was good for him. He tried not to think about her so often, but it was no use. Despite her headstrong opinions and trouble-making ways, he wanted to spend much more time with her.

Was it too much to hope for, that she might want to see more of him too?

EIGHT

"Sophie, there you are!" Gillie rose from the rocking chair on the Verandah's newly painted porch and hurried down the front steps. "I know you're on your way to that fancy reception up at Blue Smoke, but I'm hoping you have a minute. I need a favor."

Sophie took Gillie's arm, grateful for a few minutes with her friend. Their growing closeness seemed almost a miracle, considering that her work at the paper and Gillie's rounds with Doc Spencer left so little time for socializing. For the most part they had to be content with hurried visits before and after church and an occasional tea at Miss Hattie's.

"Mr. Heyward will be here soon," she told Gillie, "but of course I have time for you. What is it?"

The two of them sat in the creaking rocking chairs Sophie remembered from her childhood. The summer breeze smelled like Ada's teacakes, yeasty and moist. The rosebush beside the door sagged beneath the weight of the season's first blooms. From inside came the clank of silverware and the muted voices of the women who soon would begin new jobs at Blue Smoke.

"It's about my infirmary," Gillie said. "I want to talk to the town council about it, but Mayor Scott won't give me a place on the agenda."

Sophie frowned. She didn't know the mayor very well, though he and his wife attended services at Robbie Whiting's church every week. He had been mayor forever, accustomed to getting his way, but she had never considered him to be unfair. "Did he say why?"

Gillie took her fan from her reticule and fanned her face. "He says Hickory Ridge can't afford a free infirmary, even though that is not exactly what Dr. Spencer and I are proposing, and he also thinks it's a waste of time anyway because the women who need help the most won't take it. But how does he know?"

Sophie shook her head. "I'm sorry to say this, but he may be right. Remember the woman I met on the mountain? She was clearly sick, but she told me in no uncertain terms to leave her alone. It seems she'd rather be sick than wound her husband's pride by asking for help. I'm all for your idea, but honestly, I don't see how having an infirmary will convince people like that to come in when they need help."

"I know it won't be easy. But I'm hoping that if the leaders of Hickory Ridge show their support for the infirmary, then those husbands whose pride is standing in the way of their wives' well-being will be more apt to accept it." She shrugged. "Maybe we can shame them into seeking help."

"Maybe." Sophie chewed her lip. "I can't help but wonder if there's more to it than pride. Perhaps the men fear having to take on more of the burdens at home if their wives are indisposed." She watched a wren darting in and out of a nest. "Change comes slowly to small towns. Maybe they're simply afraid of anything new."

"Well, it isn't as if this is a brand-new idea. Infirmaries are opening in Asheville and Knoxville, and just last week Doc told me about a sanatorium opening up on a lake in New York—Adirondack Cottage. It's for treatment of tuberculosis. He says it's only one large room, but still, to the patients who need it, it's a godsend."

Sophie regarded her friend. "Suppose the town council

approves the infirmary. Where would you put it? There's not an empty room to be had here at the Verandah or at the inn. Even Mr. Webster's school is bursting at the seams."

"I've thought of that. The orphanage has been vacant for years. It's sitting there falling into disrepair. And it's perfect for my infirmary because it already has lots of rooms where I can set up beds. It has a kitchen and a dining room and an office. And it won't be too expensive. All it needs is some repairs." She huffed. "I should think the mayor and the council would rather have it occupied and useful instead of continuing to offend the eye of every visitor who comes to town."

"Can't Dr. Spencer plead your case? Or your father? I can't imagine Mayor Scott would turn a deaf ear to Mr. Gilman."

"Daddy's no help. He says this is my project, so it's up to me to make my case." Gillie wrinkled her nose. "He thinks it's good for my character."

Sophie grinned. More than once Wyatt Caldwell had told her the same thing about her newspaper enterprise. In the end, though, he had advanced her the money to get her business started. Surely Mr. Gilman would do the same for his only daughter.

Gillie sighed and fanned her face. "Dr. Spencer is all for my infirmary. He has spoken to the mayor, but Mayor Scott keeps putting him off too, and Doc's too busy to fight this battle for me. Why, just last week, Mrs. Sproule came down with consumption. And Mrs. Harper is expecting another baby and having a hard time of it. Poor Doc hardly has time to eat and sleep before he's called out again. Even with Mrs. Spencer's help, he can barely keep up." Gillie frowned. "That's exactly why we *need* the clinic. So he can spend his time with the serious cases instead of traveling all over the county treating minor illnesses."

"What about women in town? Surely Mrs. Spencer supports the idea."

"Oh yes, and Mrs. Rutledge and Mrs. Whiting and some others." Gillie made a face. "Naturally Mother thinks the whole idea is ridiculous and that I should worry instead about finding a husband. But I don't care."

"You don't want to marry?" Sophie took out her own fan. "I sure do. Someday."

"Oh, I'm all for finding a good man and settling down, but my Prince Charming is going to have to find me, because I am far too busy to go looking for him." Gillie leaned over and placed a hand on Sophie's arm. "Speaking of princes, you'd better get going if you want to be ready when the handsome Mr. Heyward gets here. I didn't mean to keep you so long. I only wanted to ask if you would write another opinion piece in the paper. Something to persuade the mayor and the council to hear me out."

"I'm not sure I have any influence with them, but of course I'll do anything I can to help." Sophie clasped Gillie's hand. "I think your idea is wonderful, and I personally would love to see the orphanage transformed into something useful."

Gillie nodded, her expression thoughtful. "It couldn't have been easy for you there."

Sophie gazed past her friend's shoulder, remembering. "It was a pretty dismal place. Only a few of us were taken into permanent homes. And nobody wanted a skinny mutt of a girl who had trouble with handwriting and only wanted to spin stories. Mrs. Lowell refused to let me go to school with the others. It still hurts to think about it. So I try not to."

Gillie placed a hand on Sophie's arm. "Maybe it would make you feel better to help turn the building into a place of hope."

"I'm willing to try. Next week's edition will be taken up with the Blue Smoke opening, I'm afraid, but after that I'll work on the mayor and his ilk."

"I knew I could count on you." Gillie jumped up and threw

both arms around Sophie just as a carriage rattled down the street. "Oh my lands. Speaking of Blue Smoke, here comes Mr. Heyward."

Before Sophie could reply, Gillie gave her a gentle shove. "Go on upstairs. I'll entertain your gentleman while you change."

"Thanks." With a backward glance at the approaching carriage, Sophie ran inside.

Lucy Partridge met her at the foot of the stairs. "You're late."

"Don't I know it." Sophie took out her handkerchief, dabbed at a spot of black ink on her hand, and glanced at her hair in the hallway mirror. "Mercy. I look like something the cat dragged in."

Lucy laughed. "You could never look that bad. Go on up. I prepared your bath and hung your dress up."

"You're a lifesaver." Sophie raced upstairs, undoing her buttons as she went. In her room, she slid into the warm, rose-scented water, wishing for more time to enjoy such an indulgence. But Ethan Heyward was waiting, and besides, she didn't want to miss a minute of the reception. She scrubbed away the day's grime, dried off, and ran a brush through her hair before fashioning it into a simple coil at the nape of her neck. She splashed on a bit of rosewater and stepped into the new dress, a whisper of cream silk that showed off her slim waist.

The sound of laughter drew her to the window. Down below, Ethan stood in the yard, his hat tucked into the curve of his arm, one foot resting on the hotel's bottom step. Beside him, Gillie pointed up the street, and they laughed again.

Sophie felt an unexpected stab of pure old jealousy, then chastised herself. She had no claim on Ethan Heyward. If he wanted to share a joke with Gillie, why should she care?

She opened her velvet-lined jewelry case, a sixteenth-birthday present from Wyatt and Ada, and took out two jeweled combs for her hair. She fastened a pearl choker at her neck, tucked a couple of pencils into her reticule, and buttoned her jacket. With a final glance into the mirror, she picked up her reporter's notebook and headed for the door.

Lucy grinned when Sophie came downstairs. "My word, you look pretty as a princess." Lucy parted the front curtain in the parlor and looked out. "That's some carriage. And Mr. Heyward looks mighty fine too."

"I'll see you tomorrow."

"I'll make flapjacks for breakfast, and you can give me a full report," Lucy said, her eyes full of mischief. "And not just the stuff you plan to print in the paper either. I want the details."

Sophie gave her a wave and then stepped onto the porch. Ethan looked up, a broad smile lighting his face.

"Mr. Heyward." She rushed down the steps, her silk skirt swirling about her ankles. "I am six kinds of sorry for making you wait. I'm usually much more prompt."

"He knows it was my doing," Gillie said.

Ethan laughed. "It was worth the wait. You look beautiful, Miss Caldwell." He offered his arm. "Shall we go?"

"Have fun." Gillie waved as Ethan handed Sophie into the carriage, then stepped in and took the seat opposite her.

The driver executed a wide turn. The carriage rocked along the main road and then began the climb to Blue Smoke. Sophie watched the scenery slipping past—the trees cloaked in late-spring green, patches of birdfoot violets growing near the road, golden sunlight filtering through the thick branches.

"Excited about the reception?" Ethan smiled into her eyes, and she smiled back.

"Oh yes. It isn't often I have a chance to talk to editors from other newspapers. I like knowing what's going on in their towns and what their readers are interested in."

He nodded. "Last time I was back in Baltimore, all the interest was about the new Equal Rights Party. I'm not sure how I feel about it."

She raised a brow. "Truly? It seems to me that any democracy should welcome the full participation of all its citizens. You don't agree?"

He blushed. "Well, when you put it that way, of course. And I recognize time won't stand still." He peered out the window. "Our world is changing faster than I ever thought possible. Who would have thought we'd have a Negro playing baseball for the major leagues? But it's happened in Ohio."

"Yes. Moses Walker gave an interview shortly after he joined the Toledo team. Several of the Texas papers reprinted it." Sophie braided her fingers and watched for some clue as to what he thought of Mr. Walker's achievement, but Ethan's face remained impassive. "I personally think it's a sign of progress."

"No doubt. But don't you think our society will become more complicated when the natural lines between the races, or between a man's world and a woman's for that matter, become blurred?"

"Is that a diplomatic way of telling me you don't approve of my owning the newspaper?"

"Not at all. I think it's fine for now. But surely you'll want a family someday?"

She fingered the cover of her notebook and swallowed the sudden tightness in her throat. He didn't know his question had touched the deepest recesses of her heart. Having grown up without a family, she couldn't imagine a more precious gift.

"Begging your pardon," Ethan said, his voice soft. "I've upset you, and I didn't intend to."

She took a long breath and smiled into his eyes. "I'm perfectly fine, Mr. Heyward."

"And that's another thing I've been meaning to mention. Do you think you can call me Ethan? 'Mr. Heyward' makes me feel old."

She relaxed, happy to have the conversation back on more neutral ground. "You don't look old."

He laughed and she smiled, enjoying the sound of it. "I'm

thirty-one. Old enough to know better than to peer too closely into a woman's feelings. I'm sorry. I didn't mean to pry. Your future plans are none of my business."

"You're forgiven. And of course I'm honored to call you Ethan, if you will call me Sophie."

"Done." He peered out the carriage window. "The view of the sunset tonight from the terrace will be spectacular. We must remind the photographers to have their cameras at the ready. Did I tell you the *Boston Globe* sent two writers and an illustrator?"

"That's wonderful. Is anyone from the Atlanta papers coming? I should think Blue Smoke will draw lots of visitors from there—from all over Georgia, really. And since you're a native son, there must be tremendous interest in—"

His handsome face darkened. "They weren't invited."

"I see. But why?"

He shook his head. "Never mind, Sophie. We're here."

NINE

A distinguished-looking man in a blue, brass-buttoned uniform stepped forward and held the carriage door open for Sophie. "Good evening, miss."

"Good evening." Sophie gathered her skirts and stepped from the carriage. A row of rigs and carriages lined the road and overflowed onto the soft grass. Pots of bright pink and yellow blooms nodded in the cool mountain breeze that wafted through the covered portico. On either side of the massive entrance, twin fountains burbled softly, reflecting the sunlight that painted the distant hills and turned the trees to gold.

Ethan followed her from the carriage and nodded to the door-man. "Thank you, John. Tell Silas I'll need the carriage later to see Miss Caldwell home."

"Yes, sir. Enjoy your evening." The doorman motioned to the driver and the carriage pulled away, the horses' hooves making a hollow sound on the road.

Ethan offered his arm. "Shall we?"

He led Sophie through the reception hall and up a short stair-case to the main ballroom. Two more uniformed servants smiled a greeting and opened the door. Inside, Sophie stood transfixed. Holy cats. No wonder folks called these present years the "gilded age." Like the mansions she'd read about—the Carnegies' palatial home in New York, the Palmers' castle-like mansion in Chicago—Blue Smoke was awash in gold. Thin golden ropes adorned three massive, gas-lit crystal chandeliers that spilled soft light into the room. Tables dressed with heavy white linens held stacks of gleaming china rimmed in gold. Goblets and wineglasses, flatware and serving platters glittered in the light.

"Well?" Ethan smiled down at her, and she was acutely aware of his nearness—the clean scent of his skin, the tiny wrinkles fanning out from the corners of his eyes.

"It's breathtaking."

"And so are you." His eyes moved from her face to her shoulders to the tip of one satin slipper peeking from beneath the hem of her dress.

She inclined her head, acknowledging his compliment, and waved a hand toward the crowd gathering at the other end of the room. "Perhaps we should join the others. I'm dying to meet everyone."

He laughed softly, and she felt her cheeks grow warmer as he continued to hold her gaze.

"Did I say something funny?" She opened her reticule and busied herself with her pen and notebook.

"Not at all. I was actually admiring your enthusiasm. Come on. I'll introduce you to the few people I know, and I'm sure they will do the rest."

Taking her arm, he moved into the crowd and motioned to a handsome, stocky gentleman who had just accepted a glass of wine from a passing waiter. "Miss Sophie Caldwell, may I introduce Mr. Edward Carmack of the *Columbia Herald*. Edward, Miss Caldwell is the new owner of the *Hickory Ridge Gazette*."

"Hello." Sophie nodded, and Mr. Carmack smiled back.

"Pleased to meet you, miss," he said. "I'm glad the *Gazette* is back in business. I thought a lot of the Greers. It was surely a sad day in these parts when Mr. Greer passed on."

A waiter came by with a tray laden with punch cups and Sophie took one. "Patsy Greer is the reason I got into newspapering. She let me try out her typewriting machine when I was a child, and I never got over the excitement of a newspaper office." She sipped the punch. "This is good. Do you know what's in it?"

"Sophie," Ethan said. "I must go and speak to my other guests. I'll catch up with you later, all right?"

Mr. Carmack smiled. "Don't worry about her, Ethan. Such a lovely lady is not likely to want for conversation."

Ethan disappeared into the growing crowd, and Mr. Carmack motioned to a handsome woman clad in a navy dress, a small flowered hat perched at a jaunty angle on her head. "Lydia, come and meet Miss Caldwell."

The woman set down her plate and cup and made her way through a knot of people gathered near the fireplace.

"Lydia McPherson, meet Sophie Caldwell. She's the new owner of the local paper."

"Indeed." The woman smiled and nodded. "I am delighted to meet another woman engaged in our profession."

Sophie returned Mrs. McPherson's nod, suddenly shy in the presence of a woman she'd long admired and hoped to emulate.

"Lydia owns the *Democrat* down in Sherman, Texas," Mr. Carmack said. "It's one of the most successful dailies in the South."

"My sons deserve some of the credit for that," Mrs. McPherson said. "After my husband died, we moved to Texas. The boys have worked hard to make the paper a success. We've done all right for ourselves."

"She's being modest," Mr. Carmack said. "Lydia here was one of the first women to join the Texas Press Association. Why, they even made her an honorary commissioner for the World Expo in New Orleans last January."

"I was there," Sophie said, delighted to have even more in common with the accomplished newspaperwoman. "My guardian spent summers with her family in New Orleans when she was growing up. The exposition provided her a good excuse to show her children the place where she spent much of her childhood."

"What did you think of it?"

"It was overwhelming, to tell you the truth. Didn't they say it was the biggest world's fair ever held in the United States?" Sophie took another sip of punch. "But I loved New Orleans. So many kinds of people, so much noise and energy on the river. I can see why Ada wanted to go back there."

Mrs. McPherson laughed. "I agree with you, even though I felt as if I walked a hundred miles just to see it all. My poor feet may never be the—"

"Lydia!" A bearded man dressed like an undertaker pushed through the crowd. "I didn't know you were coming."

"Hello, Adolph." Mrs. McPherson smiled. "I didn't either. My son planned to come, but he's ill, I'm afraid, and I didn't want our paper to miss out on a firsthand look at Mr. Blakely's masterpiece. And my cousin Deborah Patterson lives here. The opening was a good excuse to pay her a visit. Blue Smoke is quite something, isn't it?"

The man nodded. "Mr. Heyward invited me up here for a look a couple of times while the building was going up, but I had no idea it would turn out to be so fancy. Small wonder that they're calling Hickory Ridge the Saratoga of the South."

"Well, there's your lead paragraph for page one." Mr. Carmack began scribbling in his leather-bound notebook.

"Oh my goodness," Mrs. McPherson said. "Where on earth are my manners? Miss Caldwell, this is my old friend Adolph Ochs. Adolph, Miss Caldwell of the *Gazette*."

"*Chattanooga Times*." Mr. Ochs smiled at Sophie. "Pleased to make your acquaintance." He waved one hand at the crowded room. "Mr. Heyward has himself quite a turnout."

Sophie looked around. Reporters leaned against the fireplace, talking and taking notes. At the other end of the room, a photographer had set up his equipment and was busy framing a view of the mountains through the tall windows. Waiters scurried about bearing gilt-rimmed trays laden with sandwiches and tiny iced cakes. The hum of a dozen conversations filled the air.

". . . wouldn't you say so, Miss Caldwell?" Mr. Carmack smiled down at Sophie, one brow raised.

"I beg your pardon?"

"I was just saying that newfangled machine Mr. Mergenthaler patented is sure to revolutionize our business."

"The linotype, yes. I've wanted one in the worst way ever since I read about it."

Mr. Ochs laughed. "Don't we all? They say one of the New York papers will get the first one sometime next year." He shook his head. "Imagine being able to form an entire line of type as one piece of metal."

Mrs. McPherson, who had accepted another glass of punch, took a sip and sighed. "Imagining is about all I'll be able to do, I fear. No doubt that new machine will be scandalously expensive."

"But it will be worth it in the long run," Sophie said. "Think of how much faster the work will go when we don't have to set the type letter by letter."

Mr. Ochs nodded. "I might even be able to let my printer's devil go. I'd save a lot of money if I didn't have to pay his wages every week."

Sophie thought of Caleb. A linotype machine would undoubtedly be better for her, but without the small amount she paid him, what would become of him and his family?

The doors to the ballroom opened, and a portly man in a fancy suit entered with an equally elegant woman on his arm.

"That's Horace Blakely," Mr. Ochs said. "I met him last fall when I was up here touring the place."

A bell tinkled and the room gradually quieted. All eyes turned to Mr. Blakely, who held up one hand, palm out, and smiled. "Ladies and gentlemen of the press, it's an honor for Mrs. Blakely and me to welcome you to Blue Smoke, the finest resort in the South."

Applause rippled across the room.

"When I first saw Hickory Ridge back in seventy-six, she was a pretty little town fallen on hard times. But the local banker, Franklin Gilman, refused to let his town die. He organized the first-ever Hickory Ridge Race Day, which still draws visitors from all over the country."

He smiled a little ruefully. "My horse was beaten that day by the now-legendary Majestic, ridden by one of Hickory Ridge's most outstanding citizens, Mr. Griffin Rutledge—now head of our riding program. And if you know me, you know I don't like to lose. But I gained something that day too. Something about this place called to me—these beautiful, unspoiled mountains, the clear springs and grassy meadows, and . . . well, a sort of peacefulness that seems to fill the air, like a favorite hymn on Sunday morning."

All around her, reporters were opening notebooks and digging for pencils. Sophie set her punch cup on a nearby tray and took notes too.

"On the train home from that first race, I started to dream about building a place where folks from all over could come to enjoy the solitude and beauty of these magnificent mountains. Fish in the clear-running streams. Ride the trails. And partake of the finest foods and wines available anywhere." He held up his glass as if for a toast and swept his arm toward the window. "It took a long time to acquire the land, clear it, and build a rail supply line, not to mention building the resort itself. But this evening you are witnesses to the result of big dreams, hard work, and imagination. If you will follow me, we'll begin the tour."

Sophie followed Mrs. McPherson and Mr. Carmack to the door. Mr. Ochs spotted another friend across the room and soon was engaged in animated conversation, waving his hands in the air. For the next half hour, Mr. Blakely led the reporters through the public rooms and about the manicured grounds, peppering his comments with enough facts and figures to fill a government report.

They stopped at the stables, and Griff Rutledge walked out leading Majestic. Griff waited for photographers to set up their cameras and posed for pictures with the sleek black stallion before pointing out the riding trail snaking upward through the forest. Mr. Blakely then led them back to the main building by way of a lavishly planted garden just beginning to bloom. They reached the wide terrace and stood quietly, taking in the view. The sun perched atop the mountain as if suspended by a string, turning the sky to pink. The doors opened and a small band of strolling musicians came onto the terrace, filling the air with song.

"This concludes my remarks," Mr. Blakely said, "but if any of you have further questions, I'll be happy to answer them. Or you can ask my partner and managing director of this enterprise, Mr. Ethan Heyward." He scanned the crowd, a scowl darkening his fleshy face. "If you can find him."

After another round of food and drink, the photographers packed away their cameras and the reporters began gathering their things, saying good-bye. Mr. Carmack nodded a farewell to Sophie and called for his rig. Mrs. McPherson patted Sophie's arm. "I'm glad to have met you, Miss Caldwell. Perhaps one day we'll have a chance to compare notes on the New Orleans Exposition."

"I'd like that."

"Tell me. Did you write about it for anyone?"

"Only a couple of small articles for our paper in Dallas."

"Oh, so you're from Texas too?"

"Since I was a girl. I started working for the paper after I finished school. My boss, Mrs. Mills, thought I was ready to handle the reporting, but her boss thought otherwise. He said I was too young."

Mrs. McPherson shook her head. "Nonsense. I've known Prudence Mills for years. She's solid as they come. If she thought you were ready, you are. Age has nothing to do with it. A keen eye and a decent vocabulary trump age any day." She motioned for her carriage. "Have you heard about Mr. McClure's news syndicate?"

"Only that he formed one a couple of years ago."

"I hear it's doing well. Perhaps you should approach him about writing for his organization. It would be excellent exposure for your talents, and the pay is all right."

"I'd love that, but right now the *Gazette* is more than enough for me to handle."

The carriage arrived and Mrs. McPherson climbed inside. "Perhaps later, then. Good-bye, my dear."

Sophie waved as the carriage started down the drive, and then returned to the ballroom where a few reporters still leaned against the wall, laughing and comparing notes. She found a chair by the window and watched the lengthening shadows fall across the grass. Where on earth was Ethan? She hadn't seen him all night.

She was tired but eager to get home and write her story while all her impressions were still fresh in her mind. And she needed to think about the editorial she promised Gillie. How could she possibly influence the mayor and the council where others had failed?

She rose and left the ballroom, her shoes skimming the Oriental carpet, and hurried down the hall to Ethan's office. Perhaps he was working on more details for tomorrow night's ball. She lifted her hand to knock on the door, but the sound of angry voices stopped her.

The door crashed open and a tall, olive-skinned man stormed out, nearly knocking her down as he passed. Ice-blue eyes briefly met hers, and in that instant, something immediate and visceral passed between them. She had never before seen this man, but somehow she felt a kind of instant kinship.

"Pardon," he muttered before hurrying into the night, a small leather pouch tucked into the crook of his arm. A few moments later horses' hooves clattered across the brick driveway and receded into the silence.

Sophie peered into the office. Papers and books were scattered everywhere. A crystal glass lay on its side on the floor, its contents dribbling onto the priceless carpet.

Ethan sat behind his desk, his head in his hands.

"Ethan?"

He started and leapt to his feet. "Sophie. You must forgive me for being such an inattentive escort. I became sidetracked, I'm afraid." He picked up the glass and began stacking the books. "Did you have a good time?"

"Yes, but, Ethan, what happened here?"

He squared his shoulders and offered her a tight smile. "I should get you home. Wait a moment, and I'll call for the carriage."

Together they returned to the ballroom where the staff were already busy cleaning up, preparing for tomorrow night's festivities. Ethan spoke to a couple of the men and then offered her his arm. Outside, they waited beneath the portico while the driver brought the carriage around.

Ethan nodded to the driver. "Silas, I want you to see Miss Caldwell safely to the Verandah Hotel."

"Yes, sir."

Sophie looked into his face. "You aren't coming with me?"

"I'm afraid not. Something has come up that needs my immediate attention. But I'll call for you tomorrow evening for the ball, just as we planned."

She studied him in the flickering light of the gas sconces, the flames spilling gold across his troubled features. Clearly, the argument with his visitor had upset him. "This is about that man who was in your office just now, isn't it? Is he a reporter? Who is he?"

Ethan handed her into the carriage and stuck his head into the open window. "He's nobody, Sophie," he said, clearly dismissive of the stranger. "Nobody at all."

⌒

Ethan watched Sophie's carriage disappear into the darkness and silently cursed his bad luck. He'd wanted to spend more time with her this evening, help her establish herself with the other newspaper writers in the region. But then Julian showed up, a ghost from his haunted childhood, and spoiled everything.

Still reeling from the shock of Julian's sudden appearance, from the rage and the memories it evoked, Ethan crossed the portico and headed for his suite of rooms on the second floor. What he needed was a good night's sleep—an unlikely prospect now that his mind was filled with horrific images he'd spent years trying to forget.

At the top of the staircase, Horace Blakely spied him. Cigar in hand, Horace hove toward him like a battleship cutting through rough seas. "Ethan."

"Good evening, sir."

"You're to be congratulated on arranging such a successful reception. The Boston and New York writers were suitably impressed."

Ethan nodded and loosened his blue silk cravat. "I'm glad you approve."

"Didn't see much of you during the festivities, though."

"I know, and I regret it, but it was one of those nights. Li Chung's assistant dropped an entire platter of canapés and was afraid to make more without my approval. One of the Kentucky carpenters complained that someone had stolen his banjo, but it turned up in one of the other cabins. And then to top it all off, I had an unexpected visitor, a man I hadn't seen since I was a boy. It made for a chaotic evening, I'm afraid."

Blakely nodded. "I've been meaning to ask you about the workers' camp. I assume you've decided what's to be done about those cabins. Once the men are released next week, we won't have need of them."

"I put Lutrell Crocker in charge of tearing them down. Much of the lumber is still good. We ought to store it for future repairs to the stables and fences, save the cost of buying new."

Blakely nodded and chomped his cigar. "Other than the misplaced banjo, any more unrest in the ranks? The newspaper article that young woman wrote last month gave me quite a scare. Once a place gets a bad reputation, it's hard to turn things around."

Ethan leaned against the door frame and stifled an irritated sigh. Clearly he would not escape his boss anytime soon. "A knife fight last week. A couple of Irish got drunk and went a few rounds with the stableboys. Griff Rutledge took care of that one, though. And luckily, no one breathed a word to Miss Caldwell."

Blakely's cigar smoke swirled toward the ornate plastered ceiling. He flicked ash onto the carpet and peered at Ethan. "All right, boy. Out with it. What's troubling you?"

For a moment Ethan was tempted to confide in his boss. Deprived of his parents at an early age, he'd long since grown accustomed to solving his own problems, relying on no one but himself and God. But Julian's sudden reappearance had left his emotions too raw for words. He needed to be alone, to sort out his feelings and decide what to do about Julian's presence in Hickory Ridge.

Before the story erupted and blew his whole world sky high.

TEN

"So how was the reception?"

Through the Verandah's open window, the creaking of rigs and freight wagons, the shouts of children, and the barking of dogs punctuated Lucy's question. The other hotel residents had already left for their jobs at Blue Smoke or at the shops lining the street. Though it was still early, Sophie and Lucy had the place to themselves. Lucy slid a stack of flapjacks onto a plate and set it on the table in front of Sophie.

Sophie drizzled syrup over the flapjacks and took a bite. "Sumptuous."

Lucy grinned. "Are you talking about the resort or my cooking?"

"Both." Sophie sipped her coffee, then added a bit more cream.

"Well, you have Flora to thank for the flapjacks. She gave me her mama's recipe." Lucy poured herself a cup of coffee from the blue enameled pot and slid into her chair. "What does Blue Smoke look like? I heard it's like something in one of Mr. Chastain's storybooks."

Sophie grinned. "There was so much gold, I wouldn't have been surprised if we were robbed at gunpoint."

"You spent too much time in lawless Texas, my friend."

"No such thing as too much time in Texas. But I'm not joking. The whole place was dripping in gold." Sophie speared a bite of flapjack. "I met some wonderful people. Mrs. McPherson—she owns a paper in Texas—said I should submit some articles to a news syndicate."

Lucy frowned. "What's that?"

"A single source for articles from a lot of different writers that are then sold to a number of papers around the country."

"Oh." Lucy narrowed her eyes. "How big a take does the owner get?"

"I have no idea. Mrs. McPherson says the pay is acceptable. I might look into it one of these days. Right now it's all I can do to keep the paper going."

"Not to mention the ball at Blue Smoke tonight." Lucy finished her coffee and poured another cup. "Honestly, Sophie Caldwell, if you are not a true-life Cinderella, I don't know who is. Half the women in Hickory Ridge have been dying for Mr. Heyward's attention ever since he got here, but he seemed completely immune to their charms. Then you showed up, and the first thing we knew he started seeing you at every opportunity."

"I don't expect I'll see much of him after the big to-do for the mucky-mucks is over." Sophie polished off her flapjacks and pushed her plate away. Thinking about tonight's event filled her with a mix of anticipation and puzzlement.

Even though she hadn't seen all that much of Ethan, she was growing fond of his company. And last night, in the carriage, she'd supposed for a moment that he felt the same way about her. But then, after the altercation with the man in his office, Ethan had pulled away. Why? And why had he not invited anyone from the Georgia press to the reception? It didn't make sense. Maybe it was worth looking into, if she ever found the time.

"Speaking of Mr. Chastain." Lucy spooned sugar into her

coffee. "That once-upon-a-time wife of his sent another wire yesterday, after I already wrote to her explaining that the Verandah is full up. She seems set on coming back here all of a sudden."

Sophie nodded. "Robbie told me. Maybe she's looking for a job at Blue Smoke."

Lucy laughed. "That would be a first."

"You knew her?"

"Only briefly. I lived here for a time before I went west to marry Jake. She showed up one day, charmed the socks off poor Mr. Chastain, married him, and then up and left. It was all very strange." Lucy began clearing the dishes.

Sophie finished her coffee and rose. "I should get to the office. Caleb is probably wondering where I am."

"How's he working out?"

"Fine, though I'm not sure he'll ever master orthography." She shook her head. "Last week I asked him to set the type for Mr. Pruitt's advertisement, and the next thing I knew he was making up a notice for t-h-r-e-d and s-o-p-e. Luckily I caught the errors before he printed it. I can only imagine Mr. Pruitt's reaction to two misspelled words in a single sentence."

"Just be glad he's able to handle the press so you don't wind up with so much ink under your fingernails. I remember Patsy Greer's fingers were always black with ink."

"I remember that too. She was good to me. Very patient. I'm sorry she moved so far away. I'd like to see her again."

"You never know who might show up here in town now that Blue Smoke is becoming famous." Lucy finished stacking their dishes and brushed crumbs from the tablecloth. "Shall I fix a bath for you again tonight?"

"Oh, Lucy, that's sweet of you, but I don't expect you to be my personal maid. Not when you have this place and all your other guests to look after."

"I don't mind. I like helping you get all fancied up. That way I can enjoy some of the excitement of going out."

Sophie studied the hotelier. Lucy Partridge was much too young and much too pretty to keep to herself all the time. But she still mourned the death of her cowboy husband, buried somewhere in Montana territory. Lucy wouldn't hear of courting anyone else, at least not yet.

Lucy patted Sophie's arm. "Go on and get your work done. I'll have your bath ready at five o'clock. And don't get waylaid this time. Mr. Heyward might not take kindly to being kept waiting two nights in a row, even for someone as pretty as you."

"Thanks," Sophie said. "That would be a big help. Miss Hattie came by the other day and ordered new menus for her restaurant. I promised to have them ready by Monday, and my old jobber press breaks down at least once every day." She sighed. "What I wouldn't give for a new one. But I can't afford it."

"You're just getting started," Lucy said. "You can't expect overnight success."

"I suppose not." Taking up her reticule from the hall table where she'd left it, Sophie waved good-bye and headed for the *Gazette* office.

The first week of June had dawned clear and hot. Sophie dabbed her damp forehead and nodded to a couple of salesmen heading for the railway station. Down the street, Doc Spencer was just coming out of his office, with Gillie following behind. They spoke for a moment before he climbed into his rig and drove away. Spotting Sophie, Gillie waved and then went back inside.

Sophie pushed open the *Gazette* office door and dropped her reticule onto her desk. Caleb was waiting for her, a scowl on his face. "Guess what's broken again?"

"Did you try resetting the pin like I showed you?"

"Yep, but it keeps dropping back out. How am I supposed to get anything done when the equipment won't work right?"

"I know it's aggravating, but what can I do?"

He shrugged. "Some days I wish I had my old job back."

"In which case you would soon be unemployed altogether." She raised the window to let in any breath of cooling air and looked over the proof sheets he'd placed on her desk. "Blue Smoke is officially open as of tomorrow, so most of the carpenters will be let go."

Another shrug. Caleb indicated the stack of proofs on her desk. "They look all right?"

"They're fine. Go ahead and run them, and I'll work on Miss Hattie's order."

He scooped up the stack and headed for the back. "Better you fool with that ornery machine than me."

She watched his retreat and suppressed a smile. For all his grumbling, Caleb was a godsend. As soon as she was able, she'd raise his wages a bit.

She sat down at the jobber press and worked the treadle. The pin clanked onto the floor. "Oh, for mercy's sake." Bending down, she spied the errant pin and reached for it just as the door swung wide. A ragged, hollow-eyed woman stepped across the threshold, a limp infant cradled in her arms. "Miss?"

"What's the matter?" Sophie crossed the office and recognized the mountain woman and child she'd encountered on the path near Blue Smoke.

"My baby's burnin' up with fever," the woman said dully. "Hank told me not to come down here, but I got to do something for her, and you said—"

"Of course. You were right to come for help." She swept the papers off her desk. "Lay the child here. Caleb!"

He stuck his head into the room. "What is it?"

"I want you to find Miss Gilman. She's at Doc Spencer's office. Hurry."

He took one look at the mother and baby and tore out of the office.

Silent tears slid down the woman's tired face. Sophie pulled up a chair for her. "Sit down. How in the world did you get here?"

"Hank wouldn't let me have the mule. He said if God wants Rebecca to live, he'll cure her without any help from mortals." She sniffed and wiped her eyes. "So I picked her up and started walking."

"All that way?"

"A mother'll do anything for a child. You'll understand that someday."

A pang of sadness shot through Sophie. Her own mother had been unable—or unwilling—to save her from years of painful neglect. She glanced at the infant's tiny chest, which heaved with every labored breath, and sent up a silent prayer.

Caleb and Gillie rushed in. Gillie dropped her medical bag onto the floor and bent over the child. "How long has she been this way?"

"She's been sneezin' and coughin' for a week now," the woman said. "I didn't think it was the croup or nothin', so I weren't too worried. But last night she was hot and real jerky. Couldn't keep nothin' down."

"Seizures," Gillie said. "Not uncommon when a child has a high fever."

"She cried half the night," the woman said. "Finally she quieted down, and I thought the fever had broke. But this morning when I went to feed her, I couldn't wake her up."

"We must bring her temperature down." Gillie looked around the office. "Sophie, do you have any sort of washbasin we can use?"

"I bet Miss Hattie does," Caleb said. "A dishpan or something."

"That would do nicely," Gillie said. "Fill it with cold water and hurry right back."

While Caleb fetched the water, Gillie stripped off the baby's clothing and frowned at the red bumps covering the child's thin chest. "What happened here?"

The woman shrugged. "Chigger bites, I reckon. You know how young'uns like to play in the woods."

"Yes, I do. And it's good to let children outdoors when the weather is nice. But you must bathe them thoroughly with soap and water before bed to get rid of anything they've picked up during the day."

The woman looked away. "Chigger bites never hurt nobody. Me and my sisters had 'em all the time when we was young'uns."

Gillie's hands moved over the child's still form. "Do you have other children?"

"Two boys alayin' in the graveyard. Four more livin'."

"Are any of them sick?"

The woman's tired eyes filled. "No, just my baby girl. She ain't gonna die, is she?"

"I hope not." Gillie looked at Sophie, a worried expression clouding her blue eyes. "What on earth is keeping Caleb?"

Just then he returned with a faded blue towel and tin tub filled with water. A chunk of ice bobbed on the surface. "Miss Hattie said ice is better for bringing down a fever. And she sent a towel."

Gillie nodded and gently lowered the child into the cold water. Again and again she cupped her hand and poured water over the baby's head and shoulders. The child's mother waited, arms clutched to her chest.

Caleb watched until Gillie looked up and saw him staring at her. He blushed and ducked his head. "If you don't need me, I reckon I ought to get back to work." He headed for the press, the door swinging shut behind him.

In a few minutes the baby stirred, opened her eyes, and began to scream. "Stop!" the woman cried. "You're hurtin' her."

"She's feeling a sensation like you would if you pricked your finger with a sewing needle. It's a good sign, Mrs. . . . ?" Gillie lifted the baby from the water and used Miss Hattie's towel to dry her off. She cradled the little girl on her shoulder and gently rocked her until the crying stopped.

"Name's Wimberly." The woman reached for the baby and dressed her. "I thank you kindly, but I got to git on home 'fore my man comes back."

"Mrs. Wimberly, I believe your daughter may have a weak strain of influenza. You should keep her away from your other children until her cough stops. And bring her to Doc Spencer's office immediately if her fever spikes again."

The woman trailed a finger across her daughter's cheek and said nothing.

"Give her some weak, warm tea with honey." Gillie took a small tin of salve from her bag and pressed it into the woman's hand. "Please put this on those chigger bites and remember what I said about cleanliness. It's important in keeping all your children healthy."

Mrs. Wimberly shook her head. "I cain't take that medicine from you."

"Why not?"

"I just . . . cain't. That's all."

"If it's a matter of money, don't worry about it. This is a sample a salesman left for Doc Spencer last week. Didn't cost us a thing." Gillie suddenly caught the woman's wrist and pushed up her sleeve, exposing a gaping, pus-filled wound on her forearm. Red streaks radiated from the woman's wrist to her elbow. "What happened here?"

"Ain't nothin'."

"It looks like a knife wound." Gillie's expression darkened. "It needs tending. Did your husband—"

"Look." Mrs. Wimberly jerked away and headed for the door.

"I'm much obliged to you for taking care of Rebecca. But that don't give you no right to go meddlin' in my business."

"But—"

The door slammed shut, rattling the framed newspaper pages hanging on the wall. Gillie collapsed onto a chair. Sophie set the tub of water on the floor and perched on the edge of her desk.

"If I were a gambling woman, I'd bet my last dime that Mr. Wimberly is responsible for that cut on his wife's forearm," Gillie said. "But what is she going to do?"

Gillie refastened the knot of flaxen hair at the nape of her neck. "Doc Spencer says half of the practice of medicine is fighting disease and the other half is fighting ignorance." She looked up. "Mrs. Wimberly must be the woman you told me about. The one on the mountain."

"Yes. I gave her our names and told her to look for us if she needed help." Sophie paused, remembering. "I think she's afraid of her husband. He wouldn't even let her take their mule to bring the baby down the mountain."

She studied her friend, impressed with Gillie's medical skills and her passion for helping others. "How did you know to look for that wound on her arm?"

"An infected wound gives off an odor. I smelled it on her the minute I came in, but I needed to take care of the baby first."

"Will the baby be all right?"

"With any luck. Doc Spencer treated a few cases of influenza last week. Everyone recovered. But I won't be surprised if the other Wimberly children are sick within the week. I'm actually more worried about their mother's wound."

"Not that we will ever know about it."

"Right." Gillie got to her feet. "I should get back to the office. Doc Spencer is expecting Jeanne Pruitt this afternoon. She has a nasty boil that needs lancing and I promised to assist."

Sophie shuddered. "I don't see how you can bear to be around pain and suffering all day."

"It's what I'm called to do," Gillie said simply. "It isn't a burden at all. It's a privilege, really, to make people feel better."

"Well, you have a gift for it. That's for certain."

Gillie picked up her bag and headed for the door. "Think of how much more good I could do if I had my infirmary."

ELEVEN

Overnight the ballroom at Blue Smoke had been transformed from a large reception hall to an opulent dance floor surrounded by tall urns of exotic flowers. A riot of pink, blue, and creamy white blooms competed for attention with the sun-gilded mountains visible through the open French doors. Dining tables set with paper-thin china and glittering crystal were festooned with fresh garlands and miles of white and blue satin ribbons. At the far end of the room, formally attired musicians warmed up their instruments.

"Well?" Ethan, resplendent in gray formal clothes and a navy cravat, smiled down at Sophie. "What's the verdict?"

"It's enchanting. Even more beautiful than last evening."

His gaze held hers for so long and in such an intimate way that it felt like a caress. Her face warmed. Except for Wyatt Caldwell, the man against whom she measured all others, Ethan was the most attractive man she'd ever met. But she couldn't get past the feeling that he was hiding something from her. Something significant.

Not that she could fault him for that when she was keeping a secret of her own.

Tucking her hand into the crook of his arm, Sophie watched the crowd swelling around them. Ladies in their finest silks, gentlemen in frock coats and boiled shirts milled about, chatting quietly and greeting friends. Ethan pointed out the wealthy and the famous, murmuring into her ear the names of lawyers, retired generals, senators, and businessmen from across the state. Sophie spied Carrie and Griff Rutledge standing with the Gilmans and sent Carrie a tiny wave. Gillie had been invited tonight too but had chosen instead to spend the evening helping Doc Spencer with a difficult case up on the mountain.

Horace Blakely strolled over, his wife on his arm, and sent Sophie a curt nod before turning his attention to Ethan. "I thought you said the governor was coming tonight."

"He is, but he wired O'Brien late this afternoon that his train is behind schedule." Ethan consulted his pocket watch. "He shouldn't be too much longer."

"I hope he makes it," Mr. Blakely said. "I'd hate to disappoint all these folks who want to meet a genuine war hero."

Sophie's ears pricked. Since returning to Hickory Ridge, she'd been too busy to read up on the state's political situation. But when Jasper Pruitt stopped by the newspaper office that week to place his advertisement, he'd mentioned Governor Bate's war record and his work on clearing up the state's debt problem. Such a man might just be someone worth writing about.

"Hold on now, Sophie," Ethan said as the Blakelys moved on to greet others.

"What?"

"I can see the wheels turning in your head. But tonight is strictly a social occasion, so no questioning the governor for that paper of yours."

She placed one hand over her heart. "Why, Mr. Heyward, I wouldn't dream of it."

He laughed. "Would you like a walk in the gardens after dinner?"

"I'd love that."

A sudden hush fell over the crowd as a distinguished-looking gentleman entered the room in the company of an equally handsome woman. Even Ethan seemed in awe of the couple as they began greeting those nearest them.

"That's the governor," he murmured, "and his wife, Miss Julia. He got that limp at the battle of Shiloh back in sixty-two. The story goes that he got shot and the doc wanted to amputate the leg, but Mr. Bate pulled his pistol and threatened to shoot any man who tried to deprive him of it."

"What a fascinating story! I'd like—" She noted his raised eyebrow and stopped midsentence, choosing instead to study the musicians. "I think they're about to start."

Moments later a lively waltz filled the room and couples paired off for the first dance. Ethan bowed to Sophie. "Shall we?"

She nodded. He swept her into his arms. And for the next half hour, as they moved from one waltz to the next, Sophie didn't let herself think about the editorial she needed to write in support of the infirmary, the plight of the mountain woman and her child, the broken jobber press, or Ethan's reaction to the man she'd encountered outside his office last evening. Instead she gave herself over to the beauty of the music and the opulent ballroom, the luxurious feel of her royal-blue silk gown whispering about her ankles. Ethan held her close and smiled down at her, and she laughed out loud. Who would have ever believed that a mixed-up, muddleboned orphan like her would attend a ball with the governor himself?

When the dance ended and everyone was seated for dinner, Mr. Blakely made a short welcoming speech recognizing the white-haired, white-mustachioed governor who rose to greet the crowd with a wave and a slight smile. The applause died, and a small army of waiters appeared bearing the first course, a light consommé flavored with spring herbs and cream. Then came a fish course, a meat course served with an array of vegetables, and platters of small coconut cakes garnished with tiny sugar flowers. Finally the waiters appeared again with trays of cheeses, bowls of salted nuts, and tiny petits fours enrobed in white sugar icing.

When the tables were cleared and the music began again, Ethan rose and offered Sophie his hand. "Ready for that turn in the gardens?"

They made their way through the crowd and out into the deepening twilight, following a narrow pebbled pathway to a garden lit with hundreds of flickering candles. Ethan pointed out the massive beds where summer flowers were just beginning to bloom and a tiered rose garden studded with small stone benches that faced a fountain. A whippoorwill called from the branches of a gnarled hickory tree. Fireflies darted among the rosebushes.

"The gardens are magnificent, Ethan. You should be proud of everything you've accomplished here." She waved one hand. "If Blue Smoke isn't a success, it surely won't be your fault."

"I can't take too much credit for the gardens. Mr. Tyler from New York designed every inch of them, right down to the last pebble. All I did was make sure his plans were carried out."

"Still, it couldn't have been easy, given all the unrest among the workers." She settled herself on a stone bench and took out her fan. "I suppose they're all gone now?"

"For the most part. Li Chung and his assistants will remain, of course. Horace and I are retaining a small number of local men to handle maintenance on the place, and I've got a crew working on dismantling those cabins you find so offensive."

"Now you're making fun of me."

"No, I'm not." He paused and gazed directly into her face. Summer insects hummed and chirped in the grass. "Can I ask you something?"

"Certainly."

"That first day you came to my office for that interview, I

was struck by your resemblance to my mother's family. They were mostly from Italy. I'm wondering if you are too."

Her heart thudded in her chest. Italy? Is that what he thought? She'd spent most of her life dodging questions about her heritage, pretending that the persistent rumors of her African ancestry didn't exist. She'd long ago become accustomed to doing what it took to have a chance at a decent life.

But this was different. This was personal.

Sophie fanned her face, willing the truth to come but unable to speak it. Deceit was wrong and she knew it, yet she heard herself saying, "I'm Italian and French, we think. My parents both died when I was young."

"Then we have that in common." Ethan's smile was gentle. A wave of guilt and fear engulfed her, washing away all the enchantment of the evening. She had told a lie, plain and simple, and one day she would have to answer for it. She gazed past Ethan's shoulder to the line of carriages and rigs standing beneath the portico. The party was breaking up.

She rose. "I've had a wonderful evening, the best evening of my life, but I should go. Will you call for the carriage?"

"In a minute." He caught her hand and drew her close. "Ah, Sophie."

In the flickering candlelight his gaze softened and her pulse jumped. Ethan wanted to kiss her. She wanted it too. Something in the way he held her when they danced, the way he looked at her as if he could see past all her defenses, connected with her heart in a way she didn't understand. But she couldn't let it happen. A kiss promised something—a future perhaps. And how could they possibly have a future now?

She pulled away. "Please, I must go."

He dropped her hand and stepped away. "I've offended you."

"No, I—"

"No need to explain. It's my fault. I misread your feelings and I apologize." He offered his arm. "Come. I'll get the carriage."

Wordlessly he led her along the path to the portico and signaled the doorman.

Carrie Rutledge hurried over, her small jeweled reticule dangling from one arm. "Sophie, I'm so sorry we didn't have a chance to visit tonight. Wasn't this party grand?"

Sophie forced a smile for Ada's old friend. "Very grand. I've never seen so much food in all my born days."

"Me either. Griff said it reminded him of parties his parents hosted when he was a boy in Charleston. I myself came from much more humble stock. But they say it isn't where you came from that's important; it's where you're going. Don't you agree?"

Sophie nodded. Where was that infernal carriage? But the line moved slowly as the guests said their good-byes. Ethan stood a little apart from the others, talking with the Gilmans.

"Are you all right?" Carrie asked. "You seem upset."

"I'm fine. A little tired. And I still have some writing to do when I get home."

Carrie laughed. "You're just like my husband. Griff can always think of ten things that need doing at the end of the day. Oh, here's our rig." She kissed Sophie on both cheeks. "Don't be such a stranger, my dear. I'd love to have you visit whenever you can spare the time. Promise me you'll come for tea one day soon."

"Thank you. I will."

Carrie got into the Rutledges' rig and tucked her voluminous skirt around her. Griff nodded to Sophie, picked up the reins, and drove away.

"Here's your carriage." Ethan motioned to Sophie and helped her inside. "I hope you had a good time," he said, his voice stiff, "despite my behavior in the garden."

"Please, you mustn't think—"

He rapped sharply on the carriage door and called up to the driver, "The Verandah, Silas."

She turned around on the seat and watched Ethan walk away. Tears pricked her eyes. Despite the long day, her conscience wouldn't let her sleep tonight. Well, she deserved an unquiet mind after the untruth she'd just told Ethan. But his question had come from nowhere, leaving her unprepared. As had her strong feelings for him.

Oh Lord, what shall I do now?

In Texas everyone had assumed she was like the Caldwells because that was what Ada and Wyatt thought best. It hadn't felt like lying—not really. And last year, in New Orleans for the Exposition, she'd noticed dark-skinned white people mingling with light-skinned Africans and folks of every ilk, and no one seemed to give it a second thought. But such was not the case everywhere. And clearly not with Ethan.

She couldn't forget the thunderous expression on Ethan's face, the loud exchange with his visitor last night, and the pained look on the olive-skinned stranger's face as he passed her in the hall. And she understood all too well the reason for Ethan's question about her family.

He wanted to know whether her blood was pure.

Well, what did she know for certain? Everyone at the orphanage assumed she was of mixed blood and treated her as such. Caught between two worlds and belonging to neither, she would have continued as an outcast if not for the Caldwells. Still, there was no real proof one way or another. Mrs. Lowell had refused to answer any of Sophie's questions about her parents, and now the woman was dead. She hadn't really deceived him, had she?

Of course she had.

She leaned against the leather seat and closed her eyes as the carriage rattled down the mountain road. Regret weighed on her heart heavy as stone. She desperately needed to confide in someone, but who?

At last the carriage drew up at the hotel. The driver jumped down and opened her door. "Good night, miss."

"Good night." She watched the carriage disappear into the darkness. Somewhere far off a dog barked. A few lights flickered in the windows of shops and houses along the street. A horse and rig appeared at the far end of the street, heading away from the church.

Robbie. Of course. The one boy in Hickory Ridge who had never judged her.

The one person who would understand.

~

Ethan headed back into the ballroom, where a few guests still lingered over glasses of sherry and port. He smiled and nodded as he passed them but eschewed conversation. He needed to think. Very soon he would have to figure out what to do about Julian, but at this moment he was preoccupied with what had just happened in the rose garden.

He couldn't blame Sophie for refusing his advances; they were practically strangers, after all. He was not usually so quick to reveal his feelings. But with Sophie he felt as if an invisible thread, woven of their similar childhood tragedies, ran between them, binding them together. He had thought Sophie felt it too. Obviously he'd been wrong.

Even after all these years, he didn't like to think about what had happened so many years ago. The memories still lacerated his heart. For years he had asked God not for peace or understanding but for justice. He'd received neither. So he'd buried himself in work, in striving for success, in travel—anything to keep the past at a safe distance.

Then Sophie arrived, bringing with her the revival of old memories and old longings. He shook his head. Stupid. No wonder she'd taken off like a scared rabbit.

Too keyed up to sleep, he pushed through the French doors and cut through the deserted gardens. The candles had burned down to nubs; several had gone out. Only a few attenuated shadows danced against the dark walls. He paused to lift a budding rose to his nose. In a few more days, the roses would open in full beauty. He'd send Sophie an armload of them and hope for her forgiveness. Maybe she would give him another chance.

"Heyward!" a voice called from the shadows and Ethan turned toward the sound.

"Yes? Who's there?"

Footsteps crunched on the graveled walkway and a lone figure appeared on the path. Ethan peered into the darkness. "Is that you, Lutrell?"

"'Is that you, Lutrell?' Of course it's me." The wiry carpenter wove his unsteady way toward Ethan, a half-empty bottle of whiskey in one hand, a pistol in the other.

"You're drunk, my friend." Ethan kept his voice calm. "I can see how you and the boys feel entitled to a celebration now that Blue Smoke is finished. But you ought to give me that firearm before someone gets hurt."

"No, sir. I ain't givin' up my pistol till I get my money back from that no-good Irishman that stole it."

Ethan massaged his aching temples and sighed. "And which Irishman might that be?"

"Sean Murphy's cousin. Fitz."

"Fitz Murphy's never been in trouble before. I'm sure it's nothing more than a misunderstanding. We'll get it sorted out in the morning."

"In the morning, my eye. I already done finished tearin' down the workers' cabins like I was told to do, and I'm on my way to Alabama to marry my girl. You said I could have a week to get married and bring her back here."

"And so you shall."

"Besides, Murphy's already gone. Most everybody cleared out of here this morning. And now I got Mary Susan awaitin' for me in White Oak, Alabama, and no way to get to her."

Behind them, the lights inside the resort winked out. Suddenly Ethan was too tired to argue. He reached inside his jacket for his wallet. "I'll advance you the money until we can get to the bottom of this. If you still want to work here, helping take care of the place, you can pay me back out of your first month's wages."

"Pay you back?" Lutrell advanced on Ethan, his eyes wild with spirits and anger. "That ain't fair. I was robbed!"

"Can you prove it?"

"You callin' me a liar, Mr. Heyward?"

"People don't always see things clearly when they're drinking."

"Well, I saw clear enough who stole from me. Murphy was the only one near my cabin this whole day."

"Proximity does not equal guilt."

"Then why'd he take off when I yelled at him?"

"I'd run too if a half-drunk man was pointing a gun at me. It has been a very long day, Mr. Crocker. I'm very tired." He pressed several bills into the man's hand. "Go on home and marry your girl. Forget about the money."

"Onliest folks that say forget about money is the ones got plenty of it." Crocker took a long pull on the bottle and tossed Ethan's money onto the path. "I don't aim to be beholden to you, Mr. Heyward. If you ain't going to replace the money that no-good Irish devil stole from me, then I got nothin' else to say to you."

"Your choice. I appreciate the work you did on Blue Smoke.

I'm sorry you won't be coming back. And I hope you and your bride will be very happy in Alabama. Good night."

Ethan waited until Crocker disappeared into the darkness, then turned and headed back inside.

TWELVE

Sophie closed her hymn book and pressed her palm to her forehead. Was it her imagination, or was Robbie looking in her direction more than was usual on a Sunday morning?

Gillie leaned toward Sophie. "You look a bit peaked this morning. Are you ill?"

"I'm fine." Sophie forced a smile. How could she ever be fine if concealing the details of her parentage, what few she thought she knew, was to be her daily portion from now on? She closed her eyes. Heavens above, she had been six kinds of stupid to come back here. What had she been thinking? How could she have possibly believed that things would be different this time? That she could build a newspaper and live here and not have to be constantly on guard against rumor and suspicion?

Just last week, coming out of the mercantile, two farm women had stopped their conversation and frowned at her as she crossed the street, disapproval clearly etched on their weathered faces. She didn't recognize them, but perhaps they remembered her and the gossip that had ensued when Wyatt and Ada removed her from Mrs. Lowell's. Sooner or later the truth would get back to Ethan, and he would hate her for it.

She thought about last night and the ball at Blue Smoke. The entire night had been impossibly romantic—the dancing, the flickering candlelight, the faint scent of budding roses, the quiet strains of chamber music spilling onto the terrace. No wonder Ethan had gotten ahead of himself. She had felt something for him too, a longing to know more about him and where he came from. What had happened to his parents? Was their fate to blame for the haunted look in his eyes when someone mentioned Georgia?

She shook her head. It didn't matter now. There could be nothing between them. From now on, she would speak to Ethan Heyward only concerning her printing orders for Blue Smoke. Guard her heart.

She fanned her face and looked around the church. Today it wasn't as crowded as in recent weeks. Some of the Blue Smoke workers were undoubtedly using this weekend to pack their belongings and head for home. And Gillie had reported that several more families had been stricken with a nasty summer cough. She and Doc Spencer hoped it would not spread even further.

His sermon concluded, Robbie motioned the congregation to their feet and led the final hymn. Sophie closed her eyes as the words of the song washed over her.

Mercy now, O Lord, I plead
In this hour of utter need;
Turn me not away unblessed;
Calm my anguish into rest.

The people gathered their hats and reticules and squirming children and prepared to depart. Sophie still sat there, hungry for that spirit of peace but failing to grasp it.

"Can you come home with me?" Gillie clasped Sophie's arm. "Mother has invited Thomas Ryden to Sunday dinner. He's the son of one of her old school friends—a professor of bugs at some college back east and—"

Despite her anguished heart, Sophie laughed. "A professor of bugs?"

Gillie waved one hand. "You know what I mean. He studies insects, though to what purpose I haven't a clue. Mother claims Tom is just passing through, but I'd wager my last button she has recruited him as a marriage prospect for poor little old me. You must come and save me from death by tedium."

"I wish I could, but I must speak to Robbie."

Gillie's blue eyes held both curiosity and sympathy. "Is everything all right at the paper? Are the Caldwells all right?"

"They're well, at last accounting. This is a more . . . personal matter."

"Oh. I won't pry then, but you do know you can count on me."

"Yes, and I'm more grateful than you can imagine." Sophie caught Robbie's eye and waved. He grinned and waved back.

"If you change your mind, come on out to the house this afternoon. I'm certain Mr. Ryder will be holding forth on the wonders of black beetles for hours on end."

Just then Mrs. Gilman sailed over, the pink and white silk flowers on her summer hat stirring in the warm breeze wafting through the open windows. "I heard that remark, Sabrina, and I must say I find it most unbecoming." She eyed Sophie. "I see you've settled in, though I can't imagine why you would want to live in a place where you have no friends. It must be terribly lonely here for someone like you."

"Mother." Sabrina frowned. "You're being inexcusably rude."

"Sabrina is my friend," Sophie said, "a very good one. As is Reverend Whiting and his parents. And the Rutledges. And Lucy Partridge. Sheriff McCracken looks out for me as well."

"Nevertheless," Mrs. Gilman said, lifting her chin, "it seems to me that you'd be better suited elsewhere."

"Hickory Ridge needed a newspaper." Sophie tried to smile,

but her throat was tight with worry. Mrs. Gilman was just the kind of woman to foment trouble for its own sake. Why, oh why, hadn't she listened to Wyatt and started her newspaper someplace else?

"I must speak to Dr. Spencer," Gillie said. "I'll see you later, Mother." She pushed through the door and headed for her rig.

Mrs. Gilman placed a hand on Sophie's arm. "Our Sabrina does seem to be quite taken with you, Miss Caldwell. All she can talk about is you and that paper of yours." She frowned. "And her scheme for an infirmary. It's ridiculous."

Sophie took out her fan and snapped it open. "I'm afraid I don't agree, Mrs. Gilman. I hope the mayor and the council will at least listen to her proposal."

"It's an entirely unsuitable pursuit for a woman of her station, and I wish you wouldn't encourage her. She needs to find a suitable match and take her rightful place in society before it's too late." With a curt nod, Mrs. Gilman whirled away.

Sophie fanned her face and waited for Robbie to finish greeting his flock. His wife, Ethelinda, dressed in a modest blue frock with lace trim at the throat, stood beside him, talking quietly with two elderly women while Robbie exchanged greetings with the Pruitts. As they made their way up the aisle toward the door, Mr. Pruitt noticed Sophie and offered a brief nod.

"Good morning, Mr. Pruitt," Sophie said. "Mrs. Pruitt."

"Look, Jasper," his wife said. "You see the fabric of her dress? That is exactly what I was talking to you about last week. You need to order some for the mercantile. Now that Blue Smoke is open, ladies in Hickory Ridge will be wanting something a little fancier for Founders Day and the harvest festival, and not all of them can afford to have me make dresses for them."

Jasper eyed the periwinkle-blue silk frock Ada had sent the week before. "It is right pretty. I will think on it, honeybunch."

Mrs. Pruitt straightened her hat and offered Sophie a

gap-toothed smile. "When he calls me honeybunch, it's as good as done."

Remembering the storekeeper's harsh judgments when she was a child, Sophie tried to hide her surprise. Time had certainly softened Mr. Pruitt's heart. Or perhaps Robbie's stirring sermons were at least partially responsible.

The Pruitts and the elderly ladies left. Ethelinda began counting the morning's offering, the coins spilling into a leather pouch with a faint tinkling sound. Robbie hurried over to Sophie. "I'm glad you're here today. I wasn't sure you would be after two nights of festivities up at Blue Smoke. I understand the opening was spectacular."

Sophie nodded, overcome with the need to unburden her heart.

"I imagine you must be exhausted. I heard the governor was there last night. I was hoping he might turn up here this morning, but I didn't see—" He frowned. "Sophie Robillard Caldwell. Something is wrong, and don't bother denying it."

She twisted her handkerchief into a tiny damp ball. "I've done a terrible thing, and I doubt it can be fixed."

"Our Lord is the master of the impossible fix," he said. "You want to talk about it?"

"I was hoping for a word with you, but—" She glanced at Ethelinda, who had finished counting the offering and was busy retrieving her gloves and hymnal from the piano bench.

"Ethelinda won't mind. Wait here."

Robbie spoke to his wife, who stood on tiptoe to whisper in his ear before leaving through the side door. Robbie led Sophie to a tiny alcove just off the cloakroom. Barely large enough for a desk and a chair, it was filled to overflowing with books and papers stacked haphazardly on the floor. A narrow window was open to the breeze that drifted across the street, bringing with it the scents of baking bread, leather, and horses.

Motioning her to the chair, Robbie leaned against the door frame and crossed his arms. "Now, what's troubling you?"

"I have told an untruth, and my heart is about to break because of it."

"Go on."

Briefly she told him of her encounter with the blue-eyed stranger outside Ethan's office and of last night's conversation with Ethan in the garden at Blue Smoke. "He acted almost as if he hated the man, who was obviously . . . like me. When he asked whether my family was Italian, I said yes. Because I didn't want him to hate me too."

Robbie sighed. "I don't blame you for wanting to retain his good opinion. It's human to want to be accepted."

"It isn't only my personal feelings at stake. Ethan is my best customer. I can't afford to lose his account." She opened her reticule and dropped her wadded handkerchief inside.

"But, Sophie, haven't you jumped to conclusions here? You can't know what the problem is between those two men. Their antipathy might be due to any number of things. And you can't be sure he'd stop doing business with you because of questions about who your parents were."

Through the open window, she watched a buckboard rumble toward the railway station. "I suppose you're right, but I didn't want to take that chance. And now there is no going back."

Robbie smiled, his blue eyes glinting with amusement.

"What's so funny?"

"I was just thinking about how God answers prayers."

She looked up at him, her brows raised, her palms up.

"Just this morning I was trying to settle on the subject for next week's sermon. I couldn't seem to decide what I should talk about. And then lo and behold, here comes my oldest friend, wrestling with the question of deceit."

She slumped in the chair. "I'm happy to know my troubles inspired you. But honestly, I don't know what to do about it."

"Yes, you do." He pinned her with his gaze and waited.

She sighed. "I suppose you'll tell me I must confess and ask both God and Ethan to forgive me. Believe me, I rehearsed that confession a thousand times last night when I couldn't sleep. But then I kept imagining Ethan's reaction."

"It isn't easy to admit to a wrong. But the truth, however unpleasant, is hardly ever as bad as we imagine. If Ethan Heyward is half the man he ought to be, he'll accept your apology, forgive you, and you'll go on as before."

His voice softened. "We've been apart for a long time, Sophie, but I still can read you like a book. And the chapter I'm reading right now tells me you might be developing feelings for this man that are far deeper than you've admitted—and that have nothing to do with the success of the *Gazette*."

Heat crept into her cheeks. Was she really so transparent? But it was a relief to unburden herself to someone who knew her so well. "It makes no sense, really. I've seen him only a few times, but I do like him very much."

"Then you owe him a friendship based upon truth."

"I know that, but I lack the courage."

He steepled his fingers and studied her. "Maybe what you really need is the courage to believe that you are a perfect creation, just as you are. That our Creator knew what he was doing when he made you."

The train whistle pierced the quiet. Robbie took out his pocket watch. "I should go. My mother-in-law arrived here last night for a week's visit, and Ethelinda reminded me that we promised to take a picnic to the river this afternoon."

Sophie laughed. "Robbie Whiting, somehow I cannot picture you on an outing with a mother-in-law."

"Sometimes it doesn't seem real to me either. But it will be all too real if I'm late. Mrs. Wilkins is a good woman, but she can be sharp-tongued when she feels her daughter is getting less of my attention than she deserves. I ought not to keep them waiting."

She rose. "Thank you for listening to my troubles. They must seem small compared to what so many others face."

"The Lord makes no distinction among us, Sophie. He sees and feels all our suffering and is willing to offer solace if we ask." He took both her hands. "If you value Mr. Heyward's friendship, you know what you must do. Do it now, before it's too late."

THIRTEEN

For two months, the mayor and the town council have refused Miss Sabrina Gilman an opportunity to present her idea for opening an infirmary in Hickory Ridge, despite support from Dr. Ennis Spencer and many of our leading citizens.

Last week the mayor again refused Miss Gilman's request, citing an overcrowded agenda. However, he and the council members had plenty of time to discuss the purchase of a new brass spittoon for the post office and plenty of time to debate whether Sheriff McCracken or Mr. Griff Rutledge ought to lead this year's Race Day parade. If the men of this town think so little of the welfare of—

"Sophie?" Caleb Stanhope stuck his head into the office and Sophie's fingers stilled. "Sorry to disturb you when you're writing, but our shipment of newsprint arrived on this morning's train and the stationmaster wants it out of the way. You want me to finish printing the fliers for Blue Smoke or go get our paper?"

Sophie took off her reading glasses and set them aside. "I

suppose you'd better get the paper. I'll finish the Blue Smoke order."

He came into the office and peered over her shoulder. "I hate to interrupt your work, especially when you're on your high horse about Miss Gilman's infirmary."

She massaged the tight muscles at the back of her neck. These days work was her only solace. Since her conversation with Robbie, she had slept fitfully, turning his words over in her mind. She never doubted God would forgive her, but Ethan might be a different matter entirely. Perhaps Robbie was right and she needed to summon the courage to be the woman God had created, regardless of anyone's opinion. But so far that was easier said than done.

She pushed back her chair and stood. "I can finish this later. The Blue Smoke order can't wait."

Caleb nodded and brushed his unruly hair from his eyes. "Mr. Pruitt says he heard the resort's been full up this whole week, and we're still almost a month from Founders Day. He says if we keep getting a steady stream of visitors, Hickory Ridge will grow rich as Croesus. Whoever that is."

Sophie smiled. "In which case there is no reason on earth why the town council should not support Gillie's infirmary."

"They won't have any choice once people read your new editorial," Caleb said. "Shame 'em into it if you have to. The mayor is just being pigheaded, is all. He likes to remind people who is in charge of things around here." He headed for the door. "I'll find a freight wagon and get our paper over here."

Sophie went into the back room and sat down at the jobber press. She checked the troublesome cotter pin and shoved it into place, then worked the treadle. A finished sheet slid into the tray. She picked it up and glanced at the list of activities available to guests at Blue Smoke.

9:00 AM: *Coffee and tea available in the library.* Please ring the bell for service.

10:00 AM: *Tour of the gardens.* Marvel at more than one hundred species of blooming plants, but please don't pick the flowers. Leave them for all to enjoy.

10:30 AM: *Riding lessons and demonstrations.* Join Mr. Griffin Rutledge at our stables for the finest in equestrian instruction. Meet Majestic, the first Thoroughbred to win the annual Hickory Ridge race.

12:00 noon: *Luncheon* in the main dining room or on the terrace, weather permitting. Our chef, Mr. Chung, and his able assistants are happy to answer any questions regarding today's offerings. We accommodate special requests whenever possible. We use only the finest ingredients from local sources. For this reason some items may not always be available.

3:00 PM: *Hiking expedition.* Please join our own Mr. O'Brien as he leads a hike to the summit of Hickory Ridge. Experience the singular beauty of the mountains from this perch high above the valley. Hikers are encouraged to wear sturdy shoes and carry a walking stick. Photographic equipment and sketchbooks are encouraged. You'll want to capture this spectacular view.

4:00 PM: *Afternoon tea in the library.* Blue Smoke is proud to offer occasional lecturers from the worlds of art and literature. This Tuesday we are pleased to host Miss Garaphelia Swint, author of *Homes and Gardens of the Old South.* Please join us for refreshments and conversation.

7:00 PM: *Dinner in the dining room.* Menu changes daily. This week our special dessert features locally grown strawberries with buttery shortbread and whipped cream.

9:00 PM: *Concert on the terrace.* Enjoy beautiful music to

soothe the soul and inspire the spirit, courtesy of the
Hamlin Trio. Gentlemen are invited to the smoking
lounge for cigars and a selection of the finest spirits.

Sophie counted the finished copies and quickly completed
the order. Returning to her desk, she rolled a clean sheet of paper
into her typewriting machine, typed up the bill, and checked it
for errors, feeling a sense of satisfaction. Together with the revenue
from her advertising customers, the money from the Blue Smoke
account just might be enough to get the jobber press repaired—if
she could find anyone with the skills to tackle such an ancient
machine.

Caleb returned with the freight driver and they unloaded the
paper. Sophie paid the driver and set Caleb to work loading the
press for tomorrow's run, hoping that by morning she'd be able to
finish the piece in support of the infirmary. Gillie was counting
on her.

The front bell chimed and Sophie looked up to find Ethan
standing in the doorway, holding an enormous bouquet of roses. "I
brought you a peace offering."

As delighted as she was to see him, trepidation pressed on her
heart. How could she ever admit her lie? Especially now when he
was standing so close and smelling wonderfully of cedar and roses.
"They're beautiful. But, really, you didn't have to—"

"Yes, I did. I had no right to behave as I did Saturday night." He
laid the fragrant bouquet in her arms, and she noticed someone had
taken pains to remove all the thorns. "Everything about the ball was
so beautiful that I'm afraid I forgot myself. It won't happen again."
His fingers brushed her wrist. "Until we both want it to."

Tell him. She opened her mouth, but the words wouldn't come.
She buried her nose in the sweet-scented blooms. "I—thank you,
Ethan." She spun away. "I'll find a vase for these."

He followed her into the back room, where Caleb had just finished loading the press. Ignoring Ethan, Caleb grabbed his cap. "All done, Miss Caldwell. I'll see you tomorrow."

He left, the door slapping shut behind him. Ethan leaned against the door frame and crossed his ankles. "I didn't know you'd hired Stanhope."

Sophie rummaged in the cupboard for her blue enameled pitcher and filled it with water from the bucket beside the door. She set the bouquet into it. "It was my fault he lost his job. I had to do something."

"I heard that you and Miss Gilman are trying to get an infirmary established."

"Yes, but we need permission from the town council to convert the orphanage into the infirmary and funds to get it started, but the mayor keeps putting her off." She gestured toward the outer office. "I'm working on an editorial about it for this week's edition."

"Then heaven help the mayor." He paused. "The building is in bad shape. It'll take some doing to get it repaired, and that's not even considering the cost of supplies and running the place."

"Gillie's thought of all that. But first we have to convince the council to turn the building over to us. After that, we'll—" She stopped, suddenly aware of his intent gaze. "What's the matter? Do I have ink on my nose?"

He shook his head. "Your nose is perfect. I was just thinking that you always seem to do the right thing."

Tell him. "Ethan, the other night, when we—"

He held up one hand. "Can we not talk about that? I'm still mortified at my behavior, and I would consider it a great favor if you would forget about it. Let's pretend it never happened and that we are meeting today for the very first time."

Forgive me, Lord. But if it is his wish to erase from memory the events of that entire night . . .

"The Founders Day celebration is coming up in a few weeks," Ethan said. "I'll have to be up at Blue Smoke for part of the day making sure our guests are taken care of, but I'm hoping you'll join me for dinner and fireworks." He smiled. "I promise to behave like a perfect gentleman."

She fussed with the bouquet, turning the pitcher this way and that. "The last time I attended the Founders Day to-do, I was ten years old. I remember telling my guardian a story that day. I think that was the day she decided to help me."

"I wish I had known you then."

"No, you don't. I was skinny and ragged and living in a dream world. I could barely read and write. I had no future until Ada came along." She removed a couple of leaves from the rose stems. "It's breathtaking, isn't it, how quickly our lives can change."

Something flickered in his eyes. "Yes, it is. So how about it? Will you come with me?"

The hotel clerk looked up from his magazine as Ethan approached the desk. "Help you, Mr. Heyward?"

"I'm looking for a man who might have checked in a few days ago, name of Julian Worth. Tall fellow. Olive skin, blue eyes."

"He checked in all right, but then he checked right back out."

"Any idea where he might have gone?"

"He didn't say. You want to leave a message in case he turns up again?"

"No message. Thanks."

Leaving the hotel, Ethan headed toward the railway station and the supply train that was due to leave for Blue Smoke in a matter of minutes. Now that construction was finished and the passenger car delayed indefinitely, the train was used mostly for transporting fresh meat, produce, and housekeeping necessities up the mountain to the resort.

After stopping at the mercantile to buy a bag of peppermints, he found a bench at the station near the waiting-room door. He removed the lid from the box containing the print order Sophie had just finished and scanned the top sheet. He had to hand it to her. She made sure every job was letter-perfect.

He liked being able to depend on her. Aside from that, he enjoyed the sound of her infectious laughter, the hint of mischief in her eyes. True, today she had seemed more serious than usual. Preoccupied. But maybe that was because she cared so deeply about Miss Gilman's infirmary.

He'd hoped the roses would bring more of a smile to her face, but at least she had agreed to accompany him to the Founders Day celebration on July 4—well, July 3 this year since the actual holiday fell on a Sunday. Founders Day was a big occasion for the town, and Ethan had attended the festivities every year since coming to Hickory Ridge, though he didn't much care for the noise and the crowds. Invariably too many men—including his workers—imbibed more spirits than was wise.

This year, however, he looked forward to the communal picnic, the music and fireworks, the children running about and splashing in the river. Their antics put him in mind of the languid summer days of his boyhood, fishing and running wild through endless fields of cotton with Julian. Julian, who had been his closest friend and confidant until that horrific day when the world as he knew it ended and Julian disappeared, leaving behind dark clouds of hatred and suspicion.

The supply train whistle sounded. Ethan climbed aboard and found a place to sit among cartons of tomatoes and squash, boxes of flour and salt, and slabs of bacon and beef neatly wrapped in butcher paper. Sun Wong, the chef's number one assistant, got on and bowed to Ethan. He pointed to the box Ethan balanced on his knees. "You buy present for missy?"

"For . . . oh no. This is a printing order she filled for me."

The Chinaman nodded, but confusion showed in his eyes. "Ah. Pretty lady."

"Yes, indeed."

The train, spewing cinders, labored up the steep grade. Ethan stared out at the passing landscape and thought once more about Julian's unexpected appearance at Blue Smoke. Shock and rage had prevented him from saying anything other than ordering his unwelcome guest off the premises. But now he found himself haunted by the question he hadn't thought to ask. Why on earth had Julian sought him out after all this time—when it was far too late for the interloper to undo the harm he'd done?

FOURTEEN

Sophie scrubbed at her fingers with a pumice stone and soap, trying to remove the traces of machine oil from her fingers. The jobber press had broken twice today, the second time requiring a complete dismantling in order to fix it. And of course Caleb was not due to work again until tomorrow. The mutinous press seemed always to break down when she was working alone.

She swished her hands through the soapy water and inspected them. Not perfect, but she was running late for her promised visit to Mariah Whiting's bookshop. She dried her hands on the towel she kept hanging on a nail beside the basin, tidied her hair, and removed her ink-stained apron. With a final glance around the office, she locked the door and crossed the street.

She passed the bakery and Mr. Pruitt's mercantile, where half a dozen men crowded the doorway, chewing tobacco and swapping stories. Someone laughed. A skinny black-and-tan hound got to his feet and followed Sophie along the boardwalk, his brown eyes pleading for attention.

She smiled down at him. "You want something to eat, don't you?"

The dog sniffed her skirts and nuzzled her hand. She stopped to scratch his ears and his tail thumped against her skirts. "I don't have anything for you, I'm afraid. You might have better luck at the bakery."

"Hector!" A barefoot boy in tattered overalls rushed toward them. "I told you to wait for me." He grabbed the dog by the scruff of the neck. "We got to get on home." He glanced up at Sophie. "Sorry, ma'am. He knows not to bother people."

"He isn't a bother at all." Sophie smiled at the boy and stroked the dog's head. "He's hungry, that's all."

"Yes'm, I expect he is. We all are, but our mama's feeling too poorly to cook us anything. She's been down in the bed for more'n a week, and Pa can't cook worth spit."

Just then a burly man emerged from the mercantile carrying a large crate. Spotting the boy and his dog, he emitted a loud whistle and shoved the crate into a waiting wagon.

"That's Pa. We got to go."

"Just a minute. Has your mother seen a doctor?"

"No, ma'am, but Pa's been doctoring her with mustard plasters. He says mustard'll cure just about anything that ails you."

He raced toward the wagon, the dog bounding along at his heels. Sophie shook her head. What would it take to convince people to see a doctor instead of relying upon home cures? Stepping around a gaggle of children sprawled on the boardwalk with their marbles, she hurried toward the bookshop and opened the door.

The woman behind the counter looked up when the bell rang and a slow smile spread across her face. "Sophie, I'm so glad you're here. We never seem to have much time to visit these days, do we?"

"Hello, Mrs. Whiting." Sophie grinned, overcome with a rush of affection for Robbie's mother. Though they saw each other briefly around town and in church, they always seemed to be off in opposite directions. Mariah Whiting had grown rounder and her hair was threaded with gray, but her smile was just the same as when she used to come by the orphanage to deliver quilts or

Christmas stockings. Mrs. Whiting had always managed to slip Sophie an extra treat—a piece of hard candy, a hair ribbon, a pastry from the bakery. Those small gifts had made Sophie feel, at least for a moment, as if she mattered.

"Aren't you looking pretty as a picture?" Mariah Whiting came around the counter and embraced Sophie. "Thank you for coming to see me. Our conversations on Sunday mornings have been much too brief."

Sophie smiled. "They have indeed. I keep hoping you'll take me up on my invitation to come by and see the office."

"And I've meant to, but"—she swept a hand around the cluttered premises—"it's hard for me to leave the shop these days. Between keeping things going here and looking after Sage, I barely have time to breathe."

"His accident must have been hard for you both," Sophie said. "How is Mr. Whiting?"

Mrs. Whiting shook her head. "His leg has healed as much as Doc Spencer says it's going to. It's his spirit that seems to be permanently broken . . ." She looked up and smiled. "But you didn't come here to be burdened by my troubles, I'm sure. Tell me, what do you hear from Ada and Wyatt? It's been months since I've had a letter."

"They're well. Lilly is turning ten and going away to school next term. Wade is growing up so fast, helping Wyatt on the ranch."

"Yes, Ada mentioned that in her last letter to me. It seems her hat business is still thriving." Mrs. Whiting crossed the shop to a small table beneath the dusty window. "I've just made tea and I have some shortbread. I seem to remember you're partial to it."

"I'd love some. I was too busy at the paper today to stop for lunch."

Mrs. Whiting found two cups and poured tea. "I was in Mrs. Pruitt's dress shop yesterday dropping off a shirtwaist to be repaired, and everyone was talking about those opinion pieces you've been writing about Sabrina Gilman's infirmary. They say that Mayor Scott and the town council have finally agreed to let Sabrina make her case."

"Really? That's wonderful news. I hadn't heard a single thing about it."

"It only just happened is what Mrs. Pruitt said. I'm not sure even Sabrina herself knows yet."

"I'm sure she doesn't, or she would have told me right away. It's all she's thought about for months." Sophie accepted the tea and took a long sip. "On my way here this afternoon I ran into a young boy whose mother has been ill for a week, and all the treatment she's getting is mustard plasters. We desperately need a way to get up-to-date medicine to more people. Don't you agree?"

"I do. But even if we open the infirmary, some folks still will prefer the old ways. My granny used to prescribe sassafras tea and mustard plasters for everything from a cough to a stomachache. Eugenie Spencer says Ennis sometimes has a terrible time convincing folks to try the newest medicines."

"We're lucky to have him, but he can't be everywhere at once. If people will give the infirmary a chance, perhaps minor illnesses can be cured before they become much more serious."

Mrs. Whiting set her cup down and nodded. "A couple of years ago one of the boys at the mill cut his hand pretty badly. Sage sent for the doctor, but by the time he arrived, it was nearly dark and the boy had gone home. His mother treated the cut with soot and coal oil, but before the boy could get back down the mountain and into town, an infection developed and Doc had to amputate."

Sophie shuddered. "Maybe the infirmary can prevent such things from happening again. If it ever becomes a reality."

"I'm proud of you for speaking out and forcing the mayor to stop stalling. There was no excuse to make Sabrina wait this long." Mrs. Whiting sipped her tea. "The *Gazette* seems to be doing well. I noticed last week's edition went from four pages to six."

"Yes. The advertising notices have increased since Blue Smoke officially opened. I suppose the local merchants want to attract visitors to their shops. At least that's what Mr. Pruitt says."

"I should place a notice myself." Mrs. Whiting passed the plate of shortbread to Sophie. "I've recently received the latest editions of *Ladies' Home Journal* and *Harper's Bazaar* and the sheet music for a wonderful new song. 'Oh My Darling, Clementine.' Do you know it?"

Sophie, her mouth full of shortbread, shook her head and swallowed.

"Well, it's just the most fun to sing. I'll bet the guests up at Blue Smoke would enjoy it. And I've copies of two of Mr. Twain's books. Though the latest one is mostly about the exploits of an illiterate Negro and a wayward orphan."

Sophie's face heated. She dropped her gaze.

"It's called *Adventures of Huckleberry Finn.* The title is compelling enough, but I can't imagine many people will be interested in two such unsavory characters. I— Oh dear." Mrs. Whiting's cup clattered onto her saucer. Her cheeks reddened. "How thoughtless of me. I didn't mean . . . Sophie, you must forgive me."

Sophie's eyes burned. Everything—and nothing—had changed. The old prejudices were alive and well, even among those she counted as friends. She set down her cup. "I should go. Thank you for the tea. I'll be sure to remember you to Wyatt and Ada in my next letter."

Mrs. Whiting's brown eyes filled. "I've hurt you, and I didn't mean to."

Sophie stood and busied herself with her reticule, avoiding the older woman's eyes.

"You may not believe it," Mrs. Whiting added, "but since so

many outsiders have come to town, Hickory Ridge has become a little more progressive. We've had to, with all sorts of folks coming and going." She paused and laid a hand on Sophie's arm. "Have you met Mr. Rutledge yet? He's in charge of the equestrian program at Blue Smoke."

"Yes, I've been out to their farm. I liked him very much."

"We all do now. But when he first arrived here, some folks— including me, I regret to say—held his background against him for a time. He was a known gambler who blew into town with no visible means of support and immediately fell for Carrie."

Sophie nodded, remembering Ada's joy when Carrie's letter requesting a wedding hat arrived in Texas. Carrie had fallen hard for Mr. Rutledge too.

"We feared he wasn't the kind of citizen our town wanted, that he wouldn't do right by her, but of course he did. He donated money to hire Mr. Webster to return to our school. Griff Rutledge was a reminder to all of us that God calls us not to judgment, but to acceptance and love." Mrs. Whiting patted Sophie's arm. "I should not have made such a thoughtless remark. After all, we know nothing for certain about who your parents were, and even if we did, it shouldn't matter."

No, it shouldn't. But it did. And to some people, it always would.

Sophie bade Mrs. Whiting good-bye and headed for the Verandah. She had been looking forward to attending the Founders Day fireworks show with Ethan. But today's visit was a harsh reminder of the secret that would always keep them apart.

She sighed. The more she saw of Ethan Heyward, the more she liked and admired him.

And the harder it became to tell him the truth.

132

"Ah. There you are."

Sophie turned to find Ethan standing behind her, holding a wicker picnic basket. Dressed for Founders Day in a white shirt, dungarees, and brown boots instead of his customary gray suit, he seemed boyish and even more appealing. "I hope you haven't had supper yet."

She shook her head and indicated the tables set beneath the trees, each of them covered with dishes, pots, cake stands, and boxes filled with leftovers from the noon meal. Plenty of food was left for the crowd of revelers who were sticking around for tonight's fireworks display. "I'm still full from dinner. Gillie and I each had two pieces of Carrie Rutledge's pecan pie."

"Sorry I couldn't get away from Blue Smoke sooner. Horace has come up with another scheme for the resort. And once he makes up his mind about something, there's no choice but to hear him out."

Remembering the long list of activities on the fliers she printed for him, Sophie shook her head. "I can't imagine what else there could possibly be. Lectures, garden tours, teas, hiking, horseback riding. Sounds like a full agenda already if you ask me."

They walked together across the crowded park, nodding to friends and acquaintances. Gillie stood next to Caleb Stanhope in the lengthening shadows, chatting with her parents and Doc Spencer and his wife. Mariah Whiting sat on a blanket nearby, knitting and laughing with Carrie and Griff Rutledge. Their daughter, Charlotte, had fallen asleep with her head on her father's knee, a wooden toy horse clutched in one hand.

Earlier, Sophie had spotted Robbie and Ethelinda, but they'd been quickly surrounded by members of Robbie's church. Now Robbie and Sheriff McCracken and some of the men from the mill were engaged in a boisterous game of horseshoes, while children darted behind trees, playing games of hide-and-seek.

Sophie smiled, remembering the day Ada played with her and

Robbie among those same trees. Rain had turned the ground wet and slippery, but Ada hiked her skirts and chased them until they collapsed on the wet grass, laughing and breathless. Mrs. Lowell, the director of the orphanage, and Miss Lillian Willis, Wyatt's irascible aunt, frowned and harrumphed from the sidelines. The disapproval of the grown-ups made the game seem all the more delicious.

"I agree with you about the agenda," Ethan said. "Our guests already have plenty to occupy their time, but Horace worries about money even when things are going well. He thinks we should set up a photography studio at the top of Hickory Ridge and charge folks for having souvenir portraits taken there. Bring in some extra income."

Sophie nodded. "If he's bound and determined to do it, I don't see why it wouldn't be successful. Tourists at Niagara Falls always want a souvenir, don't they?"

"I reckon so. I remember seeing an old photograph of people walking across the falls the year it froze over. Not that I expect anything that dramatic to happen here."

Mayor Scott rang a cowbell and the crowd moved toward the tables, loading up plates for supper. A few minutes later a wagon rattled along the road and stopped beneath the trees, and men piled off like ants from an anthill. Ethan frowned. "What in blazes is Lutrell Crocker doing here? I thought he went to Alabama to get married."

Sophie studied the men, who were unloading supplies for the fireworks show. "Who's Lutrell Crocker?"

"He was on the construction crew. Claimed one of the other men stole his money. More than likely he spent it all on liquor and was too drunk to remember it." He switched the basket to his other hand. "It'll be dark soon. Let's head down to the river and find a good spot to watch the fireworks." He indicated the basket. "I asked Li Chung to pack something special."

He led the way along the narrow path paralleling the river. Sophie noticed that one back pocket held his leather notebook, while the other bulged with a sack of penny candies. Twists of shiny black licorice protruded from the top of the bag as he walked. She hid a smile as they wound through the trees and found a flat spot on a bluff overlooking the river.

"Is this all right?" Ethan indicated a spot near the edge.

Sophie looked around. Long shadows dappled the ground. Water bugs skittered and buzzed across the river's sun-burnished surface. A fish jumped, a flash of silver in the waning light. "It's perfect." She waved away a cloud of gnats and settled herself on the soft grass, glad now that she had worn a pretty but older calico skirt with her new blue shirtwaist. No sense in getting grass stains on one of her better frocks.

Ethan fished his notebook from his pocket and began sketching. She watched the quick movement of his hands across the heavy vellum pages. "An idea for the photographer's hut?"

He shook his head. "I was just noticing that house across the river—the one with the gingerbread trim. What it needs is a much deeper porch, raised a bit higher and cantilevered out over the river. Like so." With a few more pencil strokes he finished the drawing and passed her the notebook.

"That's wonderful. Sitting there would be like sitting in a boat on the water."

"Without the danger of leaks." He grinned. "Ah, well, maybe someday I can build what I want."

Others began arriving along the river, the children whooping and tossing rocks into the water while their parents juggled blankets, baskets, and plates of food. Several men had brought banjos and fiddles, and soon the air was filled with music. Sophie spotted Robbie and Ethelinda and the elder Whitings arriving for the fireworks. She'd seen Mrs. Whiting in church only once since her visit to the bookshop. She had forgiven Ada's old friend for her thoughtless remark, but the memory still rankled.

She and Robbie hadn't spoken again about the secret she was keeping from Ethan. Now, watching the last of the sunlight glinting on Ethan's rich brown hair, she was overcome again with regret. Ethan was becoming more important to her as the summer went on. One day she would have to tell him the truth, and then he would want nothing more to do with her. But not now. Not yet.

Ethan set aside his notebook, opened the basket, and took out a small white cloth bearing the Blue Smoke monogram. He opened a silver carafe and poured lemonade into two stemmed goblets. Touching his glass to hers, he smiled into her eyes. "To Founders Day. And to a lovely evening."

The lemonade was ice cold, tart, and lightly sweet. Sophie savored the taste of it and watched translucent bits of lemon pulp settling in the bottom of the glass. She took another sip before setting her glass onto the small silver tray Ethan had taken from the basket. After that came small water biscuits topped with glistening caviar, three kinds of cheese on crusty bread, tiny rolls of paper-thin ham, slices of fresh melon, and for dessert a feather-light pastry filled with warm chocolate.

"This was delicious, Ethan." Sophie held out her glass for a refill of the lemonade. "Please tell the cook I enjoyed every single bite."

Footsteps sounded behind them, and Mayor Scott appeared, towering over them. "There you are, Miss Caldwell."

Sophie licked the last of the chocolate from her fingers and dabbed at her lips with a thick linen napkin. "Good evening, Mayor." She inclined her head toward Ethan. "I'm sure you know Mr. Heyward."

"Of course." The mayor nodded to Ethan. "But it's you I wanted to see."

"Oh?"

"I thought you'd want to know the council plans to hear Miss Gilman's harebrained scheme for that infirmary of hers. A week from Thursday. I'm sure you'll want to be there to gloat."

"To gloat, Mr. Scott?" She set her glass onto the tray.

"Well, you kept harassing me and the boys with those editorials of yours until you got our womenfolk all stirred up, and now can't any of us have a moment's peace in our own homes."

Sophie bit back a laugh. "If I've caused people to talk about the important issues in our town, then I've done my job. But I hope you won't decide that the plan is harebrained until you've heard what Miss Gilman has to say."

"Hiram?" Molly Scott ambled over and took her husband's arm. "The music is startin'. Are you going to sit with me for the fireworks or ain't you?" She nodded to Sophie. "Hello, Miss Caldwell."

"Mrs. Scott."

Ethan got to his feet and dusted off the seat of his dungarees. "Evening, Mrs. Scott."

"Don't be getting up on my account, boy." Molly motioned Ethan back to his spot on the grass. "I only come to fetch the mayor. The Pruitts came with us, and they'll be wonderin' where we got to."

The mayor offered a curt nod, then turned and walked away. Molly winked at Sophie. "Reckon I'll see you at that hearin'."

When they had gone, Ethan packed up the remains of their feast and stowed the glasses, trays, and plates in the basket. Then they sat side by side, shoulders almost touching. The first of the fireworks exploded over the river in a shower of bright white sparks that winked out one by one as they fell. The music gave way to exclamations of awe and delight from the assembled crowd.

"I've been meaning to go up on the ridge," Ethan said, "to look for a spot for the photography studio. Why don't you come with me? We'll start early and make a day of it."

"I'd love to, but it depends on which day. The paper—"

"Stanhope can take over for one day, can't he?"

They watched another shower of red and blue sparklers streak across the dark sky.

"Perhaps. I'm caught up on your printing orders, and we've started setting type for the next issue. But I promised the Ladies Benevolent Society an article about the quilt raffle they're organizing for the harvest festival. And Mr. Webster asked me to write a piece about the new curriculum he's planning for the next school term. He's hoping parents will encourage the older children to get a head start on the required reading." She wrinkled her nose. "I told him I'd print it, but I can't imagine even the most serious students giving up their summer trying to decipher *Macbeth*. Honestly, the least he could have done was to choose one of Mr. Shakespeare's comedies."

"Oh, I don't know. The scene with the witches and the cauldron and the spooky chant holds a certain appeal."

She laughed. "Maybe you're right."

Another burst of color lit the sky. The music began again.

"That's the last of the fireworks," Ethan said. "We should start back."

He held out his hand and drew her to her feet. "I'll let you know when I'm ready to make the trip. You'll come with me, then?"

"If Caleb is available to look after things."

"Good. I'll ask the cook to pack another basket for us." He bent his head to hers. "Congratulations, S. R. Caldwell."

"What for?"

"For convincing the mayor and the council to let Miss Gilman speak." He clasped her hand and held it. "I'm proud of you, Sophie."

She couldn't meet his gaze. As much as she wanted Ethan's approval, his words were like shards of glass in her heart. Would he be proud of her if he knew the truth?

FIFTEEN

The smells of cornbread and beef stew wafted up the Verandah's stairwell, teasing Sophie's nose. Although she'd had an unusually busy day and eaten nothing since breakfast, she was too nervous to eat now. In an hour the mayor and council would convene at Sheriff McCracken's office, which doubled as the town hall, to consider Gillie's request for her infirmary. Though Sophie had done little more than write the inciting editorials, because of her friendship with Gillie, she almost felt as if it were her project too.

"Sophie Caldwell." Lucy Partridge's voice echoed in the stairwell. "If you aren't down here in ten seconds, I'm coming up there and dragging you down. You've got to eat something."

"Coming." With a last look in the mirror, Sophie tucked her notebook and a clean handkerchief into her reticule and hurried down to the dining room.

Several of the Verandah's other residents were already at their places around Lucy's table. Sophie smiled and nodded to the ones she knew by name—Mabel Potts and Merribelle Winters, young women who shared the room across the hall from hers; Miss Pritchard, the baker's ancient assistant; and Flora Burke, the stout, serious-faced woman with graying hair who came and went from her work at Blue Smoke with few words for anyone.

Lucy, her thick curls lying damp along the back of her neck, bustled about setting out fresh butter for the hot cornbread, pitchers of water and cold milk, and bowls of thick stew. "You ladies be sure and save some room for blackberry cobbler. It's Flora's recipe."

Sophie's stomach clenched. Blackberry cobbler reminded her of Robbie and their summer adventures along the river, the blackberry brambles catching at the hem of her dress, the creak of their metal bucket, the hot sun pressing on their heads. And thinking of Robbie reminded her of her dilemma with Ethan. Next week, when she accompanied him to the top of the ridge, she would tell him the truth. He would either accept her or reject her, but at least her conscience would be clear.

She took her seat and unfolded her napkin. Lucy set a bowl of stew in front of Sophie, a smile in her eyes. "Eat every bite. You'll need your strength for the meeting tonight."

Sophie picked up her spoon. "I'm going only to report on the proceedings. And to offer moral support to Gillie, of course."

"As we all are." Flora Burke buttered a square of cornbread. "Knoxville has a modern infirmary. I don't see why Hickory Ridge can't have one too."

"Knoxville is bigger'n we are," Miss Pritchard said. "And folks there have more money."

"But now that the resort is here, our town is prospering again." Lucy filled a bowl for herself and took her place at the end of the table. "When Aunt Maisie passed on, this place was a wreck. I never imagined I'd be able to fix it up. But thanks to Blue Smoke, every room has been taken for the past year." She brushed a damp curl off her face and ate a spoonful of stew. "That's why I was able to put in new windows and paint the porch."

"Now if only you could do something about this infernal heat," Flora said darkly. "My room is on the third floor, and it's like sleeping in an oven up there, even with those fancy new windows of yours standing wide open."

"I'm sorry, Mrs. Burke." Lucy poured Flora another glass of water. "It's July in Hickory Ridge. What can I do?"

Flora snorted. "Pray for rain, I reckon." She finished her stew and pushed her bowl away. "Guess I'll forget about the cobbler and get ready for the council meeting. I don't want to miss a thing."

"Me either." Mabel swiped her mouth with a napkin. "I think Miss Gilman is wonderful. I want to go away for nurse's training too, if I can ever save enough money."

Flora got to her feet. "The folks up at Blue Smoke leave extra money for the maids every night. You'll be rich as cream one of these days."

"Maybe," Merribelle said as Flora crossed the parlor and started up the stairs. "It's hard work, but the pay is good. And those Chinese cooks make the best meals." She patted her flat stomach. "I bet I've gained ten pounds already."

Miss Pritchard frowned at Merribelle over the top of her gold-rimmed spectacles. "Best keep your figure if you ever hope to marry." She motioned to Lucy. "Since I'm not expecting any suitors, I'll have some cobbler if you don't mind."

Lucy pushed back from the table. "Anyone else?"

Sophie shook her head. "I'm too nervous to eat any more. I'm going to the sheriff's office to wait with Gillie." She rose and took her dishes to the sink.

"We'll see you later, then." Lucy took the pan of cobbler from the windowsill and spooned up a heaping portion for Miss Pritchard.

Sophie checked her reflection in the hall mirror, then headed out the front door and down the street. Even this late in the day the sun was brutal, though rain clouds were gathering on the horizon. Perhaps Flora Burke's prayers would be answered.

Approaching the sheriff's office, she spotted a line of rigs and wagons parked along the street. Knots of women dressed in their best clothes and fanciest hats stood talking quietly in lengthening shadows under the trees, fanning themselves in the oppressive heat. She caught sight of Carrie Rutledge and waved, then went inside Sheriff McCracken's office. Opposite his desk, a row of chairs had been set up, five of them reserved for Mayor Scott and the council. Judging from the crowd waiting outside, the meeting was sure to be standing room only.

In the back of the jail, a cell door clanked shut. The sheriff ambled into his office, a coffee cup in one hand. He smiled at Sophie. "Evening, Miss Caldwell. Been to any riots lately?"

"Did I miss one?" Sophie took her notebook from her reticule and claimed a chair nearest the window. Not that there was much of a breeze. Already beads of perspiration were forming on her forehead. She blotted her face with her handkerchief.

McCracken grinned. "Nope. All's quiet since the transient workers left town. Except for Tad Holloway, who's back in his regular cell, sleeping off too much strong drink." He sat down behind his desk and his chair creaked. "These days about all I'm doing is rounding up drunks and serving legal notices."

"Cheer up. Maybe something spectacular will happen one of these days. A bank robbery, for instance."

He laughed. "I'd just as soon things stay quiet. How are things at the paper?"

"Busy. Caleb Stanhope is working for me part-time."

"So I heard."

The door opened and Gillie rushed in. She wore her hair in a cascade of curls held away from her face with silver combs. A dark blue skirt, white shirtwaist, and blue jacket completed her ensemble. Spotting Sophie, she hurried across the room, her skirts belling out behind her, and threw both arms around her friend.

"I'm so excited I can't stand still. Did you see how many people are waiting outside?"

Sophie grinned. "Won't the mayor be surprised to see such a show of support?"

"I hope they're here to endorse my idea and not to disparage it." Gillie turned. "Hello, Sheriff McCracken."

"Miss Gilman." He nodded. "Reckon I'll go on outside for a bit." He checked his watch. "Council ought to be arriving soon, and we'll get started."

He left, and Gillie plopped down beside Sophie. "I hope I don't forget my speech. I've been practicing all day, in between looking after Mrs. Pruitt's cough and the Mitchells' baby." She frowned. "I'm really worried about him. I've been fighting his fever for a week, and he can't seem to shake it."

"What does Doc Spencer say?"

"He's worried too. But he drove out to the Mitchells' place this afternoon, and at least the baby's lungs seemed clear." She paused. "I ran into Robbie Whiting on the way over here just now. He said someone up on the mountain is sick and the family has sent for him."

"But not for the doctor?"

Gillie shrugged. "I don't understand that. I believe in God and in his healing powers. But I also believe he gives us knowledge and skills that he expects us to use to help each other. Don't you?"

The door opened and Mayor Scott blustered in, followed by the four members of the town council. Sophie jotted their names into her notebook: Jasper Pruitt, Frank Talbot, the barbershop owner, Mr. Hammonds from the Hickory Ridge Bakery, and Dr. Young, the town dentist. They arranged themselves around the sheriff's desk while Sheriff McCracken ushered the crowd into the room.

Sophie looked around. Carrie Rutledge had taken a seat near the door that led to the jail cells. Next to her sat Mariah Whiting and Molly Scott, the mayor's wife, along with Lucy and Mrs. Pritchard.

Dr. Spencer and Griff Rutledge stood near the back next to Caleb Stanhope and Mr. Webster, the schoolmaster. Mr. Whiting stood behind his wife, leaning heavily on his cane. Sophie's heart constricted. She had seen Robbie's daddy only briefly since the day he came to Miss Lillian's to fetch Ada to the train station. He looked much older now, worn and faded as an old photograph.

When the room was full, the sheriff directed the overflow crowd to wait outside. Through the open window, Sophie saw Robbie's wife, Ethelinda, talking with Flora, Merribelle, and Mabel. A knot of men, some of them puffing on pipes and cheroots, leaned against their wagons, talking in low tones.

The mayor gaveled the meeting to order. "First order of business is to approve the minutes of the last meeting." He nodded to Jasper Pruitt, who stood and read them aloud.

The mayor growled, "Any changes or additions?"

When no one spoke, Mr. Scott said, "Approved as read. Next order of business—the new spittoon we ordered for the post office came in on this morning's train."

The men spent ten minutes arguing about who ought to retrieve the spittoon and whether there should be some sort of ceremony to dedicate it. After all, it was made of pure brass and came from New York City. Sophie took notes, her hand moving quickly across the pages. Gillie shifted in her seat and blew out a long breath. "My lands," she whispered to Sophie. "How much time can they spend discussing a stupid spit can?"

". . . is Miss Sabrina Gilman."

Sophie nudged her. "Good luck."

Hands clasped, Gillie walked to the front of the room. The last rays of sunlight slanted through the window and fell across her hair, turning it to platinum. Her eyes seemed to be lit from within.

"Thank you for giving me the opportunity to speak about our need for an infirmary. As you know, many of our families live in the hills above town, and it isn't always possible for them to get medical attention as quickly as they should. Dr. Spencer travels constantly, but he can't be everywhere at once. An infirmary would allow those who are sick to come here and stay if necessary instead of sending for the doctor and waiting for him to arrive. It would also serve as a place where nurses such as myself can treat minor illnesses and injuries, thus freeing the doctor to spend more time treating more serious cases."

The dentist made notes on a yellow sheet of paper in front of him. "Some folks don't trust doctors anyway. They'd rather look after themselves than rely on modern remedies, the same way they'd rather pull a tooth with a pair of pliers than visit my office."

"That's true, Dr. Young. I know there will be some people who still won't seek the help they need. It will take time for attitudes to change. But if we can save even one life, isn't it worth it?"

Mayor Scott waved one hand. "Go on, Miss Gilman. Get to the point."

"Lack of money also keeps some people from seeking help, even when they are gravely ill," Gillie said. "An infirmary where they could come for treatment they could afford would work wonders for the health and well-being of our entire town and for the people on the mountain too. Wouldn't the council agree?"

Gillie paused and turned her wide, blue gaze upon the mayor and his council. Sophie bent her head to her notebook to hide a smile. What a smart question. How could the council members possibly disagree without looking like a bunch of unfeeling clods?

The men nodded, and Gillie continued. "Our orphanage has been closed for years and has turned into an eyesore. Boarded-up windows and a weedy yard don't leave the kind of impression we want to make on visitors and newcomers. And now that Blue Smoke is open, we're sure to have a constant stream of them coming and going. I'm asking the council to grant me permission to turn the building into an infirmary."

Mr. Hammonds cleared his throat. "That's a noble idea, young lady, but just how do you propose paying for new windows and such? Not to mention supplies, medicines, beds, and linens. It'll cost a small fortune, and Hickory Ridge just doesn't have that kind of money."

The door opened. Heads turned as Horace Blakely edged his way into the room. Sophie frowned. What was the owner of Blue Smoke doing here? She wrote his name in her notebook and underlined it.

Gillie looked directly at Mr. Hammonds. "I don't blame you for wondering about how we can afford it. It is indeed a great undertaking. But I've been working on this idea for almost a year. I've managed to secure pledges of donated supplies from colleagues in Philadelphia, where I took my nurse's training and where Dr. Spencer studied as well. And I'm investing a small inheritance from my grandmother to cover the initial cost of medicines."

Mayor Scott frowned. "That's all very well, Miss Gilman, but if you don't charge folks for treatment, how will you keep the doors open?"

"Dr. Spencer and I have worked out a sliding scale. Those who can afford to pay will do so. Those who cannot won't be charged. We'll make up the difference in ongoing donations from the medical society and our local charities." Gillie smiled at Mrs. Scott. "Your wife's organization has already agreed to donate a quilt for a raffle this fall, and Robbie's—Mr. Whiting's church has pledged its support."

Frank Talbot raised his hand like a schoolboy at the recitation bench. "You still haven't told us how you plan to finance the repairs for the orphanage."

For the first time all evening Gillie faltered. "I—I am hoping the council will see fit to provide funds for basic repairs."

"Just a minute there, Mayor." Horace Blakely spoke from the

back of the room. "Last fall I told you I might be wanting that building for myself."

Mayor Scott nodded. "I remember. But I haven't heard another word about it. I had no idea you were still interested."

"Maybe I am and maybe I'm not. Blue Smoke has only recently opened. It's too soon to know what facilities I might need on down the line."

Mr. Talbot polished his spectacles with his handkerchief. He cleared his throat. "It seems to me if that building was promised to Mr. Blakely, then we're duty bound to stand behind our word."

Gillie braided her fingers and sent the mayor a pleading look.

Dr. Young smoothed his beard. "What I heard was a maybe from Mr. Blakely and another maybe from the mayor. Don't seem to me like promises were made at all. Now, Miss Gilman here has put a considerable amount of thought and trouble into her plan, and I for one think she deserves a chance."

Jasper Pruitt leaned back in his chair. "I'm not opposed to letting her try, but for the life of me I don't know where the money is coming from. The town treasury is mighty near empty."

"Because you bought a spittoon!" Sophie jumped to her feet, her notebook sliding onto the floor.

Heads turned in her direction. "It seems to me that you gentlemen should reconsider your priorities."

Mr. Hammonds smiled. "Don't go getting your dander up, missy. Now, listen here, I—"

"Please don't call me missy." Sophie returned his steady gaze. "I realize a spittoon is not as expensive as paint and windows, but it's all a matter of priorities. Surely if you can pay for a fancy brass spittoon, you can come up with some way to provide the necessary materials."

The mayor toyed with his wooden gavel. "I reckon we could dip into the emergency fund, but we'd expect to be paid back."

"Now, just a minute." One of the men, his large belly

protruding from the waistband of his suspendered pants, pushed his way to the front of the crowd. "Who gave you the authority to go squandering our money just because some pretty little spoiled girl wants a project to work on?"

Jasper Pruitt studied him through narrowed eyes. "I reckon you did, Charlie, when you elected us to the council. Now, pipe down and let us get on with the meeting. I haven't had my supper yet, and my stomach's growling."

Sophie sank onto her chair. Holy cats. She hadn't meant to voice an opinion, but she couldn't help herself. Had she helped Gillie's cause or hindered it?

The mayor and council leaned in, literally putting their heads together. Finally Mr. Talbot said, "Miss Gilman? How much you reckon you need?"

Gillie beamed. "Seventy-five dollars."

Mr. Blakely strode to the front of the room. "Let me get this straight. You're actually going to approve this scheme to the detriment of the most important business in the county? With no regard for my needs?"

Sophie was on her feet again. "Mr. Blakely?"

He turned to her, a frown creasing his fleshy face. He sighed. "Hello, Miss Caldwell."

She smiled. "You remember me."

"How in blazes could I forget after that article you wrote about Blue Smoke? An article based upon hearsay, I might add."

Anger spurted through her. "Based upon eyewitness accounts, sir, not hearsay. You may recall that your eyewitness was fired from his job for talking to me."

He waved one hand and his gold signet ring caught the light. "What do you want?"

"I want to tell you a story I didn't print. One based upon my direct observation."

Briefly she recounted the day she'd met Mrs. Wimberly and Rebecca on the trail above Blue Smoke and their subsequent trip to seek Gillie's help. "Your guests are hiking those mountain trails, riding their horses up to the creek, and I understand you're planning to set up a spot for souvenir photographs atop the ridge."

"So what?"

"They're bound to encounter the mountain residents from time to time. And think of your staff. You don't want sick folks exposing others to fevers, influenza, infections, and whatnot. That could be bad for business."

Mr. Blakely shrugged. "I'd say the chances of that happening are extremely remote. I've been around here long enough to know that the folks in the hills tend to keep to themselves."

Dr. Spencer cleared his throat. "You may be right about that, Mr. Blakely. But all it takes is one outbreak to foment a disaster. I'm sure you've heard about the deadly yellow fever epidemics that have plagued different parts of this state from time to time. An outbreak of influenza or typhoid could decimate our region just as quickly."

From her spot in the front of the room, Gillie nodded, undoubtedly remembering Miss Cook, her heroine from the yellow fever epidemic in Memphis. Sophie sent her friend an encouraging smile, and Gillie went on.

"Though I'm most concerned about women and children, an infirmary will benefit everyone—including you, Mr. Blakely, not to mention the men at the mill. Someone is always sustaining a cut or a broken bone or a bad sprain. Isn't that true, Mr. Whiting?"

Sage Whiting nodded. "True enough, I reckon, but most menfolk don't like being looked after by a female that isn't family. I reckon we'd rather take our chances and wait till Doc Spencer is free."

Mariah Whiting turned to gape at her husband. "Why, Sage

Whiting, I never suspected you of harboring prejudice against the female gender."

"Now, Mariah—"

"Miss Gilman's infirmary is a wonderful idea, and I believe I speak for most of the ladies in town when I say we will do all in our power to see that it succeeds." Mrs. Whiting caught Mr. Blakely's eye. "I do hope you will reconsider your objection, sir."

Mr. Blakely folded his hands over his ample stomach and blew out a long breath. "I can see I'm outnumbered here, and I must say I'm disappointed. Hickory Ridge was dying on the vine before I bought up that land and started building Blue Smoke. I've invested hundreds of thousands of dollars, and this is the thanks I get."

"We haven't forgotten," Mr. Talbot said. "And we do appreciate Blue Smoke. But we've got a Christian duty to help the sick and the injured, and if this young lady's infirmary makes it easier for folks to get doctored when they need it, then I say we give it a try."

Jasper Pruitt shifted in his chair. "Are we ready to vote yet? Because I am about to expire from this infernal heat."

Mayor Scott had been flipping through the stack of official-looking papers he'd brought. Finally he looked up. "Miss Gilman, we appreciate what you're trying to do here, but I've looked at this budget again and I am sorry to say, we don't dare deplete the emergency fund."

"I see." Gillie's voice wavered, but her expression remained serene. "Will you give me the building then, Mr. Scott? I'll trust God to provide for the repairs."

The vote came swiftly, four to one, and the ladies broke into applause. Gillie squeezed past a knot of ladies standing next to Mr. Blakely and rushed over to embrace Sophie. "We did it!"

"You did it, my friend. I only brought the situation to everybody's attention."

The resort owner fished a cheroot from his pocket and bit off the end. "So you did, Miss Caldwell. So you did." He waved his unlit cheroot in the air. "You and that little newspaper of yours have managed to stir up a lot of trouble in an astonishingly short period of time."

"That's a matter of opinion, Mr. Blakely. The way I see it, a modern newspaper should be an advocate for the citizens it serves. It's my job to call attention to a town's problems as well as its achievements, not merely to serve as a mouthpiece for one politician or another as in the old days."

She paused, suddenly embarrassed. She hadn't meant to sound so pompous. But heavenly days, the man was irritating.

He shook his head. "You aren't old enough to remember the old days."

"But I studied them. I want the *Gazette* to be much better than that."

He pointed his cigar at her. "You'd be much better off sticking to articles like the one you wrote last week on cultivating lilies. My wife quite enjoyed that one."

"I'm glad she found it entertaining."

"Don't push me, Miss Caldwell." He said it with a smile, but the expression in his eyes was hard as granite. "I will push back."

SIXTEEN

July 16, 1886

Sherman, Texas

Dear Miss Caldwell,

I trust you will remember our most pleasant conversation the evening of the press reception at Blue Smoke. Since returning home, I have received three letters from my cousin Deborah, each containing clippings of your newspaper pieces. I especially enjoyed your article on the novels of the prolific Mr. Mark Twain, and although I regret to say I have not read his most recent offering, I certainly agree that *The Prince and the Pauper* is certainly one of his most entertaining works. Likewise was I captivated by your article on ladies taking up the sport of bicycling. Though I consider myself quite well traveled and open-minded, I must say I cannot imagine engaging in such a reckless pastime. However, times change, and we must change with them.

Your editorials in support of an infirmary for your town were well reasoned and articulate, especially considering your tender years. It is my sincere hope that by the time this letter reaches you, the town council will have reached a favorable decision.

Because I believe so strongly that your work deserves a wider readership, I have taken the liberty of sending these clippings along to Mr. McClure as a possible addition to his news syndicate. While I cannot speak for him, I believe you have a very good chance of writing for him, and you will of course be paid a tidy sum for each piece published.

It was a pleasure meeting you, my dear, and I do hope our paths will cross again.

Most sincerely yours,
Lydia McPherson

Sophie folded the letter and put it in her desk drawer. In the weeks since it had arrived, she had read it so many times that she knew every word by heart. How thrilling that Mrs. McPherson thought her accomplished enough to write for the syndicate. The extra cash would be welcome. But could she keep up with running the *Gazette* and her printing business and still find time to write articles for Mr. McClure?

Footsteps sounded on the boardwalk. A dark-haired woman in a bright-yellow dress cupped her hands to the window and peered inside. Sophie frowned. Another mountain woman seeking medical help?

She opened the door. "May I help you?"

The woman clutched her reticule to her chest. "I . . . You're Miss Caldwell."

"Yes. Have we met?"

Sophie stood aside to let her visitor enter. Instead the woman turned abruptly and fled. Sophie watched her rush down the street, dodging farm wives, children, dogs, and freight wagons until she disappeared into the alley beside Sheriff McCracken's office.

Sophie closed the door and returned to her desk, intending to finish an article on the upcoming harvest festival, but the strange encounter had so unnerved her that she couldn't think.

She went into the back room where Caleb kept his coffeepot and helped herself to a cup of the bitter, lukewarm brew. Perhaps the woman had intended to place a notice in the newspaper, then changed her mind. Nothing to get upset about, especially when there was plenty else to occupy her thoughts. For one thing, her outing with Ethan was coming up. And though she had not wavered in her determination to set the record straight concerning her background, finding the right words was proving harder than she anticipated. Would he react with disgust? Anger? Or would he somehow understand?

Then there was the matter of Horace Blakely. Just yesterday she'd run into him at the post office, and he'd glared at her as if she'd stolen his last dime. It was ridiculous for the richest man in three counties to be such a dog in the manger about the orphanage. Clearly he was more upset at having his wishes thwarted than at losing a building he had no immediate plans to use. She took another sip of coffee. Why was it that most successful people, instead of being grateful for their good fortune, were often the most mean-spirited?

"Sophie?" Caleb came in, a sheet of paper in his hand. "I took a stab at writing that story about Mrs. Tanner's prize tomatoes." He blushed. "It's prob'ly not very good. I was always better at arithmetic than writing. But I like the idea of being where important things are happening and being the first to tell about it."

She set down her cup and went back to her desk. "Me too. Wyatt always told me that having a heart for your work is as important as knowing how to do it. As long as you love being a reporter, you can learn the tricks of the trade. Let's have a look."

She picked up her reading spectacles, hooked them over her ears, and scanned the page.

Aside from a few typographical errors, the beginning wasn't bad. But Caleb had made a typical beginner's mistake and stopped asking questions before the story was complete. She handed it back to him. "It's good that you remembered what I told you about getting some direct quotations from Mrs. Tanner. Folks like to hear people tell their stories in their own words. And our readers will enjoy learning about how Mrs. Tanner's grandmother taught her to grow tomatoes. But—"

"I forgot to ask her exactly how she makes them grow so big."

"*Who, what, when, where, why.* And *how.*" She ticked the words on her fingers. "Answer those questions, and your story will be complete." She handed the page back to him. "Want to give it another try?"

He shook his head. "Not right now. I need to finish printing next month's menus for Blue Smoke. Mr. Heyward's secretary was in here yesterday all in a huff because they weren't done yet."

"Well, there was no need for him to be upset. I told Mr. O'Brien when he dropped the order off that we couldn't get to it before today."

Caleb shrugged and headed to the back. "He wanted it right away. Acted like he was mad when I told him he'd have to wait. Rich people are always in a hurry, I reckon."

"I don't think Mr. O'Brien is rich."

"Compared to me he is." Caleb's shoulders sagged.

"Is something wrong?"

He turned to face her. "You know how much I love working here and how much I want to learn newspapering."

"Yes, and you're making a fine start."

"But I can't support Ma and my brothers on what you're paying me."

"I'd pay you more if I could afford to."

"I'm not blaming you. But the truth is, this job is a luxury I can't afford. I'm thinking about asking Mr. Heyward if he'll take me back on the maintenance crew up at Blue Smoke. If not, maybe I can get on at the mill."

"But, Caleb, I depend upon you week to week to help me with the typesetting and print jobs and collecting the advertising notices."

"I know it, and I'm sorry, but I have to feed my family. Ma's learned to manage the farm real well, but there's never enough money for everything we need. Joe's sick a lot. His lungs are weak. And James Henry is too young to work. So that leaves me." His breath hitched. "Maybe when they're old enough to look after themselves, I can come back and take up newspapering again." He attempted a smile. "Who knows? Maybe by then you'll have a press that doesn't fall apart ten times a day."

Sophie removed her glasses and pinched the bridge of her nose. Just when things were going so well, now she'd have to start over. Train someone else to mix ink, run the printing press, set the type, coddle the temperamental jobber press. Where would she find such a person? Maybe Ethan would know. She'd ask on Friday when they finally made their planned trip to the top of the ridge to scout for a photographer's perch. A week of rain, Ethan's obligations at Blue Smoke, and some pressing deadlines of her own had forced them to postpone the excursion again and again. At last the weather and both their schedules had cooperated.

"Hey, Sophie?" Caleb paused, one hand on the door frame. "Don't go to frettin' just yet. I have to find another job first, and it could take awhile. I'll give you plenty of notice."

Sighing, she tucked her order book and pen into her reticule and pinned on her hat, a leghorn straw trimmed with pink silk rosebuds and white netting. "I'm going out for a while. I may as well start collecting from our advertising customers now. Get used to it."

He lifted one shoulder. "Nothing to it. It just takes time is all. Most folks like to visit awhile, especially Miss Hattie and Mrs. Pruitt over at the dress shop. Just don't let Mrs. Pruitt get started on her childhood up in Muddy Hollow. She remembers everything, and she can go on and on."

"Thanks for the warning." Sophie left the office and walked along the boardwalk to the mercantile, jingling the bell as she entered. She smiled at a woman and her young daughter who were busy selecting fabric from bolts scattered across the wooden table at the back of the store. She stood aside for a couple of farmers who were shuffling up and down the aisles, selecting nails, saw blades, lengths of rope, and sacks of feed.

Mr. Pruitt emerged from behind the meat counter, wiping his hands on his blood-spattered apron. "Miss Caldwell. What can I do for you?"

"I've come to collect your advertisement for next week's issue." She opened her reticule and took out her order book and pen. "Since we're less than a month away from the harvest festival, I suggest you feature your dress goods and sewing notions and such." She smiled. "Every lady in town wants something pretty to wear to the festival."

He frowned. "I ain't set much store by that celebration since they moved it from October to September. September just don't feel like the fall of the year to me. You know what I mean?"

"I do. But in church last week Mrs. Rutledge told me the town council changed it to September so it wouldn't interfere with Race Day in October."

He shrugged. "That was the excuse, but mostly it was because Horace Blakely wanted it moved. I didn't vote for it, but Hiram Scott and the rest of 'em didn't blink an eye. Fifty years of tradition wiped out faster than you can say Jack Robinson."

She nodded. "About your advertising notice, Mr. Pruitt, I—"

"I'm not placing an ad this week."

"Oh. What about the next week, then? We may as well go ahead and write it up while I'm here and save us both some time."

Mr. Pruitt grabbed a feather duster from beneath the counter and ran it over a stack of tin cans. "Truth is, I won't be advertising in your paper anymore. And neither will my wife, so you don't need to make a trip to her dress shop."

"But why? Has my work been unsatisfactory? Is there some problem with the placement of your notice? I'll be glad to—"

One of the farmers dumped a sack of feed and a box of nails onto the counter. "Jasper? You want to add this to my tab? I'll pay you next week, soon as I take my sweet corn crop in."

Mr. Pruitt seemed relieved to have something else to do. He took his time adding up the bill and boxing up the man's order. Finally the man left, and the mercantile owner turned back to Sophie. "I'm sorry. I still think a lot of Wyatt and Miss Ada, and for her sake if nothing else I wish you good luck with that newspaper of yours. I know you want to make them proud. But I can't help you no more. That's all I got to say."

Sophie left the mercantile, her thoughts racing. What could have changed Mr. Pruitt's mind? Did it have something to do with her personally, or was something else to blame? Losing the revenue from his weekly notices was a blow, but perhaps she could convince her other customers to purchase bigger ads to make up the difference.

Two hours later, though, she sat at her desk in the *Gazette* office hot, tired, and utterly discouraged. The bakery, the Hickory Ridge Inn, even Miss Hattie had all canceled their accounts. She pressed her fingertips to her throbbing temples and fought a wave of panic. Even if she didn't replace Caleb and took on every task herself, the income from subscriptions alone would not sustain the paper until the end of the year. After such a promising start, she had failed.

And she didn't know why.

SEVENTEEN

"God does not abide liars, Sophie. They wind up in the fiery lakes of burning sulphur, same as murderers and cowards. Same as thieves. Is that what you want? To burn in the everlasting flames?"

Sophie woke, her heart pounding, her nightdress stuck to her hot skin. She sat up in her bed waiting for the dream to dissipate. It had seemed so real. She was eight years old again, and Mrs. Lowell was standing over her bed at the orphanage, insisting that she confess to taking a cornhusk doll belonging to another girl. She hadn't stolen it, but anytime something disappeared, she was the first to be blamed.

Too shaken now to sleep, she threw off the sheet and lit the oil lamp, her gaze seeking the familiar contours of her hotel room. The flickering light fell on the dull gleam of her silver hairbrush on the dresser, the blue-and-white ewer and basin on the stand by the bed, her hatboxes stacked neatly in the corner. She let out a long breath and crossed to her door.

A seam of light brightened the hallway and soft voices carried from the room across the hall. Mabel and Merribelle were still up, no doubt gossiping about the goings-on up at Blue Smoke. Merribelle laughed, and Sophie felt a pang of sadness mixed with pure old envy. The two young women shared everything.

Until Gillie came along, she had never had a true woman friend, someone who could share her fears and her confidences. But these days Gillie was so busy with plans for opening the infirmary that she barely had time to say hello before rushing off again.

Sophie lifted the curtain and peered onto the empty street. Here and there, gaslights flickered. Crickets chirped. A cat yowled and slunk down the street, casting a thin shadow on the walls. She poured a glass of water from the earthenware pitcher on the dresser and drank it down. Tomorrow she would join Ethan for the trip up to the ridge. She had looked forward to it until the unsettling dream reminded her of her guilt. Her deceit. Her hesitation in setting things straight.

Wyatt and Ada taught her that God was a Father of forgiveness and love. But they also taught her that actions were not without consequence. Were her troubles somehow the result of what she had done . . . or failed to do?

She sat on her bed a long time, pondering. But finally she crawled beneath the sheet and snuffed the light.

⁓

"Almost there."

Ethan paused and offered Sophie his hand as they ascended the steep, narrow trail. They had left his horse and rig in the clearing at the end of the river road and proceeded on foot, Ethan leading the way. In his knapsack was a picnic Li Chung had prepared for them. A faint scent of butter mixed with cinnamon teased Sophie's nose, and her stomach groaned. Last night, after hours of tossing and turning, she'd finally drifted to sleep. Then she had nearly overslept, and there hadn't been time for breakfast.

"I didn't realize this trail was so steep." Sophie clasped Ethan's hand and he pulled her up beside him. They paused for breath, listening to the sultry summer breeze moving through the stands of oak and pine.

"This looks like an old logging trail." Ethan indicated the deep ruts in the ground. "They must have abandoned it when they discovered a shorter one closer to the rail line."

Sophie took her handkerchief from her pocket and blotted her face, too worried about her loss of advertising revenue to concentrate on what he was telling her. How on earth would she face Wyatt after he'd shown so much faith in her? And how could she give up work that grew more important to her every day? The little speech she'd delivered to Mr. Blakely during the town council meeting had been more than mere words to her. Maybe it was foolish and naïve to hold on to such lofty goals, but she truly wanted to change things for the better. Now it seemed doubtful she'd have that chance.

"Let's press on." Ethan smiled down at her. "I want to reach the summit in time for lunch."

Bright sunlight filtered through the dense forest, falling across his broad shoulders and lighting his brown hair. Dressed in dungarees and a pale blue shirt, the sleeves rolled to expose his muscular forearms, he looked more handsome than ever. But she couldn't let herself admire him too much. After today he probably wouldn't want to see her again.

They clambered along the trail, stepping around tangled undergrowth and exposed tree roots, and soon grew too winded for conversation. At last they reached the top of the ridge that gave the town its name. The valley unfurled beneath their feet, a carpet of dark green dotted with patches of brown. Here and there, behind rows of fences, farmhouses lay scattered like forgotten toys. To her right, a patch of river and the church steeple glittered in the late-summer sunlight.

The air was cool against Sophie's warm skin. No wonder

Wyatt had brought Ada up here to propose marriage. What woman could resist such a romantic vista, especially when viewed—as Ada had—from a snow-dusted sleigh? Sophie inhaled another draft of air and sighed. Surely this must be how God felt when he surveyed his creation.

"Pretty spectacular, isn't it?" Ethan set his knapsack down and looked around. "I was hoping to find a more level plot of ground up here for the photographer's hut, but I suppose I can send a couple of men to take out a few more trees. Getting rid of those big tree roots would expand the space a bit."

"Seems a shame to cut them down. Wyatt says some of these trees have been here since Indian times."

Ethan nodded. "You can't stop progress, though. Once Horace makes up his mind about something, there is no going back. He's keen to get this enterprise up and running before the end of this season."

"But won't he first have to hire someone to take the photographs?"

"He has someone in mind." Ethan opened his knapsack, spread a small white cloth on the ground, and set out their feast: tantalizing, buttery cinnamon bread stuffed with raisins, a jar of raspberry jam, a hunk of cheese, and a small basket of fruit. He motioned for her to sit, then settled himself beside her. He offered her a plate and polished an apple on his sleeve. "I think he intends to offer the position to Miss Garaphelia Swint."

Sophie frowned. Where had she heard that name? She bit into the cinnamon bread and sighed. Li Chung certainly had a way with flour and yeast.

"Miss Swint gave some talks at Blue Smoke last month," Ethan said. "She published a book of photographs last year and seems quite taken with the idea of working up here on the mountain." He flipped the pages of his leather notebook and showed her a sketch of a long, low building open on three sides, a stone fireplace anchoring the middle. "It's nothing fancy, but it'll get the job done. Eventually I'll add some benches and maybe a couple of tables so guests can picnic while they wait their turn for photographs. But Miss Swint is as eager as Mr. Blakely to open for business."

"I remember that name now." A little squirrel ventured close and she tossed it a morsel. "I saw it on the flier I printed for you. Her book had something to do with Southern homes and gardens."

"That's her." He tucked away his notebook and eyed the last bit of cheese. "Are you going to eat that?"

"Be my guest. I suppose Miss Swint must be quite the genteel lady."

Ethan laughed. "Genteel? More like outspoken and intrepid. Opinionated. But I suppose those are good qualities for working up here." He finished off the cheese, plucked a grape, and popped it into his mouth. "She seems quite determined about everything she does. Sort of like you, Sophie. I admire that in a woman."

Her face warmed at the compliment. "Thank you, but I'm not sure determination is enough."

He opened a jar, poured water into two cups, and handed her one. "It seems to have worked for Miss Gilman. I understand the council gave her permission to use the orphanage for her infirmary."

"Yes. But there's no money to buy materials for the repairs. Gillie has been asking everyone we can think of for donations, but I doubt we'll raise enough to buy new windowpanes and replace the rotten clapboards."

A cardinal called from the low-hanging branches of an ancient oak, his crimson feathers gleaming in the sunlight. Ethan scooted closer to Sophie until their shoulders touched. She swallowed. It was dangerous to be alone with him this way, risking her heart for something that could never be.

"I may be able to help with that," he said. "We've some excess materials left over from the last phase of construction. There's not enough to warrant shipping back to the suppliers, just a few odds and ends. But it might be enough to repair the orphanage."

"That would be wonderful. How much would you charge for them?"

"Not a thing. Consider it my contribution to the welfare of the town."

"Oh, Ethan. Gillie will be thrilled."

"Just don't let Horace find out. He pinches every penny until it hollers."

"He does seem like a . . . difficult man."

Ethan nodded. "Horace Blakely insists on having his own way about everything. And he never forgets any perceived wrong, no matter how slight."

Sophie's stomach dropped. Of course. That was why most of her customers had suddenly deserted her. Horace Blakely had found a way to pay her back for her infamous editorial and to teach her a lesson for being on the wrong side of the argument with the town council. Anger burned inside her. An ordinary person could never win against the rich and powerful. Why had she been so reckless?

". . . let me know."

"I'm sorry." She managed a shaky smile. "I was lost in thought. Gillie will be ecstatic to learn this news. It's most generous, Ethan. How can I ever thank you?"

He grinned, leaned closer, and tapped his cheek. "Little kiss right here will do nicely."

Despite all warnings to herself, she wanted to kiss him. And this would be her only chance. Once he knew the truth, he would want nothing more to do with her. She leaned over and gave him a quick peck on the cheek.

He turned his deep blue gaze on her, and she was lost. He

clasped her arms, sending a river of warmth flowing through her. "I said once I'd never kiss you again until we both wanted it."

She nodded, unable to speak.

"Well, I want it very much right now," he said, his voice rough with emotion. "How about you?"

"Ethan—"

"I'll take that as a yes." He gave a soft little laugh and her heart sped up. Ethan seemed to have that effect on her these days. His lips claimed hers, and all caution dissipated like mountain fog. She went willingly into his arms and gave herself over to the clean, woodsy scent of his skin, the warmth of his lips on hers. How wonderful it was to be held this way, to be wanted. But this one kiss, the memory of it, would have to last forever.

At last they drew apart and sat silently, their gazes locked, afraid to speak and break the spell. At last Ethan let out a long breath and got to his feet. "Let's pack up and look around a bit more. Maybe there's a better spot for Miss Swint's hut on down the ridge."

She picked up their dishes and cups and folded the white cloth, blotting at a red smear of jam. Ethan stuffed everything into his knapsack and they set off, his hand clasping hers. A bit farther along the trail they came to a large clearing overlooking a wide expanse of the river below and the gently undulating mountain peaks beyond.

With his free hand, Ethan shaded his eyes and looked out over the valley. "This place is perfect. Plenty of space to erect a pavilion and the best view in town. I have to admit, Horace may be on to something. Not only will our guests leave with a memorable photograph; they'll show it to their friends, and then those people will want to come here too. Free advertising."

Advertising. The beauty of the afternoon vanished in the wake of new worry. Now that she knew what Horace Blakely was up to, she'd have to figure out some way around his scheme. She couldn't really blame Mr. Pruitt and Miss Hattie and the rest of them for withdrawing their business. No doubt Horace Blakely had issued an ultimatum: withdraw their notices or face his censure. But she couldn't think of that now.

"You're right. It is perfect, Ethan."

He squeezed her hand. "I'm sorry for this day to end, but we ought to start back."

"Yes." She looked up into his face and was overcome with fear and guilt. Robbie's words came back to her, filling the space between her and Ethan before settling into her heart. She had to follow through with her plan to tell the truth, even as her conflicted thoughts beat like trapped birds inside her chest.

She briefly closed her eyes. *Please, Lord, give me courage. And please let Ethan understand.*

"Ethan? There's something I must tell you. Something I should have told you long before now."

He shifted his knapsack to his other shoulder and smiled down at her. "All right. I'm listening."

"That day at Blue Smoke, when you asked about my family, I said they were Italian and French."

"I remember."

"I'm ashamed to admit that I was not truthful. I've regretted it ever since, and I want to rectify the situation."

His forehead furrowed. "Go on."

"The truth is, I have no idea who I am or where I came from. My first memories are of living at the orphanage and being called, among many other things . . . a mulatto." Even after all this time, the recollection still hurt. She lifted one shoulder. "Maybe I am."

He turned away and stared out over the valley. Tears welled up and she scrubbed at her eyes, willing them away. After the incident with the stranger at Blue Smoke that night when Ethan had been so angry, so dismissive of his mixed-blooded visitor, what else had she expected?

She took a deep breath and plunged ahead. "I don't blame you for hating me. I was wrong to deceive you, and I wish—more than you can imagine—that I'd had the courage to admit this to you from the outset."

Ethan looked at her then, his expression hard and unknowable.

"Please forgive me." Not knowing who her parents were had always made her ache inside, but the look in his eyes caused a wound just as deep. His silence enveloped her like a shroud. What was the use of saying anything more? "Please take me down to the rig. I can walk from there. I don't imagine you care for my company any—"

"Yoo-hoo!" A female voice echoed across the ridge. "Mr. Heyward? Anybody here?"

Ethan hesitated, then cupped his hands and called out, "Hello?"

A woman wearing a sturdy brown skirt, white shirtwaist, and battered gray hat appeared on the path in front of them. Buggy-whip thin and all sharp angles, she shouldered a bulky leather bag, but it didn't seem to hinder her confident stride. She clambered up beside them and wiped her forehead on her sleeve. "That is quite some climb, Mr. Heyward."

"Indeed." Ethan placed one hand on the small of Sophie's back and gave her a gentle nudge. "Miss Swint, may I present Miss Sophie Caldwell. She owns the *Gazette*. Miss Caldwell, this is Miss Garaphelia Swint."

"Pleased to make your acquaintance, I'm sure." Miss Swint bobbed her head at Sophie. "I heard a woman was running the paper these days, and I'm glad to hear it. If you ever need photographs, let me know. I'll make you a good price."

If she didn't think of some way to earn more money, there soon would be no paper. Sophie nodded. "Thank you. I will."

Ethan eyed Miss Swint's leather bag. "Don't tell me you hauled all your equipment up here."

"Just my field camera and my tripod. I want to make a few studies to see how the light hits the ridge at various times of day. I can't have the sun messing up my photographs, now can I?"

At last Ethan grinned, and Sophie breathed easier, even though his smile was meant for Miss Swint and not for her. "I suppose not." He swatted at a bug buzzing around his ear. "This ridge runs for miles. How in the world did you find us?"

The photographer produced a slender brass cylinder from her pocket. "With a compass and my spyglass, of course. Take a look."

Sophie watched Ethan put the spyglass to his eye and follow a bald eagle circling below them. He handed it back. "Quite impressive. I'd enjoy having one of those."

"Well, you won't find another one as famous as this. It belonged to Jean Lafitte, or so I was told." Miss Swint tucked it away. "If you two will excuse me, I need to get set up. The light changes fast up here." She inclined her head. "Happy to have met you, Miss Caldwell. Don't forget to call on me for all your photographic needs."

The lady photographer hurried along the ridge, her leather bag bumping against her hip.

"Ready, Sophie?" Ethan asked.

Without waiting for her reply, he led her down the trail and into the clearing where his horse stood tethered to a sapling. At their approach the horse raised his head, then went back to cropping grass. Sophie watched Ethan stow his knapsack in the rig and fought the powerful emotions surging through her. Kissing Ethan was like tasting chocolate for the first time and wanting more. But now there was no chance that he might one day love her.

"I don't mind driving you back to the Verandah," he said.

"Thank you, but I'd rather walk."

Some indefinable emotion flashed across his face, then was gone. He shrugged. "Suit yourself."

He got into the rig, clicked his tongue to the horse, and drove away, leaving her to stare after him. She waited until his rig disappeared before beginning the long walk down the mountain. She'd been foolish to hope he would forgive her lie or overlook her uncertain parentage.

He had come from a family where everyone knew who they were and where they belonged.

He would never understand the pain of being blamed for something that was not his fault.

EIGHTEEN

August 30, 1886

Hickory Ridge, Tennessee

Dear Mr. McClure,

On the recommendation of our mutual acquaintance, Mrs. Lydia McPherson of the *Sherman, Texas, Democrat*, I'm writing to inquire whether you might be interested in my writing for your newspaper syndicate. I believe Mrs. McPherson has sent you certain of my pieces, but I have taken the liberty of enclosing herewith a few more that I feel might have wider appeal. For instance, Mr. Bell's new telephone machine is sure to revolutionize communication. The dedication of the Statue of Liberty certainly engenders any American's reflections about the meaning and cost of freedom. Finally, I'm enclosing an article about the brigantine *Mary Celeste* and the unknown fate of Captain Briggs, his family, and crew. Sad though it is, people love a mystery. The fact that this one remains unsolved so many years after the ship was found abandoned at sea should appeal to your readers' sense of curiosity without, I hope, being too sensational.

I am most eager to join your syndicate and I hope for a favorable response.

Sophie R. Caldwell,

Editor and Publisher,

Hickory Ridge Gazette

Sophie blew on the pages to dry the ink, then folded the letter and enclosures for mailing, hoping they would find favor with Mr. McClure's syndicate.

She had to do something to bring in extra money. A return visit to her advertisers had confirmed her suspicions regarding Mr. Blakely. Although Mr. Pruitt refused to speak another word about it, Miss Hattie had reluctantly admitted Mr. Blakely's role in her decision. According to the restaurateur, Mr. Blakely forbade his day workers to patronize any establishment that did business with Sophie Caldwell. Since most of Miss Hattie's steady customers were men and women who took both breakfast and supper in town, she had no choice but to honor the resort owner's wishes.

Horace Blakely's actions were akin to blackmail, pure and simple, but how could she fight them? Writing for Mr. McClure's syndicate and soliciting more subscriptions were her only defenses.

"Sophie?" Caleb rounded her desk, a scowl on his ink-smeared face. "I just came from the depot, and our paper shipment still hasn't come. It should've been here a week ago."

She leaned back in her chair and closed her eyes. Why must everything be so difficult? "I'll send a wire to the supplier and find out what's going on."

"I can do it. I need to stop by the mercantile anyway. Tomorrow is Ma's birthday, and I want to buy her a present."

"I'm sure she'll appreciate it."

"It won't be much. I'm thinking new hairpins, or a card of buttons maybe. I'm about broke, and Joe and James Henry both need new shoes." He fidgeted with his cap. "I reckon I ought to tell you Mr. Blakely won't take me back, and Mr. Whiting says orders at the mill are way down since construction at Blue Smoke is finished. Reckon you're stuck with me awhile longer."

"I wish I could pay you more, but the truth is, I'm about broke myself." She had spent the last few weeks poring over her ledger and worrying about her dwindling bank balance. If Mr. McClure didn't buy at least some of her pieces, she'd be out of business by Christmas.

Caleb nodded. "Losing most of our advertisers is a bad break, all right."

She smiled at his use of the word *our*. She loved that he felt such a personal stake in the paper, despite his need to move on.

Caleb scratched his head and cleared his throat. "I was telling Ma about it the other day, and she said that what you need is an advice column where folks can write in about their problems and you say how to fix them."

She laughed. "I'm afraid I'm the wrong person for that job. I can't even fix my own problems."

"Ma says people—especially ladies, I reckon—would buy subscriptions just to read about how to get a tomato stain out of a favorite dress or how to fix everything from a broken pump handle to a broken heart. She says people read questions from the lovelorn because they like trying to figure out who wrote the letter."

"I'm certain that part is true. Folks are always curious about other people's lives."

Caleb whipped a sheet of paper from his pocket and unfolded it. "I figured we could post notices at the bank and the mercantile and over at Mrs. Pruitt's dress shop. Ma says that's where most of the ladies go for the latest neighborhood goss—uh, news."

He handed her the paper, covered with his familiar scrawl.

Attention All! Do you have a thorny problem that
needs an answer? Are you suffering from dingy
laundry or unruly children or, worse of all, a
broken heart? Then write to The Answer Lady c/o
the *Gazette* and your problem will be solved.

Sophie mentally corrected his spelling of *worst* and thought
about her days at the paper in Dallas. Writing the advice column
was considered the lowliest, most undesirable job a true newspaperwoman could undertake. Still, there was no denying the column's
appeal. Mrs. Mills and her assistant could barely keep up with the
dozens of letters that poured into the office each week. If writing
such a column would save the *Gazette*, she'd hold her nose and do it.

She looked up at Caleb. "Change the *e* in *worse* to a *t* and print
some up. Run it on page four of the next issue also. Let's see what
happens."

He grinned and headed for the printing press.

Sophie picked up her letter to Mr. McClure and her reticule
and headed for the post office. Passing the mercantile, she nearly
collided with a woman coming out of Mr. Pruitt's, her arms laden
with packages.

"Miss Swint. Excuse me. Good morning."

The photographer nodded. "Take one of these packages if you
don't mind. I've got my glass plates in here, and I don't want to
drop 'em."

Sophie took the heavy package. "Where to?"

"My rig's right over there."

Sophie looked where she pointed and recognized Ethan's black
rig and horse. Her stomach clenched. She had neither seen Ethan
nor heard from him in the two weeks since her confession. It felt
like two years. But she had no one but herself to blame. To keep her
emotions at bay, she'd thrown herself into her work, soliciting more

printing jobs and stockpiling more articles she hoped Mr. McClure might purchase for his syndicate.

"Did Mr. Heyward drive you in this morning?" She followed Miss Swint across the dusty street.

"He offered and I accepted, but he and Mr. B. were in the midst of an awful row this morning, and he told me to come on by myself." Miss Swint stowed her purchases and straightened her hat. "I didn't mind. I like solitude."

Sophie handed her the box of glass plates. "What do you suppose they were arguing about?"

Miss Swint waggled a finger at Sophie. "Oh no you don't. I'm not about to give you fodder for one of your newspaper stories. I can't afford to anger Horace Blakely. I need my job." She climbed into the rig and picked up the reins. "Come on up to the ridge when you get a chance and see how my hut worked out. I'll take your photograph for free."

After she drove away, Sophie posted her letter to Mr. McClure and ducked into the mercantile for a box of pencils. She stopped at the bakery and splurged on a couple of sweet buns. Maybe Gillie could tear herself away from the orphanage long enough for a chat and a quick bite to eat.

Exiting the bakery, she nearly tripped over a black-and-tan dog lying on the boardwalk. He gazed up at her and thumped his tail. He looked like the same dog she'd seen earlier in the summer. She bent down. "Hector, is that you?"

At the sound of the name, the hound's tail swished the ground and he licked her proffered hand. "Are you still hungry, boy?"

She reached into the bag and broke off a bit of sweet bun. No doubt Hector would have preferred a slab of beef, but he wolfed down the pastry, his eyes begging for more. She handed him another bite and started down the street. Hector trotted alongside her, his pink tongue hanging out.

Outside the *Gazette* office, she paused. "You're just the sweetest thing I've ever seen, but you need to go on back now and wait for your master. He'll be lost without you."

Hector sat on his haunches and stared at her.

She smiled, glad that somebody was happy to see her. "Go on, now, before I fall in love with you."

"Sophie?"

She whirled around. "Ethan."

He touched one finger to the brim of his hat. "How are you?"

The memory of their kiss washed over her like a rogue wave. "I'm all right." She nodded toward the street. "I just saw Miss Swint, driving your rig."

He nodded. "She was in a hurry to get on down here to pick up her supplies. We've an entire family from North Carolina on their way up to the ridge today to get photographed."

She reached down and scratched Hector's ear. "Mr. Blakely's idea must be paying off. It seems that everything he touches turns to gold."

"He's got an instinct for business, all right." He bent to the dog. "Who's this?"

"I think his name is Hector. He belongs to a farm family. I gave him a bite to eat, and now he's my friend for life."

"He couldn't have chosen a better one." Ethan's gaze held hers. "I came to apologize. I should never have allowed you to walk home from the ridge that day. And I shouldn't have behaved so coldly."

"I suppose you had a right to be angry. Nobody likes being duped. I should have been truthful from the beginning. But I was afraid." She dropped her gaze. "I wanted you to like me."

"What made you think I wouldn't?"

She hesitated. "I saw the way you looked at that man who came to your office the night of the reception, the way you dismissed him as a nobody." She swallowed a knot in her throat. "The moment I saw him, I recognized that he's of mixed blood too."

His lips tightened. "I'm sorry you were witness to that night. But believe me, Julian is nothing like you." He paused. "And I do like you, Sophie. I like you very much. Anyway, I didn't come down here to talk about Julian." Ethan nodded to a man hurrying past them on the boardwalk. "I came to ask whether you'll forgive the way I acted and come with me to Race Day. I know October is a ways off yet, but I wanted to get my bid in early."

She stared up at him. Was it too much to hope for, that he had forgiven her?

"Griff Rutledge has a horse in the race," Ethan went on. "Blakely figures him to win."

"If Mr. Blakely says so, then I'm sure it will happen. He seems to control everything in this town."

Ethan leaned against the wall and jammed his hands into his pockets. "You're referring to your advertising clients."

"How did you know?"

He shrugged. "I read your paper cover to cover every week. I find it entertaining and informative, even when I don't necessarily agree with your opinions. I couldn't help noticing the lack of advertisements in the last couple of issues, and I assumed Horace had something to do with it. This morning I asked him flat out, and we had a very colorful discussion about it." Ethan shook his head. "I had no idea Horace knew so many curse words. It may well have been the most inventive dressing-down I've ever received in all the years I've known him."

She frowned, trying to make sense of it. Was Ethan saying he didn't care about her ancestry? That he had defended her against his vindictive boss? "I'm sorry to have been the cause of so much trouble between you."

"Horace Blakely is one of the most successful businessmen

in the country," Ethan said. "You could write the worst kind of accusations, and it would make no difference to someone with his money and influence, especially here in Hickory Ridge. There was no need for such pettiness, and I told him so."

"He's about to drive me out of business," Sophie said. "All because of one editorial and because I dared to contradict him at the council meeting."

"I know it. But don't worry." Hector nuzzled Ethan's hand, and he stroked the dog's head. "I have an idea."

NINETEEN

The parlor at the Verandah was so jam-packed, Sophie could barely move. Before dawn, thick clouds moved in, obscuring the mountains, and now a torrential rain had forced the cancellation of Race Day. Townsfolk and visitors alike sought shelter wherever they could find it—beneath the overhangs of the buildings along the main road, in shops and offices, in Mr. Tanner's livery. And a sizable number, it seemed, had sought out the Verandah Hotel for Ladies.

Sophie moved through the crush of whining children, harried mothers, and disgruntled visitors, offering cups of tea and plates of the hot biscuits Lucy had been preparing since the first roll of thunder. Mabel and Merribelle, lucky girls, were already up at Blue Smoke, seeing to the needs of the guests who had had better sense than to venture out in such weather.

A fire crackled in the fireplace, warding off an autumnal chill that seeped through the walls of the old building. Wet umbrellas leaned against windowsills, dripping water onto the pine floor.

Sophie carried her empty tray to the kitchen. "We need more biscuits."

"This is it." Lucy, her face shiny with perspiration, took another pan of biscuits from the stove and motioned to Sophie. "I'm nearly out of flour, and I am not about to go to the mercantile for more."

Sophie peered out. Rain fell so hard it was impossible to see anything. "I don't blame you. It isn't as if these folks are paying guests anyway."

A child let out an ear-splitting shriek that brought the buzz of conversation in the parlor to a temporary halt. Lucy closed her eyes. "Sweet sassafras! Who are all these people anyway?"

Sophie gazed around the room. In the small entryway, Mariah Whiting and her daughter-in-law, Ethelinda, stood sipping tea and chatting. Carrie Rutledge sat on the bottom step of the staircase, her arms wound around her small daughter's waist. Sophie recognized the mayor's wife and a few ladies from her church. Several women wore simple calico skirts and shirtwaists that marked them as local farm wives, but most of the others were strangers who had arrived on the train expecting a horse race, a parade, a picnic, and fireworks. Annoyance and disapproval clouded their faces. As if anyone other than God himself controlled the weather.

Lucy piled the hot biscuits onto a tray and added more boiling water to the glass jugs filled with tea. "I heard that Mr. Blakely wanted to hold the horse race tomorrow, but Mr. Rutledge refused. Even if the rain stopped right this minute, the race course will be too dangerous for the horses."

"Mr. Blakely thinks he owns this town now." Sophie's empty stomach protested and she helped herself to a biscuit. "Sometimes I think Hickory Ridge would be better off without Blue Smoke."

"Maybe." Lucy poured two cups of tea and offered one to Sophie. "But then you wouldn't have met Mr. Heyward."

An image of Ethan the day of their hike to the ridge rose in her mind—the sunlight falling on his broad shoulders and his hair, the curve of his lips when he smiled. Now they were talking again, laughing together like old friends when one errand or another brought Ethan to town. And yet from time to time she still sensed in him a holding back, a private grief he was unwilling to admit or share.

A couple of boys, smelling of apples and wet wool, raced into the kitchen, swiped a handful of biscuits from the tray, and thundered back into the parlor. Lucy shook her head. "When my husband was killed, my first thought was regret that I would never be the mother of his children. But, I declare, if I'd had children and they turned out like those two . . ."

"Ada always said that as the twig is bent, so grows the tree." Sophie refilled her cup and leaned in the doorway, watching the two boys wrestling each other for a place above Carrie's on the crowded staircase.

Another clap of thunder rocked the building. The door opened and Gillie rushed in, her dress and shawl dripping water, her hair plastered to her skull. She shook out her umbrella and scanned the crowd.

"Go on and take her up to your room," Lucy said. "I put some fresh towels in the upstairs cupboard last night. She needs to get out of those wet clothes before she catches her death of cold. I'll bring up some hot tea in a minute."

Sophie made her way through the crowd. Gillie collapsed against her. "Thank goodness you're here. I wasn't sure where I'd find you. People are holed up everywhere waiting out this storm." She unlaced her muddy boots and set them beside the fire.

"Come on." Sophie took her friend's hand, and they squeezed past the knots of people sitting on the staircase. In the upstairs hallway, Sophie took a stack of clean towels from the cupboard and opened the door to her room.

Gillie shivered and stepped out of her wet things, draping her skirt, shirtwaist, and vest over the bed post. She peeled off a wet petticoat, added it to the pile, and laughed. "At least my unmentionables are dry."

Sophie handed her a towel, and Gillie blotted her face and squeezed water from her thick, white-blond braid. "That feels better."

"I'd give you something of mine to wear, but I don't think I have anything that will fit."

"That's all right." Gillie eyed Sophie's bed. "But I wouldn't mind warming up beneath that quilt."

Sophie waved one hand. "Be my guest."

Gillie wrapped a towel around her wet hair and slid beneath the covers. "Much better. Reminds me of when I was little and Mother tucked me in at night."

Sophie perched on the foot of the bed. "I'd read you a story-book, but I don't have one."

Gillie grinned and pulled the covers up to her chin. "I've missed you."

"I've missed you too. But I hear you've been busy."

"Yes, the repairs on the orphanage are going well. Just yesterday Dr. Spencer received more donations from the hospital in Philadelphia. And Mrs. Scott stopped at the bank to give Daddy the money raised from the harvest festival. I hope we can open by Thanksgiving."

"That soon?"

"Mr. Heyward has been over several times to bring materials and help the men with the heavy work. And you know what they say: many hands make light work. I only wish—"

Someone knocked on the door. Sophie rose. "That'll be Lucy, bringing tea."

But a strange woman stood there in a rain-spattered silk dress, her umbrella dripping water, an enormous veiled hat shadowing her face.

"I'm sorry," Sophie said. "This is a private room. You'll have to wait out the storm in the parlor like everyone else."

"But, Sophie," the woman said in a voice that reminded Sophie of moonlight and magnolias, "I'm not everyone else. I'm your mother."

~

Ethan set down his coffee cup and stared out at the pouring rain. He didn't care about the canceled horse race, but he had counted on seeing Sophie today. On his trips to town, he made a point of seeing her, but with the resort so full, he had a hard time getting away. And the truth was, he missed her. He loved her saucy grin, her keen intelligence, her tender heart. And though he had apologized to her twice over, he still regretted the way he'd treated her when she confessed her deceit to him. Her admission had triggered an old resentment he'd spent a lifetime trying to tame.

In recent years he hadn't thought much about the elderly aunt who took him in after his parents died. But here lately, every time he thought about Julian and felt the old hatreds rising up, he remembered the day Aunt Eulalie caught him destroying a neighbor's crabbing pots in an effort to exhaust his rage. After making him apologize, she had paid for the damages and taken Ethan home. And warned him: "Don't grow up angry, boy. It'll make it harder to find your place in the world."

Well, he had tried to let go of his anger, but sometimes that old helpless rage still overpowered him. If only Sophie had trusted him enough to be truthful from the outset. But maybe she was angry too, angry at the circumstances of her life. Certainly she was struggling to find her place in the world.

He picked up his pen and flipped through the stack of papers O'Brien had left on his desk. He signed bills of lading, supply requisitions, and payroll withdrawals, then scanned the monthly financial report. After only four months in operation, Blue Smoke was showing a healthy profit. From the beginning every room had been filled, and guests seemed not to blink an eye at a daily rate that was more than most of the staff earned in a month. The photographer's hut had been a stroke of genius. Every guest, it seemed, wanted to make the trek to the mountaintop to pose for a photograph.

Lightning flashed and a clap of thunder rattled the window. Ethan glanced out at the roiling sky. Surely Miss Swint had had the good sense to stay off the mountain today. Not that Horace would be concerned. If there was money to be made, he wouldn't care if the poor soul caught pneumonia.

Ethan smiled. As personally repugnant as Horace Blakely had become to him over the past few months, he had to admit the man had no peer when it came to making money. Ergo, there was no reason why he shouldn't contribute, albeit unwittingly, to Sophie's bottom line.

He poured another cup of coffee from the silver carafe O'Brien had brought and opened the latest issue of the *Gazette*. He perused front-page stories about Race Day and about last month's America's Cup yacht race in which the *Mayflower* defeated the British challenger, *Galatea*. Sophie R. Caldwell was nobody's fool. The people of Hickory Ridge might be more interested in local affairs, but for many of Blue Smoke's moneyed guests, yacht races—especially the America's Cup—amounted almost to a religion. Every guest was sure to buy a copy of this edition.

He turned the page. A pen-and-ink illustration of a kind-faced woman in a pert, flowered hat was accompanied by a large headline. "Ask the Answer Lady."

Dear Answer Lady: My mother passed on unexpectedly last month, and Pa has already taken himself a new wife. They're too old to bring more children into the world, so I do not understand the big hurry. This woman is after nothing but Pa's hundred acres and his mule, plus my ma's good teacups, which she used only for company. How can I get him to come to his senses?

Ethan frowned. As serious as Sophie was about her newspaper, an advice column must be a desperate attempt to earn more money. He set the paper aside.

Once, long ago, he had been too young and powerless to help those who mattered the most. That was over and done with, buried deep in his heart. Nothing could change the past. But he was no longer alone, young, and afraid. He could help Sophie Caldwell, and he would, no matter the cost.

Perhaps then, at last, he would feel washed clean.

Redeemed.

TWENTY

The woman at Sophie's door removed her rain-splotched hat and shook out her hair. Numb with shock and disbelief, Sophie stared at her. She was the same person who had appeared months before at the *Gazette*, only to run away with scarcely a word.

Sophie opened her mouth to speak but had no voice. Was the woman's claim true, or was this some cruel hoax?

The woman gestured toward the room. "May I come in?"

"Sophie?" Gillie draped herself in the quilt from Sophie's bed. "What's the matter? Who's there?"

"I . . . Come in."

The woman swept into the room, her damp skirts dragging across the worn carpet. She spun around, taking in the furnishings, then lifted the curtain and let it fall. "Why, the old Verandah hasn't changed a bit since I lived here. My room was number nine, just across the hall. Of course I didn't stay here long. I married Nate Chastain and got out of this place—not a moment too soon, let me tell you."

Sophie blinked. This was the woman who had wed dear Mr. Chastain and then abandoned him?

The woman grabbed both of Sophie's hands and drew her close. "Dear little Sophie, if only you knew how long I have waited for this moment. There were days when I despaired of ever seeing you again."

Sophie looked into the woman's face, an older version of her own—the same green eyes framed with brows that swept upward like dark wings, the same cheekbones and forehead. It was easy to believe this stranger could be her mother. For years she had imagined this moment, prayed for it, longed for it. Now she felt completely detached, as if she were encased in ice.

"Don't you remember me at all, Sophie?" the woman asked. "I know you were just a baby when I . . . but don't you remember the songs I used to sing to you? Remember when we sat on the lawn counting fireflies? Remember the stories I used to tell you about the princess from Africa?"

Sophie's heart jolted. She did recall a fragment of just such a story—the same one she had spun for Ada Caldwell one bright October afternoon. The childhood memory rushed over her like a chill wind. *"Onct they was a princess, lived all the way in Africa. One day a ship came and the princess was kidnapped. They took her to a big white house on a island. The sand was white as sugar . . . They was a big storm . . ."*

Her eyes filled, and the woman embraced her. "I knew you would remember. I knew it."

Gillie gathered her wet clothes and touched Sophie's shoulder. "Are Merribelle and Mabel at work today?"

Sophie nodded.

"I'll slip into their room across the hall."

Sophie clasped Gillie's hand. "Please stay."

"We'll sort it out later, I promise." Gillie left and closed the door softly behind her.

The woman perched on the edge of the bed. "I suppose you have questions."

Now that the shock had abated, a thread of anger wove its

way through Sophie's heart. How dare this woman disappear for her entire life, subject her to the hurts and indignities of being an orphan, and then waltz in here as though she'd only been away on some casual errand?

"It might be nice if I knew your name."

"It's Rosaleen. Dupree. Chastain—though Mr. Chastain and I have been divorced for years."

"Where is my father?"

Rosaleen shrugged. "Anybody's guess. He . . . I thought he loved me, but I was mistaken. The moment I told him I was with child, he flew the coop." She fluttered her fingers, mimicking a bird in flight. "Never saw or heard from him again. Take my advice, Sophie. Never depend on any man. Especially a Frenchman. They are constitutionally incapable of telling the truth."

"So you dropped me at the orphanage and never looked back?"

"It wasn't that simple. I was young. I had no money and no skills. I couldn't find work as a dressmaker or a milliner or a shop-girl. The war had begun, so most of the menfolk had enlisted and went off to fight the Yankees." Rosaleen took a handkerchief from her reticule and dabbed at her eyes. "It wasn't as if I could find someone else to marry me and provide for us. By the time you were three, we were near to starving. Then my sister Nola married a man from North Carolina and offered to take you with her. I thought it was the best thing. But I never heard from her again. And I never dreamed she'd give you away. I missed you every day of my life."

Sophie's throat throbbed with unshed tears. "I thought you were dead."

"I can understand your bitterness. But this isn't the first time I've looked for you. Ten years ago I hired a detective to find out what had happened to you. I came here to search for you, but by that time the orphanage had closed and you were gone."

Sophie went numb. Was this the woman Wyatt had hired Pinkerton's to find?

The visitor smoothed her skirts. "Eventually I ran out of money. I went back to New Orleans and tried to make peace with the notion that you were gone forever. And then last year during the world exposition, I saw a lovely young woman coming out of the exhibits building with a handsome man I supposed might be her husband, though he seemed much too old for her. And somehow— call it a mother's instinct—I knew it was you."

Sophie closed her eyes, remembering the crisp January afternoon in New Orleans when Wyatt accompanied her to the Exposition exhibits while Ada and the children rested at the hotel. She had always imagined that the bond between mother and child was unbreakable, that she possessed some kind of special antennae that would allow her to recognize her mother if ever their paths should cross. But she had brushed shoulders with Rosaleen Dupree that day, walked right past her and hadn't felt a thing.

Rosaleen went to the window and pressed her palms to the rain-smeared glass. "You were so beautiful it nearly stopped my heart. I couldn't lose you again. But I couldn't simply walk up to you and announce myself. So I followed you to the hotel and watched while your escort retrieved your keys. Then all I had to do was sweet-talk the desk clerk into letting me take a look at the guest book, and I saw your signature. Miss Sophie Robillard Caldwell."

She looked at Sophie, her eyes full of regret, a sardonic smile playing on her full lips. "Sweet-talking gentlemen seems to be the one thing I am good at."

Sophie's anger cooled. What a sad and wasted life this woman had led. Perhaps it was better that she had grown up apart from Rosaleen's influence. But where did they go from here? What did Rosaleen expect would happen now? Sophie was grown, with a business and a life of her own. It was far too late to undo past wrongs, to make up for everything they had missed.

"That day you came to the *Gazette* office—"

"I had to be sure it was you. I wanted to tell you then, but I lost my nerve. I was afraid of being turned away." Rosaleen lifted one shoulder. "Not that I deserve anything else."

Sophie felt the sting of tears building behind her eyes. Why hadn't Rosaleen stayed away? That would have been kinder than opening wounds that could never be healed. She met the older woman's eyes. "I'm not sure what you want from me."

"I only wanted to . . . see you once more. To explain myself in the hope that you can forgive me."

"That's a tall order after all this time."

"I know it is. And I know it must have been hard, thinking you were all alone, wondering about who your parents and grandparents were. Where you came from." Rosaleen opened her worn tapestry bag and handed Sophie a small journal, its leather covering cracked with age. "It's all in here."

Sophie stared at it as if it were a live thing. After a lifetime of wondering and wishing, here at last was the truth.

"It belonged to your great-grandmother Elena Worthington. She was born in 1740. But our story goes back even further than that."

Sophie sank onto the bed and ran her fingers over the journal. Outside, rainwater poured from the eaves and splashed onto the boardwalk, nearly drowning out the sounds of the restless crowd still gathered below.

Rosaleen sat down beside her. "There was a ship called the *Henrietta Marie* that traveled here from Africa, bringing slaves to the plantations in Jamaica. It sank off the coast of Key West after dropping off its human cargo in Kingston. One of them was a young African princess who had been sold into slavery after being captured by a rival tribe. They say she was so beautiful that a plantation owner took her for his own wife, and she went to live with him in a huge house perched in the green hills above the sea. From her window she could see plants and birds and the fields of sugar cane stretching as far as the eye could see. I can imagine how she longed for freedom and her home."

"Sophie?" The door opened and Lucy came in with a tea tray. "I brought—oh. Forgive me. I didn't know you had a visitor."

She set down the tray and her eyes went wide. "Rosaleen? Is that you?"

"Hello, Lucy." Rosaleen studied the hotelier. "Last time I saw you, you were just a slip of a girl. I thought you went to Wyoming."

"Montana." Lucy frowned. "Didn't you get my wire? I told you the Verandah is full."

"Oh, I'm not staying. I only came to see Sophie."

"It's all right, Lucy," Sophie said. "Thanks for the tea." Lucy nodded to Sophie and withdrew.

Rosaleen resumed speaking. In the small, close room, with rain beating against the windowpanes, her voice was hypnotic. Sophie listened to the story with the hunger and rapture of a small child, the tea all but forgotten.

"Where was I? Oh. The princess had a daughter named Emily, who married a Spaniard, and then her daughter married—" Rosaleen got to her feet. "Well, it's all there; you can read it for yourself. That's all I came for, really. I was never able to give you any sort of gift when you were a child. I hoped at least to give you the gift of knowing where you came from."

Sophie swallowed. "Thank you."

"I'd best be going."

"You can't go out in this storm."

Rosaleen laughed. "Honey, compared to the storms I've been through in this life, a little rain is nothing." She retrieved her umbrella.

"But you can't just disappear again. I . . . I might have questions. I might want to see you again."

"I'd like that." Rosaleen took out a pencil and scribbled on a calling card. "Here's my address. If you're ever in New Orleans again, please come and see me." She pressed a warm palm to Sophie's cheek. "You are more beautiful than I dreamed. And more forgiving than I deserve."

Sophie's throat went tight with emotion. Rosaleen Dupree wasn't perfect. Far from it. And it was too late to recover everything her decision had cost them both. Still, she hadn't given up her quest to find her child. That counted for something. "If you ever need anything—"

Rosaleen released Sophie, her mood suddenly lighter, her green eyes dancing. "Now that you mention it, I am short of cash. The trip up here took nearly everything I had."

Sophie opened the drawer where she stashed the extra money Wyatt had given her on the day he took her to the train station in Fort Worth. She'd been saving it for emergencies. But her mother—her mother!—needed it now. She pressed the bills into Rosaleen's hand. "This isn't a fortune, but it should be enough to get you home."

Rosaleen folded the bills without counting them and tucked them into her bodice. "I'll be seeing you, Sophie."

She pinned on her hat and left, picking her way down the crowded staircase. Sophie leaned against the door frame, too stunned to think.

The door across the hall opened and Gillie came out, still wrapped in the quilt. "Are you all right?"

"I guess so."

"Come inside. You've had quite a shock." Gillie slid an arm around Sophie's shoulder and they returned to Sophie's room. Gillie poured tea, and Sophie recounted her conversation with Rosaleen.

Gillie shook her head. "All this time your mother was alive, and you had no idea."

"No. When I was still at boarding school, Carrie Rutledge told Wyatt and Ada that someone was here asking questions. Wyatt hired Pinkerton's to investigate, but nothing ever came of it."

"Weren't you curious?" Gillie poured another cup of tea. "I would have been dying to know what was happening."

"I didn't know about any of it until I was much older. The Caldwells thought there was no point in telling me about a fruitless investigation while I was still at school." She inhaled the faint scent of ginger tea and wrapped her hands around her cup to warm them.

"Still, I imagine you were shocked when they finally told you."

"Actually, I found out by accident. Wyatt asked me to retrieve a bill of sale for some cattle from his desk, and I stumbled across the old Pinkerton's report. He'd forgotten it was there. I was shocked at first, and angry. But then I realized they had been right not to say anything. The wondering and worry would have made it impossible to concentrate on my studies." She smiled. "I had a hard enough time with mathematics as it was."

"So what happens now?" Gillie asked, her blue eyes serious.

"I gave her money for a train ticket home. She asked me to visit her in New Orleans."

"Will you go?"

Sophie shrugged. "Maybe someday."

"Well, you don't have to decide that right now."

Later that evening, after the storm had passed and Gillie had gone, Sophie ate a supper of cornbread and beef stew and retired to her room. She lit the fire to ward off the damp, turned up the wick in the oil lamp, and opened the journal.

The Journal of Elena Worthington, Being an Account of her Life.

Kingston, Jamaica, 9 September 1778. Here begins an account of my days and the history of my ancestors, pieced together from the stories my mother told me when I was but a child. I set them down before life and memory are lost . . .

The handwriting was thin and precise, the ink faded to a reddish brown. Sophie touched the brittle pages, nearly overcome with wonder and reverence. Here in her own words was her great-grandmother's story. The answer to the mystery of her ancestry.

Knowing where she came from would make all the difference to her. But what would Ethan think?

TWENTY-ONE

New York

October 29, 1886

Dear Miss Caldwell,

   I am in receipt of your clippings and those Mrs. McPherson forwarded to me. Although your work is quite accomplished, I am afraid I cannot offer to syndicate it at this time. We expect to serialize certain of Mr. Twain's writings in the near future, and thus our space for other work is necessarily limited. I quite enjoyed your piece on the unfortunate brigantine *Mary Celeste* and am prepared to publish it in my magazine for the sum of five dollars. Please let me know whether this is agreeable to you.

Yours truly,

Samuel S. McClure

Sophie slumped in her chair and took off her spectacles. Though she was happy at the thought of being published in Mr. McClure's publication, he might as well have said five cents. Five dollars would do nothing to alleviate her situation. Her bank balance was dwindling faster than the days of autumn.

She wouldn't ask Wyatt for more money. It wouldn't be fair. Besides, she hated to admit failure. But she was out of options.

Ethan had said he had an idea for helping with her money situation. But that was weeks ago, and he hadn't mentioned it since. Just what did he have in mind, anyway?

She picked up her shawl and reticule, locked the office, and headed for the orphanage. Last night, over steaming bowls of chicken and dumplings at Miss Hattie's, Gillie had mentioned that Ethan was bringing a couple of his men from Blue Smoke to help Mr. Whiting and the local men finish the repairs. If all went as planned, the infirmary would officially open the week of Thanksgiving. Sophie planned a special edition of the *Gazette*, complete with Miss Swint's photographs, to mark the occasion. Assuming she could hold on to the newspaper until then.

A chill breeze rattled the trees, and a swirl of fallen leaves crunched underfoot as she turned onto the river road. Nearing the orphanage, she spotted several wagons loaded with stacks of lumber and cans of paint and a crew of men milling about. Ethan's rig was parked beneath the trees.

She saw him then, his shirtsleeves rolled to the elbows, helping Mr. Whiting and another man carry a long table up the steps and into the building. One of the men said something. Ethan laughed in response, and she smiled. Almost from the beginning, she had been attracted to that sound, to the way his hair curled over his collar, to the light in his deep blue eyes when he looked at her. But it was his bone-deep goodness, his desire to help her and to ensure the success of the infirmary, that touched the deepest recesses of her heart.

Ethan spotted her and waved, and her heart jolted as the truth dawned. She loved him. Plain and simple. And maybe it was all right that he hadn't yet shared with her everything from his past. Maybe Carrie Rutledge was right that the future was more important than what had gone before.

She pushed through the newly oiled and painted gate, following Ethan and the others up the front steps and into the long, narrow room that had once served as the dining room. The wooden walls had been painted a soft cream color that caught and reflected the sunlight streaming through the new windows overlooking the street. Partitions had been erected to form separate rooms where patients could be seen and treated. Lined up along the walls were wooden crates filled with medical supplies. The office that once belonged to Mrs. Lowell, the orphanage director, had been transformed into an office for Dr. Spencer.

Ethan helped the men place the table beneath the windows, then walked over to greet Sophie, wiping his hands on his dungarees. "I'm glad to see you. I was just about to call on you at the office and invite you to take a look."

He swept his arm toward the new staircase and the large room beyond. "My crew is nearly finished. All that's left is a little bit of painting and the cleaning up."

"It's marvelous. I never imagined this place could look so cheerful. You've done a wonderful job, Ethan. The whole town owes you a huge vote of thanks."

He smiled into her eyes. "It was Miss Gilman's vision. I only helped with the practical things. But I'm glad you're pleased. I can well imagine what it was like, living here."

"I thought it might make me sad, coming back inside. But I'm not. It seems like a hopeful place now."

He took her arm. "Come on. I want to show you the second floor."

He guided her past a couple of workmen who were busy sanding the newel posts, and they ascended the staircase to the upper hallway. Sophie went still, overcome with memories of the years when it seemed her life would never change. Her gaze went to a nook in the far corner, where her bed had been tucked beneath the eaves, apart from the other girls. She had spent countless hours there with only Mrs. Lowell's cat for company, inventing fanciful dreams to ease the lonely ache in her heart. Many nights she drifted into sleep imagining long sea voyages beneath billowing white sails, the ship loaded with bright silks, parrots in cages, baskets of gleaming pearls. A crew of gypsies who played sad songs on violins. Ladies dressed in purple silks, holding fringed parasols to ward off the blazing sun.

But mornings brought the insistent clanging of the breakfast bell and Mrs. Lowell's strident voice, pulling her back to reality.

She thought of the other human castoffs who had lived there with her. What had happened to them? And what had become of the wooden treasure box filled with a hair ribbon she was forbidden to wear, a treasured piece of colored glass, some arrowheads Robbie Whiting had given her? Had she taken it with her to Texas all those years ago? She couldn't remember.

"Sophie?" Ethan murmured. "Are you all right?"

"I suppose I'm not as unaffected as I thought. But I'm fine."

"Look at me." Ethan placed a finger beneath her chin and lifted her face to his. "The things that happen to us in childhood are the hardest to overcome. They mark us forever. But somehow we keep going."

He drew her into his arms and kissed her, his lips warm and demanding on hers. She leaned against him, wishing with all her heart that she could undo the past and sweep away the secrets and deceptions, the pain that had marred them both. Start fresh, like the Bible said, washed clean and whiter than snow.

"Mr. Heyward?" One of the men stood at the top of the stairs, a box in his hands. "Where do you want this?"

Ethan released her and cleared his throat. "Just over there in that alcove will be fine, Joel."

He winked at Sophie. She smiled back.

Joel set the box down. "I reckon that about does it, Mr. Heyward. Soon as they get done sanding the stairs, we'll paint 'em, then get this place cleaned up." He wiped his hands on his shirt. "We done a right good job of it if I do say so m'self."

Ethan nodded. "I appreciate your help. I'll be sure you all get paid out of my personal account."

"Me and the boys ain't worried about that." Joel stroked his bushy beard, dislodging a handful of wood shavings. "It feels good to be doing something for the town. 'Specially the womenfolk." He leaned against the wall and fished a plug of tobacco from his shirt pocket. "My sister died last year, right after her boy was born. She wadn't but twenty years old. Had a real hard time of it. Reckon she might have made it if there'd been someplace like this she could come 'stead of waiting for Doc Spencer." He bit off a plug of tobacco. "It wadn't his fault. He was off tending to other folks and couldn't get to Jenny in time. Miss Gilman is a saint, if you ask me."

"Joel, will you excuse us?" Ethan took Sophie's arm. "I want to show Miss Caldwell the children's ward."

"Sure thing." Joel made room for them on the stair. "Oh, boss?"

Halfway down the stairs, Ethan turned. "Yes?"

"I saw Lutrell Crocker at the mercantile this morning. He's looking for you."

Ethan frowned. "I haven't seen him since Founders Day. I figured he'd gone back to Alabama for good. What does he want?"

Joel shrugged. "Don't know. He seemed awful mad about something."

"Maybe Mrs. Crocker kicked him out."

"Maybe." Joel shifted his plug of tobacco to his other cheek.

"You know he's got a temper on him. You oughta be careful around him, 'specially when he's drinking."

"I will." Ethan took Sophie's arm as they reached the ground floor. He led her through half a dozen rooms already set up with cots and washstands. At the far end of the building was a playroom equipped with a table and a bookcase. New doors led out to the old playground, which had been swept clean. Ethan smiled at her. "Like it?"

"I do. It's wonderful. The children will love it."

"I hope it will make a difference, but I did it partly for you." He drew her into the shadows and took her into his arms again. "I want you to be happy, Sophie."

"I know. And I'm grateful." She brushed a couple of wood shavings from her skirt. "But I came here to discuss something else."

"And what is that?"

She took a steadying breath. "You mentioned a plan to help me replace the income I've lost because of Mr. Blakely. As much as I prefer handling my own problems, I do need your help. I was hoping—"

"Ethan Heyward!"

A skinny man in a dirty gray shirt strode across the playground and grabbed Ethan's shoulder. "I been looking for you."

"Lutrell." Ethan pried the man's hands away and stepped back. "I'm happy to talk to you, but not in front of this lady. I'm heading back to Blue Smoke in a little while. We can talk there."

"What if I don't want to go up to Blue Smoke?"

Sophie touched Ethan's arm. "I should go and let you talk to this man."

Lutrell Crocker glared at her. "That is exactly what you should do, missy, because what I've got to say to him ain't fit for a woman's ears."

Ethan turned to her and winked. "We'll have to finish our talk later, Miss Caldwell, if that's all right."

"That will be fine, Mr. Heyward."

Leaving Ethan to deal with Mr. Crocker, Sophie crossed the yard, went out through the gate, and headed to the office, her thoughts racing faster than her feet. Ethan had said he wanted her to be happy. And he'd kissed her just now in a way that left her breathless. That proved he had at least some tender feelings for her, didn't it?

She paused beside the road as a farm wagon clattered past, a towheaded boy at the reins, a shaggy black dog beside him. Would Ethan still care for her once he knew about her family? As long as there was doubt, she could pretend to be anything. But her great-grandmother's journal left no room for what-ifs.

Sophie had read the little book so many times, savoring the quaint spellings and turns of phrase, that she knew it all by heart. Elena's father was a Spanish soldier "fond of ale and musick." Elena herself had married a British merchant in 1770. Her daughter Anna, who was Rosaleen's mother, had wed a Frenchman in New Orleans in 1820. And according to Rosaleen, Sophie's own father was a Frenchman too.

The children at the orphanage were right. She was indeed a mixed-up muddlebones. But at least now she knew her own story. She knew her mother. And that knowledge gave her a certain kind of peace.

She reached the main street and hurried along the boardwalk toward her office, her footsteps hollow on the wooden boards. If Ethan loved her, maybe the one drop of long-diluted African blood was not enough to matter. Maybe his idea for helping her, whatever it turned out to be, would allow her to keep the newspaper.

Maybe everything would be all right after all.

"Now, Lutrell, what was it you came here to discuss?" Ethan pushed open the rear door leading to the children's playground and motioned his visitor outside. "I thought you decided to stay in Alabama."

"I wanted to, but what woman wants to hitch herself to a man who's poor as a church mouse?" Lutrell Crocker jammed his hands deep into his pockets. "I was counting on that last bit of money from Blue Smoke to get us started out in life. Then Murphy stole it from me, and you wouldn't do nothing about it." He pulled a sack of tobacco from his pocket and took his time rolling himself a smoke. "Mary Susan sent me back here to get what's mine. She won't marry me until I do."

Ethan pressed a hand to his eyes. "Lutrell, we have had this conversation already. Nothing has changed. Murphy is gone, and you have no proof that he stole anything."

Crocker peered up at Ethan, his walrus mustache forming a set of parentheses around thin, tobacco-stained lips. "My word ain't good enough for you, I reckon."

"My offer to lend you the money still stands," Ethan said. "Far be it from me to stand in the way of wedded bliss."

"And my refusal still stands. I ain't about to borry what's already rightfully mine. But I got a business proposition for you."

Ethan studied the man for a long moment, torn between exasperation and pity. "All right. I'm listening."

Crocker fished a watch fob from his pocket and slid his fingers over the dark leather. For a moment, Ethan saw a spark of pride in the man's faded eyes. "My granddaddy taught me how to weave leather when I was a young'un. Used to weave all sorts of things—belts, coin purses, and the like. He learnt it from his daddy, is what he told me."

Ethan nodded. The mountains near Hickory Ridge were populated by fine crafters and fine musicians the rest of the world had yet to discover. He'd never imagined Lutrell as one of them, but he had to admit the watch fob was a superior piece of work.

"I reckon I could make you some more of these for that fancy gift shop up at Blue Smoke," Lutrell said.

"The guests would pay a good price for something that well made," Ethan said. "I'll take half a dozen to start at, say, two dollars apiece. I'll pay you half now and half on delivery. If they sell as well as I think they will, I'll order more for next summer. Some of those belts and coin purses too." He stuck out his hand. "You want to shake on it? Might be the start of a whole new line of work for you."

Lutrell spat. "I got to get at least five bucks for 'em. At two dollars apiece, I'll be old and gray 'fore I can save up enough to marry Mary Susan."

Ethan's patience snapped. He turned and started back inside. "Then we have nothing more to discuss. I'm sorry you came all this way for nothing. Now, excuse me; I've got to check on my crew and help them pack up."

He was turning on his heel when Crocker lunged at him. Caught off guard, Ethan twisted and fell, his shoulder cracking against the hard-packed dirt of the playground, his spectacles skittering three feet away. Crocker fell across him and landed a solid blow to Ethan's face. Warm blood spurted from his nose, spattering the front of his shirt.

Ethan grabbed the smaller man's forearms and, with a sharp twist, ejected him onto the ground. Crocker rolled away and got up, his fists clenched, a murderous look in his bloodshot eyes.

Ethan reached for his glasses, then pulled out his handkerchief to stanch the flow of blood. A sharp pain needled his shoulder as he got to his feet and dusted off his dungarees. "Hit me again,

Lutrell, and you'll find yourself keeping company with Sheriff McCracken."

Crocker laughed. "That don't surprise me none. Hiding behind the law rather than settling differences like a man."

"I'm telling you to clear out now. And don't come back. Understand?"

Crocker slapped his hat against his thigh to dislodge the dust. With a final glance at Ethan, he spat and sauntered down the road.

TWENTY-TWO

The back door squeaked open, letting in a blast of cold air. Caleb pushed inside, his arms laden with stacks of vellum. Sophie looked up from the jobber press, where she'd worked all afternoon making up a new stationery order for Mariah Whiting's bookshop. Sophie couldn't really afford such expensive paper, but Robbie had convinced her to establish a mail-order business selling stationery and business cards, and she needed something nicer than newsprint for corresponding with her new customers.

Caleb dumped the paper onto the counter and brushed his fingers together. "You still here?"

Last night both she and Caleb had worked late, poring over Miss Swint's photographs for the special edition of the *Gazette* due out on Friday. Thanks to Ethan and his crew, all that remained before the official opening of the infirmary was to add the finishing touches. Sophie, Gillie, and several other ladies from Robbie's church were meeting today to hang curtains and make the beds with the new linens and quilts the Ladies Benevolent Society had sewn. Mariah Whiting had promised to stock the children's bookshelf with storybooks from her shop.

"I went home for a little while, but I couldn't sleep. I've been here all day." Sophie took her foot off the treadle and rubbed her tired eyes. Thinking about everything that needed doing at the office had been only one reason for her wakefulness. Ethan, and their unfinished conversation, was the other.

"Gillie says Mr. Heyward sure did a fine job on the infirmary." Caleb set about mixing the ink, pouring a cup of powder into the bucket, and carefully stirring in water. "She's real excited about it."

"It's a wonderful thing for Hickory Ridge. And for Gillie. A dream come true for her."

Caleb nodded. "I reckon. Only I wish she could think of something else sometimes."

Sophie looked up at his earnest face. Holy cats. Caleb had gone sweet on Gillie, and Sophie hadn't seen it coming. Not that she wasn't pleased for him. But Gillie was older than Caleb, and so single-minded about her infirmary, Sophie wasn't at all sure her friend had room in her life for a man, even someone as hardworking and honest as Caleb Stanhope.

She gathered the finished stationery order, stacked the sheets neatly, and placed them into a sturdy box for delivery to Mrs. Whiting. "Does Gillie know about your feelings, Caleb?"

"My—" He stopped stirring the ink and glanced away. "Does it show?"

"Only when you mention her name." Sophie grinned and retrieved the set of business cards she'd just printed for a gentlemen's emporium in Knoxville.

"I haven't said anything to her, and I wish you wouldn't either." Caleb tossed some broken pieces of type into the bucket to be melted and recast. "I mean, I think an awful lot of her, but she's older than me, and she's educated, and I'm—"

"One of the smartest, kindest men I know," Sophie said. "I'm not much older than you, so maybe I'm not the most qualified person to give advice—"

"You do pretty well as the Answer Lady," Caleb said. "I happen to know we got ten new subscription orders yesterday, not to mention that bag of mail I picked up from the post office."

"Don't change the subject. If you want to court Gillie, then make a plan for your future. Show her that you intend to look after her, even if she doesn't think she needs it." She smiled. "Every woman wants to feel that her man will cherish and protect her, no matter how much schooling she's had."

"I reckon so." Caleb leaned against the counter, the last of the oyster-colored light falling on his shoulders. "And I've been thinking about that. The truth is, I like newspapering an awful lot. I know I'm not much of a speller, but I'm good with the presses and selling advertising and such. And since there's no room for me at Blue Smoke or at the mill, I've applied to Mr. Ochs over at the *Chattanooga Times*. If he takes me on, I can send money home to Ma and the boys. And maybe someday I can save up enough to ask Gillie to marry me."

Sophie's mind whirled. Even though Caleb worked only two days a week at the *Gazette*, doing without his help would be difficult. But others had made her dream possible. How could she hold him back from reaching for his?

"I shouldn't have dropped the news on you like this," Caleb said. "Should've waited till I heard back from the *Times*." He shrugged and went back to picking broken type from the wooden trays. "They may not have a job for me anyway."

"If they do, then you must take it. I'll manage somehow." Sophie sighed. "I may not be able to publish the *Gazette* much longer anyway, despite those new subscriptions. Paper and ink are getting more expensive all the time. And so far, Mr. McClure has bought only two of my articles."

"I thought Mr. Heyward was going to help you."

"He said he had an idea, but he never said what it was. And I haven't seen him in over a week. Too busy at Blue Smoke, I imagine."

"I saw him at the post office yesterday," Caleb said. "He was with that tall, dark-haired fellow. They seemed mad as two old roosters."

Sophie nodded. So Julian Worth, whoever he was, was back in town. Or maybe he never left. At any rate, maybe that explained why Ethan had not stopped in to see her.

Caleb loaded a stack of newsprint onto the press. "Might as well get this first page printed up before I head home."

Sophie shook her head. "It'll keep. It's late. Go home and get some rest."

"You're not sore at me about leaving?"

She mustered a smile for him. "Someone else gave me a chance to learn this business. I can't very well stand in the way of your taking your chance."

"I'm real happy you understand. But please don't say anything to Gillie about—"

"Would I steal your thunder on something as important as your future?"

Caleb grabbed his cap off the hat tree and went out the back door, whistling.

Sophie lit the lamp against the November gloom and took a seat at her desk. She sorted through the mail, setting aside a stack of bills, a couple of subscription payments, and a thick letter from Ada, which she tucked into her pocket to read later. Then she opened the bag of mail addressed to the Answer Lady, picked up her silver-handled letter opener, and slit open the first envelope.

Dear Answer Lady,

When was Daniel Webster born and where did he grow up? Why did he rite a dictionary? Please anser in next Monday's *Gazette*. My report is due Thursday. Thank you.

Sophie smiled at the misspellings and the nature of the question. It wasn't the first letter she'd received seeking a shortcut to a school assignment, but it was the most honest.

She opened another envelope and took out a single sheet written in pencil.

Dear Answer Lady,
My baby died. Why does God allow suffering like that? Thank you.

Sophie closed her eyes. Why indeed? Just last Sunday Robbie had preached a sermon on suffering. He spoke of the suffering of Job and the trials of the apostle Paul and reminded his flock that God didn't promise a shield from suffering, but rather spiritual sustenance in the midst of it. Ada often said that suffering made one stronger. Maybe it did. But such an answer seemed inadequate, a pale thing to offer this heartbroken mother.

Footsteps sounded outside, followed by a sharp knock on the door. Sophie lifted her lamp and went to answer it.

"Miss Caldwell?"

Julian Worth stood in the doorway, backlit by the streetlamps just coming on, a leather pouch tucked under his arm. He wore neither a coat nor gloves. "I apologize for barging in like this, but I need your help. It's about Ethan Heyward."

Her heart lurched. "Is he all right?"

"He isn't sick or hurt, if that's what you mean. But the truth is, Ethan hasn't truly been all right since we were children. I've been trying to fix that ever since June, but he's too angry with me to listen."

"I'm sorry, but I don't see how I can help."

He leaned forward, his ice-blue eyes bright in his dusky face. "Until my first trip here a few months ago, I hadn't seen Ethan since he was twelve years old. So I can't claim to know him very well."

The wind caught the door and sent it crashing against the wall with a sound like gunfire. Mr. Worth shivered in the deepening chill. "But the one thing I do know is that he loves you."

Her stomach dropped. Ethan loved her? She hoped with all her heart it was true. But perhaps Mr. Worth's claim was a ruse to get inside. Should she trust a perfect stranger, especially one Ethan so clearly disliked? Despite her apprehension, something in those eyes convinced her to hear him out. She motioned him inside, set the lamp on her desk, and took her chair, keeping the desk between them.

Mr. Worth indicated the other chair. "May I?"

"Please."

He sat, holding the leather pouch on his lap, and studied her intently. "I remember seeing you outside Ethan's office the night I visited Blue Smoke."

"I remember you too. Ethan was furious that you'd turned up, but he wouldn't tell me why." She toyed with the letter opener, watching it catch the lantern light. "To this day, he still hasn't. But then, whatever is between you is hardly my business."

"As boys, we were very close, but he hates me now. He thinks I'm responsible for the worst thing that ever happened to him." Mr. Worth tapped the pouch. "I have proof that I'm not to blame. Ethan won't hear me out. But he might if you ask him to."

"I see."

"Miss Caldwell?" The man bent forward, elbows on his knees, until his eyes were level with hers. "Just answer me one thing. Do I look like a man who would murder his own father?"

Ethan slid into his chair and pressed the button on the floor to summon O'Brien. A ten-hour round trip to Nashville earlier in the week had put him behind on his paperwork. It would take the rest of the afternoon and half the night to catch up, but in the long run, it would be worth it.

He opened his desk drawer just to be sure the pale blue jeweler's box was still there. Ever since their kiss at the infirmary that day, he had thought of little else but Sophie. He loved everything about her—not only her considerable beauty and poise, but her passion for her work, her belief in the importance of it. Her determination to keep the paper afloat despite Horace Blakely's petty interference.

At least he had solved that problem. Coupled with the increased subscription orders in the wake of her Answer Lady column, the money Blue Smoke would pay her to write stories about and for the resort would more than compensate for the loss of her advertising accounts. Horace had given Ethan the task of increasing the public's awareness of Blue Smoke before the start of the next season. He would have to hire someone to write articles and stories, so why not Sophie? She was a good writer and someone he trusted. He'd commission the pieces, and soon her work would appear in newspapers and magazines around the country, with Horace none the wiser.

Ethan couldn't help feeling his plan would right a wrong. Horace had caused Sophie's problem. Now, however unwittingly, he would fix it.

Ethan's only worry now was whether Sophie's feelings for him were as tender as his were for her. She'd kissed him as if they were. But secrets still lingered between them, and secrets were a perilous foundation for a marriage he hoped would last a lifetime.

He shuffled a stack of papers on his desk, too preoccupied to concentrate. Half a dozen times he'd been on the verge of telling her about the day he'd stumbled from his parents' room, half-mad with terror and powerless to do anything except hide and wait for death or rescue. But shame had silenced him—that and the fear of letting go of the careful fiction he'd created and believed about his own life.

O'Brien knocked once at the door and entered, carrying a stack of mail and the latest issue of *Scribner's Monthly*. "Here you go, boss."

The secretary pointed to the magazine. "There's a good article in there about Geronimo's surrender. They sent him and the others to Florida, you know, but General Miles says they might be moved to somewhere out west before too much longer."

Ethan hid a smile. O'Brien knew Ethan preferred to discover the magazine for himself rather than receive a synopsis, but sometimes the Irishman couldn't help himself. Ethan flipped through the mail, setting aside a couple of letters for later. "Thanks for the tip. I'll be sure to read that piece."

O'Brien blushed. "Sorry. I meant to read only the first couple of sentences, but I got caught up in the story and couldn't stop." He shook his head. "Somehow I can't imagine old Geronimo and all those Apaches living in Florida. Doesn't seem natural, if you ask me."

Ethan nodded. "Anything going on around here that I should know about?"

The Irishman shrugged. "Not especially. Mr. Rutledge says one of the Blue Smoke horses is sick—colic or something." He shook his head. "That man sure sets a lot of store by those horses. He's planning on spending the night with that horse, walking it around and such and making sure it doesn't go down."

O'Brien crossed the room and lit the lamp. "It's getting dark in here, boss. You don't want to strain your eyes." He set the lamp on the corner of Ethan's desk. "Li Chung is making fresh-caught trout and wild rice for the staff tonight. I imagine it's done by now." He eyed Ethan's cluttered desk. "From the looks of things, you're going to be here awhile. Shall I be askin' one of the cooks to bring you a tray?"

"I'd appreciate it. I want to get this cleared away. I'm thinking I might take tomorrow off."

"Seein' Miss Caldwell, are you?"

"Maybe."

"Ha! You're smitten, and you know it."

"Try to keep it under your hat, will you, O'Brien? It'll be awfully embarrassing if she doesn't return my affections."

"Sure, sure. But I'm guessing she's about as besotted as you are." O'Brien glanced around the room. "If there's nothing else you're needing . . ."

Ethan waved a hand. "That should do it for now."

The secretary left, whistling. Ethan drew the lamp closer to his work and quickly dispatched a stack of bills. He signed the weekly payroll report and the bank draft to pay the maintenance crew and approved Li Chung's weekly order from Pruitt's mercantile. He finished his report for Horace and signed off on an elaborately worded request from Miss Swint for a stack of warm blankets to be delivered to her photo hut.

Though the resort was closed, a steady stream of curious tourists with time to kill between trains still made the trek to the ridge. Any day now cold weather would shutter the operation until spring. But in the meantime Miss Swint was eager that her customers should not catch cold while posing for her camera.

At last Ethan closed his ledger, surprised to find it was already past eight o'clock. By now the Blakelys would be seated for dinner, enjoying Li Chung's trout and wild rice and anticipating the chocolate pastries the Chinese cook baked fresh every afternoon.

Ethan's stomach rumbled. Where was his dinner? He was partial to those pastries too. In another ten minutes he'd simply help himself to a plate in the kitchen. The cooks and the Blakelys' staff were for the most part a congenial bunch, mostly locals, and Ethan enjoyed their company.

He rose from his chair just as a huge stone crashed through the French door leading to the terraces. Shards of glass flew across the room.

"Heyward!"

Ethan's shoes crunched on the broken glass as he crossed the room. The shattered door flew open, and Lutrell Crocker stood swaying in the doorway. Ethan saw at once that the man was half-drunk. It took a bit longer to realize that he carried a gun. And it was aimed straight at Ethan's heart.

TWENTY-THREE

Was Julian Worth a murderer?

Sophie peered into his face, her heart thudding, her mind racing to make sense of the question he had just asked. Had she been foolish to trust him? She surreptitiously slid the letter opener into her lap, her fingers curling around the handle. It wouldn't be much protection, but it was better than nothing.

"I'm sorry, but I don't understand Ethan's concern for whatever might have happened between you and your father."

For several moments, his eyes held hers. "I think you do."

Except for the ticking of the office clock, the room was silent. Far off, a dog howled.

Julian Worth whispered, "Look at me."

Her whole world tilted. She sucked in her breath. The truth was staring her in the face, plain as day. It was there in the man's strong, even features and his blue eyes. "Ethan is your brother?"

"Half brother."

"And he thinks you killed his father?"

"And his mother. But I can prove it isn't true, if he can get past his hatred long enough to listen. I need you to go up to Blue Smoke with me and prevail upon his better instincts. I know I have no right to ask, but—"

Sophie's mind reeled with the irony of the situation. All this time, as she'd walked around guilt-ridden and ashamed, berating herself for deceiving Ethan, he'd been deceiving her too. And when she confessed her fears about her past to him, fearing his rejection, he had never once hinted at the connection between Mr. Worth and himself.

She should have felt angry, but instead her heart ached for Ethan. She'd grown weary of hiding a part of herself from him. Maybe he was weary too. "Very well, Mr. Worth. We'll go first thing in the morning."

"I can't wait till morning." He took a yellow sheet of paper from his pocket and slid it across her desk. "This wire came just an hour ago. My son has fallen gravely ill. I've booked a ticket home on the morning train."

He leaned forward in his chair. "It isn't only because I want to get this monkey off my back. I think it will help Ethan. He blames himself for what happened. I'd like to relieve him of his burden too."

Sophie nodded. Now Ethan's reticence to talk about his child-hood in Georgia made sense. His parents had been murdered. Who could bear to repeat the details of such a tragedy, even one that had happened years ago? Some wounds never healed.

"Miss Caldwell?" Julian Worth stood, fanning the flame in the lamp. "May we go now?"

She rose, fighting the apprehension building inside her. It was foolish to go off into the night with a stranger, especially one sus-pected of murder. But something told her he was trustworthy. And if she could help Ethan . . .

"I'll get my wrap."

She doused the flame and locked the door, and they left the office, crossing the quiet, darkened street. Wind tore at her cloak and a swath of frosty stars blanketed the sky. She glanced toward the infirmary, barely visible through the trees lining the shadowed road. Lights glimmered in the windows on the first floor. No doubt Gillie was still there, making preparations for the opening.

"I paid the supply-train driver to take us up." Mr. Worth's breath clouded the cold November air. "It isn't much of a conveyance for a lady like yourself, but it's faster than taking a horse and rig up the mountain at night. And safer too, I expect."

Sophie pulled her cloak around her and hurried to keep up with his long strides as they passed the shuttered shops and headed for the supply train. She watched him from the corner of her eye. He seemed sincere, and the reason for his haste seemed believable enough, but he was still a stranger. She was grateful for the train and the engineer.

They reached the station and hurried to the supply train. The engineer, his face illuminated in the weak lantern light, nodded a greeting. Mr. Worth helped her aboard and made room for them on a wooden bench. The engine hissed and groaned, and they clattered up the mountain.

Sophie shivered in the unheated train car, too stunned for conversation. For once, her reporter's instincts and her curiosity had deserted her. She could think only of Ethan, of the deep hurt lodged in the very marrow of his bones, and her affection for him grew even stronger.

She folded her hands in her lap and stared out the window at the darkened landscape. As the train labored up the track, she caught glimpses of farmhouses, their windows aglow with lamplight, and an occasional sliver of moon riding the bare branches of the old oak trees. A wave of uneasiness moved through her. Assuming Julian Worth's story was true, could she persuade Ethan to hear his brother out? Suppose Ethan got angry with her for coming with a man he clearly despised. Suppose he wouldn't listen to her at all?

At last the train slowed and, with a screech and grinding of wheels, lurched to a stop. Mr. Worth rose and helped Sophie to her feet. "This won't take long," he said to the engineer as they left the car.

"I'll be here." The engineer pulled his hat lower over his ears and blew on his knobby hands. "Got nowheres else to be."

Mr. Worth took Sophie's arm and they crossed the railway tracks. Skirting the horse barns, where a solitary lantern burned, they walked up a gravel path to the side lawn bordering the terrace and the garden.

"We're in luck," he said. "Ethan's still at work. The lamps are burning in his—"

A gunshot cracked the air above their heads. Sophie yelped and threw up one hand. "What's going on?"

"No idea. Stay here."

He raced across the lawn, his leather pouch tucked tightly to his chest.

"Mr. Worth, wait!" Sophie clutched at her skirts. Keeping to the shadows, she hurried after him. She rounded the corner, spotted Ethan, and stopped short.

He stood in a circle of yellow light from the terrace lantern, his hands loose at his sides. His shirt was untucked, his cravat askew. In front of him stood Lutrell Crocker, so full of alcoholic spirits she could smell it from where she stood. The barrel of his gun wobbled in the lambent light.

Desperate to help Ethan, she looked toward the heavy doors leading to the ballroom. Surely someone—Mr. O'Brien, Mr. Blakely, or one of his staff—had heard the gunshot and would come to his aid. Where was Mr. Worth? She strained to catch a glimpse of him, but he seemed to have vanished.

Then everything happened at once. Mr. Worth emerged from the shadows, shouting Ethan's name. Ethan's head jerked, and he turned just as Crocker stumbled toward them and fired again. A bullet whined past her head, cracking a small tree branch that crashed into her shoulder as it fell. Sophie screamed and fell to her knees. *Oh, dear God, please save him. Please don't let him die.*

Then Ethan was beside her, folding her into his warm, strong embrace, his lips in her hair, whispering her name. Over his shoulder she saw Julian Worth lying in a widening pool of blood, the crimson stain seeping into the cold stone terrace.

TWENTY-FOUR

The doors to the ballroom opened. Tim O'Brien and several members of Mr. Blakely's staff spilled onto the terrace and fanned out into the darkness, searching for Crocker. Griff Rutledge raced along the path from the stables, his hair mussed, his shirttail flapping, and bent over Mr. Worth.

Mr. Blakely pushed through the small knot of onlookers. "Is this man alive?"

Sophie massaged the burning pain in her shoulder and strained to hear Griff's reply.

Ethan grabbed her by both shoulders, his fingers pressing into her flesh so hard she yelped. Instantly he released her. "What in blue blazes are you doing here?"

"Mr. Worth asked me to come. He wants to talk to you about—"

"I know what it's about. How did you get here?"

"The supply train. It's waiting on the siding."

He nodded. "Go tell the engineer to make a place for a wounded man. Then stay there, Sophie."

"What about you?"

"I'll take my saddle horse and alert Dr. Spencer. I want him ready to treat Julian as soon as we can get him off this mountain."

"But—"

"Go on!"

She raced toward the train and called for the engineer. "Mr. Worth has been shot. They're bringing him here."

"Lord amighty. What's the world coming to?" The driver pushed off from his perch in the chilly train car, shoving boxes and coils of rope out of the way. "Did you see who did it?"

"Lutrell Crocker. He was drunk as a skunk."

The driver nodded. "He's a tough customer, all right. Mebbe some jail time will sort him out."

"If they can catch him. He ran into the trees. They're looking for him now. Ethan—Mr. Heyward sent me here to alert you."

She rubbed her shoulder and peered into a pile of gear in the corner. "Do you suppose there are any blankets in there?"

"I don't think so. It's mostly stuff I've been meaning to throw away." He blew on his hands and rubbed his arms. "It's cold as a well-digger's grave in here, that's the truth."

Lantern light flickered in the trees. Griff Rutledge and three other men arrived at the siding, carrying Mr. Worth on a litter. Mr. O'Brien, armed with a pistol and a lantern, followed them. He nodded to Sophie.

"Bring him aboard," the driver said. "I'll get the engine to going."

The men laid the injured man on the floor, and she saw the gaping wound in his thigh where the bullet had shattered bone and lacerated his flesh. Someone had wrapped a belt around his thigh, but blood still oozed onto the leg of his trousers. More blood dripped from a cut on his forehead. She swallowed hard as black spots danced before her eyes.

Griff sent her a sympathetic look. "What an awful thing to have happen. Miss Caldwell, are you all right?"

"I'm fine." She took in a deep draft of cold night air and sat on the floor beside Mr. Worth. "Where is his leather pouch?"

"What pouch?"

"He had it when he was shot. It's important."

"I'm sure someone picked it up. I wouldn't worry about it just now."

The engine hissed, rattling the train car. The men took their litter and jumped off as the train began to move.

"Please. Find that leather pouch and give it to Mr. Heyward."

"We'll find it." Griff Rutledge ran after the train and thrust a towel into her hands. "You just keep pressure on his wound and keep him calm till you get to town."

"I will." Sophie removed her cloak and draped it over the injured man.

The train lurched and sped down the mountain. Everything passed in a blur. Sophie sat beside Mr. Worth, one hand pressed to his bleeding thigh, willing him not to die. How cruel it would be if redemption and reconciliation—now so close—were lost forever.

That is, if Julian Worth was telling the truth.

It seemed that hours passed before the train slid into the Hickory Ridge depot. A group of men waited with lanterns and another litter to take Mr. Worth from the train. Sophie waited while they lifted him and placed the litter on a wagon. She stumbled onto the platform in her blood-spattered skirt, light-headed and boneless as a fishing worm.

"Sophie." Gillie hurried over and embraced her. "Are you all right?"

"Yes. Is Ethan—"

"Waiting with Dr. Spencer at the infirmary. We figured now is as good a time as any to start seeing patients there."

They climbed into Gillie's rig and made the short trip to the infirmary. As they neared the building, Sophie spotted Caleb and Robbie Whiting standing near the entrance. She followed Gillie up the steps.

"Sophie," Robbie said. "Are you all right?"

"You had me worried sick," Caleb said. "I came back to the office to get my dictionary and saw you leaving with a stranger. I thought—"

"I'm all right." She smiled at Caleb and patted Robbie's sleeve. "Thank you both for your concern. But it's Mr. Worth who needs our attention."

"Of course," Robbie said. "I happened to be at Doc Spencer's when Mr. Heyward arrived with news of the shooting. I wanted to be here if you needed me."

Despite her fatigue and her worry, Sophie felt a rush of affection for her old friend. "Thank you."

Caleb turned to leave. "Don't even think about coming into the office in the morning. I can get that print order for Blue Smoke done and finish composing the first page. Unless you want to write up a story about the shooting."

"I don't think so."

He and Robbie disappeared into the night.

The wagon carrying Julian Worth arrived. The men lifted him and took him inside. Sophie and Gillie followed them into the room where Ethan and the doctor waited.

Gillie squeezed Sophie's hand. "I need to wash up and help the doctor. Why don't you stay and keep Ethan company? This may take awhile."

Suddenly Sophie found it hard to breathe. Her shoulder was on fire. She drew the sleeve of her shirtwaist tight against her arm and a circle of blood bloomed on the fabric.

Gillie saw it too and grabbed Sophie's arm. "What happened here?"

"A branch fell when Mr. Crocker's shot went wild. It hurts. I—" Her stomach fluttered. The room spun. She crumpled to the floor.

A freight wagon rumbled past the infirmary, setting off a chorus of barking dogs. Ethan roused himself from the chair where he'd half dozed, waiting for news. What time was it anyway?

He stood, crossed to the window, and pulled back the curtain to peer out onto the street. Gas lanterns illuminated the shuttered storefronts and cast deep shadows into the alleys. At the far end of the deserted road stood a half-empty freight wagon. Another wagon rattled along the street and drew up at the bakery. Ethan watched as the lamps inside were lit, sending pale streams of light into the cold November darkness.

He rubbed his gritty eyes and rolled his neck to get the kinks out. What was taking the doctor and Miss Gilman so long? Off and on all night he'd heard their voices, low and calm, behind the closed doors of the rooms where Julian and Sophie lay.

Sophie. When she fainted, he'd scooped her up and followed Gillie to one of the rooms on the first floor. He took in the scent of her skin, the sweet, warm weight of her in his arms, and his heart stirred. Not for the first time, he regretted the way he'd treated her that day on the ridge. He'd been more angry with his failures—and with the memories her confession stirred—than with anything she had done. But it had been easier to blame her than to face his own shortcomings. So he had gone silent, let her think the fault was hers. It was a wonder she had ever spoken to him again.

And now she was hurt, and it was his fault. If he'd been willing to listen to Julian in the first place, had the courage to face the past, all of this might have been avoided. He hadn't wanted to consider that Julian might be telling the truth about what had happened on that hot summer day in Georgia. To hear a new version of events would mean that he had wasted his entire adult life holding on to hate and blame and a smoldering desire for revenge.

Strange, though, because now that Julian might actually be dead, he didn't feel the satisfaction he'd expected. Instead, he felt empty. Diminished.

He flopped into his chair and glanced down the deserted hallway, tamping down his growing impatience. What was happening back there? Did the long delay mean hope for Julian's survival?

As the minutes dragged on, Ethan came to a decision. If Julian survived the bullet meant for him, he would hear his brother out.

The prospect brought a kind of peace he hadn't realized he'd been missing. Where had this feeling come from? Regardless, he was grateful. Maybe it had taken violence to bring him back to reality, to prepare him for his moment of grace.

~

"What happened?" Sophie blinked against the wavering lamplight and tried to sit up, but Gillie shook her head.

"You fainted. Now, hold still." With practiced fingers, Gillie unbuttoned Sophie's shirtwaist and peeled back the sleeve, exposing the wound on her arm. "Holy cats."

"What is it?"

"You didn't get this from a falling tree limb. You've been shot."

"But—" Sophie turned her head and peered at the fiery red welt that ran from her shoulder to her elbow.

"The bullet grazed you. Lucky you were wearing your heavy cloak or it would have been worse." Gillie poured water into a basin, dampened a small towel, and touched it to the wound. Sophie clenched her teeth and drew in a sharp breath. The towel felt like sandpaper against her raw skin. Her eyes watered.

"There." Gillie finished cleaning the wound, then opened her medical bag and took out a jar of salve. "This will sting for a moment, but then you'll feel much better."

Sophie braced for the application of the salve, then watched as Gillie expertly bandaged her wound. "What about Mr. Worth?"

"Dr. Spencer is tending to him. Soon as I finish this, I'll check on him." Gillie tied off the bandage and helped Sophie button her shirtwaist. "What on earth were you doing at Blue Smoke in the middle of the night?"

"It wasn't the middle of the night when we started. Julian Worth asked me to go with him. He wants to talk to Ethan, but Ethan doesn't want to hear it."

"I see."

"I wish Ethan would listen. It might resolve a lot of things for him. I hate to see him so closed up inside. He's a wonderful man."

Gillie replaced the lid on the salve jar and smiled. "I think there's more to your feelings than mere admiration."

Sophie nodded. "I love him. I think he has feelings for me too, but something always gets in the way of his declaring them."

"He's only waiting for the right moment to tell you."

Sophie sat up on the cot and brushed her hair away from her face. "What makes you so sure?"

"When you fainted, he scooped you up and carried you in here. I've never seen a man look so worried, or so besotted either." Gillie grinned. "He kissed you when he thought I wasn't looking."

"He kissed me? And I missed the whole thing. Just my luck."

"Don't worry. Something tells me you'll have plenty of opportunities to enjoy his affections."

"I must look awful." Sophie fished for her hairpins and tried to impose some semblance of order upon her thick mane. "Be honest. Do I look as terrible as I feel?"

"You're definitely a little peaked, but that's to be expected." Gillie patted her hand. "I want you to rest here while I assist Dr. Spencer. I'll tell Mr. Heyward you're awake and good as new."

A door opened, and Gillie Gilman came down the hall, drying her hands on a white towel.

Ethan got to his feet. "How are they?"

"Dr. Spencer is finishing with Mr. Worth now."

"Is he—"

"Alive for the moment. The tourniquet helped, but he's lost a lot of blood. The bullet damaged a vein and shattered the bone." Gillie arched her back and briefly closed her eyes, and Ethan saw how exhausted she was. "It took awhile to pick out the fragments. I hope we got them all."

"Me too. What about Sophie?"

"A bullet grazed her shoulder. But she's fine. She's resting now."

"A bullet?" Shock and rage moved through him. "I ought to kill Crocker."

"Violence begets violence, Mr. Heyward." She crossed the room and opened the curtains, letting in the pale morning light. "Sheriff McCracken will deal with him."

Dr. Spencer came in, his trousers and shirt spattered with blood. "Mr. Heyward."

"How is he?"

"Sleeping. I've given him enough laudanum to keep him quiet for several hours."

"But he will be all right?"

"If we're lucky, and if sepsis doesn't set in. His thigh bone is blown to smithereens. He also had a bad concussion when his head hit the ground, but it's the leg I'm most concerned about. Even if he pulls through this, I'm afraid Mr. Worth won't ever walk normally."

"May I see him?"

The doctor shrugged. "He won't know the difference, but it

certainly won't do any harm." He turned to his assistant. "I'm dead on my feet, and so are you. Go on home, Gillie."

"I want to stay with Sophie."

"I'll stay," Ethan said.

The doctor consulted his pocket watch. "Nearly seven. I need to clean up and get something to eat. I'll be back soon."

"Take your time. I'll watch over them."

They left. Ethan walked down the hall and peered into the room where Julian lay, the curtains drawn against the light. A sharp medicinal smell permeated the air. He stood for a moment in the heavy silence, watching the rise and fall of Julian's chest, then closed the door and went to find Sophie.

TWENTY-FIVE

Ethan opened the door and peered in. Sophie lay curled onto her side, sleeping softly, her fist beneath her chin. The sight of the thick bandage beneath her sleeve sent another surge of anger coursing through him. If Crocker wanted to shoot at him, fine. But none of this was her fault.

She stirred and opened her eyes. "Ethan."

"Sorry to wake you."

"I was just resting my eyes."

He smiled. So like her to deny any vulnerability.

She sat up and scooted her feet along the floor, looking for her shoes.

"Here. Let me help." He crossed the room, fished her shoes from beneath the infirmary cot, and helped her with the tiny buttons, trying to ignore the effect the sight of her small delicate feet had on him.

She put her hands up and fussed with her hair. "I'm a fright."

"You look fine. I'm sorry you got into the middle of my feud with Lutrell Crocker."

"How is your brother?"

His stomach lurched. "So you know about Julian and me?"

"Yes."

"How much did he tell you?"

"Only that you think he committed murder. He says that he can prove he didn't, but you won't listen."

"You disapprove."

"I think one should always give another the benefit of the doubt." She thought of her one and only conversation with her mother. "Even if you are disappointed in the end."

Ethan held the door for her, and they went down the hall to Julian's room. "You're right. I've been sitting here all night, and I finally realized that. When Julian wakes up—if he wakes up—I'll listen to his evidence."

"You sound as if you don't want to be proven wrong."

"I suppose it's never easy to have one's assumptions challenged, but it's time. I see that now."

He opened the door to Julian's room and they went in. Sophie moved to open the curtains, but Ethan stopped her with an upraised hand. "I want to tell you everything. It'll be easier in the darkness."

"All right."

He motioned her to a chair and leaned against the door frame, ankles and arms crossed. "Promise you won't hate me."

"I don't think I could," she said, her voice soft, "even if I wanted to."

"All right then." He focused on Julian's face and began.

"Julian is nine years older than I am. As a boy, I couldn't remember a time when he wasn't around. His mother, Martha, looked after my mother at Ravenswood. Mother allowed Martha and Julian to sleep in the house instead of the servants' quarters. She taught Martha to sew. And to read—a secret she took to her grave because my father would surely have disapproved or forbidden it.

"Julian was the only boy his age who was not sent to the fields every morning. Father allowed him to remain behind, and

I thought he did it for my sake. My only sister died when I was five, and he saw how lonely I was. Then one day I overheard my parents arguing and realized that my father and Martha were in fact Julian's parents. Though, of course, he denied Julian his name."

Sophie nodded. "That must have been a shock."

"It was. I was furious with Father for betraying my mother. But after my parents died and I grew older, I realized I had no memories of ever seeing affection pass between them." A long sigh escaped his lips. "I don't know, Sophie. Perhaps my mother was aware of my father's assignation and turned a blind eye. Perhaps she even encouraged it. She wouldn't have been the first woman of her station to do so."

Julian made a soft moaning sound and they both turned, watching and waiting until he quieted.

"Julian knew about his mother and my father. We talked about it one time, and he made me promise never to mention it again. He resented the fact that I was denied nothing while he and his mother lacked for almost everything."

"Even so," Sophie said, keeping her voice low, "resentment is not the same thing as murder. What made you think Julian was responsible?"

"Because I saw him. Or I thought I saw him . . ." Ethan's voice faltered, and he began again.

"When the war came, we heard rumors of slave uprisings, of plantation owners being killed in their beds. It happened to my mother's second cousins, the Witherspoons. Union soldiers were riding through the countryside, setting fire to everything, urging the slaves to revolt, promising them their freedom. But somehow we never thought such violence would touch our home. Then one morning it did."

Despite the intervening years, the memories of that day

overtook him with such force that he couldn't speak. He balled his fists and swallowed hard until his composure returned.

"Go on, Ethan." Sophie's calm gaze found his. She folded her hands and waited, her green eyes bright with unshed tears.

"That morning started out like any other. The overseer, Jonas Carpenter, came to the door to tell Mother that several of the slaves were too sick to work. One was about to deliver a child. Mother gathered her things and went down to the quarters to tend to them. Father finished reading his paper and retired to his study to work on his account books. Julian and I went fishing, but nothing was biting. After a while we got bored. He said, 'I'll race you home,' and took off down the road.

"I tried to catch him, but he was older and faster, and I lost sight of him. I'd heard him talk about a shortcut through some woods behind the slave cemetery. Mother had told me to stay away from there, but that day I decided to try it. Julian had been teasing me all morning about not being able to keep up with him, and I figured the shortcut might put me back home ahead of him.

"Later I asked myself a million times why. Why that day of all days did I make that choice? If only I had taken the road, I wouldn't have been delayed by the two Yankee soldiers who appeared out of nowhere. They stopped me and asked all kinds of questions that scared me half to death. Then they finally got tired of terrorizing me and told me to get on home. When I got to the yard, the slaves had left the fields and were running in every direction. Yankees were helping them load wagons with things from the house—my mother's settee, the painting my father kept above the fireplace in his library, even the wooden rocking horse that my mother still kept in the nursery. I wondered where the overseer was, where my father was, why he wasn't making any attempt to stop them.

"I ran inside, calling for my parents. I looked into every room downstairs and couldn't find them. Then I went up to their bed-rooms, and—"

Sophie's face paled. She slowly shook her head. "No."

Ethan swallowed the burn of tears in his throat. "Father was lying in the hallway, facedown. Mother was in her room, partially hidden behind the curtains. Her head was turned to the wall, and I could see blood flowing from a wound in her chest. I screamed. Then Julian stepped out of the shadows, holding a knife.

"He said, 'I didn't do it.' He dropped the knife and ran. And that was the last time I saw him until this summer when he showed up at Blue Smoke."

"No wonder you were so shocked." Sophie shifted in her chair. "I know it looks as if he's guilty, but can you blame him for running away? He'd have been lynched on the spot—or given a kangaroo trial and then lynched. Even if he is innocent, he did the only thing he could have done to save his own life."

Ethan's shoulders slumped. "I know that now. But why come back after all this time, when it's too late?"

"It's never too late for reconciliation. For forgiveness. Julian wants you to know the truth for your sake as much as for his." She glanced at Julian. "If he—"

Shouting erupted in the street, stopping her words. Ethan opened the curtain and peered out onto a chaotic scene. People were running toward the opposite end of the road, voices raised in fear. Wagons rattled along the street. A whistle blew.

"What the devil?" Ethan glanced at his brother. Julian was still in a deep sleep. He grabbed Sophie's hand. "Let's go."

At the front entrance to the infirmary, they collided with a red-faced and breathless Caleb Stanhope.

"Sophie!" he yelled. "Come on. The *Gazette* is on fire."

Sophie lifted her skirts and sprinted down the road, dodg-ing knots of curious onlookers. Men carrying buckets and shovels elbowed her aside and rushed toward the fire. She reached the main street ahead of Ethan and pushed through the growing crowd.

Black smoke rolled from the roof. Flames snaked along the sides of the *Gazette* building and curled toward the windows. Heat waves shimmered along the boardwalk. Someone had organized a bucket brigade stretching from the *Gazette* to Mr. Tanner's livery on the opposite side, bringing water from the horses' troughs to douse the fire.

A water wagon from the railway station rattled up the street. Ethan climbed up. He and Sheriff McCracken dipped buckets into the big water barrels and tossed them onto the flames while Caleb and Robbie shoveled dirt onto the smoldering boardwalk.

Sophie sank to her knees and let the tears come. So many months of work and effort, gone. Any chance of paying Wyatt and Ada back, of making the *Gazette* into the kind of paper she could be proud of, gone. Maybe she deserved it. Maybe she'd been too sure of herself. Maybe . . .

She wept for Ethan, for his lost innocence and for his long, lonely grief. Her tears flowed for Julian too, for his damaged life, and now for the infirmity that would always be his to bear.

A cheer arose and she looked up. The fire was out. Part of the roof was caved in and one of the windows had shattered in the heat, but at least the building wasn't a total loss. Ethan, his face blackened with soot and grime, sought her gaze and sent her a crooked smile—half sympathy, half triumph. For some reason, she felt better.

Lucy rushed over from the Verandah, the ties of her blue checked apron flapping behind her. "I was in the bath when I heard the commotion. What on earth happened?"

Sophie shook her head and waved one hand toward the burned-out building. Lucy put her arm around Sophie's shoulder, then drew back. "Mercy, what's that under your shirtwaist?"

"A bandage. I got between a stray bullet and a drunken work-man up at Blue Smoke." Briefly, she filled Lucy in on the night's events.

Lucy shook her head. "A shooting and a fire in the same night. I'm sure I do not know what this town is coming to."

Caleb pushed through the crowd. "Sophie, are you all right?"

"I suppose." She felt faint again and completely disoriented. What day was this? When had she last eaten? She couldn't remember.

"The good news is that the presses aren't damaged. We'll be down for a while, but Ethan says the building can be salvaged and made good as new."

"But surely my files, my typewriting machine, our type trays, our paper and ink are all damaged or gone." She shrugged. "I haven't the money to replace those things, let alone pay for the building repairs." She placed one hand on Caleb's arm. "I couldn't ask for a more able assistant, and I appreciate everything you've done. We gave it a good try, but—"

"Wait a minute. You're saying you're giving up? Just because of a bit of bad luck?"

She laughed. "A bit of bad luck? My advertisers have deserted me, thanks to Mr. Blakely. Mr. McClure has rejected most of the articles I submitted to his syndicate. I have hardly any money left in the bank. And now this. I'd say that's more than a bit of bad luck."

Lucy patted her hand. "When bad things happened to me, Aunt Maisie would say God uses everything that happens for the good. He sees every sparrow that falls. That's what got me through the bad days when my Jake died."

Sophie dropped her gaze, feeling suddenly ashamed. The fire was another bad blow, no two ways about it. But Lucy's loss, and Ethan's, were much worse than the loss of paper and ink. And

Wyatt would be more disappointed if she quit than if she kept trying and failed. She could almost hear his soft drawl in her ear. *"When you fall off a horse, darlin', there's nothing to do but dust off your britches and climb right back on."*

"All right." Though she felt about a hundred years old, she smiled at Caleb. "Let's find out just how bad the damage is and make a list of what we need in order to get up and running again. We'll find the money somehow."

Caleb grinned, his teeth stark white against his soot-smudged face. "Yes, ma'am. I'll get right on it."

The crowd dispersed. The water-wagon driver vaulted onto the wagon seat and headed to the railway station. Mr. Pruitt caught Sophie's eye and nodded before returning to the mercantile. Lucy patted her back as Mariah Whiting and Jeanne Pruitt hurried over.

"My dear," Mrs. Whiting murmured. "I am so terribly sorry. Is there anything we can do?"

"If you need anything from the mercantile, you just say the word," Mrs. Pruitt said. "Jasper will set you up a tab."

"That's very kind." Sophie smiled at the dress shop owner. "I'm sure I'll have a list of necessities once I've had time to think."

"You are going to keep the *Gazette* going, aren't you?" Mrs. Pruitt asked. "Me and my sisters look forward to reading the Answer Lady every week."

Mrs. Whiting nodded. "It's the first thing I read each week too. I'd miss it if you stopped."

Sophie smiled. "I hope to keep the paper going, Mrs. Pruitt, but with the loss of my advertising revenue—"

"That's another thing—and please call me Jeanne. I've been meaning to stop by and tell you that I, for one, have had just about enough of Horace Blakely telling me and everyone else in this town what we can and cannot do. Christmas is coming, and I've got a lot of pretty things in the shop that ladies need to know about. If you get that paper of yours going again, I aim to take out an advertisement notice, and Mr. Horace High-and-Mighty Blakely can like it or lump it."

Lucy and Mariah Whiting burst into laughter. Mrs. Whiting patted Jeanne's arm. "I've known you for twenty years, and I believe that's the longest speech I've ever heard from you."

"Well, that Blakely fellow gets my dander up." Jeanne brushed cinders off her sleeves. "The very idea that he thinks he can tell me what to do just because of that fancy hotel of his makes me madder than a wet hen."

"Come on, little hen," Mrs. Whiting said. "I need you to finish pinning up my hem."

Lucy took Sophie's arm. "And you, my friend, need a nice warm bath and a good, long nap."

"I am tired," Sophie said. "But someone should check on Mr. Worth. He's alone in the infirmary."

She looked around for Ethan, but he had gone.

TWENTY-SIX

"Mr. Heyward, you busy?"

Ethan looked up from his ledger to find Joel Tipton standing in the office doorway, lunch-bucket in hand. "Joel. Come on in."

Joel crossed the room and handed Ethan a smudged paper. "I worked out that estimate you wanted."

Ethan scanned the list. Lumber, nails, paint, glass—it added up, not to mention the labor costs. But the estimate could have been ten times the sum, and it wouldn't have made any difference. "Thanks. When can you start?"

"Next Monday ought to be good." He indicated the half dozen workmen hurrying about on the terrace. "Once we get those stones replaced, there won't be as much to do around here for a while. Aside from keeping everything in good shape, of course."

Ethan nodded. In the three days since Julian's injury and the fire at the *Gazette*, his small crew had replaced the shattered glass in his office door and repaired the damaged lock. Now they were replacing the bloodstained stones on the terrace, matching them stone by stone. All visible traces of the shooting soon would be erased, but the events had left an indelible mark on Ethan's soul.

Joel shifted his weight and glanced out the window. "Heard

some talk this morning down at the depot. Fellow said he heard Sheriff McCracken arrested Lutrell Crocker last night."

Ethan's gut twisted. "I hadn't heard. But I hope it's true. Lutrell has a lot to answer for."

"Yes, sir, I reckon so." Joel stroked his beard. "How is that fellow that got shot? I heard he was in a bad way."

"He lost a lot of blood, but the doctor thinks he'll make it." Ethan swallowed the unexpected knot in his throat and again thanked God for sparing his brother. "He won't ever walk without a cane, though."

"I just don't understand such meanness. Lutrell is lucky he won't be sent up for murder." Joel indicated the list. "You want me to go on and order those materials? I've got to go to the mill this afternoon anyway."

"I'd appreciate it. Thanks."

"You're welcome." Joel went to the door, then turned back to Ethan, his hand on the cut-glass doorknob. "Me and the boys were talking last night, and, well . . . the truth is, we think you're too good-hearted for a place like Blue Smoke. And we liked the way you treated us when we worked on the infirmary. Me and Chester and them, we'd quit Blue Smoke and work for you, if you ever wanted us to."

Ethan smiled. "Thank you, Joel. That's good to know. I'll keep it in mind."

Joel left. Ethan stood, shrugging into his jacket. He picked up the season-end report he'd just finished and headed for Blakely's office. Horace had been in a foul mood since the shooting. Ethan wasn't looking forward to this meeting.

He headed down the hall, nodding to the Blakelys' daughters, who were returning from the riding stables, their cheeks and noses pink from the brisk wind. He passed the library, where the serving girls were pouring tea for five or six of Mrs. Blakely's friends seated in the overstuffed chairs oriented to catch the loveliest views. A fire hissed and crackled in the grate.

At the door to Horace's office, he squared his shoulders and knocked.

"Enter."

Ethan went in. His boss was still wearing his silk dressing gown, a cheroot clenched in his teeth. His breakfast tray, barely touched, sat on the edge of his massive polished walnut desk. Horace set aside his magazine and motioned Ethan into a chair.

"The boys got those bloody stones taken out yet?"

"They're working on it now. They'll finish soon."

"Let's hope so. Mrs. Culpepper is arriving this afternoon with a few friends. She wants to host a chestnut roast and some fool costume party for Thanksgiving."

Ethan winced at the mention of the resort's most difficult guest. Elvira Culpepper had arrived in late June and stayed all summer, hosting groups of her friends who arrived almost weekly by train from Baltimore or Richmond or New York. The woman seemed to possess unlimited money and an enormous capacity for demanding the most outlandish things. Ethan had been relieved when the season ended and she packed up and went home. Now she was back, acting as if Blue Smoke was her own private residence.

"Isn't it a bit chilly to be hosting an outdoor affair?"

Horace shrugged and picked up his coffee cup. "It's her money and her posterior that will be affected. Not mine." He downed his coffee and held out his hand. "That the final report?"

Ethan handed him the papers and watched a couple of squirrels chasing along the lawn while Horace, wire spectacles perched on the end of his florid nose, perused every jot and tittle.

"How come the gift shop revenue is down so much?"

"Miss Swint has closed her photography hut on the ridge until we reopen in the spring."

"So? What's that got to do with the sale of doodads and such?"

"When we opened the hut, you told me to account for her sales in the gift shop report. If you consider the figures apart from her sales, you'll see the income remained constant over the season." Ethan leaned over Horace's shoulder and tapped the paper. "Our handmade items sold very well, especially the quilt tops and the wooden toys. We ought to consider paying our craftsmen a bit more next season."

"Pay them more? Why should I?"

"When you're standing in the shade, you ought to remember the one who planted the tree. The way I see it, the folks whose labor is responsible for our success ought to share in it."

Horace snorted. "That's why you'll never be a millionaire, Ethan. You're too softhearted."

A pang of regret moved through Ethan. If only he'd been more softhearted toward Julian, his brother might not be lying in the infirmary, his leg permanently damaged. Suppose Julian really was innocent? How could Ethan possibly make amends?

Horace took off his spectacles and set aside the report. "I understand Eli McCracken's got Crocker locked up."

"I heard that too. Maybe Lutrell can shed some light on the fire at the *Gazette* office."

Horace looked up. "You think he's responsible?"

"Eli told me he thinks the fire was set, but of course he can't prove anything."

"Why would Crocker do a thing like that?"

Ethan shrugged. "A man is capable of almost anything when he's in his cups. And Lutrell seems to stay that way most of the time."

Horace took up his cheroot and puffed to get it going again, sending a cloud of smoke drifting toward the ceiling. "Well, I'm sorry that stranger got shot. But the truth is, Crocker did us a favor."

"What are you talking about?"

"Can you imagine the sensationalistic stories that girl would have written about the goings-on up here? Preaching about how it isn't a fit environment for the workers and so on? Exhorting me to do something about the unbridled violence at Blue Smoke?" Horace took another long draw on his cheroot. "She's a pretty little thing, but so full of high-mindedness."

Ethan nodded. Sophie's belief in the power of words, her passionate sense of fairness, were among the many qualities he'd come to love about her.

Horace shook his head. "She hasn't any idea how the real world works. I'm sure Miss Caldwell was upset, watching her building going up in flames, and I do sympathize, but it's a lucky break for us, Ethan. Maybe now she'll head on back to Texas and stop meddling in my affairs."

Anger spurted through Ethan's veins, heating his blood. "Then you'll be disappointed to learn that the damage to her presses is minimal. As soon as the building can be repaired, she'll be back in business."

"Well, with her advertising clients cut off, she won't last long. Besides, she'll need a work crew. Where's she going to get boys willing to cross me for the sake of one measly little repair job?"

Ethan thought of the money Sophie soon would be earning through her Blue Smoke magazine work, once he had the chance to tell her about it. Once the contract was signed, her income would be assured. And if he had learned anything about the people of Hickory Ridge, it was that they pulled together to help out a person in need. He had a sneaking suspicion that some of her lost advertising clients just might make their way back to the *Gazette* office once it was up and running again, despite Horace's ban. He thought of Joel's offer to quit Blue Smoke and come to work for him. "You might be surprised. About a lot of things."

"What in blue blazes are you talking about?"

Ethan headed for the door. "I've got a crew all lined up and the materials on order. I'm seeing to the repair myself."

Horace rose from his desk, rattling the delicate bone china on his breakfast tray. "You're turning against me? Against Blue Smoke? After all I've done for you?"

"I've given you a good day's work for every day I've been here."

Horace frowned. "Just whose side are you on, Heyward?"

Ethan pictured Sophie's dear face the way it had looked in the light of the dancing flames, so full of worry, defeat, and fear. He paused, one hand on the doorknob.

"Hers."

TWENTY-SEVEN

Sophie burrowed into the folds of her borrowed coat and tilted her head, watching Joel Tipton and two other men walking gingerly across her burned-out roof. The sounds of hammers and saws filled the air as the men removed the charred timbers and cut new ones. Caleb and Mr. O'Brien were busy carting the old timbers to a waiting wagon and helping hoist the new ones onto the roof.

Down below, Ethan and Jasper Pruitt lifted a new window into place. Sophie watched as Ethan tapped his hammer, patiently setting the new window into its frame. Behind her, Mariah Whiting, Carrie Rutledge, and Robbie's wife, Ethelinda, were busy setting out platters of fried chicken from Miss Hattie's, dozens of homemade dishes, and baskets of bread from the bakery.

The morning train chuffed into the station and a steady stream of travelers surged toward the platform. Now that Blue Smoke had closed for the season, a number of the waiters, gardeners, stableboys, kitchen helpers, and housekeepers had headed home until spring. Most of the ladies from the Verandah were already gone; only Flora and Merribelle had nowhere else to go. Lonely for them, perhaps, but Sophie was grateful for their company. The old hotel seemed too quiet already without the constant squeak of the stairs, the groaning of the water pipes, and the residents' friendly banter.

Sheriff McCracken ambled up the street, his coattails flapping in the sharp November wind. He sent Sophie a crooked smile. "Morning, Miss Caldwell."

"Sheriff." With a sweep of her hand, she took in the busy scene. "Can you believe all this?"

"Doesn't surprise me in the least. We look after our own." He pushed his hat to the back of his head. "Believe me, when word got around about the fire, I got an earful from the ladies. They're ready for me to hang Lutrell Crocker from the nearest tree."

Sophie nodded. "For shooting Mr. Worth."

"Nope. For nearly burning down the Answer Lady's office."

Her stomach dropped. "Mr. Crocker is responsible for this?"

"He confessed, though he claims it was an accident."

Just then Gillie arrived. She jumped from her rig and crossed the street, her hands jammed into her pockets. "Sophie, I have big news. Hello, Sheriff."

He tipped his hat. "Miss Gilman. I reckon I ought to give the boys a hand hoisting those rafters."

"I appreciate your help, Sheriff McCracken," Sophie said. "And thanks for telling me about Mr. Crocker. I feel better knowing who is responsible for this fine mess." She paused. "May I ask a favor?"

"Go ahead."

"Would you please not mention this to Wyatt and Ada? It's over now, and I'm all right, and it would only worry them to think someone wanted to burn me out. I'll write to them later, after I'm up and running again."

"If that's what you want." The sheriff took a small leather pouch from inside his coat. "I almost forgot. Caleb Stanhope said you were looking for this."

Her fingers closed over Julian's missing evidence. Maybe now he could prove his innocence, and Ethan would regain one small part of his lost family. Did he truly realize how important that one connection could be?

Sheriff McCracken joined Joel and the other men who were nailing new rafters into place. Ethan and Jasper finished with the window and starting picking up their tools. The clang of hammers, Ethan's low banter, and Jasper's raspy laugh filled the air. So much busyness, so much generosity, gave Sophie hope. Maybe the paper would survive after all. Maybe she'd try Mr. McClure's syndicate again.

She grinned at Gillie. "What's your news?"

"You first. What did the sheriff want?"

"Mr. Crocker, the would-be assassin, confessed to burning my building. He claims he didn't mean to do it."

Gillie whistled softly. "Do you believe that?"

"It's possible. He was stinking drunk that night. I'm surprised he remembers anything."

"He's probably trying to avoid a longer stretch in jail," Gillie said. "Daddy says Judge Madison is much harsher than old Judge Blackburn was. Maybe this Crocker fellow thinks he'll get a shorter sentence if he admits to everything."

"Maybe." Sophie clutched the leather pouch. Should she wait until Julian was stronger and return it to him, or should she hand it over to Ethan?

Gillie snapped her fingers. "Are you listening to me?"

"Sorry. What?"

"I delivered a baby last night all on my own. A strapping boy. Mother and son are in fine fettle over at the infirmary. I was just about to go out there to check on them and on Mr. Worth."

"That's wonderful, Gillie. Congratulations. Is Mr. Worth any better?"

"He managed to sip some broth yesterday, and he was awake for most of the morning. Dr. Spencer has weaned him off the laudanum. We are much encouraged."

"That's good news."

Gillie nodded. "He's worried about his little boy back home."

"Ethan wired Julian's wife about the accident. We're waiting for a reply about his son. I do hope the boy is all right."

"Sophie?" Ethelinda Whiting made her way through the small knot of women gathering near the food tables. "Mariah wonders if you can give us a hand."

"Of course. I'll be right there."

"I should go check on my new patients," Gillie said as Ethelinda bustled away. "I stopped to ask whether you'll come out to the farm for Thanksgiving. Mother has planned enough food to feed the Confederate army. All my dreary cousins will be there, and I'm sure Mother will round up some more gentlemen in hopes of finding a suitable husband for me. I could use a friend to help me ward them off."

Sophie laughed. "You're the only girl I know who's trying desperately *not* to find a husband."

Gillie blushed and lowered her voice. "Can you keep a secret? There is someone I like, but I know my parents won't approve."

"Caleb Stanhope?"

Gillie's eyes widened. "How did you know?"

"A lucky guess."

"I don't believe you." Gillie clutched Sophie's arm. "Has he said anything? About his feelings for me, I mean."

A couple of workmen brushed past them carrying boxes of nails, perfuming the air with the smells of sweat and new wood. Sophie wrinkled her nose as they passed. "Mr. Stanhope thinks most highly of you. He's afraid you might find him unsuitable."

"Oh, that dear man! But what should I do? I can't very well

walk up and declare my feelings, can I? You're the Answer Lady. Give me some advice."

"I'm afraid I'm not very good at giving advice in matters of the heart." Sophie looked for Ethan and spotted him standing with Joel near the water buckets, dipper in hand. Joel said something that made Ethan laugh, and Sophie's breath caught. Despite all her troubles, she couldn't stop imagining a life with Ethan.

"I see," Gillie said. "You don't know what to do about the love of your life either."

"It's confusing. He loves me—I'm sure of that. Though he hasn't precisely said so." Sophie sighed, thinking of everything that had happened between them, everything that they still didn't know about one another. "Perhaps he simply can't imagine a future with me."

"I think you worry far too much," Gillie said. "Ethan's had a lot on his mind lately repairing the infirmary, and then poor Mr. Worth's injury, and then the fire. Not to mention taking care of his work at Blue Smoke." Gillie grinned. "However, you are fairly irresistible, so I imagine Mr. Heyward will come around sooner or later."

"Maybe." Sophie glanced toward the food tables. "I should go help the ladies get dinner ready."

"And I must check on my new mother and help Dr. Spencer change Mr. Worth's dressings. But do say you'll come out for Thanksgiving. I need some reason to get out of bed that day."

Sophie laughed. "I promised Lucy I'd go to church with her and Flora on Thursday morning. But I could drive out after that, if it isn't too late."

"Heavens, no. We won't get to eat until three at the earliest." Gillie started for her rig. "Tell Mr. Heyward he's invited too."

"What am I invited to?" Ethan's breath was soft on her ear.

Sophie spun around. "You startled me."

"Sorry. I was trying to see Miss Gilman before she got away. Is there any news about Julian?"

Sophie gave him Gillie's report and handed him the leather pouch. "The sheriff recovered this. From Mr. Crocker, I presume."

She watched Ethan run his fingers over the smooth leather. How could he bear not to open it, to see for himself the evidence of Julian's innocence—if, indeed, that was what it contained? But he tucked it into his coat pocket, the expression in his eyes unreadable. "Do you have a moment?"

"I must help the ladies with the food, but I can spare a few moments."

"Then I'll be quick. Remember when I told you I had a plan to help you recover your lost revenue?"

"I remember. But it's been so long, I thought you might have forgotten."

"I never forget a promise, Sophie."

Briefly, he told her about the articles he needed for the magazines. "Horace told me to take care of it, and you're the best writer I know. So the job is yours if you want it."

"Of course I want it! Ethan, I can't thank you enough."

"Believe me, the pleasure is all mine." He paused. "I've got the contracts ready for you. But I want to see Julian this afternoon. Will you come with me?" His voice cracked, and she saw just how much he wanted to make things right with his brother.

"I'll come with you."

He squeezed her hand and went to join Joel, Jasper, Caleb, and the others who had finished repairing the hole in the roof. Ethan took off his hat and stood back, his coat unbuttoned, one hip cocked, and admired their handiwork. She couldn't help noticing that Flora and Merribelle had stopped their preparations to admire him.

Well, she could hardly blame them. Even in dusty dungarees and a faded work shirt, his sleeves rolled to his elbows despite the chill, Ethan Heyward was the most appealing man in Hickory Ridge. And the kindest. And the most complicated.

Sophie helped Mrs. Whiting and the others set out stacks of plates and uncover the platters and bowls of food, but her thoughts were for Ethan and his estranged brother.

After so many years of bitterness and hate, could they find a way home?

TWENTY-EIGHT

By the time the men were fed and the empty bowls and platters stacked away, the sun had slipped behind the mountain and the wind picked up, bringing with it the smells of wood smoke and rain.

While Ethan helped Joel and his crew load their wagons, Sophie helped Ethelinda pack the last of the food. She held one end of a long tablecloth while Ethelinda folded it in halves and then in halves again.

"I'm so glad the damage to your office wasn't worse," Ethelinda said. "Robbie was frantic when he saw the smoke billowing." Her eyes met Sophie's. "He's very fond of you."

"As I am of him. Even as a boy, he was kind and thoughtful. His friendship was a gift to me in those days."

"I hope it still is."

"Of course." Sophie handed Ethelinda the folded tablecloth and picked up a blue-and-white checked one. "He's a talented preacher. His sermons always give me food for thought." She smiled. "Wyatt used to say Robbie could talk the legs off a mule. I wasn't a bit surprised to learn he studied law. He'd have made a fine lawyer too."

"Yes, but I'm very glad he chose the ministry. I feel I can be more useful to him than if he were writing up wills and deeds and such."

Sophie watched Joel, Caleb, and Jasper head for home. Most of the ladies were packing up too, loading baskets and dishes into wagons and rigs. Ethelinda drew her shawl around her shoulders and picked up the folded tablecloths. "I think that does it. I should be getting home."

"Thank you for helping with this."

Ethelinda nodded. "I'll see you in church tomorrow—and Thanksgiving too?"

Sophie smiled. "I'll be there. I'm looking forward to it."

Ethelinda hurried away, passing Ethan, who touched the brim of his hat as he headed toward Sophie.

"Ready to go?"

"In a minute." Sophie stood with her hands in her coat pockets and studied her building. Once the new wood was painted and her new typewriting machine, paper, and ink arrived, she could begin publishing again. It would take the last of her savings to do so, but the fire had taught her just how committed she was to this community and to the paper. She couldn't quit just because the job had become harder.

"God will provide," Ada often said. He would provide for her now.

She took Ethan's arm. He helped her into his rig, and in the growing darkness they drove the short distance to the infirmary. Ethan guided the horse through the wrought-iron gate. Gillie's rig, and Dr. Spencer's, stood in the side yard. Lamplight glowed in the first-floor windows.

Dr. Spencer met them in the entry hall. "Evening, Miss Caldwell. Mr. Heyward."

Ethan shook the doctor's hand. "How is he?"

"He had a slight fever this morning, but it seems to have abated. I'm still treating his wound with the carbolic acid compresses. They're painful, I'm afraid, but necessary. Miss Gilman tells me his appetite has returned. A good sign."

Ethan let out a long sigh. "That's good news. But isn't there anything we can do to hasten his recovery?"

Dr. Spencer passed a hand over his tired-looking face. "I'm afraid not, son. Unfortunately, a soft lead bullet like that tends to inflict the most damage to human flesh. Mr. Worth is over the worst of it, but his wound will have to heal on its own. What he needs now is bed rest and good food. Time will take care of—"

A blast of cold air interrupted him as the door flew open to admit an anxious-looking young man.

"May I help you?" the doctor asked.

"Oh. No. I mean yes! That is, my wife had a baby yesterday, and I'm here to take 'em home. If you think it's all right."

"It's fine." The doctor pointed down the long hallway. "First door on the right. I think my assistant is with them now."

"I can't thank you enough," the new father said. "We lost a baby before we moved to Hickory Ridge. My wife was afraid it would happen again. I'm glad we had the infirmary this time."

He headed down the hall, and the doctor retrieved his coat, hat, and medical bag. "If you folks will excuse me, I think I'll go on home. I was up half of last night with the Purdys' little girl and out at the lumber mill all morning tending to Davy Blevins." He shook his head. "The boy got careless with the saw and nearly severed a couple fingers."

The young father and his wife came down the hallway, the baby swaddled and tucked into the crook of his mother's arm. Gillie, grinning from ear to ear, followed them. Sophie smiled, too, at her friend's happiness.

The young man paused, turning his battered felt hat around and around in his hands. "Doctor?"

"Yes?"

"I'm sure it's not the first time, but me and Anna want to name our boy Gilman Spencer, after the two of you. Because Miss

Gilman delivered him, and she says you're the one who taught her how to bring a baby into the world. We aim to call him Spence if that's all right with you."

The doctor smiled. "I'm honored. I hope he grows into a sturdy young man."

"Well, it's the first time a baby has been named for me," Gillie said, "and I think it's completely wonderful."

"Come on, honey." The new father ushered his little family into the darkness. Gillie, her arms folded across her chest, beamed at them.

"I'm going home," Dr. Spencer said, "before Eugenie forgets what I look like. Send for me if you need me, Gillie."

"I will."

"And congratulations on your first delivery. You did a fine job, as I knew you would."

"I had a good teacher."

"Just don't go thinking they will all be this easy. They won't."

"No, sir."

"Well, good night, all." The doctor pointed a finger at Ethan. "Don't keep Mr. Worth up too late. He needs his rest."

He left, the door slapping shut behind him.

"Mr. Worth is awake," Gillie said. "You can go on in. I'll be here awhile longer. Our salesman is due to arrive on tomorrow's train, so I need to inventory our supplies and make up a new order." She squeezed Sophie's arm. "I'll see you on Thanksgiving, I hope. You too, Mr. Heyward."

Ethan nodded. "Wouldn't miss it for anything."

Gillie disappeared into the office she shared with Doc Spencer. Ethan headed down the hall toward Mr. Worth's room and Sophie followed, her heart flailing like a bird in a box. Now that the leather pouch had been recovered, perhaps Mr. Worth could prove his innocence once and for all.

Ethan pushed open the door. Gillie had lit the lamp. Inside the clear glass globe, the flame burned blue and white-hot, its light giving Julian the appearance of a finely carved statue. He turned his head on the pillow and motioned them inside.

Without thinking, Sophie grasped Ethan's hand and felt it tremble. She squeezed, and he squeezed back before approaching the bed and pulling up a chair for her. He drew the curtains and perched on the deep windowsill, still wearing his woolen coat.

The brothers took each other's measure for a long moment before Ethan said, "How are you, Julian?"

"Tired. But the pain is better today." He hitched his shoulders. "Is there any word from home?"

Ethan shook his head. "I checked at the telegraph office earlier today. No news is probably good news. But I'll go by there again before the office closes and see if anything has come in."

"I appreciate it." Julian winced. "Today my head hurts worse than the bullet wound." He touched the thick bandage that covered most of his forehead and smiled at Sophie. "I heard you were wounded. Are you all right?"

"Fine."

"I owe you a great debt for taking care of me on the train."

"There wasn't much I could do."

"If I ruined your cloak, I'll gladly get you another."

She shook her head. "No harm done."

Ethan cleared his throat and produced the small leather pouch. "The sheriff returned this today."

Julian studied it for a long beat. Finally he said, "Have you opened it?"

"It isn't mine to open."

"Open it now," Julian said. "Over here by the lamp so you can see."

Ethan opened the pouch, took out a sheaf of papers and news clippings, and bent toward the light. Sophie watched his face as he read each one, slowly stacking them on the bed as he went. Did these few wrinkled pages hold the key to healing his past?

She thought of the diary Rosaleen had left to her. Of course it hadn't magically erased every bitter memory, every deep scar on her heart, but knowing the truth had set a part of her free. She now could accept her history with all its burdens and imperfections. If only Julian's papers would do the same for Ethan.

Ethan finished reading. He looked up and Sophie saw tears standing in his eyes. She glanced at Julian, who waited calmly, hands folded atop his coverlet.

"How long have you known this?" Ethan asked at last.

"I first got word of it a couple of years ago, when I went home for my mother's funeral."

"Martha is dead?"

Julian nodded. "It was quick. A shock to me, but a blessing really. Her mind was gone. She kept calling out for your mother. I think she imagined she was at Ravenswood. Back when we were boys together."

"Well, I'm sorry to hear that. She was a comfort to my mother for many years."

Julian didn't answer that. He turned to Sophie. "I heard you had a fire."

"Yes, but Ethan has seen to repairs. I hope to begin publishing the paper again very soon. Perhaps by Christmas, if my supplies arrive."

"What happened?"

"The sheriff thinks that the man who shot you is also responsible for the fire."

Julian shifted his injured leg and sighed. "My, my, I seem to have wreaked all sorts of havoc in pursuit of truth."

Ethan shrugged out of his coat and draped it across the foot of the bed. "You got the short end of that stick, Julian. I'm sorry you got mixed up in the dispute between Crocker and me. If I had listened to you when you first showed up back in June, none of this would have happened."

Julian lifted one shoulder. "I reckon everything happens for a reason, brother."

"Maybe." Ethan picked up the sheaf of papers and sorted through them again. "I knew the Yankees were responsible for destroying most of Georgia. But that day when I saw you in Mother's room holding that knife, after what had happened to our Witherspoon cousins, I assumed that you—"

"I know how it must have looked to you. Everything that day was in chaos." Julian closed his eyes, as if summoning the scene again. "By the time I beat you back to the house, they had already stolen everything out of the toolshed and the smokehouse. They slaughtered the chickens and turned the cattle out and started taking things out of the house. Paintings, silver, anything of value. Mr. Carpenter had run off. They told the field hands to load up wagons with everything they could carry. Told 'em all they were free to go."

"Father," Ethan said. "Where was he while this was happening?"

"I found him in the upstairs hallway, lying atop that pistol he kept in the library. I expect he was trying to fend off the Yankees when they shot him. Then I heard Miss Rachel scream and I ran into her room." Julian swallowed hard and glanced at Sophie. "This next part isn't fit for a lady's ears."

Sophie sat on the edge of her chair, trembling and near tears. She could well imagine what came next. She stole a glance at Ethan. He sat on the windowsill, his head bowed, his elbows on his knees.

She licked her lips. "Go on, Mr. Worth."

"I pushed open the door, and I saw one of the soldiers was . . . trying to have his way with her. I tried to scream, but my mouth was dry as cotton. Miss Rachel grabbed his arm, but he was a lot bigger than her and he . . . he cut her. At first she just looked surprised, and I thought, soon as he leaves, I can help her. But she made an awful choking sound, and then she just lay down on the floor like she was tired and taking a nap."

"Dear God," Ethan whispered.

"The soldier ran out of there, and I was thinking I'd go out the window, jump off the roof, and go get her some help, but then I heard footsteps on the stairs. I was scared that man was coming back and would kill me too. I grabbed the knife and hid behind Miss Rachel's curtains."

Gillie tapped on the door and stuck her head in. "Everything all right in here?"

Sophie nodded. "We're fine."

"I'm headed home. Don't keep my patient up too late."

She closed the door.

"That was where I found you," Ethan said to Julian, "standing behind Mother's curtains, holding a bloody knife."

"I could see the pure hate in your eyes," Julian said. "I knew you wouldn't believe me. And I knew if I stayed there I'd be hanged, no questions asked. So I ran."

"You're right. After what happened to our cousins, I wouldn't have believed you." Ethan smoothed the front of his dungarees. "Still, I wondered what became of you." He glanced at his brother. "We had some good times when we were boys. Before the war ruined everything."

"We sure did. 'Member the time we both got chicken pox and your mama made a fort for us out of her old blanket, and we nearly caught fire to it?"

"I forgot about that." Ethan sighed. "I tried to forget everything about Ravenswood and what happened there. I haven't set foot on Heyward land since the day Aunt Eulalie arrived to take me to her place in Baltimore."

"I heard that's where you went. Mama and I headed north too—Ohio first, and then Pennsylvania. When the war ended and freedom was official, she went back home to Georgia, but I didn't want anything to do with that place. I got a job stocking groceries and then went to school. After that I opened myself a bookshop on one of the fanciest streets in town."

"A bookshop? I never would have guessed."

"We were both more in love with fishing and climbing trees than books back in those days," Julian said. "After everything that happened, I suppose I buried myself in other people's stories so I wouldn't have to think about my own. Anyway, it suits me now."

Outside, the horse neighed and rattled his harness. Ethan peered out the window. "We should go soon."

"I am getting tired," Julian said, "but I want to tell you the rest of it."

"Go on."

Julian waved a hand toward the papers. "When I went home to bury Mama, I saw the article in the Atlanta paper about former Union soldiers who were finally being brought to justice for the atrocities they committed during the war." He looked up at Sophie, his ice-blue eyes glittering in the lamplight. "It's one thing to shoot an enemy on the battlefield. It's another to murder a helpless woman just for sport. I saw that one of the men, a Sergeant Hollis from Indiana, had confessed to burning out a family over in Cobb County about the same time as Father and Miss Rachel were killed. I figured he might have something to do with what happened at Ravenswood too, so I hung around till the trial. When he saw that he might be sent up for life for his crimes, he confessed to being at Ravenswood that day. And he named the murderer."

Ethan picked up the papers and shuffled them again. "Roscoe Peck?"

Julian nodded. "He died last year, but not before admitting his guilt. That paper there, the one with the seal on it, is signed by the priest and the judge who witnessed his confession. I've been trying to find you ever since."

Ethan smoothed the paper and shook his head. "All this time, I hated you. I hated myself for not saving them."

"We were boys, Ethan. They were grown men, soldiers with swords and guns. All the time I was on the run, I thanked God it was me who got home first that day, and not you."

"How did you track me down?"

"I remembered your mother had family in Baltimore. I took a trip out there and asked around. Someone remembered your aunt, but then I found out she's long dead as well."

"Yes, she died when I was sixteen."

"Last January I bought a bunch of books at an estate sale in Baltimore, and I went back to supervise the shipment. Got a couple of first editions, but I'm not inclined to part with them." Julian sighed and drew up his covers, and Sophie saw how much this long conversation had cost him.

"Ethan, maybe we could come back tomorrow."

"No," Julian said. "I'm tired, but I'll sleep better when this story is done." He sent her a wan smile. "After all, I've waited most of my life to tell it."

The lamp was nearly out. Wind whistled around the corner, rattling the iron gate outside. Sophie shifted in her chair and listened as Julian finished his story.

"I saw an article about Blue Smoke in the *Baltimore Sun*, and your name was listed as the manager for the whole thing. I came to the opening in June. You know the rest."

"I turned you away. I'm sorry. I should have listened."

"Mama used to say that when the learner is ready, the teacher will appear. Maybe that applies to truth telling too. Maybe it all happened to prepare your ears for this story." Julian sat up in the bed and clasped his brother's hand. "I'm glad your life turned out so well."

Ethan nodded.

"Listen," Julian said. "I understand this is a lot to take in all at once. And I don't expect we'll go back to being friends overnight. Maybe we never will. Too much to work out in your head. Too much water under the bridge. I'll be heading home to Philadelphia as soon as I'm fit to travel. But my door is open if you ever want to visit."

"Maybe I will."

"Anytime." Julian gathered up the papers and stuffed them back into the leather pouch. "I reckon I'll hold on to these. I've been a free man for more than twenty years, but still—" He gestured to Sophie. "Ethan, I expect you'd best get this lady home."

Ethan took Julian's hand. "I'm glad you told me. I'm sorry it came at such great cost."

"So am I. Now, get on away from here and let me sleep."

Ethan blew out the feeble flame in the lamp and they left the infirmary.

Sitting next to him on the short ride to the Verandah, Sophie snuggled into her cloak and thought about the beautiful and terrible ways people had of dealing with the past. Until now, she'd never thought about the layers of secrets, the complexities of human relationships, the subtexts and shadows of half-remembered lies and half-truths that separated people from each other. It was a wonder anyone survived it.

"Here we are." Ethan halted the rig and helped her out. "I'm glad you were there with me tonight. I hope the story wasn't too upsetting."

They walked up the steps to the door. The hotel was dark, save for a single lantern burning in the parlor window. "I'm sure it was much more difficult for you to relive such a terrible day."

"It was a long time ago. I'm all right, just tired. I need some time to think about things."

"Thank you for all you've done to repair the office. If you hadn't offered, I'd have had to shutter it for good, I'm afraid."

"Couldn't have that." He drew her into his arms and kissed her with her such longing that she would have sunk to the floor if he hadn't held her so closely. "I'll see you Thursday at the Gilmans'."

"All right." She clung to him a moment longer, savoring his strength and his warmth. If only such moments might last forever. At last she released him. "Good night, Ethan."

She went inside and stood at the parlor window watching his retreat. At the bottom of the steps he paused, one hand on the railing. Then he sank onto the steps, his shoulders heaving.

TWENTY-NINE

Thanksgiving morning dawned cold and damp. At first light, Sophie woke to the smells of frying bacon and coffee. Through the rain-smeared window, she watched veils of gray clouds drifting across the valley. Not the best day for a drive to the Gilmans' farm.

She dressed and went down to the kitchen to find Lucy at the stove in her stocking feet, a white apron protecting her Sunday dress.

"Good morning, Sophie." Lucy smiled as she poured coffee into a thick white mug. "Bacon and eggs?"

"Please." Sophie slid into her chair and took a sip of the scalding, bitter brew before adding sugar and a generous splash of cream. She helped herself to a biscuit from the basket on the table and reached for the butter plate.

Lucy slid a couple of eggs onto Sophie's plate. "There you go." She served her own plate and sat down. "Is Flora awake?"

Just then Flora Burke hobbled into the kitchen, her round face contorted with pain. She fell heavily into her chair and motioned for coffee.

Lucy poured. "What's the matter, Flora? Don't you feel well?"

"Something's wrong with my knee." Flora shifted sideways in her chair and lifted her skirts. "Look at it. It's all swole up, and it feels like there's a sack of water under my skin. It hurts to walk."

Lucy frowned. "Have you seen Dr. Spencer?"

"Certainly not." Flora smoothed her skirts and took a sip of coffee. "I'm not about to show that man my knees."

"I'm sure he's seen plenty of ladies' knees, Flora."

"Well, he ain't seein' mine." She took a deep breath and frowned. "I don't see how I can get to the church this morning. I could barely walk down the stairs just now."

Sophie finished her eggs and stood. "Flora, you can't suffer in silence. If you won't see the doctor, I'll ask Gillie to come here."

"Would you?" Flora shifted in her chair. "I sure would like something to make the pain go away."

Sophie gathered her coat, hat, and gloves and headed for the door. "I'll be back as soon as I can."

"Don't forget, church starts at eleven o'clock," Lucy said. "I'm sure it'll be packed today, and I want to get there early so I can sit down front and hear the preacher."

"So you can look at him, you mean," Flora said. "Can't blame you, though. Robbie Whiting is cute as a button."

"And married." Lucy arched her brows. "I'm surprised at you, Flora."

Flora shrugged, then winced and grabbed her bad knee.

Sophie took an umbrella from the stand beside the door. Leaving the Verandah, she hurried along the rain-slicked board-walk toward Gillie's tidy cottage, which sat behind the doctor's office.

She knocked and Gillie appeared, barefoot despite the chilly morning and still in her nightdress. The light coming through the window fell onto her flaxen hair, giving her the ethereal look of an angel. Her cheeks were pink, but Sophie noticed faint shadows beneath her eyes.

"Sophie! Come in out of this rain." Gillie ushered Sophie into a small parlor ajumble with books, papers, and medical journals.

A large bouquet of purple asters sat atop the tiny kitchen table. Gillie pushed her hair off her face. "What brings you out in this weather?"

Sophie folded her umbrella and shook the rain from her hair. "I've come about Flora Burke, over at the Verandah. Something's wrong with her knee and she refuses to see Dr. Spencer."

"I'll get dressed and see to her. I won't be long." Gillie disappeared into a small bedroom off the parlor, leaving the door open. "Have a seat, if you can find room."

Sophie perched on the edge of the floral settee and paged through a well-thumbed copy of *Scribner's Magazine* until Gillie appeared wearing a dark-blue dress with tight leg-o'-mutton sleeves trimmed in white lace.

Sophie looked up from the article she was reading. "Pretty fancy dress for making a house call."

"I won't have time to change before going home. Mother expected me last night, but the little Gibbons girl is sick, and I stayed with them until she felt better."

Gillie stood before her small mirror to pin her hat into place.

"Nothing serious, I hope," Sophie said.

"I don't think so. Mrs. Gibbons was worried that she might be coming down with croup, but luckily it was nothing more than a bad cold." Gillie picked up her medical bag. "Peppermint tea and a few drops of honey was all she needed. Now, let's go see what's ailing Flora."

They returned to the hotel. Flora had moved to the settee in the parlor, her swollen knee propped up on pillows. Lucy was in the kitchen, washing the breakfast dishes.

"Hello, Flora," Gillie said. "What's the problem here?"

"Take a look." Flora drew up her skirt, her expression glum.

Gillie probed Flora's knee until Flora sucked in a breath and jerked. "That hurts."

"I don't doubt it for a moment," Gillie said. "You've got housemaid's knee. It's common among ladies who spend a lot of time on their knees scrubbing and such."

Flora nodded. "Up at Blue Smoke the head housekeeper, Mrs. Ingram, made us scrub the floors every day whether they were dirty or not. Wouldn't let us use a mop either. She said hands and knees was the only way to be sure we got all the corners clean."

"You'll have plenty of time to recover before next season, but you might want to ask Mrs. Ingram for a different assignment next year," Gillie said. "In the meantime, you should apply warm, moist compresses and stay in bed for the next couple of days."

"But what about Thanksgiving? I was planning to eat with my cousins up in Muddy Hollow this afternoon."

Lucy came into the parlor, drying her hands on a red checked towel. "Don't worry, Flora. You can eat here with me. I have plenty of food. I'll invite Mrs. Riley and Mrs. Welty from church to share our meal too."

Flora brightened. "I reckon that'll be all right. Wouldn't want to miss my pumpkin pie." She smiled at Gillie. "Much obliged for coming to see me."

"No trouble." Gillie slid her arms into the sleeves of her coat. "Get started with those warm compresses and you'll feel better in a day or two."

Sophie walked Gillie to the door, and Gillie peered out. "Looks like the rain has stopped. I hope the road home won't be too muddy."

"Are you staying for church?" Sophie asked.

"I wish I could, but I promised Mother I'd help with her preparations and I'm already a day late. I'll see you this afternoon. You and the charming Mr. Heyward." She paused. "I've been wondering about inviting Caleb. I know he has a mother and two brothers at home, and I don't know whether he's coming into town today, but—"

"He said he might stop by the *Gazette* this morning. You could try catching him there."

"I don't want him to think I'm being too forward."

"Oh, I see what you mean," Sophie teased. "Heaven forbid he should think you like him."

Gillie blushed. "I think he might know. Did you see the flowers on my kitchen table?"

"Caleb brought them?"

Gillie nodded. "Last night, when I got home from the Gibbons' place, he was waiting on my front porch. I was going to invite him then, but I lost my nerve."

"My word, Sabrina Gilman. You have more nerve than any woman I know. You certainly wouldn't find me lancing boils and sewing up wounds."

"This is different."

"It's easy. Simply open your mouth and say, 'Mr. Stanhope, would you care to join my family and guests for Thanksgiving dinner?' Now you try."

Gillie burst into peals of laughter.

"What's so funny? They say Queen Victoria proposed marriage to Prince Albert. A dinner invitation pales in—"

"Sophie?" Lucy came into the parlor wearing her fanciest hat. "We should start for the church soon."

"I'm ready."

The three women left the Verandah. Sophie and Lucy turned toward the church. Gillie headed to Mr. Tanner's livery to retrieve her horse and rig.

As Lucy had predicted, the church was packed. Sophie followed her down the crowded aisle and squeezed into a pew next to Robbie's parents. Mrs. Whiting bobbed her head in greeting before turning around to speak to Carrie Rutledge, who was seated behind them. Carrie leaned forward and patted Sophie's shoulder.

"Happy Thanksgiving, my dear. I hope you aren't too homesick for Wyatt and Ada."

Sophie turned around. "I do miss them, but things have been so hectic here, I've had little time to dwell on it."

"No doubt. But I hear the newspaper will be up and running again soon," Mrs. Whiting said. "I, for one, am looking forward to having the Answer Lady back."

Ethelinda Whiting entered from the side door, took her place at the organ, and began to play. Voices softened and stilled.

Sophie closed her eyes. This silence before the start of the service was one of her favorite moments in the week. Sitting in the cool stillness of Robbie's church, she felt her spirit grow calm and her heart opening.

"Lord of heaven and earth," Robbie began, his voice rich with feeling, "give us a pure, still heart, a humble mind, and for every breath a thanksgiving and a song."

Sophie stood with the congregation as Robbie led the hymn. She imagined Wyatt and Ada worshipping at their church back home, Wade and Lilly beside them. No doubt Ada would wear her fanciest fall hat for the occasion, something trimmed with flowers and ribbons after the latest fashion. Last year she'd worn a tall, round hat adorned with burgundy velvet roses trimmed in gold cord. Wyatt teased her about it, but after the service, three of Ada's friends placed orders for similar hats and Ada teased him right back. What did he know about ladies' fashions?

As the last notes of the hymn faded, Sophie battled her wave of homesickness. After all, she had chosen to come here, to try to make a difference, to prove her mettle. She wouldn't feel sorry for herself despite everything that had gone wrong.

As the congregation settled in for Robbie's sermon, Sophie glanced to her right and saw Ethan sliding into the far end of the pew. Since the close of the season at Blue Smoke, he'd attended services almost every week. He balanced his hat on his knee and sent her a smile that warmed the empty places in her heart. How she would miss him if the paper didn't make it and she had to leave town. But why dwell upon things that couldn't be changed? And at least she'd see him this afternoon at the Gilmans'.

Robbie motioned the congregation to stand for the closing prayer. "Lord, on this day of thanksgiving, let thy merciful ears be open to the prayers of thy humble servants. Make them to ask such things as shall please thee, through Christ our Lord."

What prayers would please the Lord? Sophie closed her eyes.

Lord, may Ethan find peace and regain his love for his brother. May Julian's wounds heal. May you forgive me for my lack of courage, for waiting so long to tell the truth. Her breath hitched. God could forgive any sin, but that didn't mean he would erase the consequences. She had confessed her deceit, but was that enough? Maybe Ethan would never truly trust her. Or maybe his wounds went too deep for them to find a lasting love. Not that she had put all of her own doubts to rest. Could she overcome her own wounds and her own uncertainties?

She stopped herself, reined in her runaway thoughts, turned them around. *Forgive my lack of trust in you. You've brought me this far. Please keep your hand on me and those I love.*

Then, in the prayerful stillness, her thoughts turned to Rosaleen. *Wherever my mother is on this day, forgive her and protect her.*

"Amen." Robbie's voice filled the room.

Ethelinda struck a chord and played a soft hymn as people gathered their hats and cloaks, spoke to friends and neighbors, and left the church. Sophie said good-bye to Lucy and Mrs. Whiting and started for Mr. Tanner's livery to hire a horse and rig.

"Sophie?" Ethan strode toward her, a smile in his eyes, looking impossibly handsome in his pressed gray suit, his brown hair curling onto the collar of his crisp white shirt.

"Good morning." She returned his smile. "With Mrs. Culpepper and her party descending upon Blue Smoke today, I didn't expect to see you here."

"The staff is prepared to deal with her. And it was better for me to stay out of Horace's way. We had another disagreement yesterday. He's still angry that I helped with the repairs at the *Gazette*."

"I'm sorry for causing so much trouble."

"No trouble at all. I wanted to help. Besides, it doesn't really matter anymore." He took her arm as they crossed the street. "I quite enjoyed Reverend Whiting's sermon."

Sophie smiled. "It still feels so strange to hear my oldest friend called 'reverend.' When we were growing up, I could imagine him doing lots of different things, but never preaching." They skirted a group of children dressed in their Sunday best, playing chase outside the bank. "Have you seen Mr. Worth this morning?"

Ethan nodded. "I went by the infirmary first thing. Julian has been anxious for news of his son, and his wife telegraphed that the boy is recovering. I wanted to deliver the good news right away. Dr. Spencer says Julian can leave the infirmary next week and continue his recuperation at home."

Sophie lifted her skirts and stepped around a muddy spot in the street. "He's fit to travel, then?"

"Not just yet, but maybe by Christmas. Julian's planning to rent a room at the inn until the doc releases him."

"I'm sure he's more than ready to get out of the infirmary."

"He's turned cantankerous—a sure sign he's feeling better." Ethan grinned. "I suppose you're headed to Miss Gilman's."

"Yes. I asked Mr. Tanner to reserve a horse and rig for me."

"Let me drive you." He motioned toward the mercantile where a handsome rig and an even more handsome horse stood. "Griff Rutledge lent me one of his best Blue Smoke mares for the occasion."

"Thank you. I'd love some company. I wasn't looking forward to driving out there alone. Especially since Mr. Tanner seems to have only Miss Pearl available for me, and she is slower than Christmas."

Ethan grinned and helped her into his rig and they set off for the Gilmans'. Sophie drew her coat about her shoulders and pulled on her woolen gloves, watching him from the corner of her eye. He held the reins loosely in one hand, his eyes fixed firmly on the narrow road. He seemed preoccupied, wound tight as a watch spring.

"Ethan, I—"

"I've quit Blue Smoke," he said. "I handed in my resignation yesterday."

So that was what accounted for his strange mood. She turned in her seat and searched his face. "I thought you loved it there."

"I loved building it. I don't love what it's become, or how its success has changed Horace Blakely. It has made him callous, ruthless, not the man I first met when I was seventeen." He glanced at her. "I can see why the Good Book says love of money is the root of all evil. It has turned Horace into someone I hardly recognize."

"I see. I suppose you'll go back to Baltimore, then."

"That's one possibility. I haven't decided yet."

Sophie folded her hands and willed herself to be cheerful, though all the joy had drained from the day. Ethan was leaving Hickory Ridge, and most likely she would never see him again. How could she bear to spend all afternoon at the Gilmans', pretending to have a wonderful time when her heart was breaking?

Ethan guided the rig around a mud puddle. "Of course, the minute I gave Horace notice, I started second-guessing myself, thinking maybe I'd made an enormous mistake. But this morning, when the reverend called upon us to ask what would please God, I got the answer I'd been looking for without even knowing I was seeking it. I realized that my heart is in building things, in fixing things that are broken and making them whole again."

They passed beneath a stand of stately pine trees pulsing with late-autumn light. The Gilmans' house loomed in the distance, and farther along the road Sophie could see Carrie and Griff Rutledge's place. Horses stood behind miles of whitewashed fences, placidly cropping the grass. A gaggle of noisy children, still dressed in their best clothes, chased each other in the brown meadow, oblivious to the chill wind coming off the mountain.

Charlotte Rutledge fell facedown in a puddle and began to cry. In an instant, Carrie ran across the meadow and picked up her small daughter. An unexpected lump lodged in Sophie's throat. What a lucky child, to know the comfort and safety of a mother's arms.

The little mare trotted smartly along the road. Ethan glanced at Sophie, a smile playing on his lips. "Anyway, now that I've given Horace my notice, I'm looking forward to the future. More than I have in a long time."

"What will you do now?" Sophie asked, dreading the answer but unable to stop her question. Why were human beings determined to seek the very answers that would destroy them?

"When I was repairing your office, I realized that for the first time in a long time, I was truly happy. I think I might form a company of my own—build and repair houses and such. Joel and a few other men would rather work for me than for Horace, even though I couldn't pay them as much. And I'd like to make a trip home. To Ravenswood, or to the place where it used to be. Seeing Julian again has made me realize how much I've missed home. Despite the bad memories."

They turned into the wooded drive leading to the Gilmans', the road parting the dense forest like a comb parting hair. A collection of rigs and buggies were parked in the yard. A knot of men stood on the front porch, smoking cheroots and swapping stories, their voices rising and falling on the afternoon air.

Sophie gathered her skirts and prepared to leave the rig, but Ethan stopped her. "Sophie? I know this is sudden, but now that I've made some decisions about my future, I think maybe this is the right time."

He clasped her hand so tightly she could feel his heart racing, even through the fabric of her glove.

Her mouth went dry. "Yes, Ethan?"

"Would you do me the honor of marrying me?"

THIRTY

Sophie looked up at Ethan, lips parted, her heartbeat whooshing in her ears. Had she heard correctly?

"When I spoke just now about fixing things that are broken, I wasn't speaking only of buildings, Sophie." His eyes, the color of the gentians growing beside the road, caught hers and held. "Ironic, isn't it—my blaming you for hiding your family's past, when I was guilty of the same thing? I realize now that I was afraid too, afraid that if people knew Julian and I were kin, they would judge me. I'm terribly sorry that Julian got shot on my account, but I'm glad he showed up here. Otherwise I would have missed out on the greatest gift of my life."

Sophie blinked back tears. That they had gone through so much to arrive at this moment made his proposal even more endearing. And of course she loved him. Wanted him with a longing too deep for words. Had secretly longed for this moment. But now that it was happening, she didn't know what to say.

Would marriage be a wise choice? Was it even possible? Old prejudices were still alive and well, and she was weary of hiding from the truth. Suppose he took her home to Georgia? What if her background—her very self—proved to be a detriment to him? She couldn't bear it if he had to suffer because people didn't like her. And what if he wanted her to give up newspapering?

He clasped both her hands and drew them to his chest. "I haven't misread your feelings, have I? You do love me?"

"Yes, Ethan, I do. And I've prayed for this moment, but now that it's actually happened, it feels so . . . so sudden. I—"

"You don't have to say yes right this minute." He kissed her gloved fingers. "After all, I am now without means to support you. Take some time to think about it. Tomorrow will be soon enough."

"Sophie!" Gillie ran toward them, her rustling silk skirts hiked to her ankles. "Thank goodness you're here. My mother is in the parlor with my Aunt Livinia, and I do believe they are conspiring to announce my engagement to my third cousin William Fortis this very afternoon." She glanced at Ethan. "Hello, Mr. Heyward. Please excuse me. I need my best friend right this minute."

Ethan released Sophie and winked at her. "By all means, Miss Gilman. I reckon I'll just join the menfolk there on the porch." He touched his index finger to the brim of his hat. "I'll see you ladies later."

He helped Sophie from the rig, handed off the reins to one of the stableboys, and loped toward the house.

Gillie looped her arm through Sophie's. "I'm sorry to have interrupted your conversation with Mr. Heyward, but this is an emergency. You must help me."

Sophie's mind reeled. Ethan Heyward had just proposed marriage. How could she possibly think of anything else? But Gillie needed her. She forced her mind back to the present crisis. "Of course I'll help. But how?"

"I've told Mother and Aunt Livinia that someone else has my heart, but they don't believe me. They think I'm making up a beau just to get out of marrying William. When you meet him, you'll understand why any girl would want to avoid him. Of course Mother thinks he's perfect, just because he has money. But you know I care much more for my infirmary than for fancy things. I'd rather look after my patients and live in a cabin with Caleb than in a mansion with William the Silent."

"He doesn't talk much?"

"Much? He doesn't talk at all. Can you imagine dinner with such a man, night after night? I'd go mad."

They reached the house. Ethan and the other men paused in their stories and tipped their hats as Gillie opened the massive front door and ushered Sophie inside.

They passed the large dining room where the table was set for the Thanksgiving meal. Candlelight reflected polished silver and sparkling crystal. Massive bouquets of gentians and yellow asters anchored each end of the table. Two serving girls in starched black dresses and white aprons bustled to and fro from the kitchen, delivering soup in Chinese-patterned tureens and silver platters loaded with sweet potatoes and roasted corn. The smells of roasting turkey and mince pie wafted into the carpeted hallway.

Gillie swept past the dining room and paused outside the closed doors leading to the parlor. "You must convince Mother that I'm telling the truth. I'm not asking you to name Caleb. You made a promise to him, and I won't ask you to break it. But maybe if you tell her there is someone who likes me, she'll give up this ridiculous plan to marry me off to someone I can't abide."

Laughter erupted from inside the parlor. Gillie frowned. "That's Mother and dear Auntie, conspiring to ruin my life."

"I don't want you to marry someone you don't love, but wouldn't it be better for Caleb to tell her himself?"

"Of course it would. But I can't be sure he'll even come out here today. After I saw Flora this morning, I dropped by the *Gazette* on my way to the livery on the off chance I'd find him delivering supplies or something. The door was open and his hat was lying on the counter. The coffeepot was still warm, but he wasn't there. I suppose he'd already left to spend the day with his mother and brothers at the farm. But I left a note inviting him here just in case."

The parlor doors slid open just then and there stood Mrs. Gilman sparkling like a human Christmas tree in a moss-green gown, a suite of deep ruby jewelry adoring her neck, earlobes, and wrists. "Sabrina, it's about time you got back here. I was about to send someone to look for you."

Gillie nudged Sophie forward. "Mother, you remember my friend, Sophie Caldwell."

"Of course." Mrs. Gilman nodded a greeting, but her expression was cold as a trout. "Welcome to our home."

"Thank you for inviting me," Sophie said, although it was Gillie who had invited her.

"I was sorry to hear about the fire at your newspaper office. Such a frightening thing, right there in the middle of town. It must be very difficult for you, losing your business. Though in all candor, I can't say I approve of the trouble you caused for dear Mr. Blakely, after he's done so much to move Hickory Ridge forward."

"No more trouble than he has caused me," Sophie said. "His forced boycott by my advertising clients nearly put the paper under. Luckily, some of my clients have returned."

"Don't tell me you're reopening."

"As soon as my new equipment and supplies arrive." Sophie couldn't keep a note of triumph from her voice.

"And not a moment too soon either," Gillie said, clearly enjoying defying her mother. "Everyone is clamoring for the return of the Answer Lady."

Mrs. Gilman clicked her tongue. "Some may choose to air their petty grievances in the pages of the newspaper. But ladies of quality would never do such a thing, nor would they waste their time reading such drivel."

"I'm sorry our answer column doesn't appeal to you, Mrs.

Gilman," Sophie said, "but I hope you'll find other things in the paper to enjoy."

Just then a slight, white-haired woman wearing a severe black bombazine dress appeared in the parlor doorway and frowned at Mrs. Gilman. "Kindly come into the parlor and sit down like civilized people. You know I can't hear a thing from way out here. Hello, Sabrina. I thought you'd flown the coop."

Gillie kissed the older woman's cheek. "Aunt Livinia. The thought had occurred to me."

"Oh, pish-posh." The older woman waved one mottled hand and ushered them into the parlor. She lowered herself into a wingback chair next to the fireplace, drew a lace shawl around her thin shoulders, and peered at Sophie. "Who the devil are you?"

"Oh, sorry," Gillie said. "Where are my manners? Aunt Livinia, this is Sophie Caldwell, editor and publisher of the *Hickory Ridge Gazette* and my dearest friend in all the world."

"You're that newspaper girl?"

"Yes." Sophie liked the older woman despite her brusque manner. "I can't afford much of a staff yet. But I enjoy the work." She peeled off her woolen gloves and tucked them into her reticule.

"Sophie's the reason I got the infirmary open," Gillie said. "If she hadn't convinced the mayor and the council to give me a hearing, it never would have happened."

Livinia frowned. "I heard the newspaper office burnt plumb to the ground."

"It wasn't quite that bad. The roof and one wall were severely damaged, but my printing press was unharmed. I hope to resume publishing again by Christmas."

Gillie sent her mother a defiant look. "I can't wait to read the next Answer Lady column. I loved the one about forcing a shy child to sing in church. Sophie advised her mother to wait until the girl feels ready."

"I quite agreed," Livinia said. "A trauma like that could scar a child for life. If I remember correctly, the child in question was only nine years old. Of course, the column about how to keep a husband from snoring was much more entertaining. I laughed till I cried when I read that one."

"Livinia Merriweather." Mrs. Gilman drew herself up and glared at her sister. "You don't mean to tell me you waste time on that silliness."

"I'm sure those who write to the Answer Lady take it quite seriously indeed. And I think it's inexcusably rude of you to denigrate this young woman's work while she is a guest in your home. Besides, we have a much more serious matter to discuss." She turned to Gillie. "Now, I know how you feel about that infirmary of yours, but really, Sabrina, a woman of your age ought to be thinking of finding a husband and making a home. Your mother and I only hope it isn't too late."

Mrs. Gilman nodded. "You should have married Franklin West when you had the chance."

"Mother. I was barely seventeen, and still mourning the loss of Jacob Hargrove."

"So? I was only nineteen when I married your father, and look at what I have now. A fine home, a man to protect me, enough money to live comfortably in my old age. No need to go about sewing up wounds and birthing babies and cleaning up . . . bodily waste." Mrs. Gilman shuddered. "I can't imagine it."

"But I love taking care of people," Gillie said. "Opening the infirmary was the best thing I've ever done."

"And the town is grateful, I am sure. But now it's time to turn it over to the doctor and take your rightful place in society."

Gillie sighed and rolled her eyes at Sophie. "The infirmary is my rightful place. I'm sorry if you don't agree."

Mrs. Gilman stood and paced the room, her slippers whispering on the thick wool carpet. "You know who I blame for this? Your father, that's who. He never should have given in to your request for medical training. But he was so sure that you'd see what a filthy, thankless task it is and come to your senses." She paused in front of Sophie, her dark eyes blazing. "I don't want to seem impolite, but this is a private matter. Perhaps you could wait with the other guests in the library?"

Gillie stiffened. "If she goes, I go."

"But, Sabrina," Livinia said, "this is a family crisis."

Gillie folded her arms across her chest. "You and Mother are the only ones who think it's a crisis."

Mrs. Gilman waved her hand. "Very well. Here is what has been decided. At dinner this evening, your father and I will announce your engagement to William Fortis of Louisville. He has agreed to marry you providing your father settles a decent dowry on you, which of course he is more than prepared to do."

Gillie frowned. "In other words, you're paying him to marry me. How much am I worth, Mother?"

"That's a vulgar question and doesn't deserve an answer. Now, next month Livinia and I will accompany you to Nashville to select a wedding gown and a trousseau and whatever else you might require. Mr. Fortis has been a bachelor all his life, so I imagine his house, fine though it is, could use a woman's touch. The wedding will be held next April. You may choose the date."

"I may choose?" Gillie broke into mirthless laughter, her pale blue eyes brimming with tears. "The only thing you're leaving to me is to pick the day I give up the most meaningful thing in my life so that you won't be the embarrassed mother of a spinster daughter?" She shook her head. "Short of your kidnapping me and tying me to the altar, this wedding will not happen. It will be far more embarrassing for you to explain to a church full of guests why there is no bride."

The parlor had grown cool. Livinia stood and poked the fire, sending up a shower of sparks.

"Besides," Gillie said, "I told you I have fallen in love with someone. I have reason to hope that he loves me too, though he has not yet declared himself. So you see, Mother, I don't need you to purchase a groom for me. Despite my advanced age and unsavory occupation, I am not as undesirable as you think."

Mrs. Gilman shook her head. "How convenient that you have fallen in love just as I've made plans for you. I'm sorry, but I don't believe—"

Sophie rose, her gloves and reticule tumbling to the carpet. Never had she met such a cold, uncaring woman. Even Rosaleen had shown more feeling. "It's quite true, Mrs. Gilman. Gil—Sabrina has indeed caught the attention of a fine young man right here in Hickory Ridge. She asked me to come here today to assure you of his regard for her."

"Is that so? Then where is he? Why can't he speak for himself?"

"William Fortis is not here to speak for himself either," Gillie said.

"William was delayed in his travels. He'll be arriving this evening." Mrs. Gilman turned to Sophie. "What does this suitor do for a living?"

"I can't tell you that without giving away his identity."

"Of course you can't, because he is simply an invention you and my daughter cooked up to postpone the inevitable."

"He's quite real, I assure you. But I promised to let him speak for himself when the time is right."

In the hallway a dinner bell chimed and someone knocked at the parlor door. "Ma'am? Dinner's ready."

Mrs. Gilman placed an arm around her daughter's shoulders. "Believe me, Sabrina, I want only the best for you. After you're married, William will open up to you, I'm sure of it. A year from now, perhaps a child will be on the way. And you'll see I was right to make this decision for you."

"Come along, girls," Livinia said. "Let's put all this aside and join our guests. It's Thanksgiving, after all. And I am purely famished!"

THIRTY-ONE

I now set my hand to the end of my story. My only daughter, Anna, rests in a churchyard in New Orleans. She was but eight and twenty and the mother of a babe when called to eternal rest. It seemed unjust to me, but what shall I say? There is an all wise Being who orders events, who knows what is best for us and determines accordingly, and we must patiently, if not cheerfully, submit to his will. As to the final resting places of those who went before us, I know naught. I pray they received God's mercy and passed from this earth into his loving care. Here ends my story. Elena Worthington in the year of our Lord, 1820.

Sophie closed the journal. Unless she saw Rosaleen again someday, here was all she would ever know of her heritage. But Ethan loved her no matter what, and his devotion had at last filled the empty places inside her heart.

In the weeks since his proposal, they had spent time together nearly every day. With the residents of the Verandah who worked for Blue Smoke away until next spring, Lucy had hired Ethan to replace a rickety stairway banister and repair zigzagged cracks in the plaster ceiling of the dining room.

In the evenings when his work was done and she was home from the *Gazette*, she ate with Ethan, sharing a tray before the fire in Lucy's cheerful parlor. She loved watching his hands move as he described his vision for a new house on his family's land near Savannah, the way his eyes lit up when he spoke of Palladian windows, fanlight doors, lintels, corbels, and spiraling staircases.

He hadn't pressed her for an answer to his proposal, but the look of expectation in his eyes when they said good night said plenty about his hopes for their future. But as much as she loved him, she still couldn't bring herself to say yes or no, to break this sweet bubble of possibility they were living in, to face her fears.

So she kept putting it off. And so far he had been patient.

Occasionally, they bundled themselves against the cold and walked to Miss Hattie's for dinner and then to the Hickory Ridge Inn to visit Julian. Just last Sunday Dr. Spencer had pronounced his patient well enough to travel. Though Julian spoke of going home to Philadelphia in time for the holiday, she hoped he'd stay. Julian would have many more Christmases to spend in Philadelphia. But Julian was all the family Ethan had left. Surely Mrs. Worth would understand. Or perhaps she and her son could come to Hickory Ridge for the holiday.

She tried not to think too much about Christmas in Texas. Every year Ada decorated the ranch house with fresh garlands and dozens of white candles. Silver bowls of clove-studded oranges filled tables in the dining room and parlor. She would miss all of it this year—the smells of citrus and cedar, the sound of Wyatt's booming laugh, Wade's mischief, and Lilly's excited chatter—the sounds and sights and smells that meant home to her.

She put away her great-grandmother's journal, parted the curtain, and looked onto the bustling street. Horses, rigs, and freight wagons lined the street near Mr. Pruitt's mercantile. Clusters of farm wives hurried in and out of shops while knots of noisy children paraded along the wooden boardwalk. The doors to Mrs. Pruitt's dress shop and Mariah Whiting's bookshop were dressed in fresh cedar garlands.

She released a long sigh. Despite her loneliness, her troubles and doubts, this year had been a season of gifts. Ethan Heyward loved her. She'd met her mother at last. And her dream of owning a newspaper had come true despite Mr. Blakely and the fire.

She'd reopened the *Gazette* on the first Monday in December and some of her advertising clients had returned. The Answer Lady column was more popular than ever and was gaining a following outside of Hickory Ridge. Caleb went to the post office every afternoon to pick up the letters that arrived from as far away as Louisville and Birmingham, and every week he took a bundle of papers for delivery out of town. Just yesterday she'd mailed the first of her articles for Blue Smoke to a magazine in Boston. Perhaps one day she'd write more articles for Mr. McClure's magazine too. If she was frugal, and if her good fortune continued into the new year, the *Gazette* could be running in the black by next summer.

These days her life seemed like a fanciful story, made up to chase away the dark of night. Until the day Ada Wentworth walked into her life, Sophie had had nothing of her own, not even a name. No home. No family. No toys or books, and no companion save Robbie Whiting and the orphanage director's haughty cat. Even her threadbare dresses had first belonged to someone else.

But all that was behind her now. Now the *Gazette* was hers, the best achievement of her life. Now she had a home, a name. How could she be anything but grateful?

Downstairs the front door slammed shut, rattling the windows. "Sophie? Are you up?" Lucy's voice echoed in the stairwell.

"Coming." Sophie grabbed her shawl and hurried downstairs past the freshly cut Christmas tree Caleb had lugged into the parlor last night. Homesickness and childlike anticipation mingled inside her. On Christmas Eve, after services at church, she and Lucy would gather with Ethan, Julian, Caleb, and Gillie to decorate it. Already Lucy's cozy kitchen smelled of Christmas spices. Dozens of gingerbread and raisin cookies filled the jars on the counter.

She crossed the empty parlor and found Lucy in the kitchen putting away supplies.

"Good morning." From her perch atop her step stool, Lucy smiled at Sophie, her eyes bright, her cheeks and nose still pink from the cold. "I've never seen Mr. Pruitt's mercantile so crowded. Christmas shoppers everywhere." She handed Sophie a sack of sugar. "I guess that's what happens when folks wait till the last minute. I saw Caleb Stanhope just now, shopping in the ladies' department."

Sophie laughed and put away the sugar. She had completed her own shopping just after Thanksgiving: a red woolen shawl for Lucy, a delicate enameled bracelet for Gillie. More modest gifts than they deserved, but after giving Rosaleen her emergency money and writing a check for a new typewriting machine, there was barely enough left for the gift she wanted for Ethan—a polished brass spyglass like Miss Swint's. The lady photographer had given Sophie the name of a manufacturer in Boston. Of course this one had never belonged to a famous pirate, but she still couldn't wait for the look on Ethan's face when he opened it.

She peered into Lucy's shopping bag and took out a pound of rice and a box of beeswax candles. "I suppose Caleb was shopping for Gillie. She's so in love he could give her a sack of pebbles for Christmas and she'd be perfectly happy."

Lucy stood on tiptoe and shoved a sack of cornmeal into the pantry. "Have the Gilmans come to terms with her choice of a husband?"

Sophie set the candles on a shelf. "Mrs. Gilman isn't exactly thrilled with the match. She thinks Caleb is beneath them."

"Caleb is a fine man, from what I can tell, and besides, Gillie is a grown woman. The only opinion that counts is hers." Lucy finished putting away her supplies and set the teakettle on to boil. "I only hope she doesn't leave town once she's married. We need her at the infirmary. Hickory Ridge keeps growing. Doc Spencer is getting older. And who knows how long it will take to replace him, when that day comes."

Sophie took two mugs from the pantry and poured a pitcher of milk from the jug in the icebox. She filled a platter with cookies and tossed another log onto the fire in the fireplace. "I don't think you have to worry about Gillie leaving her infirmary. It's very dear to her heart."

The kettle whistled. Lucy spooned tea leaves into the teapot and poured the water in, filling the room with the heady scent of bergamot. She pulled out her chair and sat down. "What's the matter? You look much too glum for this time of year. It's almost Christmas, for goodness' sake."

"Ethan wants to go home to Savannah. Reclaim his family's land. I can't blame him for that." She swallowed the sudden lump in her throat. "People don't realize how important home is, until it isn't there anymore."

Lucy touched her shoulder. "You're missing the Caldwells."

Sophie's eyes burned. "Yes. This will be the first Christmas we've spent apart since I was a child. It hardly seems like Christmas without them. But I suppose I have to grow up sometime. I'm not a ten-year-old orphan anymore."

"I don't think Mr. Heyward is headed for Georgia anytime soon. He told me yesterday that half my roof is about to cave in. He can't take the old one off until warmer weather, and then who knows how long it will take him to put on a new one? I'd say you're safe until at least next spring." Lucy's eyes glittered like copper pennies. "But I wouldn't wait too long to say yes to his marriage proposal." She lifted the tea strainer and poured the fragrant brew into their cups. "After all, Ethan Heyward is the handsomest man in Hickory Ridge. When Blue Smoke reopens next spring, there will be a whole passel of young women parading through here, looking for a husband."

Sophie nodded and stirred milk into her tea. Very soon she would have to gather her courage and make a choice. But not yet. "We saw Sheriff McCracken at Miss Hattie's last night. He says Mr. Crocker's trial is scheduled for the end of January. Both Ethan and Julian will need to be here for that."

"Will you have to testify too?"

"I'm not sure. Ethan says it's possible Mr. Crocker could admit to everything and avoid a trial altogether. Supposedly Mr. Crocker has a lawyer, a cousin from Birmingham, coming from Alabama to talk to the judge next week."

"My stars. I hadn't heard a word of this. That's why I love having a newspaper reporter under my roof. Keeps me up-to-date on all the goings-on around here."

The parlor clock chimed. Lucy got up and bustled about the kitchen. "It's ten o'clock already, and I still have a ton of things to do. I need to bring that box of decorations down from the attic and wash my good cider glasses and find Aunt Maisie's crystal candle-holders. I use them only for special occasions."

"I'll help you." Sophie finished her tea and brushed cookie crumbs from her fingers.

"No, you won't. You're a paying guest—the only one until spring. I don't want to run you off."

"I don't mind. I'd rather keep busy doing something useful so I won't miss my family quite so much."

A wagon rattled along the street and drew up outside the Verandah. Lucy parted the curtain and peered out. "It's Mr. Heyward with a load of planks. I didn't expect to see him here so close to Christmas. That man sure does love his work."

She poured a cup of tea and handed it to Sophie. "Take this out to him. It's cold as a banker's heart this morning." She winked. "Unless you can think of some other way to warm him up."

Sophie blushed and took her coat from the hall tree in the parlor. "The tea will do nicely, thank you."

Lucy laughed and propelled Sophie out the door.

Ethan looked up, his handsome face lit with pleasure. "Good morning. I figured you'd be out shopping for Christmas like the rest of Hickory Ridge."

She shook her head and handed him the steaming cup of tea. "I had to ship presents home to Texas anyway, so I took care of everything all at once."

He took the tea and sipped it gratefully. "Makes sense."

"What are you doing here this morning? Lucy wasn't expecting you today."

"I know it, but I got to thinking about the rotten boards on the back porch and figured I'd replace them before somebody falls through and breaks a leg." He gestured toward the wagon that was piled high with new boards and a box of carved posts. "Then I figured as long as I was replacing the boards, I might as well build a new railing too."

Ethan drained his cup and handed it back to her. He picked up one of the delicately carved rail posts. "I borrowed Sage Whiting's shop, and we made these. I think Sage enjoyed the chance to escape his desk for a while."

"I'm sure he did." Sophie ran her fingers over the satiny wood. "They're beautiful. Lucy will love them. But, Ethan, I'm not sure she can afford this—not after all the other repairs she's already made. And not when she still has the roof to replace."

"I don't expect payment. It's my present to her. She's my first customer since I left Blue Smoke, and I'd like to do something to show my appreciation. Besides, it's good advertising for my new company."

"Well, it's very generous. She'll be thrilled."

"I hope so." He pulled on his heavy gloves and began unloading the wagon, sliding the new boards onto the frosty ground. "I brought you a present too." His blue eyes caught hers and held. "I know it's still a week until Christmas, but I couldn't wait."

He looked so hopeful and so earnest, like a young boy smitten for the first time. Her heart expanded with love for him. How could any woman resist such a sweet show of affection? "If you chose it, I'm sure it'll be perfect."

He left his task, clasped her hand, and led her to the rear garden where a tiny gazebo stood amid a tangle of winter vines. He took a small, elaborately wrapped package from his coat pocket and pressed it into her hands. "Happy Christmas, my love."

She placed a hand on his sleeve. "I have something for you too. Wait just a minute. I'll go get it."

He drew her close, his arms solid and strong around her, his breath warm against her cheek. "Later, Sophie. Stay right here with me. It's the only present I really want."

She stepped into his embrace and lifted her face for his kiss, oblivious to the cold mist that began to fall. He settled his lips on hers in a tender, lingering kiss that left her breathless and wanting more.

At last they drew apart, and he smiled down at her. "Open your present."

She fumbled with the paper and ribbon. Inside a small velvet box, a fine gold locket on a matching chain winked in the dull light. "Oh, Ethan, it's exquisite."

"I had it made for you in Baltimore." He took it from her and turned it over. On the back, their initials were engraved, entwined among delicately carved flowers and vines. "You know my heart. I hope this will turn out to be an engagement present—something you will wear every day of our life together and pass along to our granddaughter someday. But even if you decide not to marry me, I want you to keep it as a reminder of how much I love you. How much I will always love you."

Her eyes and her heart too full for words, she turned her back to him and lifted her hair. He fastened the locket around her neck, his gloved fingers lightly brushing against her skin. She released a long sigh.

"You do love me?" he asked. "You haven't changed your mind?"

"Of course I haven't," she whispered.

"Just don't keep me waiting too much longer," he said, drawing her close again. "The suspense is killing me."

THIRTY-TWO

"Sophie. Wake up. It's Christmas Eve."

Sophie burrowed further into the feather mattress and willed herself to stay inside this beautiful dream where Ada was calling to her, gently rousing her from sleep. Ten minutes more beneath the warm covers and she would rise to help Lucy finish her holiday preparations. Later they would dress for the evening service at church. Sophie was looking forward to it.

"Sophie?"

Sighing, she opened one eye and looked out the window at a leaden sky. The icy rain that had lashed the Verandah all night had turned to snow. Soft flakes drifted past the window and formed lacy patterns on the windowpane.

She threw back the covers and felt around on the floor with her feet, searching for her shoes as the last vestiges of her dream dissipated, leaving her feeling melancholy. How she missed home. Ada's voice had seemed so real it was almost as if she were standing right there beside the bed.

She found her shoes and shoved her arms into the sleeves of her woolen dressing gown.

A knock sounded at her door.

"In a minute, Lucy." She reached for her hairbrush and gave her hair a couple of hasty strokes. "I'm barely awake."

The door opened. She looked up. Her hairbrush slipped from her fingers and clattered onto her dressing table. "Ada?"

"Darling." Ada Wentworth Caldwell rushed across the room and embraced her. "Happy Christmas."

Sophie blinked, overcome with happiness and astonishment. "You're here? I was . . . I thought . . ."

"Lucy let me come up to wake you." Ada's wide gray eyes shone with love and amusement. "Apparently you were sleeping quite soundly."

"I heard your voice, but I thought it was just a wishful dream." She clasped both Ada's hands, her questions tumbling out. "Why didn't you tell me you were coming? When did you get here? Did Wyatt come? How are Wade and Lilly?"

"Wyatt saw how much I was missing you, and he gave me this trip as a Christmas present. We've only just arrived. He and the children are still at the depot collecting our baggage, but I could not wait another moment to set my eyes on you." Ada laughed and drew back, eyes appraising Sophie. "You look wonderful. Being in love agrees with you."

Sophie felt for the gold locket resting beneath her gown. She hadn't taken it off, even to sleep. Maybe she never would. "Ethan is a wonderful man. I can't wait for you to meet him."

"From the descriptions in your letters and Carrie's, I feel I already know him." Ada perched on the edge of Sophie's rumpled bed. "Wyatt approves as well. He says Ethan sounds like a man who isn't afraid to go after what he wants."

"That's true." Sophie bent to the fireplace, lit the kindling, and blew on it until the flame caught. The wood hissed and crackled in the grate, chasing away the early morning chill.

Ada folded her hands, her expression expectant. One brow arched. "But?"

"He's working on the Verandah and a few other things right now. But eventually he wants to marry me, leave Hickory Ridge, and build a new house on his family's land in Georgia. He plans to open an architectural office in Savannah."

"Which means you'd have to let go of the *Gazette*."

"Yes." Sophie drew her dressing gown tightly about her shoulders.

"And you aren't sure you want to give up something you've worked so hard to earn, not even for love." Ada smiled. "It's my story all over again, isn't it? When Wyatt proposed, I was certain I never wanted to depend upon a man for my well-being."

Sophie nodded. "That's what my mother—Rosaleen—said when she showed up here last fall."

"Was it too awful for you, my dear, seeing her at last? You didn't say very much in your letter."

"It was unsettling. All those years at the orphanage when I dreamed she'd find me, I expected to feel overwhelming love for her. But looking into her eyes was like looking at a stranger." Sophie shrugged. "It was a big letdown."

Ada rose and embraced Sophie. "I'm sorry, sweetheart."

"Don't be. I'm glad to put the mystery to rest."

"Anyway, it's wise to remember that there are good men and not-so-good ones in the world. Wyatt is the good kind, and so, I've been told, is Ethan." She patted Sophie's hand. "And the world is changing, you know. Just look at how the suffrage movement is growing."

Sophie nodded. Here lately, newspapers and magazines from everywhere had published pieces about it. Many people were convinced women soon would have the vote.

"A woman who is determined and resourceful can always open another hat shop or another newspaper office," Ada said. "But finding the one man who wants to cherish and protect her, to love her and build a life with her, is a gift from God that can never be replaced."

"I know that."

"Well then?"

"I'm worried about what would happen down there if anyone found out I'm of mixed blood."

"That was never a problem in Texas."

"Because we kept everything a secret. I don't want to live like that anymore." She touched the locket at her throat. "You know how it is. A person with even a drop of African blood is considered a Negro. It's a cruel alchemy, and I don't want Ethan to suffer because of it."

Footsteps sounded in the hall, then Lucy peeked through the open doorway holding a laden tray. She grinned at Sophie. "Surprise."

"You knew about this?"

"Not until an hour or so ago. But I think it's the most wonderful thing ever—right up there with Mr. Heyward's marriage proposal." She set the tray on the small table next to the fireplace, rattling the china cups in their saucers. "Brought you two some breakfast."

"Thank you." Sophie took a wrapped package from the walnut wardrobe in the corner and pressed it into Lucy's hands. "This is for you. Merry Christmas."

Lucy opened the package, unfolded the red woolen shawl, and wrapped herself in it. She checked her reflection in the mirror. "It's perfect. Thank you, Sophie. But honestly, I wasn't expecting anything."

"Sometimes the most perfect gifts are the ones we aren't expecting," Ada said.

Lucy left, closing the door behind her. The fire danced in the grate, sending out warmth and the smell of hickory wood. Sophie offered Ada the only chair in the room and poured coffee for them both. Then she piled her pillows on the floor and lounged at Ada's feet, balancing her plate on her lap. While they made short work of flapjacks with maple syrup, sausages, and fried eggs, Ada brought Sophie up-to-date on their train trip from Texas and everything going on back at the Rocking C Ranch, including the new ponies Wyatt had recently bought for Wade and Lilly.

"I do miss the ranch, especially the horses," Sophie said. "And especially dear old Cherokee. Robbie Whiting mentioned her to me after church one day. He loved that mare as much as I did."

"I'm looking forward to seeing Robbie," Ada said. "He was away at school when Wyatt and I came back here for poor Henry Bell's wedding." She took a last bite of flapjack and poured more tea. "I still can't quite believe Henry came to such a tragic end."

Sophie nodded. "Caleb Stanhope was talking about it just the other day—about how Griff and Carrie and his mother waited until after Christmas to tell him and his brother that Mr. Bell had died."

Ada added sugar to her tea and stirred. "Tell me, how are things at the paper since the fire? You haven't written much since Thanksgiving."

"I meant to write more often, but I've been so busy."

For the next hour, Sophie told Ada about Gillie's infirmary and the Gilmans' efforts to marry her off. She showed Ada her great-grandmother's journal and told Ada about Julian's arrival in Hickory Ridge, the shooting, Mr. Crocker's impending trial, and Ethan's Thanksgiving Day marriage proposal.

Ada laughed. "Heavenly days. No wonder your letters have been scarce lately. Whoever says nothing ever happens in a small town ought to spend a few weeks in Hickory Ridge. Now, you should get dressed, because Wyatt and the children are dying to see you."

It didn't take long. Within minutes, Sophie and Ada set off for the Hickory Ridge Inn. Sophie spotted Wyatt the minute she walked through the door of the inn. He was standing in the lobby with Wade and Lilly, his dark head bent to theirs, his expression grave as he listened to their excited chatter. Her heart lifted. Wyatt Caldwell was as dear and as handsome as ever, his eyes very blue in his tanned face, his grin when he saw her as wide as the Texas prairie. He crossed the lobby in long strides, lifted her off her feet, and twirled her around just as he had when she was ten years old and in the throes of an enormous crush on him.

"Well, darlin'," he said, setting her on her feet again, "I reckon newspaperin' agrees with you. You are one sight for sore eyes. Isn't she, son?"

Wade ducked his head and nodded. "Yes, sir."

Lilly pulled a rumpled package from her pocket and handed it to Sophie. "I brought you a present."

Sophie bent to the little girl and gave the package a gentle shake. "That's very thoughtful of you. Goodness, I wonder what it could be?"

"Open it and find out."

Sophie unwrapped a small glass vial filled with dirt. "Well. This is certainly—"

"It's some dirt," Lilly said, gray eyes shining, "from our ranch. I brought it all the way on the train, didn't I, Daddy? So you can keep a piece of Texas with you wherever you go and you won't be homesick. Or much, anyway."

Sophie swallowed the tears building in her throat and hugged Lilly tight. "It's the best present ever, and I will keep it until I come back to the Rocking C."

"When are you coming? Daddy said you won't ever live with us again because you're a grown-up now."

"Sometimes I don't feel very grown up. But I'll come back to the ranch to visit, because the people I love are there."

Wyatt shepherded them all toward the door. "I don't know

about you ladies, but Wade and I are starving for a platter of biscuits and Miss Hattie's fried chicken."

Ada linked her arm through his. "Fried chicken for breakfast?"

"Sure. Why not?"

Ada smiled up at her husband. "You and Miss Hattie's. Some things never change."

~

"More coffee, Mr. Heyward?"

The waiter hovered at Ethan's shoulder, his silver coffeepot gleaming beneath the crystal chandelier. The dining room was filled to capacity with the inn's regular guests, farm families in town for an early supper before tonight's church service, a few nattily dressed salesmen eating alone, their newspapers and dime novels propped against bread plates and water glasses.

"Yes, please." Ethan waited until his cup was full again before turning back to his notebook, which he'd left on a vacant chair during dinner. He took out his pencil and flipped to the drawings of the house he planned to build in Georgia. Now that the idea had captured his imagination, an intense longing for home gripped his heart and refused to let go.

Last night, unable to sleep in the room he'd rented just down the hall from Julian's, he had thought long and hard about his future—and about the unwelcome possibility that Sophie, despite her great affection for him, might refuse his marriage proposal. Maybe the thought of giving up the only thing that was truly hers was holding her back. Having grown up an orphan himself, he understood the need to achieve something important, to be noticed, to matter. And to cast off the feeling, however unwarranted, that having no parents made a person somehow inferior. Regardless of where one came from.

He had loved her at first sight, loved her even when she admitted she'd kept the truth from him. And it grieved him that she thought keeping her family history hidden was the only way to win his heart. Had he really seemed that hard and unforgiving? Probably.

He set down his pencil and sipped his tepid coffee. He couldn't stop thinking about the way she'd trembled in his arms yesterday, her voice husky with emotion, their longing for each other shimmering in the air around them, fragile as a moth's wing.

It wasn't only her beauty that captivated him. He'd come to appreciate her fine intelligence, her curiosity, her determination to run her newspaper for the good of the community despite the stumbling blocks Horace threw into her path and the fire that had come close to shutting down the *Gazette* for good. Sophie not only had a gift for words; she had a true passion for her work. Such a passion should never be wasted or ignored.

Which was why he was revising his plans for the Georgia house. A woman of Sophie's talents should have a proper place to nurture them. He envisioned a lovely room filled with sunlight, with a carved walnut desk, a place for her books and her beloved typewriting machine, a fireplace, and a cozy settee for thinking and writing and reading. He sketched it with double Palladian windows opening onto the plot of ground that had once been his mother's garden. It would take a lot of work and a king's ransom to restore his home to its former glory, but for Sophie he would do whatever it took.

He could picture her there already, bent over her work, the Georgia sunlight falling on her shining black hair, the windows open to the sounds of the birds and the summer insects singing in the tall grasses beside the river. Maybe she'd write only for the newspaper syndicate. Maybe she'd start up another paper. Or write poems.

He finished his coffee just as a group of snow-dusted carolers, their cheeks red from the cold, entered the packed dining room. Conversations stilled as the first notes of "God Rest Ye Merry, Gentlemen" filled the room. After the first line, the diners and waiters joined in.

Ethan sang along despite the sweet ache that squeezed his heart. Somehow the words of hope and promise seemed to be speaking only to him.

"O tidings of comfort and joy!"

He almost laughed out loud, amazed at how happiness had changed him. If only he could hold on to that feeling for the rest of his life. But he had done all he could do to convince Sophie to join her life with his. The rest was up to God.

THIRTY-THREE

In the gathering dusk, Sophie and the Caldwells made their way along the snowy street to the church for the Christmas Eve service. Indigo light draped the foothills as a half-moon peeked out from beneath the snow clouds, and the evening sky seemed to shiver with the beat of wings. As they crossed the street, candlelight appeared in every church window, first a tentative flicker, and then a steady glow that spilled onto the busy street.

Sophie's heart expanded with a sense of peace. How beautiful Hickory Ridge looked, all dressed up for Christmas with wreaths on every door and candles burning in the windows. The new coat of red paint on Mr. Tanner's livery stood in stark contrast to the white church, giving the whole street a festive air. Passing Sheriff McCracken's jail, she noticed he had hung a wreath on the door, albeit a bit crookedly. Even the thought of Mr. Crocker and the impending trial couldn't dampen her spirits.

"Ada, is that you?" Carrie Rutledge, holding her daughter Charlotte, by the hand, hurried to catch up to them. "What a wonderful surprise. Why didn't you tell me you were coming? Hello, Wyatt."

Wyatt smiled and touched his hat brim. "Mrs. Rutledge."

Ada took both Carrie's hands in hers. "Once we decided to

make the trip, I was so busy with preparations I had no time to write. I'm thrilled to see you, though." She bent to the child. "This must be the Charlotte you're always writing to me about."

"One and the same." Carrie smoothed her daughter's curls. "She keeps me busy."

Ada introduced Wade and Lilly. "And where's Griff? Wyatt and I are dying to see him after all these years. Aren't we, darling?"

Wyatt nodded. "Yes, ma'am."

"My husband is around here somewhere." Carrie scanned the crowd heading into the church. "Probably at Mr. Tanner's livery. He never can resist any conversation about horses, and Mr. Tanner is interested in buying a foal next year."

"How is Mariah?" Ada asked. "I've been so worried about her since Sage's accident."

"Darlin'?" Wyatt took Ada's arm. "We're going to be late for the service, and Robbie Whiting will never let me hear the end of it."

Sophie laughed. "Robbie will be glad to see you. He talks about you all the time."

"That boy and I had ourselves a time back in the day," Wyatt said. "I never figured him for a preacher."

"We'll catch up later," Carrie said to Ada. "Don't you dare go back to Texas without stopping for a visit first. I'll invite Mariah too. It'll be just like old times when you first came to Hickory Ridge and we had our quilting circle."

"I'd love that." Ada waved to her old friend and looped one arm through Sophie's. "Now, Sophie Caldwell, when are we going to meet your young man?"

Sophie's stomach jumped. She pressed her fingers to the gold locket hidden beneath her collar. "He will be here tonight."

They reached the church and slid into a pew near the back. Wyatt entered first, followed by Ada and their children. Sophie took the seat nearest the aisle, removed her cloak and gloves, and looked around the packed room. To her left and a few rows closer to the candlelit altar, Caleb and Gillie sat with an older woman and two younger boys—Caleb's mother and brothers. Behind them sat the Gilmans and Jasper Pruitt with his wife, Jeanne. Jasper spotted the Caldwells and lifted one hand in a little wave. Ada inclined her head. Jasper grinned and whispered to his wife, who also turned and waved to them.

A group of children assembled down front, whispering and giggling together. Sophie thought of the Christmas when she was ten years old, singing with the other orphans for the church program. She had been the only child on the program without a last name. But Ada Wentworth had penciled the name Robillard, her own mother's name, next to Sophie's name in the program, a gift like no other. A gift that had been the beginning of her new life.

Robbie's wife, Ethelinda, hurried down the aisle to the organ and began to play. Sophie scanned the crowd again. Where was Ethan? Excitement and apprehension warred inside her. Had her lack of courage and her indecision turned him away?

The door opened. Lucy closed it quickly behind her and edged past Carrie and Griff to find a seat near the window.

At Ethelinda's signal, the children came to order and sang, their voices high and sweet and only slightly off-key.

What can I give him, poor as I am?
If I were a shepherd, I would bring a lamb,
If I were a wise man, I would do my part.
Yet what I can I give him—give my heart.

When the children had filed off to join their parents, Robbie walked to the pulpit and opened his Bible. Sophie leaned forward and stole a glance at Wyatt, who was obviously enjoying the sight of the young man whose life he had once saved, now all grown up and preaching to his flock. Wyatt winked at Sophie. She smiled back.

Robbie motioned the congregation to their feet as the first hymn began. Sophie was surprised at first—it wasn't a traditional Christmas hymn. But then, Robbie Whiting liked choosing the unexpected. She closed her eyes and sang the words from memory:

> *All good gifts around us*
> *Are sent from heaven above,*
> *Then thank the Lord, O thank the Lord,*
> *For all his love.*

"Please be seated." Robbie's voice, deep as the church organ, filled the room.

The door opened again, and Julian came in, leaning on a crutch, Ethan following patiently behind him. Ethan helped Julian find a seat across the narrow aisle. Then he turned to Sophie, a smile on his lips, one brow raised. She scooted closer to Lilly to make room for him, her heart tripping at the sight of his beloved face. Ada looked past her young daughter and sent Sophie a pointed look.

". . . gifts of gold, frankincense, and myrrh." Robbie leaned forward, his hands grasping the lectern. "Tomorrow we celebrate the most holy of days. Many of us will give and receive gifts great and small."

Ethan reached for Sophie's hand. His fingers closed around hers, his thumb brushing the underside of her wrist. And her heart stumbled. How on earth could she have ever considered a life without him? Ada was right. Nothing was more important than the love of the man God had chosen for her.

"Tomorrow," Robbie said, "let us remember that every good gift and every perfect gift comes from the Father of lights, with whom there is no shadow of turning. Let's not forget that the ultimate gift was a baby born in a manger, a child whose love and light shine in our hearts tonight and forever. Let us pray."

They bowed their heads. Ethan pressed his lips to her ear. "Well, Sophie?"

She looked at Ethan and saw all her hopes and dreams reflected in his eyes. Her heart swelled with the understanding of how deeply God cared for her. Even during those endless nights in the orphanage, when she had prayed for the mother who never came, he had watched over her, planned for her. He had brought her to this place—to Ethan, who loved her just as God made her. Whatever difficulties they might encounter in the future, they would face them together. And the Father still would be there, guiding them.

"I love you," Ethan whispered. "Please say you'll marry me."

"Yes, Ethan. I will."

And the people said, "Amen."

ACKNOWLEDGMENTS

As this series comes to an end, I'm deeply grateful to everyone who had a part in bringing it to life: my publisher, Allen Arnold, and the entire fiction team at Thomas Nelson; my line editor, Anne Christian Buchanan; the sales and marketing teams; my wonderful posse (you know who you are); and my family, whose love inspires me every day.

To every reader who has chosen to spend time in Hickory Ridge, thank you. I hope you enjoyed the town and her people. It was my pleasure to bring them to life.

A NOTE FROM THE AUTHOR

Dear Readers,

It seems impossible that with Sophie's story, our stay in Hickory Ridge has come to an end. Since beginning this series in the spring of 2010, I've fallen in love with my fictional town and her people. In addition to my three protagonists, Ada, Carrie, and Sophie, I will miss Jasper Pruitt, Sheriff McCracken, the Whitings, Doc Spencer and Gillie, Mayor and Mrs. Scott, and of course my three handsome heroes, Wyatt Caldwell, Griff Rutledge, and Ethan Heyward.

With all of my Southern historical novels, I strive to weave together the historical and the personal in a way that allows readers to experience life as it was in the nineteenth century. I hope you've enjoyed these stories. I hope they've made you laugh and cry. And I hope they've given you new insights into the struggles and joys of Southern women during that time.

As this book goes into production, I am already at work on my next novel for Thomas Nelson. Set on a rice plantation along South Carolina's storied Waccamaw River, it's inspired by the life of an actual woman rice planter who stayed on her land until the turn of the twentieth century. It's scheduled for publication in the fall of 2013. I hope you'll enjoy it.

To every reader who has taken time to write to me, to post a review, or to chat with me online, thank you so much. Each of you is a treasure. As always, I welcome your letters and e-mails. It's easy to get in touch. Simply head over to my website, www .DorothyLoveBooks.com, and click on "Contact." You can also log onto my Facebook author page at www.facebook.com /dorothylovebooks or write to me in care of Author Mail, Thomas Nelson Inc., PO Box 141000, Nashville, TN 37214.

Till then, may the Lord bless you and keep you. May his light shine upon you and give you peace.

Blessings,
Dorothy

READING GROUP GUIDE

1. This book is called *Every Perfect Gift*. What spiritual gifts and practical gifts do Sophie and Ethan possess? How do these gifts help or hinder their growth throughout the novel?

2. Both Sophie and Ethan experienced difficult childhoods. In what ways have those difficulties shaped their character? How have difficulties in your own life shaped the person you are becoming?

3. Sophie observes that Ethan is a complicated man. What characteristics did you find most appealing in him? Were there any you didn't care for? Why?

4. Near the end of the book, Ada remarks that unexpected gifts are often the best gifts of all. What unexpected gifts do Sophie and Ethan receive? Have you ever given or received an unexpected gift that changed you in some fundamental way? Is there any gift that you would be unwilling to part with? Why?

5. In this novel, we get glimpses of the lives of Ada Caldwell and Carrie Rutledge, the two protagonists of *Beyond All Measure* and *Beauty for Ashes*, years after we first met them. Imagine the lives of Sophie and Ethan ten years hence. Where are they living and what are they doing? Do they have children?

6. It's often said that the line separating laughter and tears is a fine one.

Were there any parts of this story that you found particularly moving? Why?

7. Sophie's family history causes her much concern because of the prevailing social attitudes. Do you think attitudes about such issues have truly changed since the 1880s? Why or why not?

8. Robbie tells Sophie that she should develop the courage to accept herself as she is. Do you think self-acceptance is less an issue in modern times or more of an issue? Why?

9. Sophie at first keeps an important truth from Ethan because she wants him to like her. Do you think such deceit could be justified, given Sophie's circumstances? Have you ever been in a similar situation? How did you handle it?

10. What do you enjoy most about reading historical fiction? When you reach the end of any novel, what emotion do you most want to experience?

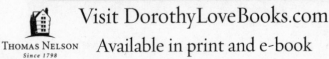

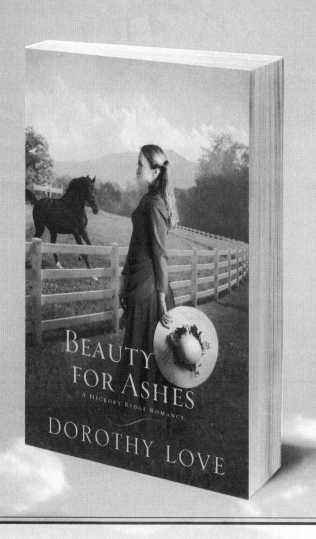

She's a beautiful young widow.
He's a Southern gentleman with a thirst for adventure.
Both need a place to call home.

VISIT DOROTHYLOVEBOOKS.COM
AVAILABLE IN PRINT AND E-BOOK

ABOUT THE AUTHOR

Author photo by Amber Zimmerman

A native of west Tennessee, Dorothy Love makes her home in the Texas hill country with her husband and their two golden retrievers. An accomplished author in the secular market, Dorothy made her debut in Christian fiction with the Hickory Ridge novels.